DETROIT PUBLIC LIBRARY

3 5674 05680030 4

P9-EMH-172

DELILAH

CHASE BRANCH LIBRARY
17731 W. SEVEN MILE RD.
DETROIT, MI 48235

DEC 16

CH

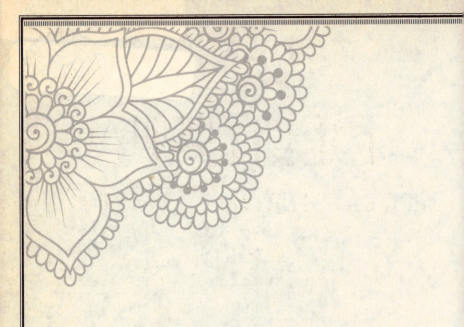

CHASE BRANCH LIBRARY
17731 W. SEVEN MILE RD.
DETROIT, MI 48235

DELILAH

TREACHEROUS BEAUTY

A DANGEROUS BEAUTY
NOVEL

ANGELA
HUNT

BETHANY HOUSE PUBLISHERS
a division of Baker Publishing Group

© 2016 by Angela Hunt Communications, Inc.

Published by Bethany House Publishers
11400 Hampshire Avenue South
Bloomington, Minnesota 55438
www.bethanyhouse.com

Bethany House Publishers is a division of
Baker Publishing Group, Grand Rapids, Michigan

Printed in the United States of America

ISBN 978-0-7642-1697-8

Library of Congress Control Number: 2016930778

All rights reserved. No part of this publication may be reproduced, stored in a retrieval
system, or transmitted in any form or by any means—for example, electronic, photocopy,
recording—without the prior written permission of the publisher. The only exception is
brief quotations in printed reviews.

Unless otherwise indicated, Scripture quotations are from the Holy Scriptures, Tree of
Life Version, Copyright (c) 2011, 2012, 2013 by the Messianic Jewish Family Bible Soci-
ety. Used by permission of the Messianic Jewish Family Bible Society. "TLV" and "Tree of
Life Version" and "Tree of Life Holy Scriptures" are trademarks registered in the United
States Patent and Trademark office by the Messianic Jewish Family Bible Society.

This is a work of historical reconstruction; the appearances of certain historical figures are
therefore inevitable. All other characters, however, are products of the author's imagination, and any resemblance to actual persons, living or dead, is coincidental.

Cover design by Paul Higdon
Interior design by Paul Higdon and LaVonne Downing

Author is represented by Browne & Miller Literary Associates.

16 17 18 19 20 21 22   7 6 5 4 3 2

Angela Hunt Presents
The DANGEROUS BEAUTY Series

"The Hebrew text has two words that are typically used to describe personal appearance. One, *yapeh*, is rather mild and means 'good looking.' The other, *tob*, when applied to women's looks, conveys sensual appeal. This woman is so beautiful that she arouses the desire of men who see her."

—Sue Poorman Richards and Larry Richards,
Every Woman in the Bible

Beauty does not always benefit the woman who possesses it. On occasion it betrays her, and at other times it endangers her, even to the point of death.

These novels—*Esther*, *Bathsheba*, and *Delilah*—are the stories of three *tob* women.

Heat not a furnace for your foe so hot

That it do singe yourself.

—William Shakespeare, *Henry VIII*

Chapter One

DELILAH

Circa 1200 BC

No woman sets out to be wicked. I'm not sure I can say the same thing about men.

At present only two men are my daily companions: Adinai, a kind Philistine businessman my mother married three months ago, and his son, Achish, whom I distrusted immediately. Adinai displayed nothing but compassion and thoughtfulness as he moved Mother and me from our home in Egypt to his spacious villa in Gaza. Achish, however, has never uttered a kind word in my hearing.

One particular day began like any other. I slept the morning away and woke as the sun reached its pinnacle. Zahra, my handmaid, brought a tray of bread and fruit to break my fast. As I nibbled on a melon slice, she reminded me that I was to accompany my stepbrother and stepfather to a banquet that evening. "I'll be back later to help you dress," she said, giving me a shy smile. "One does not visit the ruler of Gaza in everyday clothing."

I thanked her, then picked up another melon slice and closed my eyes as the sweet juice ran over my tongue. Fruits like this always reminded me of Egypt. Even when we struggled to feed ourselves, Mama had managed to find fruit for our table.

I broke the small loaf on my tray, then felt the pressure of an intruder's gaze. I lifted my head and saw Achish, my stepbrother, lounging in my doorway. Some girls might have considered him handsome, but beneath the curled hair and smooth skin, his eyes brimmed with an unattractive resentment.

"What do you want?" I asked, not bothering to disguise my irritation. Achish and I had agreed to despise each other almost as quickly as our parents decided to marry. "If you want food, I'm sure your servant will get something for you."

His upper lip twisted. "I'm not interested . . . in food."

I knew he wanted to engage me in some sort of argument, but I refused to take the bait. "Run along then. I have nothing for you."

Anyone else would have scowled, but Achish gave me an oily smile and moved away.

I lowered my head to breathe deeply and calm my agitated heartbeat. Achish was a near-constant annoyance. Adinai had promised that we would be equals in the household, but Achish made little effort to hide his dissatisfaction with the current domestic arrangement. Mother kept saying that he would accept us in time, but she still viewed the world through the rosy haze of love. In six months, or twelve, I did not think she would be so tolerant of Achish's rude behavior.

I finished my breakfast, then closed the drape over my door and moved to the washstand. I washed my face and rinsed my mouth and slipped into a clean tunic Zahra had hung on a peg. The Egyptian garment was simple, straight, and the color of washed sand, completely unlike the varicolored skirts worn by Philistine women.

I found my mother sewing in the sunny room that looked out onto a busy Gaza street. Wide windows at the north and south allowed the breeze to pass through, so it was the most pleasant room in the house.

I bent to kiss my mother's cheek and then sat next to her. Achish, who had arrived before me, sat in the opposite corner, wearing a colorful tunic and a bored expression. Since he obviously found our presence distasteful, I wondered why he didn't go out and visit one of his youthful cronies.

"About time you got up," Mama said, a note of reproof in her voice. "Don't forget you are to attend the ceren's banquet tonight. I would like you to wear one of the full skirts Zahra made you. And ask her to braid your hair into something . . . more elaborate." She beamed at me while I resisted the urge to groan. "You'll be the loveliest girl there."

I gave her the most pitiful look I could muster. "Surely you don't expect me to attend the feast without you."

She tilted her head toward the couch, where Achish reclined on one elbow. "Your brother will be with you."

I refused to look at him. "But Achish will be with the men. If you don't come, I'll have to eat alone."

"I understand that the ceren of Gaza has many daughters, so I'm sure you will dine with them." Mama reached out and cupped my chin. "You worry too much, Delilah. You are going to give yourself wrinkles."

I made a face, then tucked my legs beneath me and frowned at the prospect of an evening with people I didn't know and with whom I had little in common.

Across the room, Achish caught my eye and smirked. At eighteen, he considered himself a man, so he would not do anything to ease my way. Adinai would do his best to make me feel comfortable because he was good and generous. But once we reached the ceren's home, custom would demand that he and Achish join the men while I went in search of the women.

"Why won't you come with me, Mama?" I muttered the words in a low whisper, not wanting Achish to realize how much I still depended on my mother.

"Delilah." She stopped sewing. "You know why I can't go. I don't want to make things awkward for your father."

"But," I whispered, "if the people of Gaza cannot accept your black skin, what makes you think they will accept mine? I am nearly as dark as you."

She resumed sewing, sliding her needle through beads she was adding to a garment. "You are young, dearest one, and so breathtaking that everyone will think of you as an exotic flower. Go out tonight with Adinai and Achish, have a good time, and make friends with the ceren's daughters. I will wait here, and tomorrow you can tell me all about the big event."

I blew out a breath and stood, walked outside, and wandered in the moon garden. Citrus blossoms perfumed the spring air, along with several varieties of white flowers. I would have been perfectly happy to spend the evening playing my harp here, but my stepfather had insisted Achish and I accompany him to the banquet. Mother had added that Achish and I would honor Adinai in different ways. I would honor him with my beauty, and Achish would reflect his father's strength and vitality.

I cared little about honoring Adinai. I admired the man, but why should I worry about his reputation among his Philistine peers? So long as he left me alone and treated Mama kindly, I would be content.

"Mistress?" My handmaid's voice filled the quiet of the garden, and I knew it would be futile to hide from her. In Adinai's olive-skinned household, as in most of Gaza, Mother and I stood out like fleas on a linen sheet.

"Coming, Zahra." I lifted my chin, took a deep breath of the fragrant air, and moved toward the gate.

CHAPTER TWO
SAMSON

"You think she lives here?" I studied the mud-brick building near the road. A stone wall enclosed the place, and animal troughs lined the wall. The perfect setup for an inn.

Rei, my manservant, crossed his arms and gave me a warning look. "You know this is a bad idea."

"There's no harm in visiting a woman."

"One of our women, maybe. But this one is a Philistine and a heathen. Your parents—your tribe—will not approve."

"Can't a thirty-five-year-old man make his own decisions?"

"Probably not, in your case. You must consider who and what you are."

Again with the reminders. I was not an ordinary man; I had been chosen and set apart. I was special. I was blessed. I was *alien*. And so on and so forth.

On days like this, I would have given my right hand to be like one of my brothers—completely ordinary.

"Can't a judge," I began again, "take a wife and have a family? Other judges have done so."

"You are rarely home. You are always traveling between villages, spending a night here, two nights there—"

"My wife can travel with me."

Rei shook his head. "She will not want to travel once Adonai blesses you with children. And then what will you do? Stay home?"

"Then people can come to me." I looked down the road to where the morning sun stood like a dazzling blur against the sky. "I am lonely, Rei. Did Adonai not say that it is not good for man to be alone?"

After a long moment, Rei rolled his eyes, then gestured toward a spreading terebinth tree outside the wall. "If you insist on going inside, I'm waiting there in the shade. I'll not sully my hands in a Philistine establishment."

I snorted. "You're too pious for your own good."

"You should be more like me."

"You should keep quiet."

Leaving Rei to sit in the dust, I approached the sprawling red-orange building with a wary step. Two bronze markers stood by the door, one featuring the image of Baal, the other the image of Ashtoreth, Baal's wife. Baal held a scythe in one hand and a stalk of wheat in the other, signifying his control of fertility and the harvest.

I snorted in derision and turned my eyes away. On my travels to the various tribes of Israel, I saw similar images in front of Israelite homes—another proof that many of my kinsmen had begun to worship the pagan gods of the Canaanites. If my chosen bride worshiped such idols, I would teach her the ways of HaShem, the one true God.

A half-dozen square windows looked out at the corral, where a few pack animals had been allowed to mingle—a pair of mules, a camel, and a beautiful black gelding. I whistled in appreciation and brushed the dust off my tunic. I hadn't come to Timnah to admire horseflesh. I had come to admire a woman.

Confident that I didn't look too bad for a man who'd been walking for the past hour, I stepped across the building's threshold and entered a wide, open room. Several long tables occupied the space, and a half-dozen men occupied the benches—Philistines, mostly, several of them clad in the brass armor of Philistine warriors.

I sat on a bench at a mostly empty table, nodding to the solitary figure at the other end. The man greeted me by lifting his chin, then stared morosely into his copper cup. At least he was sober enough to acknowledge a visitor.

I shifted my gaze as the innkeeper shuffled toward me. "What can I do for you, shepherd?" he asked, taking my measure in one disdainful glance.

I ignored the insult in his tone and continued to look around. I had hoped his daughters would be working in this room. I had seen one of them as she rode by my pasture. With a single glimpse of her shapely form, yellow hair, and white smile, I'd been smitten. After asking around, I'd learned that she was the daughter of the man presently regarding me as if I were something on the sole of his sandal.

"I'd like stew, if you have it," I said, peering past the innkeeper for some semblance of a feminine form. "And wine."

The man grunted. "And what have you brought to pay?"

From the leather pouch at my belt I produced a carved wooden whistle. I offered it for his inspection. "For calling the sheep. Dogs too." The man gave the whistle a tentative toot, then laughed when every man in the room turned toward him. "Just the thing for calling my daughters. All right, but you'll have to wait a bit."

I turned to stretch my legs and take a slower survey of the room. At the table farthest from me, a group of Canaanite merchants were eating cheese, bread, and honey. They wore robes too garish for an ordinary day and were probably hoping to sell the colorful cloaks they wore.

The table next to them held a group of Philistine soldiers, by far the rowdiest bunch in the room. Judging from their level of inebriation, I wouldn't have been surprised to learn that they had been sitting and drinking for most of the day. The five Philistine lords ruled from their respective cities, but joint cooperation enabled them to maintain mobile forces in the conquered Israelite territories. The foreigners had thoroughly occupied our Promised Land by robbing and raping, taxing and terrorizing.

But none of them had robbed or terrorized me.

Near the soldiers sat a pair of shepherds, and from the way they furtively dipped their bread in their bowls, I gathered that their flocks were nearby . . . and probably unguarded. They'd better eat quickly or one of the soldiers might claim a lamb for his dinner.

The only other guests were the morose fellow and me.

My pulse quickened as an odd thought reared its head. What if one of these other men had come about my woman? What if we had all been entranced by the sight of golden hair and red lips?

I refused to lose her due to a lack of initiative.

I straightened my spine, stood and went through the same doorway the innkeeper had used. I found myself inside a proper kitchen where a kettle bubbled over a cook fire near a table loaded with a bowl of dough, a platter of dried meat, a mortar and pestle. The young woman I'd seen stood with her fingers in the dough, and she froze at the sight of me, her eyes going wide.

"Don't worry." I lifted both hands to calm her fears, though my own heart did a double beat. "I'm looking for your father."

"He's . . ." She jerked a dough-covered finger toward another door. The man had probably gone outside to relieve himself.

"I can wait." I leaned against a wooden beam and tried to smile, not an easy task in the face of such breathtaking loveliness. "I'm

Samson, from Zorah." I crossed my arms, feeling as awkward as a lad. "I saw you the other day—you rode by my field. On your mule."

"Did I?" She had begun to knead her bread again, but she glanced at me and smiled.

My pounding heart stuttered. I was accustomed to women—I had a mother, and half the girls in Zorah had fancied themselves in love with me ever since my voice deepened—but the girls of my acquaintance were shy and withdrawn, with low murmuring voices, quick flushes, and nervous smiles. In all my years, never had a woman looked me directly in the eye. Even my mother tended to be withdrawn in my presence.

But this one was different. My smile broadened. Maybe this woman didn't see me as some kind of freak. She wouldn't have heard the stories, so she wouldn't treat me like an outsider. She saw me for the man I was, *as* I was, and she smiled at me.

By the time her father returned, I was ready to offer half of Canaan in exchange for his daughter.

"You!" He hurried toward me in a rush, his brows drawing together. "You should not be in here."

"In truth, I didn't come here for stew," I said, pulling myself off the beam. "I came to ask for your daughter. I saw her the other day, and just now I've spoken with her. She seems to like me, and I know I like her. So with your permission, I think we should marry."

The wide-eyed innkeeper backed away, then turned to his daughter. "Is this true?"

The girl fluttered her lashes in my direction. "He looks like a good man. And he's wearing a very nice tunic."

The innkeeper studied me more closely. "Who are you, and where are you from? Who are your people?"

One question at a time, the easiest first. "My father," I began, "is Manoah, and he's a prosperous farmer in Zorah. We are Israelites, from the tribe of Dan."

The innkeeper's eyes narrowed. "We don't get many Israelites in here."

I shrugged. "Most of my people keep to themselves."

"What about you? If I let you marry my daughter, will I ever see her again?"

"I'm not like most of my people." I grinned at the girl, whose answering smile set a dimple to winking in her cheek. "And I plan on living in Zorah, so she won't be far from you. I'll take good care of her."

The innkeeper looked at me again, then sighed and lifted his hands. "Who am I to stand in your way? If Kesi agrees, then yes, you may have her. But this thing must be done properly. Send your father to me, so we may draw up a betrothal contract."

Kesi. A nice name.

I gave the girl a broad smile, then clasped her father's hand. "It shall be done. I will go see my parents at once." I turned and moved toward the doorway, but the innkeeper's voice stopped me. "What about your stew?"

"Give it to the sad fellow at my table," I answered. "And keep the whistle as a pledge of good faith. I'll be back before you can train your dogs with it."

CHAPTER THREE
DELILAH

WITH A SHAWL DRAPED modestly over my bare shoulders, I followed my stepfather's wide form as we entered the sprawling estate belonging to Zaggi, Lord of Gaza. The brick house I glimpsed through the wide ornamented gate was the largest private residence I'd ever seen. Torches burned on the exterior walls, an extravagant waste of fuel. No fewer than eight armored guards stood in dual lines at the entrance, their heavy iron swords tugging at their leather belts.

I felt the pressure of their gazes on me as I followed the men of my household. Since maturing into a woman, I had become aware of a certain expression in men's eyes. Now I was so attuned to it that I could sense it even through a crowd. Like hungry vultures, men would stop moving and remain still, their gazes fastened to me. If I happened to glance at their faces, their expressions made me feel that I was something other than a girl—an animal to be hunted, perhaps, or an opponent to be humbled.

Though I had grown accustomed to that look, I didn't like it.

"Adinai, welcome to my home." Our host, the ceren of Gaza, greeted my stepfather in an unusually nasal voice and gripped Achish's hand. A smile twisted my mouth as Achish's cheeks glowed beneath the ceren's attention. He looked like a grateful puppy receiving praise for urinating in the right spot.

I dipped my knee in a bow when our host turned his eyes upon me. He did not leer at me like the men in the courtyard, but gave me a warm welcome. "Ah, Adinai, now I understand why you were so eager to return to Egypt. If your new wife is half as lovely as her daughter, you are indeed a fortunate man." The ceren nodded at me. "My wife and daughters are eager to welcome you. You'll find them beyond the fountain in the courtyard."

He moved aside to greet the next guest, and we entered the house. My jeweled sandals moved silently over the polished stone floors until we entered a large room where guests were accepting food from trays offered by white-robed servants. A female servant caught my eye and gestured toward another doorway. I understood at once— a woman had no business socializing with men. The servant would escort me to my proper place.

I followed the maid through the painted doorway and found myself in a small courtyard where a mosaic fountain sprayed purple water high into the air. I stopped to gaze upward, but the servant cleared her throat and led me into another room where three trays stood in the center of the space. Large pillows had been scattered over the floor, and women of varying ages sat on them. As I entered, a group of younger girls stood, squealed, and hurried to my side.

"Oh, what a lovely skirt!"

"Such a pretty linen!"

"Does your father really allow you to wear linen? It's so expensive."

"Is it true? You live with Achish? He is *so* handsome!"

The girls scattered when a taller girl approached. "Ignore my silly

sisters," she said, smiling, "and come sit by me. Sometimes I grow
tired of talking to these spoiled children, so you are most welcome.
It's good to see a new face."

The taller girl gestured to the empty pillow at her side, so I sat.
When the younger sisters gathered around to pepper me with questions, she waved them away. "Go spy through the courtyard and tell
me what you see. I understand that Achish is inside with the men."

Like a flock of starlings they flew past the fountain to the first
doorway, where they clutched at the curtain and peered out in
hushed anticipation.

A reluctant grin tugged at my hostess's mouth. "I am Sapha, the
ceren's oldest daughter. I understand you are called Delilah."

I nodded in pleased surprise. "You know my name?"

Sapha chuckled. "Father confides in me far more than he should.
Since he has no male heirs, I have become the son he always wanted.
I knew who would be on the guest list even before my mother knew
she had to plan a banquet."

I found it impossible not to return her disarming smile. "How
nice to be so close to your father."

"Are you not close to yours?"

"My father died four years ago when his ship sank in the Great
Sea. Adinai is my stepfather."

Sapha's eyes softened. "I am genuinely sorry to hear that, but my
father thinks highly of Adinai. I trust he treats you well?"

"He is quite generous with me. More important, he is good to
my mother."

"Then you are twice blessed. Not every girl can say as much about
the man who chooses her mother."

The girls in the doorway squealed again. Sapha looked at them
and sighed. "I daresay my sisters have spotted your brother. Achish makes quite an impression when he rides through Gaza in his
chariot. My father—and my sisters—have certainly noticed him."

Unimpressed, I lifted one shoulder in a shrug, eliciting a look of surprise from the older girl. "Do you not like Achish?"

I hesitated. How honest could I be? Instinct told me to watch my tongue, but this girl had given me no reason to mistrust her. "Achish is older than me," I began, "so we have little in common. For the most part, he remains occupied with his interests and I with mine. I spend the day with my mother; he travels often with his father."

"Nothing unusual in that. But soon Adinai will arrange a betrothal for you, and then you'll have your own household." Mischief lit Sapha's eyes. "May the gods help you find a good husband . . . and a rich one."

I laughed. Then, lowering my voice, I asked, "Have you been betrothed?"

Sapha's smile dimmed a degree. "Father says he has chosen my future husband, but he will not let me be married until the young man has grown a bit older."

"You make it sound like he's still a toddling child."

"He's eighteen, the same age as me," Sapha said. "But he is definitely not ready to marry. Two of my younger sisters are betrothed too, but Father says we must wait for our future husbands to grow into their responsibility." She tilted her head. "My father says Adinai is wealthy. Do you think he will be generous with your dowry? You are not really his daughter, after all. And clearly"—her gaze ran over my cocoa-colored skin—"you are neither Philistine nor Israelite. Where do you come from?"

My smile chilled. Sapha's question had raised two interesting concerns. Would Adinai be generous with my prospective husband? And where would he find a suitable suitor, since I was not a full-blooded Philistine, Hebrew, Egyptian, or Cushite? Who would agree to marry a mixed creature like me?

"Delilah?" Sapha's expression sharpened. "Are you all right? For a moment, you looked ill."

My answering smile trembled. "I . . . had not given much thought to my betrothal. My mother married Adinai only three months ago, so we are still getting used to each other."

"Don't worry." Sapha took my hand and patted it. "I apologize for making you feel uncomfortable. This evening is a celebration. My father admires your stepfather, and your brother will have a marvelous time drinking and belching with the men. Come, let me offer you some delicacies. Our cook loves to sweeten with Egyptian honey; have you tried it? Try the bread with honeyed almonds. I'm sure you have never tasted anything like it."

I bit into the biscuit she offered and pasted on a smile as I chewed. I had tasted such dainties before; my mother often baked them. Because she had come from a land south of Egypt, Egyptian honey had always been a staple in our household.

But I would not share my personal history with the girl from Gaza. I had learned many lessons from Mama, and chief among them was to guard one's secrets closely.

⌖

Mother met me outside her bedroom, her dark eyes searching my face. "Did you have a good time at the banquet?"

I nodded, acknowledging once again that she'd been right. "I met the ceren's daughters."

She smiled and took my hand. "How many daughters has he?"

"Too many. But the eldest, Sapha, was quite congenial. She is older, but not much." I tilted my head, a little reluctant to mention a topic that had been weighing on my mind since the banquet. "Sapha is eighteen and already betrothed. Have you or Adinai made any plans for my betrothal?"

Mother looked at me, an odd mingling of caution and amusement in her eyes. "So soon? You are still so young."

"I'm in no hurry to be married," I said, trying to reassure her. "But seventeen is not so young in Gaza, so perhaps Adinai should consider his role in my future. After all, the sooner I am married, the sooner he can have you all to himself."

Her grip on my hand tightened. "No one wants to be rid of you."

"I didn't mean that. I meant—"

"Don't worry about such things, Delilah. Adinai will do whatever is best for you." Mama released my hand, then pressed a kiss to my temple. "Get some rest, my darling girl. I will beg the gods to provide the right husband when you are ready."

I kissed her cheek and moved down the hallway. By the dim light of an oil lamp burning on the wall, I saw a masculine silhouette and the glimmer of narrowed eyes within Achish's chamber.

"De-li-lah," he called softly. "Did you have a nice time with Lord Zaggi's daughters?"

Experience had already taught me that I would never have the last word in a verbal match with my stepbrother, so I ignored him and went into my room.

"Delilah!" His tone sharpened. "What did you hens talk about? Did the girls ask why your skin is the color of mud? Did they ask about your black mother?"

I turned and pulled the curtain between us, blocking his view. But the frail screen did nothing to prevent me from hearing his mocking laughter.

CHAPTER FOUR

SAMSON

"I CANNOT BELIEVE MY SON—my *Nazarite* son—would marry a Philistine."

Father did not hesitate to vent his displeasure when I gave him my news. Mother didn't say much when I announced my intention, but she had not smiled since. Apparently she felt as Father did, unless her disapproval surpassed his, but I gave my parents no choice in the matter. When they suggested I take another look at the women of my tribe, I told them the truth—none of the women from my tribe excited me. If they wanted me to be happy, they would have to allow me to marry the girl from Timnah.

"Why can't you be more like your brothers?" Father fixed a stern eye on me. "Each of them married a girl from our own tribe. Each of them already has children—"

"Because I am not like them," I answered, clenching my jaw. "And you know that full well."

Father pressed his lips into a thin line and turned away, unable to argue further.

Grudgingly, my parents agreed to accompany me to the inn at Timnah, where Kesi lived. They walked in front of me, a pair of bent heads whispering and no doubt wondering where they had gone wrong in raising me.

I remained behind them, careful to hide my excited smile whenever they glanced over their shoulders. Indignation fueled their pace—they were walking faster than usual, and if they kept moving at this speed, they would arrive in Timnah well before dinnertime. That was fine with me. The sooner we completed our negotiation, the happier I would be. If my fair-haired girl desired it, I would have willingly run the distance. If she wanted silver or gold or fine leathers as a betrothal gift, I would find a way to fulfill her heart's desire.

When we came to a fork in the road, I glanced at Rei, who walked beside me. He read my intentions and lifted a warning brow, but I laughed and took the steeper path. It would also take me to Timnah, but it passed by a vineyard. The vines were bearing fruit now, and the owner might not mind a few missing grapes. . . .

Though the hot sun packed a punch only a serpent could love, I was far too excited to be slowed by the heat. "Just think," I said, startling Rei out of his reverie, "in a few weeks that gorgeous woman will be my wife. Every man in Israel will be smitten with jealousy."

"Now *that's* a good reason to marry a Philistine." Rei's voice dripped with sarcasm. "You think you love her, but how could you? You don't even know her!"

"Someone that beautiful cannot help being good." I scooped up a handful of pebbles and sent one ricocheting off an overhanging rock. "And if she is not completely good, I will lead her in the ways of Adonai. We will live near my parents, and Mother will teach her all she needs to know."

Rei heaved a dramatic sigh. "Do you think she will want to live near a disapproving mother-in-law? I've a feeling your precious mother and your pagan wife will make your life miserable."

"You're wrong about that. Mother wants me to be happy."

"Oh, yes, by all means—let's be happy. Our happiness is all that matters." Rei's dark brows lowered. "Has it occurred to you that our people have good reasons to be *unhappy*? For thirty years the Philistines—like your true love—have made our lives miserable. You are one of our leaders, but you want to *marry* one of our oppressors! How does that make sense?"

Rei's words echoed against the rocky walls along the path, but I paid them no mind. All I could think of was Kesi; all I wanted to do was lie in her arms and imagine our future together.

"There!" Leaving Rei on the path, I sprinted to the vineyard, then darted into one of the long green rows. Thick vines cascaded over wooden supports, and diligent bees hummed around the thick purple clusters. I grabbed the top of a stalk and broke it off, then held it above my head, nibbling at the lowest grapes. The ripe fruit popped when I bit into it, raining sweet juice over my tongue.

I turned, about to toss the bunch to Rei, and saw that his eyes had widened. "Samson, behind you!"

Even without Rei's warning, I would have heard the low, quivering growl. I dropped the fruit and turned. A lion—a young male, his ruff only beginning to fill in—crouched ahead of me in the row. His whiskers twitched as his throat rumbled, and experience warned that I had only a few seconds before the animal sprang—

Adonai!

With a cry, the lion roared and launched himself toward me. Claws pierced the skin at my shoulders and scraped my belly as his powerful jaws sought my throat. Somehow I caught his teeth and held a row of fangs in each hand. Though the claws on all four feet ripped at my calves, stomach, and neck, I strained, pulling the animal's jaws apart until I heard the snap of breaking bone. As a primal scream echoed between the rock walls, I twisted the massive head until the spine snapped and forever eased the creature's pain.

The lion went limp in my arms. I released him and stepped back to view the carcass lying motionless amid the grapevines.

Rei crept up beside me, his face pale. "Impressive," he said, eyeing the sleek body. "And you killed it without a weapon."

I lifted my hands, now streaked with blood. "When your hands are powered by the *Ruach Adonai*, why bother with a weapon?"

Like a fussy woman, Rei clucked against his teeth. "What are you going to tell your parents? Your legs are running with blood, and your tunic is torn."

"I'll wash at the creek." I shrugged. "And it won't be the first time Mother has had to mend one of my tunics."

Rei slammed the heel of his hand against his forehead—one of his more frequent gestures—then strode toward a boulder where he could rest while I cleaned up.

I found a nearby creek and knelt at its edge to splash the blood from my arms and legs. Fortunately, the lion was young—an older beast might have inflicted more damage once he decided to strike. My bold attacker was impulsive and the attack hardly worth mentioning.

When I finished, I waved for Rei's attention, then pointed to the valley below. "Yonder lies Timnah where a beautiful woman waits for me. You'll see, Rei—you will find her a feast for the eyes, so let's hurry!"

Rei shook his head yet again, but then he slid from the rock and followed.

Chapter Five

DELILAH

I SAT ON A STOOL, my chin propped in my hand as Zahra wound my long hair around strips of linen, rolled them up, and tied them in my hair. The Philistines, I had noticed as soon as we arrived in Gaza, were crazy for curly hair, a fashion trend that favored me more than my Egyptian maid. They were also wild about color, which explained the varicolored, multilayered skirts wealthy women wore over light linen garments. I had just removed such a skirt, and now I wore a simple cotton sheath, an Egyptian style that suited my long, leggy form.

"What did you see at the party?" Zahra asked, always curious about what lay beyond the walls of Adinai's house. "Did the women wear perfumed cones on their heads like they do in Egypt?"

"No." I stifled a yawn, then gave her a guilty smile. "Sorry. The women wore lots of colors, lots of curls, and many of them wore hats. Only older women, though. The girls my age just—" I yawned again—"wore curls."

"There." Zahra tied the last roll and stepped back. "I don't know why you do this, but tomorrow your hair will look like all the other girls'."

"Maybe that's why I want to do it. Since we have to live here, it would be nice to fit in." I stood and moved toward my bed. "Tomorrow I'll see if I can remake some of my tunics. The Philistines have a way of cinching the waist—"

I froze when an anguished cry filled the house and seemed to go straight to the center of my head. Was that Mother? Alarmed, I moved to my door and hesitated only because Achish might still be sitting in his room. But why should I worry about him?

Desperately concerned for Mama, I flung back the curtain and hurried to the chamber she shared with Adinai. The heavy wooden door was open, its occupants shadowed in flickering lamplight.

"Delilah." Mother knelt on the bed, clinging to Adinai's shoulders, her face twisted with fear. "Call Achish. Call someone!"

I beheld Adinai lying on his back, his face red, his chest gleaming in a sheen of sweat. His manservant stood nearby, his fists clenching and unclenching while Mother clung to her husband and pleaded for help. "Can't you do something?" she asked the servant. "Can't you fetch a physician?"

The terrified servant shook his head.

With fearful clarity, I saw that Mama was too frightened to be forceful. "Light more lamps," I commanded the servant as I moved farther into the room. "We can't help him if we can't see."

I glanced around and spotted Achish standing behind me in a shadowed corner, his eyes wide, his body hunched and quivering. Was he as panicked as the servant?

"Achish! Do you know your father's physician?"

His wide eyes focused on me, then his brows lowered. I had irritated him—probably by taking control—but I had no time to worry about his prideful sensibilities. I hurried to Adinai's side and pressed my palm to his perspiring forehead.

My stepfather stiffened, drew a stuttering breath, and then re-laxed, color draining from his flesh even as the breath left his body. I waited a long moment, hoping he would revive, but he did not move. His eyes remained open while my mother pressed her head to his chest and wept. I slid my hand over his face, gently lowering my stepfather's eyelids.

Cold reality hit me like an overpowering wave—Adinai, master of this household and a prosperous shipping business, breathed no more. He had not been particularly old or weak, nor had he been ill. At the ceren's banquet he had been the picture of wealth and success, his smile as broad as his expansive waistline.

But even in my short lifetime, I had learned that death often arrived unexpectedly.

Zahra stepped into the room and pulled my sobbing mother from the deathbed. Murmuring in Egyptian, she helped Mama into a chair and then handed her a soft cloth to wipe her tears away.

"She . . . Mama can sleep in my room tonight," I said, stepping away on legs that felt like wood. "I don't think she will be able to—"

"I will take care of the master," the manservant said, finally prov-ing himself useful. "With Achish's permission." He tipped his head toward the foot of the bed where Achish now stood, his arms braced on the footboard, his eyes wide, his head lolling back and forth like a bull stunned by the slaughterer's blade.

At a sudden realization, a tremor scooted up the back of my neck: Adinai was no longer master of this household. That honor had passed to his son.

❦

After Zahra and I helped settle my grieving mother in my bed, I spread several blankets on the floor and lay down. The exhaustion I'd felt earlier had been replaced by an edgy watchfulness, and as my bones grated against the hard tile I thought I might never sleep again. Questions and anxieties raced through my mind, chasing each other in an endless loop.

What would become of me and my mother? After marrying Mama in the shadow of the pyramids, Adinai had brought us to Gaza and promised us a good life among the people of Philistia. We had enjoyed our short time in his house, but we had not lived in Gaza long enough to make friends or establish strong connections. Instinct assured me that Achish would not tolerate our presence for more than a few weeks, but I couldn't think of anyone who would willingly take us in, even temporarily. Achish had managed to disguise his disdain for us in front of his father, but when Adinai was away, Achish had been openly contemptuous of me and cool toward Mama. Clearly, he was not happy about his father's marriage.

No, Achish would not want us to remain in his household. He'd tell us to take our servants and go, and we'd have to obey. Achish would have fewer mouths to feed if we left, and he would be free to establish himself in business and society. As Adinai's heir, he would have full control of his father's shipping and import business. He could grant us safe passage back to Egypt, but I did not think his generosity would stretch that far.

Mama and I would have to find another way home. I could visit Sapha, the closest thing I had to a friend in Gaza, and ask her father to intervene on our behalf. As ceren of the largest and most prosperous city in Philistia, surely he could find someone who would return us to Egypt either by ship or caravan. Mother and I would go back to our friends and the little stall where Mama wove the straw hats and mats we exchanged for food and shelter. We had not been wealthy in Egypt, but neither had we starved.

I hugged my pillow and wiped away a tear. If only Adinai had never noticed my beautiful mother . . .

Sunrise found me with red-rimmed eyes and heavy eyelids. At

some point I had drifted to sleep, and on rising I felt old, even older than my mother, who sat on the edge of my bed and regarded me with bleary eyes.

"I thought we would have years together," she said, her mouth twisting in something not quite a smile. "I would have done things so differently had I known . . ."

I pulled a loose linen strip from my hair. "No one can know such things, Mama."

"Achish will be distraught," Mother went on, fingering the silver necklace at her throat. "I must try to comfort him, if he will let me. Later, when his grief is not so fresh, we must ask him about his plans. Perhaps he can find a little house for us, someplace near the sea where we can live quietly."

I heard the sound of Zahra's footsteps, followed by a soft cough outside the curtained doorway.

"Come in."

Zahra stepped inside, letting the curtain fall behind her. "Master *Adinai*," she said, "rests in the front room awaiting visitors, then he will be transported to his tomb and buried before sunset. His manservant assures me that this is the usual practice in Gaza."

I blew out a breath, startled by the difference in burial rites. In Egypt, a wealthy man like Adinai would have been mourned for seventy days, the time required for the proper embalming of a body. During our mourning period, we would have gathered items he might need in the afterlife and placed them in his tomb. I found it hard to imagine a funeral as a hurried affair.

Mother bent her head in a stiff nod. "I will arrange whatever must be done."

"No need, my lady. Master Achish has already made the arrangements, and he plans to lead his father's funeral procession." Zahra's gaze met mine. "I will bring a breakfast tray for both of you. Later I will return to help you dress."

I was about to say that we would prefer to eat on the loggia, but the maid shook her head in a barely perceptible movement. "It would be best, mistress, if I bring a tray to you."

I pressed my lips together and watched her go, then went to my basin and pitcher. After splashing my face, I patted my skin dry and turned to my mother. She had not moved, but remained on the edge of my bed, her gaze lowered, her hands folded in her lap.

"Mama? Would you like to wash your face?"

"I will go to my own room."

She stood and walked toward the door, but Zahra interrupted with our breakfast. She set a tray of bread, fruit, and cheese on my dressing table, then stepped back, her hands trembling. Mother looked at the food, but I couldn't help noticing Zahra's distress. "What's wrong?"

"Oh, lady." She closed her eyes as if she could not bear to watch my face while she answered, "Master Achish . . . did not sleep last night."

"The boy must be tired." Mother took another step toward the door. "I'll urge him to get some rest. With guests coming to the house—"

Zahra reached out, daring to lay her hand on her mistress's arm. The unexpected breach of protocol halted Mama in mid-step.

"The young master has been busy." Zahra's voice quavered. "And he bade me command you both to appear on the loggia."

Mother's brow rose in surprise, but a different feeling chilled my blood. I had not expected Achish to begin issuing orders within hours of his father's death.

"We'll see him after we eat," I told Zahra. "We haven't had an opportunity to break our fast."

The maid bit her lip. "I would hurry, mistress. The young master has never demonstrated much patience."

Mother extended a restraining hand. "The lad is undoubtedly in shock. He needs to sleep, eat, and take some time to collect himself. I know grief—" she paused to clear her throat—"and I know how it affects the heart. I will comfort him and—"

"Lady, I would not—"

A gesture from Mama cut off Zahra's protest, then my mother raised her chin and moved out of the room, striding gracefully toward the loggia. With nerves strung as tight as a harp string, I followed.

As we approached, I spotted my stepbrother sitting in the chair Adinai had often chosen when he wanted to think or study the garden. Achish's broad shoulders rose above the back of the chair and his arms rested on the wooden armrests. Though he had to hear our approaching footsteps, he did not move or even turn his head until we stood only a few paces away.

Mother stepped toward him, her arms open, but she froze when Achish commanded her to stop. "You will come no closer."

Mama tilted her head and gave him a weary smile. "Dear Achish, we all struggle with the dreary aftermath, but our struggle is lessened if we share our sorrows—"

"I have not given you permission to speak." Achish's eyes narrowed. "You, woman, have spent your last day in this household. I have no need of a black slave."

Paralyzed by sheer disbelief at the cold expression on his face, I couldn't move. What was he saying? My mother had never been a slave.

Shock flickered over Mama's face like summer lightning. "Achish, are you not feeling well?"

"I have never felt better." He gave me a bright-eyed glance, filled with cunning. "My father purchased both of you in Egypt three months ago. Now that he is gone, I do not need so many servants."

"You lie!" Shocked out of stillness, the words flew from my lips. "How dare you proclaim such falsehoods! Everyone knows that my mother was Adinai's legal wife."

"Do they?" An amused light danced in Achish's eyes. "Produce witnesses to the marriage."

"I was a witness!" I lifted my chin. "As was Makamaru, the master of the ship that brought us from Egypt. He witnessed the ceremony before we set sail."

"Makamaru's ship frequently transports slaves," Achish said, "and the ship and its captain are no longer in port. As to your testimony, the word of a slave holds no weight with authorities in Gaza. A slave will say anything to escape his bonds, therefore a slave's testimony cannot be trusted."

Though my head swarmed with words of defiance, my astonishment was so great that I couldn't answer. I knew Achish resented us, but I had underestimated the depth of his bitterness. I hadn't expect him to act against us so quickly—or so severely. I needed time to study his argument and I needed to seek counsel about how to counteract whatever mischief he had in mind. Everyone knew that Adinai had legally married my mother.

But who could testify on our behalf? The servants, of course, were slaves. Adinai's business associates? I didn't know if he ever discussed his personal life with his clients, and even if he had, Achish would probably bribe them to support his case. My stepfather's friends? Perhaps, but Mother had never gone out with Adinai in public. Fearing what people might say about her ebony skin and foreign features, she had thought it best to remain at home a few months to give people time to adjust their thinking. I had not gone out much for the same reason, but just last night my stepfather and I had visited the ceren's home—

"Last night." Summoning up a confidence I didn't quite feel, I dared to meet Achish's gaze. "Last night I went with you to a banquet at the ceren's house. I spent the evening with his daughters, and the eldest, Sapha, will confirm that I spoke of Adinai as my stepfather."

The corner of Achish's mouth twisted. "I will tell Sapha that you are an inveterate liar."

"Why would she believe you?"

His smile turned into a chuckle. "Because our fathers were in the midst of negotiating our betrothal. She and her father will believe anything I tell them."

An odd roaring filled my ears, a rush of blood and anger. "If I am not Adinai's stepdaughter—" I drew a deep breath—"then why did I accompany you and your father to the ceren's banquet?"

He leaned forward on the armrest of his chair as his eyes lit with an inexplicable flame. "You came with us because you are my extremely spoiled and often unpleasant concubine. Since we will be sharing a house together, I wanted my future wife to meet you."

"I would never agree to be your concubine." I looked at him with revulsion. "The only thing we ever had in common was Adinai, and now he's gone."

"Indeed he is." A glow rose in Achish's face. "Now I own everything that was my father's—his business, his house, his women. Men will bow before me on the street, and others will help me multiply my wealth. I will have many friends, and many of them are powerful."

"You think you can inherit respect?" Tremors of mirth fractured my voice. "You may inherit your father's possessions, yes. But you will never have the respect your father enjoyed because you are nothing like him!"

Achish scowled, his brows knitting together. "You don't think I'll be respected? Then let me be feared. Let others rush to do my bidding and tremble at my approach. The result is the same."

"Achish, is this what your father would want?" Mother spoke, a faint line between her brows as she felt her way into the conversation. "He would be so disappointed to hear you say these things."

A muscle clenched along Achish's jaw. "Three months," he said, his chest rising and falling as he seethed. "You think you should inherit after only three months in my father's house? After only three months, could you possibly expect to share in the fruits of his lifetime? No! It would not be right! And I do not listen to my slaves."

As Mother gasped, Achish gestured to his manservant. "Take Delilah to the master's room and lock her in. If she does not remain quiet, you may bind and gag her. I will not have her disturbing the household while my father lies in the foyer."

I broke free of my paralysis and screamed as the burly servant gripped my arm. I slapped at him, but the man feared Achish far more than me.

"You had better cooperate." The grim line of Achish's mouth relaxed. "If you want things to go well for your mother, you will calm yourself and go willingly to my room."

I glanced at Mama, who appeared to be swaying on her feet. Shadows of distress circled her eyes as she looked at me and shook her head. *Don't fight,* she was saying. *Don't give him an excuse to harm us further.*

I turned my head, unable to bear the wounded look in her eyes. She probably thought Achish was acting out of grief and he'd soon come to his senses. She hadn't accepted what I realized on our first day as a family—Adinai's son was a cruel and tyrannical monster.

For Mama's sake, I managed to subdue the passions raging in my breast. I clamped my lips together and held my head high as the servant tugged on my arm. Tomorrow, after the burial, I would talk to Mother and we would devise a plan. We would arrange some sort of compromise with Achish, and then we would leave.

But Achish's next statement destroyed my plans. "Bring in the mourners," he told another servant, "and the slave trader. He is to take the old woman away at once."

I spun on my heel and shrieked, fury pulsing through my veins, but Achish had already stood and was moving toward the door. He did not see my display of temper, and my jailer did not loosen his grip. While I struggled in vain, the slave trader stepped onto the loggia, and my mother fell to her knees. As the manservant pulled me around the corner, I saw Mama reach out to me, tears flowing over her cheeks in mute appeal.

⁓⁂⁓

I was not born to be a prisoner.

Locked into my mother's former bedroom, where the dead man had lain only a few hours before, I paced the tiles and beat on the walls to no effect. The bricks bore my blows without complaint, and because I'd been locked away barefoot, my feet made no sound as I strode the room's length and breadth. I wanted to scream, but did not doubt that Achish would send his servant to bind me and stuff a cloth in my mouth if I made any noise that could be heard by funeral visitors.

How dare he? Anger and frustration energized me throughout that long day, providing me with the strength to stomp and fume and grit my teeth. I called down curses upon Achish, but since Mama and I had never worshiped any of the Egyptian gods, I didn't know which gods I should address. No one brought me food or water, so I drank from the washbasin and told myself I was too upset to eat. Several times I pressed my ear to the door, straining to hear sounds of activity, but apparently the thick wood guaranteed privacy.

I did not know much about Philistine funeral customs, so I could only guess at what might be happening in the rooms beyond my prison. Because Adinai had been a well-connected merchant, I was certain Achish would spend most of the day receiving guests. Occasionally, when the wind shifted, I heard the keening of mourners at the front of the house. I supposed they would follow the corpse to its tomb or grave and then would return to receive whatever Achish had promised to pay. I wasn't sure how long he would keep the mourners—Adinai deserved a full month of mourning, but Achish might be too tightfisted to pay for the entire month. Anyone who would sell a father's beloved wife as a slave had no conscience, no sympathy, and no honor.

By the time darkness filled the master's chamber, a profound weariness had settled over me. I sat on the floor in the corner, far from the deathbed, my legs stretched over the cool tiles. I lifted my head when I heard someone fumbling with the lock at the door, but though I shifted to cover my bare legs, I did not rise. I would never stand to honor a man like Achish.

The door opened and I glimpsed a masculine figure, backlit by a lamp in the hallway. The door closed quickly, then I heard creaking from the ropes that supported the straw mattress.

Was it Achish who entered? What was he doing?

I sat for a long while, straining to hear sounds of breathing or movement from the bed. A deep silence filled the chamber, a quiet so intense that I nearly convinced myself I had only imagined someone entering the room. But no . . . someone *had* come in, and only Achish would play a game meant to torment me.

Was this some sort of trap? Surely he didn't intend to go to sleep, not with me free to wander about. He knew I was furious, and he had to know I despised him. I wasn't strong, but I could probably smother a sleeping man with a pillow.

I stared into darkness, trying to remember every object in the room that could be used for a weapon. Achish was probably lying on the only blanket, and I hadn't seen any cords or ropes . . . but why kill him if I could escape?

I stood, fervently hoping that Achish was asleep, then padded across the tile until my fingertips touched the wooden door. Moving soundlessly, I slid my fingers down the wood until I encountered the iron hasp. I placed both hands on the mechanism and pulled with all my might.

Nothing. With the help of his servant, the monster had locked himself in with me. Either that or he had sent someone else in to torment me.

Behind me, a man laughed, the sound ominous, low, and vaguely musical. I whirled around to face my adversary, but I couldn't see anything except shifting shadows.

I heard a soft sound, then a small clay lamp glowed on a man's palm and threw his face into shadows. Achish! He held the lamp aloft, spotted me by the door, and placed the light on a bedside table. "Delilah." My name was a purr in his throat, reminding me of the way a cat toys with a mouse. "Did you think I would let you escape so easily?"

Silently he stood and loosened the brooch that fastened his cloak. The fabric fell to the floor with a soft *swoosh*.

"Achish—" I stepped backward until I hit the wall, then I slid over the bricks, moving back to my corner. "Let me be, brother. Tomorrow I will leave this house and you need never think of me again. I will not ask for anything. I only want to go home."

He smiled and mirrored my movements, sidestepping and keeping pace with me as I moved over the wall. "Beautiful Delilah. Do you think I would send you back to Egypt? I wouldn't. Actually I'm quite sure my father purchased you to be my concubine. Your mother pleasured my father; now it's only right that you should do the same for me.

"Why should I think of you as a shadow"—his sly mouth twisted, and I glimpsed something feral in his eyes—"when you are made of such desirable flesh? Have you not noticed the way men stare at you? You are the sort of woman who makes a man crazy. For three months I have lain awake and dreamed of this moment."

"You're not yourself," I said, finally reaching my corner. "You have not slept, so you are not thinking clearly. If you will get some rest, you will see things differently in the morning."

"I don't think I will." A look of malign satisfaction crept over his features, a look of gloating. "The best thing my father ever did for me was dying when he did. I did not think myself capable of waiting much longer for you."

He lunged for me, and though I scrambled and clawed and kicked, he was stronger, faster, and far more cruel. And when his attack was finished, when I lay violated and bleeding on the cold tile floor, he got up and went to bed, apparently sleeping like an innocent baby.

And why wouldn't he? We were locked in the room together. I had no weapons, and he had greater strength.

Afraid that I might wake him, I crawled to the place where he had dropped his cloak. Then, slowly, I crawled back to my corner and wrapped the cloak around my bruised body. I lay silent for a long time, my eyes fixed on nothing, until weariness mercifully took me away.

Chapter Six
SAMSON

I HAD JUST FINISHED LEADING the flock into the southern fold when I saw Rei approaching. I closed the latch on the gate and exhaled a deep breath—my servant was coming from the direction of my parents' house, which could only mean one thing.

Rei confirmed my suspicions a few moments later. "Your mother wants to see you," he said straightaway, without any preface. "She would speak with you today."

Resisting the urge to vent my frustration, I shook my head. "I suppose I should go over there soon."

"Aye." Rei's eyes shone with humor. "You know your mother."

"Indeed I do."

My parents were both righteous people, but when my father was not in the room, Mother was far more outspoken. My father's nature was practical, sometimes skeptical, but Mother regarded every breath of wind and every drop of rain either as a blessing or a sign from

Adonai. If she wanted to speak to me, she must have seen or heard something she regarded as a divine message, a communication she would be more than happy to share.

I braced the sturdy branch that held the gate in place. "The sheep are safe. I might as well go see her."

"I think," Rei said, smiling, "that would be a good idea."

I found Mother inside the house, kneeling in prayer. Her eyes were lifted toward heaven, and her lips moved silently, for Adonai did not need ears to hear the petitions of His people. She did not see or hear me come in, so I leaned against the wall, folded my arms, and watched until she had finished. Her prayers, combined with her discipline, had shaped and grounded me as a youth, and though I had become a man, she saw no reason to stop praying for me.

Though sometimes I wished she would.

Finally, she lifted her hands, closed her eyes for a moment, and stood. Turning, she saw me and her preoccupied expression surrendered to a smile. "My sunny Samson," she said, coming forward to place her hands on my cheeks. "May those who love Adonai be like the rising of the sun in its might."

I forced a smile, reluctantly acknowledging her play on words. She had named me Samson because of its similarity to our word *shemesh*, which meant *like the sun*. The name had suited me in childhood, but as an adult the name sometimes grated. How could I be expected to be taken seriously when my mother still called me "sunny boy"?

"Mother." I took her warm hands and pressed them together. "Did you want to see me?"

"Always." Her smile widened. "How bright you are! Yes, I would like to speak to you, but not here. Let's walk outside."

I released her hands and watched her open the door, silently inviting me to accompany her. What else could I do? I blew out a breath and followed.

She waited until I walked to her side, then a secretive smile softened her lips. "I know you've been told a few things about your birth," she began. "We've made no secret of the fact that Adonai told us that you would be a Nazarite from birth, set apart for the Lord's service."

I nodded, all too familiar with the story I'd heard since childhood.

"I hope what I'm about to tell you will help you see your responsibilities more clearly. Listen, Samson, and understand—Adonai will do great things through you for our people."

I lifted a brow, because though I had been a judge for some years, Adonai had not yet used me to do any particularly great thing. I made myself available to hear His voice, and after the harvest I traveled the land to judge between His squabbling children, but the angel of Adonai had not appeared to me, nor had I heard the Lord's voice in the night—or in daylight, either, for that matter.

"I am not so sure about that, Mother." I stopped and turned to face her. "The other judges have delivered Israel from her enemies. Yet when Israel went out against the Philistines in Aphek, I wondered if Adonai meant for me to join them, but Father said no. Israel was sorely defeated, the Ark of HaShem captured, and the High Priest Eli died soon after. If HaShem wanted to use me as a judge and deliverer, why didn't Father allow me to join that battle?"

"And have you die like all the others?" Mother's tone sharpened. "You were only eighteen and inexperienced in battle. You would not have survived."

"If I truly am set apart for the Lord's service, Adonai would have protected me."

"Would He protect you from your own foolishness?" Irritation narrowed her eyes, then she reached out and touched my hand. "Honor your father and mother, Son. You chose to honor us, and you did the right thing. Your father and I believe God wanted to protect you for a greater purpose. But I did not bring you out here to talk about unfortunate battles."

"My wife, then." I crossed my arms. "You want to chide me about my choice of a wife."

She tilted her head, and from the look in her eyes I knew she was tempted to agree with me. Instead, she smiled and gestured to the spot where her millstone lay in a circle of large rocks. "Sit, my son. Yes, your father and I wish you had chosen a woman from our people, but I have not brought you here to talk about that Philistine woman. I have brought you here to tell you the entire truth about who and what you are."

She sank to the straw mat next to the millstone while I sat on a rock across from her.

"It happened here." Her gaze roved over the spot, and her hand fell to the circular pair of millstones on the ground. "This may look like a simple mill to you, but this spot has become sacred to me. I was kneeling here, grinding grain, when the angel of Adonai appeared to me. He said, 'Behold, you are barren and have not borne children, but you will conceive and bear a son. So be careful not to drink wine or strong drink, or eat any unclean thing. For you will conceive and bear a son. Let no razor come upon his head, for the boy will be a Nazarite to God from the womb. He will begin to deliver Israel from the hand of the Philistines.'"

Mother looked away and chuckled. "I ran to your father, of course, and though he did not openly doubt my word, I saw uncertainty in his eyes. I wasn't surprised when he asked Adonai to send the man again so that he could learn how to raise the boy who would be born."

For a moment I wondered why she wanted to tell me about this, then a window of understanding opened. As an adult man, I understood why my father might have doubted a wife's word. My mother was extraordinarily beautiful, and if she had been unfaithful, or if someone had raped her in the field, a less righteous woman

might have claimed a supernatural source for a child who looked
nothing like its father.

But I was a younger version of my father, so any question of
infidelity had long been moot.

"Adonai heard your father's prayer," Mother went on. "And the
angel of Adonai came to me in the field and waited while I went
to fetch your father. When your father offered to prepare a young
goat for a meal, the man replied that we could offer a sacrifice to
the Lord instead. Your father asked for the man's name, and the
man smiled. 'Why do you ask for my name?' he said. 'It is secret . . .
and wonderful.'"

"Your father went off to prepare the sacrifice," Mother said, her
gaze traveling to some field of vision I could only imagine, "and I
thought of our ancestor Jacob, who wrestled the angel at Peniel.
Jacob asked that angel *his* name, and the man replied, 'Why are
you asking my name?' And when he had spoken, Jacob realized that
he had seen God face-to-face. Your father and I felt the same way
after talking to the man who visited us."

I looked at her in amused wonder. "Mother, if he was flesh and
blood—"

"Can a man of flesh and blood rise in the flame of a burnt offering?" She gave me a lopsided smile. "Because that's what the angel
of Adonai did. As your father burned the sacrifice, the angel of
Adonai ascended in the smoke. We fell on our faces, your father and
I, because we knew we had seen the same man Jacob saw. We had
seen Adonai. I don't know how He clothed himself in human flesh,
but He was with us, He spoke to us, and His word to us was true."

She looked at me, her eyes shining like twin lamps. "I have held
these memories in my heart and pondered them for years, Samson.
And I have seen a pattern, a pattern you should understand because
all the days of your life have been woven into it."

She waited, clearly expecting some sort of response, so I nodded.

"The Lord our God led Israel out of Egypt," she said, her voice dropping to the low tone she reserved for sacred things. "And the children of Israel followed Adonai under Moses and Joshua, who died when we were dwelling in the land Adonai promised to Abraham. But then our people did evil in Adonai's sight, and the king of Mesopotamia oppressed us until we repented and Adonai raised up Othniel to save us. Then we did evil again, worshiping idols and forgetting our God. Eglon, the king of Moab, oppressed us until we repented and Adonai raised up Ehud to save us. Then we did evil again, following after strange gods, and Adonai sent Jakin, king of Hazor, to oppress us for twenty years. Then we repented, and Adonai raised up Deborah and Barak to save us."

Her eyes bored into mine. "Again we committed evil in Adonai's sight, even sacrificing our babies to false gods. And the Lord brought the Midianites to oppress us until we repented, and Adonai raised up Gideon to save us. I could tell you about Jephthah, Ibzan, Elon, and Abdon, but you know those stories. Adonai chose all of them to judge Israel and remind us of His holy ways."

I nodded to let her know I was listening.

"But after Abdon died, Bnei-Yisrael again did evil in Adonai's eyes, and HaShem gave us over to the Philistines as a result. They swarmed through the land in the months before you were born. I understood then that they would be with us a long time. If we had needed only a little discipline from Adonai's hand, He could have brought forth a grown man to conquer the Philistines and rid the land of their oppression. But He didn't send a grown man. He sent a baby. He sent you."

She placed her hand on her abdomen, as if she could still feel the kicking infant I had once been. "When I realized I was with child, I remembered what the angel of Adonai had said. You were sent to begin to deliver Israel from the Philistines, and you would not commence your work until Adonai provided the opportunity.

That's why I knew we would endure many long years of Philistine oppression . . . because our sin against Adonai was extremely great."

Silence fell between us, a thick quiet in which she watched to see how her words had taken hold. I felt the weight of her expectations on my shoulders, and the burden of them was so heavy I nearly slid off the rock.

"How can one man rid the land of so many Philistines?" I asked. "They are not headed by a single king, but by a confederacy of kings! They have ships and armies, walled cities and chariots! They have iron while we only have brass and copper—"

Mother lifted an interrupting finger. "The messenger from Adonai did not say you would deliver us," she pointed out, "but that you would *begin to* deliver us. Rest in that promise, my son. Once Adonai leads you to act against our oppressors, you will have help. He will call others to aid in your cause, and Bnei-Yisrael will repent and return to the Lord." Her eyes softened. "Perhaps one of your helpers is sitting with his mother even now, hearing stories of how he was born into Adonai's service. Perhaps he is praying for a sign that his time has come, or perhaps he is as yet unaware of the Lord's plans for him. But you can trust HaShem, my son. He has already written every page in your book, and He will do the same for the ones who will work beside you and behind you. Never fear. Always trust."

Silence, as thick as wool, wrapped itself around us. Mother closed her eyes, and I thought she might be praying again.

Then, with an effort, she pushed herself up off the mat, stood in front of me, and wrapped her arms around my neck. "I love you, my sunny son," she said, a smile in her voice. "But you are mine no longer. You are a man, with a man's concerns, and I trust that Adonai will lead you. He called you, He fashioned you, and He will use you. Obey the nudging of His Spirit, and know that your father and I will always stand beside you."

With a heart too full for words, I caught her hand and squeezed it.

Chapter Seven

DELILAH

My life underwent a seismic shift after Adinai's death. Instead of having the freedom to go where I wanted, say what I thought, and control my own person, I became a slave to my stepbrother. When he woke every morning, he would leave the room to eat and dress, then he would leave the house. I never knew where he went, for he did not speak to me except in taunts or curses.

Once Achish had gone, one of the servants—usually Zahra—would enter the room and help me repair whatever had been damaged the night before. Sometimes my face needed cleaning; once my nose needed straightening. She would bandage anything that had been cut and apply salve to areas that had been bruised. And always she would have me drink a concoction that was reported to keep babies away. The stuff tasted awful and always made me sick, but the thought of enduring Achish's abuse with a baby in my belly compelled me to drink it.

Zahra brought food and water; she also brought clean clothing, though nothing as fine as I had worn before Adinai's death. "The master sold your fine tunics, along with those of your mother," Zahra explained, "so we have nothing else for you to wear."

"Not even shoes?" I looked pointedly at my bare feet.

"I'll try to find something for you." She offered a small smile. "At least you don't have to go anywhere."

She meant to comfort me, but confinement tormented me in a way Achish's fists never could. In my youth I had explored shorelines, climbed hills, and meandered through marketplaces, making friends with all kinds of people. Mama had never tried to rein me in, so to be confined to a single room, with no hope of escape, was torture.

"Do you think he will let you out?" Zahra asked one morning as she scrubbed drops of blood from the tile floor. "Maybe if you gentle yourself a bit. Show him you're not going to run or fight. Accept your place, please him, and perhaps your lot won't be so bad—"

"What are you saying?" I turned on her in a flash of indignation. "I was not born a slave. I am a free woman and I will never surrender to him. I will fight as long as I have breath, and I will run the first time I have an opportunity. He can kill me, and he may, but I will never be compliant before him."

Zahra straightened, put her hands on her hips, and gave me a look I'd never seen on her face before. "Then I will pray for you," she said. "Because your past is no longer important. If you resist your master, he will try to break you. In the end, he will do it."

I retreated back to my corner and faced the wall, grieving for the loss of my freedom . . . and my mother's. Where was Mama? Was anyone caring for her? The Egyptians had recognized her exotic beauty and treated her like a princess, and my father had adored her. Adinai had been equally protective, so how could she survive the brutality of the slave market?

Slaves and their masters lived on opposite sides of a great gulf, and a slave had no more rights than an animal. I had never considered the world from a slave's perspective, but Achish forced me to shift my point of view. After repeated nights of brutality, I realized I was no longer a pampered, spoiled girl, but something of only a little more value than a horse.

That thought brought a memory in its wake. Once, at an Egyptian market, my father and I had watched as a group of men brought a gorgeous black stallion off a ship. Wide-eyed and terrified on the dock, the magnificent beast tossed off every rope thrown at its neck and trampled two grooms who got too close. Finally they penned the stallion in a small enclosure, and three men looped ropes around the creature's neck. When another man approached with a whip and a red-hot branding iron, the terrified stallion reared back, pulling the ropes from his handlers. For a moment he stood upright on two legs, towering above all those who would hold him captive, then he fell backward and struck his head on one of the fence posts.

I had burst into tears at the sight of the beautiful, lifeless animal, and even now the memory had the power to render me speechless with grief.

That afternoon I decided that all of Gaza—or at least the homes nearby—should hear my protests. I screamed like a wild woman and pounded on the door, knowing that such hysterics would thoroughly disturb the household. I don't know which of the servants reported my behavior, but Achish came home in a fury. After unlocking the door, he bound my hands and feet and stuffed my mouth with a linen strip, leaving me on the floor.

As I lay there, I kept seeing the beautiful black stallion standing upright, front hooves striking the air, head high, nostrils flaring, until he toppled backward. And afterward, lying on the dock with his eyes open to the sky, his long mane rippling over his body like a silken shroud.

I remained on the tile floor for hours, sometimes drifting into sleep, sometimes staring at the ceiling and wondering why the gods didn't stop toying with me and simply strike me dead. Years before, when Mother and I received word that my father's ship had gone down in the Great Sea, I wept for hours, certain that my life had reached its lowest point. But this was worse. The linen fabric stole every drop of moisture from my mouth and throat, the tile grated against my bones, and my imagination tormented me with thoughts of what Mama must be enduring.

Finally, after darkness filled the room and the servants had gone to bed, the door creaked and swung open. Having lain in one spot all day, I was soiled and hungry, but I would not give Achish the pleasure of seeing me lift my head as he entered the room. I was not a dog that longed for the return of his master.

Instead, I closed my eyes and lay perfectly still.

I heard his sandals brush the stone floor, and then the little oil lamp shone weakly from the bedside table. When Achish's breathing slowed to the deep, steady rhythm of sleep, I opened my eyes and struggled to sit up, but I couldn't see above the mattress. My empty stomach had tightened like a fist, and my nostrils recoiled from the stench of my stained garments. My fingers were blistered from earlier efforts to untie the rope that held my wrists behind my back, but I went to work again. If the servants were asleep when Achish came home, none of them had been around to lock him into this room. If I could get free, I could escape. I would find my mother, gather what we needed, and make our way to the coast where we could board a ship and go back to Egypt or even Crete, anywhere but this cursed Philistia.

I stopped struggling when I realized I could no longer hear Achish breathing. I had been so focused on untying the knots that I had not been listening for movement. I waited, head lowered in concentration, then Achish sank his hand into my hair and dragged me toward the light. "Finally," he said, his voice as cold as the grave, "the half-breed is beginning to break."

He released my hair, dropping me back to the floor. I grimaced when my head hit the tile, and as I rolled onto my back, a tear ran from my eye into my hairline.

Tears . . . Achish must have seen the glimmer of wetness on my cheek and assumed that I'd been weeping with defeat. But if I could have spoken, I'd have told him my tears were merely an overflow of determination.

He wanted me to grovel. For some reason he wanted me to lick his feet like a dog.

But I would not. Not in this life, or any other.

⁓✻⁓

For two months Achish was my captor and tormentor. The servants, of course, knew what he was doing, but they were too terrified to interfere with the young man who held their lives in his hands.

Perhaps it was his use of the word *half-breed*, but in that shadowy chamber I realized why Achish hated me. I was not a mistress, not a slave. Not a Philistine, an Israelite, or even a Canaanite. Not a Cushite, not an Egyptian. Not worthy of any kind of respect or recognition.

I was an *other*. An alien who fell between the cracks. He could abuse me because I had no one to support me. No friend, no clan, no god.

I had been an innocent maiden when my stepfather died, but after eight weeks of Achish's debauchery and abuse I knew I would never think of myself as innocent again. When he focused his sadistic attention on me, I coped by diving into memories, hiding my true self among remembrances of my mother and father when we lived near the Great Sea. Oblivious to Achish and his torments, I would linger in happy imaginings, trailing my fingers in the water or hiding my toes in the warm sand.

Only when I heard the steady sounds of Achish's snoring would I swim up from the depths and break the surface of my dark reality. The only reason I came back at all was the knowledge that my mother needed help. She needed me to escape, find her and free her. I had no idea where she was, but I could not bear the thought of her suffering.

One day Zahra brought me a tray of food and caught me weeping. I tried to hide my tears, but she lowered the tray, then sat on the floor in front of me. I studied her, realizing the girl who had once been my servant had become my peer . . . or even my superior.

"How do you manage it?" I asked, looking into her brown eyes. "And why do you stay here? You were our slave, but since Mother and I have been debased . . ."

She looked away for a moment, then met my direct gaze. "As you have pointed out, I was born into slavery, so I'm accustomed to belonging to a master. And while even the best master can have cruel moments, Master Achish has never been cruel to me. I'm sorry that he's chosen to take out his frustrations on you."

I swiped angrily at my wet cheeks. "I might have been thoughtless or occasionally hard on a slave, but I don't think I was ever cruel."

Zahra's cheek curved as she smiled. "You were not. You and your mother were always kind."

"But if I escape . . ." My voice trembled. "I'm going to get away, mark my words. I am not spending the rest of my life in this room."

Zahra hugged her knees. "What will you do?"

"I'm going to find my mother. But I'm afraid for you. What if Achish turns to you when I'm gone?"

The muscles of her throat moved in a hard swallow, then she pushed herself up from the floor. "You should eat your lunch," she said, moving toward the door. "I'll be back for the tray."

I ate the meat and bread she'd brought, then nibbled at a piece of cheese. The door opened again after only a few minutes, and for an instant I was afraid Achish had come home in the middle of the day.

But Zahra entered, and she carried a clean tunic, a pair of papyrus sandals, and a square of cloth that could be used as a shawl or head covering. "You have to go," she said simply, her gaze moving to the tray. "And you need to eat every bite of that. No one will bring you dinner when you're away from this house."

I stared at her, not comprehending.

"Take these clothes," she said, dropping them onto the bed. "Leave the old clothes, and I'll get rid of them. Avoid the main roads during the day, but stay in well-traveled areas at night. If possible, try to look like a man. If that's not possible, walk like you're in a hurry to get home. People aren't likely to stop a servant who looks like she's on an important errand."

I blinked. "Where did you learn these things?"

"What do you think slaves do when we travel with our masters? We talk."

"You've known all this, you live in an unlocked house, and you stayed? Why didn't you run?"

Zahra's eyes filled with sadness. "I had no place to go and no reason to run. But you need to rescue your mother."

Struck by a sudden and irrational conviction that Achish would soon be home, I stood and yanked off my old tunic, then put on the new one. It was a plain garment any servant might have worn, but it was clean.

I had just slipped my feet into the sandals when I halted. "I can't do this. Achish will know you helped me escape."

She shook her head. "He'll know I left the room unlocked, but he might believe I was only forgetful. And even if he beats me, I don't think I'll suffer the way you have. We're different. I'm just a slave to him, but you are . . . something more. I don't understand why he delights in tormenting you, but no one should have to bear what you have borne."

I reached for her hand. "Come with me, Zahra. We'll leave together."

Her brows rose, then she smiled. "You think I can just walk away from here? I am property, and I belong to Achish."

"But Adinai bought you for me and Mama. We need to hurry. The day is slipping away and Achish will be back soon. If you want to come—"

"I can't." Her voice was firm and final. "I'm—I'm not as brave as you are. But you go, find your mother, and live the life you were meant to live."

I hesitated, then threw my arms around the girl. I knew Achish would make her pay for this, and Zahra knew it, too.

I released her, picked up the remains of my lunch, and tied the food into the fabric square. Moving quickly, I slipped through the doorway and headed toward the back entrance the servants used. I slipped through the gate, then gathered up my wild hair and wound it into a knot.

I stared at the street ahead—a path bordered by stone houses and courtyards, all of which were occupied by Philistines. I had no friends, no home, and no wealth, but I had a plan. I would find my mother, then I'd work to expose the injustice that had been committed against us. At some point I would visit the house of Zaggi, ceren of Gaza, and beg his eldest daughter to support my claims against Achish. If Achish planned to marry Sapha, she should know the sort of man he was.

Only if she listened and if her father believed my claims would justice prevail in Philistia.

CHAPTER EIGHT
DELILAH

FOR THE NEXT THREE DAYS I remained out of sight, hiding during daylight hours and lurking in alleyways after sunset. I scavenged food from the marketplace, slipping fruit under my mantle when no one was looking and begging for old bread from the baker's booth. I did not enjoy begging and thieving, but I had to eat.

When my father lived, we had a house in Heliopolis, so I was comfortable in large cities. I knew, for instance, how to remain close to walls and cloak myself in shadows. I knew to avoid men who staggered and groups of men who spoke too loudly. I knew that plump women were more generous than thin women, and that it was never a good idea to linger near any woman's children. Roaming the streets after dark didn't unnerve me nearly as much as the idea of wandering through the wilderness outside the city walls.

I would have to leave the city eventually, but before I did, I had to find my mother.

Several slave traders called Gaza their home, and all of them operated near the docks. Knowing that Achish would send men to look for me, I rubbed dirt on my face and hoped to pass for one of the street urchins who begged at the loading docks. No need to worry about my figure giving me away—I had lost weight during my captivity, and my arms looked like sticks. I wound my linen square into a turban and used it to cover my wild, tangled hair.

The first slave trader I found managed a market near the northern boundary of the city. I lingered in the shadows of a nearby building for two days, hoping to slip into the stone building where he kept his human cargo, but a guard stood at the door whenever the market was open. Finally, driven by desperation, I waited until the guard had locked the barn and departed, then I approached and rapped on the door. "Hello?" I called, bending to place my lips near the keyhole. "I seek a woman called Monifa. Has she been here?"

I heard the sound of clinking chains, followed by a gruff voice. "We don't have names in here, child. Where is this woman from?"

"She's my mother." My voice broke on the last word. "She was born a free woman, but she married a Philistine and was sold into slavery by a treacherous stepson. If you've met her—"

"We don't speak of the past in here," the voice answered again. "How would I recognize this woman?"

"She's beautiful." I answered with the first thought that occurred to me. "And she's black. She speaks with an accent."

I heard the murmuring of several voices, then the voice replied, "Sorry, child. We have no one like that in here."

I trudged away, trying to remain in the shadows as I sloshed through muddy tracks and navigated a path around various animal pens. A group of donkeys watched with only mild interest as I climbed into their pen to steal a handful of grain, but a pair of big-bellied rats stood on their hind legs and glared as I carried away part of their supper.

With a heavy heart I approached the next slave market. The makeshift barn could not be accessed from outside, but only through a more substantial structure that had been locked up tight. I had no choice but to walk to the back of the barn and look for gaps in the brickwork. Unfortunately, the structure was solid, and the bricks well-mortared. I couldn't find any openings large enough to speak through, but when I looked down I noticed that the masons had created openings above the foundation—probably for ventilation or drainage. I dropped to the ground, and in a stream of moonlight I saw the shackled ankles of at least a dozen slaves.

I slid closer to the building and pressed my face to the opening. "Hello! Can anyone hear me?"

For a moment no one answered, then a pair of feet shifted so that I could see ten toes. "Who's there?"

"I'm outside, and I'm looking for my mother. Do you have a black woman in there?"

I heard mingled murmurs and exclamations before a smaller pair of feet approached the wall. "No one like that here now," the high voice of a woman or child responded, "but there was a woman like that."

I groaned in frustration. "Where did she go?"

"She was sold." Ten dirty toes shifted as their owner knelt in an attempt to get closer. "Yesterday."

"Do you know who bought her?"

"Maybe somebody else does."

I moved even closer as a stream of whispers trickled out of the building. Someone objected to whatever was being said.

At last the small feet returned. "We think she was sold to a man who works with the iron."

I closed my eyes, suddenly aware of my own ignorance. I knew nothing about iron or the men who worked it, so how was I supposed to find the man who bought my mother?

A masculine voice seemed to vibrate the earth beneath my fingertips. "Iron is the strength of the Philistines," a man said, "so the ironworkers guard their sheds day and night. If your mother is with an iron man, you'd better be careful. They use iron to make weapons and tools, and the fellow who bought your mother will not be defenseless."

I thanked the man for the warning and pulled away from the wall, overwhelmed with the information I'd just received. Why would an ironworker need my mother? She was not physically strong, nor was she young. But she was beautiful and female, and the past weeks with Achish had taught me why men sometimes wanted women.

I hoped her owner was nothing like my stepbrother.

By the time the moon climbed high in the sky, I realized that the ironworker's shop wouldn't be easy to find. The owners of the waterfront huts and sheds closed up their businesses at sunset, and most of the workers slept in their shops. I could not tell one building from another in the dark, so I would have to search for the ironworker in daylight. I would start at the end of the docks and move down the row until I located him and, hopefully, my mother.

But first I had to find shelter.

Drawn by the moonlight, I moved toward the water and found myself at the docks again. The waterfront felt like home. The sounds, smells, and sights reminded me of mornings spent aboard my father's ship. Though Mother and I never traveled with him, we boarded his boat whenever he'd come into port. While Mama and Father visited in his cabin, I would play on the deck as pelicans dived and gulls shrieked among the wooden masts.

A half-dozen boats lay moored in the Gaza harbor, and several boats had been tied to a dock. I walked over to the closest vessel and called to see if anyone was hiding in the shadows. When no one answered, I dropped into the vessel and found an empty space near the stern. I snuggled up with coils of rope and covered myself with sail fabric, breathing in the odors of mildew, seawater, and age.

The sounds of rhythmic creaking and groaning made my eyelids grow heavy. Finally I relaxed and drifted into sleep, rocked by the cradle of the waves.

I woke to the sound of men's voices, and for an instant I didn't remember where I was. Then the scent of fish assaulted me and I sat up, flinging off the sailcloth. The action startled a pair of men at the far end of the dock, but I leapt onto the planks and ran toward the waterfront, ignoring their shouts and the curious looks of fishermen onshore.

When I was convinced no one had followed me, I darted into a narrow alley, bent forward and took deep, gulping breaths. Covered in dirt and smelling of mold, I knew I looked worse than the most humble house slave in Gaza. But there was no help for it.

Straightening, I pushed hair out of my eyes and saw that the sun had fully risen. I should have left that boat at the first sign of sunrise, but I'd slept like a dead woman. Stepping out of the alley, I startled a pair of sailors mending their nets, then darted into the street, barely avoiding a chariot driven by a man who wore the colors of Lord Zaggi's estate.

Breathless, I leaned against a wall and closed my eyes, trying to still my thumping pulse. I had to calm down and think. I was not an uneducated slave; I was a free woman who'd been unjustly robbed and personally attacked. And I had a noble mission to fulfill.

As the evening stars faded and the morning skies turned blue, I wandered through mostly deserted streets. I found a public fountain and splashed my face, idly wondering if Lord Zaggi would recognize me if he happened to ride by in his chariot. If he didn't, surely his daughters would, and they might convince the ceren to hear my plea. Sapha and I had made a connection. No matter what her relationship with Achish, I hoped she would be willing to tell her father that my mother and I had been cheated. Since she and her father were close, I could restore justice if I could win her over.

I straightened my tunic, then dipped a corner of the hem into the fountain and used the fabric to scrub dirt from my arms. If I had an opportunity to appear before Lord Zaggi, I would need to look as presentable as possible.

After washing, I smoothed the wrinkles from the plain tunic and tried to remember what Adinai had told me about the city. From a point not far away came a cacophony of sounds—the rumble of mule-drawn wagons, the babble of men's voices, and the chink of chisels striking stone. Careful to remain in the shadows, I followed the noise to a construction site so large I couldn't tell where it began or ended. From my limited viewpoint, I saw craftsmen hauling huge stone blocks while others mixed mortar and built scaffolds. Men in white tunics bent over scrolled parchments as they pointed and argued, even at this early hour.

Then I remembered—Adinai had mentioned that Gaza was building a new temple for Dagon, the Philistine god of fertility and prosperity. Lord Zaggi wanted his city's temple to be more impressive than any other, so he had engaged the best architects in Egypt for the job.

With nothing to do but wait until the shops opened, I stepped into an out-of-the-way corner and watched the city come to life. The streets filled as the sun climbed higher, and the construction crew grew with each passing hour. Shirtless men hauled stone blocks on sleds, their donkeys braying with exertion, and overseers rode horseback, their whips snapping at the bronzed backs of slaves. Citizens of Gaza carefully negotiated the foot traffic around the construction site. Pedestrians tried to remain on the established footpaths while litter-bearing slaves carried their masters' wives and concubines through the few open spaces, trusting the fluttering fabric curtains to shield the wealthy citizens within.

Only a few weeks before, my mother and I had ridden in such a litter.

By the time the sun was one-quarter of the way across the sky, I turned and tried to get my bearings. Last night I'd learned that the ironworks were near the waterfront, so where was the sea in relation to the rising temple? I shifted my gaze to the sweating slaves. Such grand work must require iron, shouldn't it? Obeying an impulse, I walked along the edge of the construction site, figuring that it would eventually circle back to the waterfront.

As I walked, I struggled to imagine how I might find an ironworker's establishment. Since my mother knew nothing about iron, her new master probably wanted her to handle domestic duties—cooking, cleaning, tending to whatever belongings an ironworker possessed. Because Mama was old enough to have a nearly grown daughter, I hoped he would not use her as a concubine, but who knew what sort of man he was?

Finally I stood on a street between the construction site and the docks. My stomach rumbled as I slowed and peered into each open tent or shack. Here was a warehouse, there a stable, here a tax collector's office. I spotted a market for farmers' produce and an importer's warehouse where sailors unloaded merchandise from Crete and other islands of the Great Sea. For all I knew, the warehouse had belonged to Adinai and was now under Achish's control.

I turned and spotted what had to be an ironworker. Despite the heat of the bright morning, a heavyset man in a leather loincloth sat before a standing log. The top of the charred log was covered with glowing coals and rocks. The man held a red-hot piece of metal in a pair of tongs. He squinted at it, hammered it, then held it aloft and squinted at it again. On the wall behind him hung what I assumed were finished products: a pair of heavy swords, a half-dozen knives, and several farm implements.

Aware that I might soon see my mother, I pulled the turban off my head, shook out the fabric square, and tied it around my shoulders as a shawl. No matter what her condition, Mama would not want to see me wandering the streets like an orphan. I circled the ironworker's lot and saw a small building behind the man's tent. The windowless structure was not large enough to qualify as a house, but a table and cot could fit inside. It certainly had room for a woman.

I stepped aside to avoid an oncoming man with a pushcart, then walked toward the building. I decided to circle the property again to glean information and build up my courage before approaching the ironworker. I would explain the injustice that had been done to me and my mother, and perhaps he would be sympathetic. If he wasn't, I would warn him that I planned to appeal to the ceren, a personal friend. If *that* statement didn't convince him to release my mother, I would sit in front of Zaggi's beautiful home and cry out for mercy and justice until someone grew weary of my complaints and acted on my behalf.

I was so intent upon my plan that I nearly stepped on a heap of rags behind the ironworker's building. When I stepped aside, the rags moved—and my mother lifted her head. The rags were her only blanket, and I hadn't seen her because she'd been huddled into a ball, her hands chained to a post behind the little building.

My mind went blank with shock. I saw metal bands on her wrists, a chain that ran from her wrists through a hasp on the post, the ragged tunic she wore. I gasped and knelt next to her. "Mama! It's me. I'm here."

I noted her frail form, the fresh marks on her arms, the bruises on her face. When she turned toward me, I saw swollen lips and what looked like a broken nose. Dark circles ringed both eyes, and her gaze was cloudy with pain. "Delilah?"

My fingertips fluttered over her, afraid to land lest I aggravate some bruise or injury. "Mama . . . what happened? Why—?"

"You shouldn't be here." My mother's ragged voice held a note of reproach. "Run, Delilah. Go find a place where you can be safe." Her eyes widened. "Are you still . . . living at the house?"

Tears welled in my eyes. I didn't want her to know what her stepson had done to me.

"Mama, what happened to you?"

She scanned my form, and her expression filled with anxiety. "You should leave Gaza at once! Run, Delilah, and never come back to this place."

"I'm not going back to Achish, and I'm not leaving you." I took her hand and held it as gently as I could. "What sort of master would beat you?"

"An owner has the right to do as he pleases with his slave." Her eyelids drooped above her swollen lips. "My life is spent, Delilah, but you are young still. Get away from Gaza, find a place to thrive. Go back to Egypt if you can. And may the gods go with you."

"Mama, I'm going to the ceren's house—"

"No." Her voice sharpened. "We are not like these people, and he would only turn you over to your stepbrother. Do *not* venture near that man's house. You must leave the city. There is no safety for you within these walls."

"But I can't leave you!"

"Delilah." Mama's mouth thinned in a familiar look of disapproval. "You will not argue with me. Go."

The urge that had driven me all this way now had a sharper spur—I needed someone to help my mother before her cruel master killed her.

"I will go," I told her, "but I will come back once I have found a way to free you. I won't let you live like this a day longer than necessary."

"I have had a good life." She closed her eyes as a beatific smile lifted the lines of her face. "Perhaps it is my turn to suffer. But you, Delilah—you mustn't think about me. Get away while you can."

"I'll speak to your master—"

"And have him claim you, too? No. If we are not Achish's mother and stepsister, then we are his slaves. And unless you can prove who you are, you have no right to approach a Philistine official. Leave, lest you find yourself in chains along with me. Go quickly . . . and know that I love you."

I remained beside her, still torn by indecision, until she lifted her head again. "If I raise my voice," she said, using the firm tone she had always used when disciplining me, "my master will come back here and beat me. I don't want you to see that, so don't make me tell you again."

Feeling as though invisible hands were forcibly twisting the hope from my heart, I whimpered, kissed her forehead, and stumbled away.

⁓❦⁓

With every step that carried me away from my mother, I repeated a refrain: *I need help. I need help.*

But who would be willing to help a seventeen-year-old girl who had been in the city only three months? No one. Lord Zaggi ruled over Gaza, but Mama had been firm about staying away from him. She knew more about the ceren's relationship with Adinai and Achish than I did, so if she meant for me to stay away from Lord Zaggi, I would. But who else could help?

No one. I was nobody, and I had no rights in Gaza.

My dream of freeing Mama surrendered to common sense. If I were to help my mother, I would need time . . . perhaps months. Mama had been sold, so to free her, I'd have to buy her. To do that,

I would need some sort of currency, either goods or silver. And I could not earn that kind of wealth overnight.

I thought about hiring myself out, but hired workers had skills—they were either scribes or dressmakers or bakers. They excelled at their trades, and the very best worked for the wealthiest families in Gaza. Skilled people bartered their goods and services for jewelry, clothing, and ornamentation for themselves or their homes. Others used their skills to bribe people in authority—Zaggi's house had been filled with more alabaster objects and fine furnishings than any man could accumulate solely through the work of his hands. Adinai once said that wealthy people were always welcome at a ruler's home. They could whisper in his ear and promise to provide him with treasure, then watch their desires come to life. Men like Adinai were granted respect; people listened to their opinions.

Slaves, on the other hand, performed unskilled labor and worked to stay alive. Every slave in Gaza fell into one of two categories: either they were subjects of a nation conquered in war, or poverty had forced them to sell themselves for survival. If I could not develop a skill, I'd find myself at the slave market again, begging to be allowed to exchange my life and freedom for food and shelter.

I had to support myself. I'd had a taste of slavery in Achish's house, and I would rather die than endure that again.

I walked toward the marketplace, armed with nothing but a vague idea of buying and selling. My stomach was empty and my feet ached from walking.

What could I sell? An obvious answer rose in my mind, but I shook the idea away. Mother had always told me that harlots surrendered a bit of their soul every time they opened their legs to a stranger, and my days in Achish's house had already devoured too much of me. I had seen harlots in Egyptian temples and at roadside shrines to Baal, and something about their overpainted faces and false behavior convinced me that they hid their true selves behind their smiles. They were neither happy nor free, so their occupation seemed only another form of slavery.

I had to find a way to support myself as a free woman. Once I had secured food for my belly and shelter for my head, I would learn a trade and work hard to buy my mother's freedom. I would not place my life into the hands of a husband unless he was willing to help my mother. After securing Mother's freedom, I would accumulate enough treasure to win an audience with the ceren of Gaza. If my gifts pleased Lord Zaggi, I might be able to wrest my stepfather's fortune from Achish and return it to my mother.

Feeling light-headed, I glanced up at the white-hot sun. My skin was slick with sweat, my heart pounding within its cage of ribs. My future depended on a string of *ifs*, yet in that moment I would have bartered my future for a drink of water. My mouth felt like cotton and my throat ached. Muscles complained because I'd been sleeping in odd positions on unforgiving surfaces. My body desperately wanted a full meal, a gourd filled with cool water, and a comfortable bed.

So how was I to find any of those things?

I leaned against a stone wall, paralyzed by stark reality. If I wanted to live, I would have to learn a trade. "Trade one, store one," my mother used to say, and I could follow her example . . . once I found a safe place to live. But where could I be safe from Achish? And how could I eat until I had goods to trade?

I stepped out and looked at the city looming all around me. I would never be safe from Achish in Gaza. But the road out of Gaza was well-traveled, so I might be able to join a caravan to Zilkeg or Beersheba, even Egypt. Until I found a place to settle I would have to live by my wits . . . and on charity.

I turned toward the east and the city's broad gates. I would leave Gaza because Mother told me to go, but one day I would return to free her and make things right.

CHAPTER NINE
DELILAH

"WAKE, WOMAN. Open your eyes so I can see if you're dead or alive."

The words came to me through a thick fog. I batted them away, not willing to lift my eyelids, but then something cold and wet splashed across my face. Sputtering in confusion, I sat up, pressed my hands to my sunburned skin and tried to coat my tongue with the moisture.

"Are you all right?"

I peeked out between my fingers. A man squatted in front of me, his head lowered to avoid the fronds of the palmetto I'd chosen for my hiding place.

I blinked as memory returned. I had stretched out beneath this short palm because I was too thirsty and exhausted to take another step. I had curled up in a ball, ignoring the roaches that scrambled across my legs, because I was ready to die.

I was still ready, but I wouldn't surrender before I defended myself from this annoying vagabond. I narrowed my eyes at the bearded traveler, then slapped at the ants on my arms and neck. They were everywhere, probably drinking the sweat on my limbs—

"Arrrrgh!" Screaming in frustration, I dove out of the palm and kept slapping. The man who'd spoken crawled out from beneath the palmetto and offered me a wet cloth. I hesitated, but only for a moment. The wetness felt wonderful on my dry skin as I wiped the ants away.

When I had finished, I stood before my interrogator breathless, humiliated, and covered in dozens of insect bites.

"You're gonna need help with those," the man said, nodding at my afflicted arms. He pulled a small pouch from a leather satchel and tossed it to me. The pouch contained some kind of sour-smelling salve.

"Ants like sweet," he said, noticing my skeptical look. "They don't like that balm. But your skin will."

Could I trust him?

I took another look at the bearded stranger. Two other bearded men stood several paces away, their heads bent in conversation as they checked a line of donkeys. Two camels knelt at the head of the caravan.

When one of the other men glanced in my direction, I saw that he wore the same sort of unadorned tunic as the man in front of me. These strangers were definitely not Philistines. They wore full bushy beards, while the Philistines preferred theirs clipped and curled.

"Hey." The first man waved for my attention. "When someone gives you an ointment, it's customary to use it."

"I will." I intended to spit out my answer, but my voice cracked and the words sounded raw.

The man turned and called to the others. "Regnar! Bring a gourd with water. And bread. Maybe some grapes, too."

The thought of food made my empty stomach gurgle, and the sound brought a smile to my new acquaintance's face. "I am Hitzig," he said, his dark eyes crinkling at the corners, "and those are my brothers, Regnar and Warati. We've finished our business at the marketplace and are heading home." He leaned forward, his eyes searching my face. "And you are . . . ?"

I rubbed ointment on my neck and arms, grateful for the opportunity to look away and be free of his penetrating gaze. His eyes were dark like Achish's, yet there was no smirk on his lips, no gleam of desire in his expression. His hands were calloused but clean, and his complexion ruddy, like my father's after a long journey.

"I am Delilah." I tossed the pouch to him and forced words over my parched throat. "And I must leave Gaza or die."

"Did you steal something?" Hitzig's eyes narrowed. "Are you a thief?"

"A thousand times, no!" I met his query with honest indignation. "I don't want to talk about the reason I must leave. Even if I explained my situation, you wouldn't believe it."

Hitzig waggled his thick brows. "I believe in an invisible God. I believe in love. I believe I can beat my brother Regnar in a wrestling match, though I have yet to do so. So you see, I believe a great many improbable things."

I blew out a breath. "I have to leave Gaza because my traitorous stepbrother sold my mother into slavery and held me captive. He lies, but I cannot prove him a liar because I am not a Philistine, nor have I lived long in the city. I have no . . . power."

"If this youth locked you up, why are you here?"

I shrugged away my shame—I could not speak of what I had endured. "A servant helped me escape."

Hitzig regarded me with a speculative gaze, and then he looked at the brother who was advancing with water and fruit. "What say you, Regnar—can we take a passenger?"

Regnar came closer, handed me the fruit and a gourd, then propped his hands on his hips and looked me over. "She looks harmless enough. She'd look better with a bath."

"Wouldn't we all." Hitzig turned back to me. "Where do you wish to go?"

"Anywhere I can be safe." I looked him directly in the eye, sensing that he might be more honest than most men. "That's all I want—safety until I can obtain freedom for my mother. If you can help me, I won't make any trouble for you."

"Women always cause trouble." Hitzig smiled, then went to talk to his brothers. I drank deeply of the water in the gourd, then filled my hand with grapes and brought them to my mouth. I tried to hear the brothers' low voices, but found it nearly impossible.

Finally, one of the men—Warati, I think—nodded, and Regnar moved to a donkey carrying two clay pots. Removing the covers, he pulled another stalk of grapes from one and a loaf of bread from the other. My mouth watered as he approached and offered more food.

I hesitated. What would these men want in exchange for their hospitality?

From his place by a camel, Hitzig laughed. "Regnar won't bite, despite his gruff appearance. He's actually quite tame."

I ignored the jibe, took the bread and fruit, then turned and stuffed chunks of the loaf into my mouth. I ate a few grapes between each bite of bread, allowing the juice to wet my tongue and parched lips. I didn't know where these men had come from, but I was grateful for their kindness. Whether they agreed to take me with them or not, tonight I would beg whatever gods there were to rain blessings upon them.

Hitzig came over and propped his hands on his hips. "We have decided. My brothers and I are concerned for your safety. Women should not travel alone within Gaza, and the dangers for a woman are even greater outside the city. Lawlessness prevails in the wilderness, and Regnar fears you will not survive if we leave you unprotected. So we would be pleased to take you with us as far as the Valley of Sorek."

I drew a deep breath, about to thank him, but a niggling doubt remained. What if their intentions were not honorable? Achish had overpowered me when I was strong and fit. In my current state of exhaustion, I could probably be overcome by a child.

I swallowed the last of the bread and then looked up at Hitzig. "I do not look like much," I admitted, "but I am not a runaway slave. I was born to a free woman of Cush and a Cretan sailor, and I have never had to beg for my dinner."

Only when Hitzig lifted a brow did I realize how pompous my little speech sounded. "Until now, eh?"

I shook my head. "What I'm saying—what I want you to understand—is that I will not allow anyone to—"

"You're saying you're not a whore." Hitzig smiled, revealing a gap where a front tooth should have been. "I'm sure you've a good reason for warning us, but my brothers and I have beautiful wives at home. We've never stopped on the road for an evening's entertainment, if you know what I mean."

His words soothed my fears somewhat, but as I walked toward the donkeys, with a heavy heart I realized that I *did* know exactly what he meant. My innocence had vanished forever.

CHAPTER TEN
SAMSON

I WAITED AS LONG AS I COULD, but a man in love is as rest-less as a lion and as impatient as a puppy. My father frequently made comments about the dangers of marrying an outsider, but his words fell away from me like leaves from a tree in autumn. I was in love.

"Lust," Rei insisted for the thirtieth time. "What you are feeling is lust."

"How would you know?" I gave him a scornful glance. "You have not married, you have never been in love—"

"Not true," he said. "I love Adonai with all my heart, soul, and strength."

I snorted and waved him away.

In truth, sometimes my servant was like an annoying fly—always buzzing about, whining in my ear, and appearing when I least wanted to see him. But he had been with me since childhood, and he would probably stay with me until death, especially if I grew irritated enough to strangle him.

One of a bridegroom's duties was to prepare a home for his bride, so I spent several weeks building a small home near my parents' home. I selected a spot that faced the rising sun, then framed out a house large enough for a couple and three or four children. I engaged a carpenter, who framed several windows, and I built a wall around the space that would be our courtyard and garden. The carpenter installed a gate as I thatched the roof with the wide fronds of a palm tree. Mother helped me choose plants and flowers to fill the garden, and by the time we had finished, I was well pleased with our work.

I hoped Kesi would be, too.

When I had finished preparing the house, I put on my finest tunic and robe and walked over to my parents' home. "I am ready to fetch my wife," I announced. "Will you come with me?"

My mother blanched and withdrew into the dark veil she wore like a shell around her face. Father looked as though he would also like to curl up and disappear, but he did not have that luxury. He had arranged my marriage, so it was his duty to accompany me and witness the fulfillment of the *shitre erusin*, the nuptial contract.

He sighed heavily. "When?"

"I'd like to go today."

Father shook his head. "Impossible. I have to find a suitable gift for the girl's father. And we really should invite some of our friends and neighbors to represent our tribe at the feast—"

"Gather whomever you will," I answered, making my decision in an instant, "because I am leaving at sunrise tomorrow."

When the sun peered over the horizon the next morning, Rei and I stood alone in front of my parents' house. Father came to the door with bleary eyes, nodded at me, and gripped his walking stick. Mother followed, her hair covered with a dark veil. None of my brothers appeared.

We set out together, just the four of us, and Father didn't have to explain why none of our kinsmen had come along. Marriage to a foreign woman was offensive, but I could have softened the insult by also taking a wife from my own tribe. When I refused to do so, my kinsmen saw my marriage as a snub to every daughter of Abraham, Isaac, and Jacob.

At the fork in the road, my parents again took the southern path where the walking was easier. Weary of enduring their stony silence, I chose the northern route.

"I'll meet you at the inn," I told my parents, "and together we will see this through."

Father grunted in response. I drew a breath, ready to chide him for his lack of support. Shouldn't a father want his son to be happy? I opened my mouth to gently rebuke him, but Rei stepped between us and shook his head.

I exhaled my indignation. Ah, well. When even my servant knew that I should keep quiet, perhaps I should bite my tongue.

I watched my parents until the road turned and led them out of my sight, then I climbed the steeper trail. My thighs bulged and stretched as I stepped over large stones, yet my soul expanded with the physical exertion. I increased my pace, leaping from rock to rock and avoiding the footpath entirely. Behind me, Rei shouted in complaint, but I laughed, enjoying the exercise. God had given me strength and agility, so why shouldn't I celebrate His gift?

I stopped at the vineyard. The grapes were gone now, the harvest over. I would find no juicy treats here today, unless the harvesters had overlooked—

An unusual sound caught my ear, a buzzing. Not the thin sound of a rogue bee, but the ferocious roar of a hive. I peered down one row, then another, and finally located the source of the buzzing—and my old enemy. The lion I had killed months before lay between the vines, its body desiccated by the arid climate. Bony ribs poked through the leathery skin, and bees flew in and out of the animal's rib cage.

Oblivious to the insects, I knelt and peered into the carcass. The little creatures had made a home of the animal's corpse, and inside the ribs I could see the golden stickiness of a good-sized hive.

Grinning, I waited until Rei came up the path, breathing hard and perspiring. "Look." I motioned to the carcass. "Have you ever seen the like?"

He leaned against a boulder and stared at the corpse with wide eyes. "Never."

"Find something for a torch, will you? This will be a wonderful gift for my bride."

Rei bent forward and braced his hands on his knees. "Sorry, but if you expect me to climb this rocky trail, you have to give me time to catch my breath."

I rolled my eyes at his cheeky answer, then searched among the hedgerows until I found a branch with green leaves. I thrust the end of the branch into a pile of dried weeds and then started a fire with pieces of flint from my satchel. A spark caught the dry tinder and burst into flame. I then picked up the branch and held it close to the body of the dead lion.

The bees flew out in a near-continuous stream, allowing me to slide my hand into the corpse and pull out the dense honeycomb, dripping with golden sweetness. I wrapped the comb in a piece of leather, tucked it into the satchel at my waist. "An unexpected prize," I told Rei, who had barely managed to pull himself off the rock. "How many bridegrooms go to their weddings with sweets for the sweet?"

"A dangerous precedent," Rei said, shooing bees away from his neck. "For bridegrooms—ow!—and their servants."

Smiling, I led the way to Timnah.

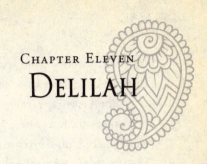

Chapter Eleven
DELILAH

EVERY WOMAN, Mama often told me, eventually learned that one must suffer to be beautiful. She often repeated that saying as she untangled my unruly hair or scrubbed rough patches from the soles of my feet. As a young girl I complained about beauty rituals, but after my mother was taken from me, I saw the wisdom in her words.

Mama certainly earned her beauty. Born in Cush, a nation on the southern border of mighty Egypt, as a young girl she was captured by Egyptian slave handlers and taken to Thebes. Her captors meant to sell her, but an observant handler recognized her nascent beauty and sent her to the palace instead. She attended school with the pharaoh's children and learned the fine art of social graces. Her handlers assumed a royal marriage was in the offing, until a sailor from Crete appeared before Pharaoh and presented the king with valuable spices, silver, and jewels. His gifts were so appreciated that when he left the royal court, he was allowed to take my mother with him.

Mama did not often speak of those long-ago days, but I cherished the story and spent the lonely hours of desert travel reliving my earliest memories. When I grew tired of walking—a common occurrence in those first days of the journey—one of the brothers would call a halt, then command a camel to kneel so I could climb onto its saddle. As we continued on the dusty road that led northeast out of Gaza, I would lean back and close my eyes, swaying to the camel's gait as I floated over the streams of time.

Though I had only lived seventeen years, I had experienced periods of plenty and periods of want. When my father brought his ship into port, we would celebrate, and for weeks we would eat the finest foods available. Mama would order new clothing for all of us, and we would walk through Heliopolis as if we were royalty ourselves.

But Father always took his ship back out to sea. After saying good-bye, Mama and I would become frugal, stretching our stores of grain and oil. We wore only old clothes to preserve our best for special occasions, and sometimes we had to sell our fine tunics. Mama would always smile and say that we would find something better when Father came home, but sometimes he stayed away for months. When our stores of food ran out and we had nothing left to sell, Mama would weave straw baskets and hats to trade at the marketplace. I would sit next to her and wear one of the hats. When people remarked that I was pretty, Mama would insist that the hat had the power to make any wearer look better. We sold dozens of hats because she had the gift of persuasion.

When Father did not come home after a year, we knew that his ship had been lost at sea. We had to leave our house and live under a lean-to at the marketplace. We were not supposed to live at the market, but the manager there turned a blind eye to our makeshift home. Mama and I sold baskets, straw mats, and hats for four years.

Then Adinai spotted Mama. He bought everything she had and treated us to a meal aboard his ship. Before I knew it, he had asked

Mama to marry him, bought Zahra to be her maid, and arranged
for our move to Gaza. I didn't like to think about what happened
after that. Neither did I want to talk about it.

Whenever our small caravan stopped at an inn, a brook or a
well, the brothers were kind enough to share their meager meals
with me. At first I kept all three of them at arm's length, but after
several nights of undisturbed sleep in one of their tents, I relaxed
and began to enjoy their good humor. After ten days on the road, I
felt as though they were the stepbrothers I *should* have had if Dagon
or whatever gods there were had smiled more favorably on me.

Regnar, the tallest of the three, rarely spoke, but his thoughts were
easy enough to discern. He was the one who called a halt when one
of the donkeys lay down and refused to move. Hitzig and Warati
got into an argument over what should be done when a donkey
proved to be more stubborn than usual, but Regnar quieted them,
lifted the animal's foreleg and pointed to an abscess near the hoof.
Hitzig pulled out a salve—probably the same one he gave me—and
smeared it on the animal's wound while Warati unhitched the other
animals. We spent that day in the shade of an olive grove, because
Regnar believed that even a donkey deserved time to heal.

Warati, I learned, was the youngest son, and the only one with
two wives. Both of Warati's wives had proven uncommonly fertile,
and his house held two sets of twins, two singletons, and one set
of triplets. "Warati's tent is so noisy that he sleeps outside," Hitzig
told me as we sat by the fire one night. "And it's a good thing or he
might have another set of triplets in the house."

Hitzig, the eldest, was as clever as he was outspoken. He and
his family had lived on their land for generations, he told me, and
his father had not forgotten the day they saw their first Philistine.
"My forefathers had already moved their flocks to make way for
the Israelites," he said, "but then the Philistines came inland, too.
They were not interested in raising sheep and cattle—they came to

tax the people and terrify our flocks. But if we pay what they ask, they usually leave us alone."

"Don't forget the Israelites," Warati added. "Tell her how we were terrified of them."

"Ah, yes." Hitzig threw another log on the fire. "The Israelites brought their invisible God with them. Before we had seen even a single son of Abraham, we had heard stories of rivers drying up, water turning into blood, plagues of frogs and flies and locusts. And death, always death. We had heard of this God before. Some claimed he struck the cities of Sodom and Gomorrah, turning them into piles of ashes. But no one in our tribe knew whether the stories were true."

"Have you been to those places?" I asked, amazed by the tale. "Are they piles of ashes now?"

"I have not been there," Hitzig answered. "But one day I will go see the proof of this miracle for myself. In any case, my great-grandfathers dressed in old clothes and old sandals, then packed their donkeys with worn-out wineskins. They rode out and met the Israelites at Gilgal with only dry, crumbly bread in their provision baskets."

"That's all we'll have left if we keep moving at this pace," Warati grumbled.

Hitzig shushed his brother, then went back to his story. "My people told Joshua, the Israelite leader, that they had come from a land far away because we had heard about their God Adonai. My father's grandfather said that we Gibeonites would serve the Israelites if Joshua would make a treaty with us. He did, and we agreed to it. But after three days, Joshua learned the truth—we did not live far from the Israelites' promised land, so we would be neighbors. He was angry, of course, but he and his people had already agreed to the treaty. So they did not harm a hair on our heads."

"But—" Regnar reminded his brother.

"Yes. But." Hitzig stirred the fire with a green branch. "Because we had deceived Joshua, we were to be woodchoppers and water carriers for Israel forever. So that is what we do, whenever we are asked."

I forced a laugh. "I thought you were going to say you vowed to show kindness to girls hiding under palm trees."

"Not exactly." Hitzig pressed his lips together, unsuccessfully repressing a smile. "But being a servant has made me mindful of others' needs."

We sat in a thick night silence broken only by the snap and crackle of burning branches and occasional snorts from the animals.

"I have heard of this God," I said, timidly offering a story of my own. "My mother lived in Egypt most of her life. She told me the Egyptians could not speak of the Israelites without shuddering. They preferred not to speak of the invisible God at all, but some of the older people whispered about the plagues that brought Egypt's gods to their knees. As you said—frogs, insects, bloody water, bad weather, boils . . . and Mama said one morning the firstborn in every Egyptian home was found dead. On that very day the Egyptians exiled the children of Abraham from their land."

Regnar lifted a brow. "If the Israelites' God was able to conquer mighty Egypt, why does he allow the Philistines to enslave his people?"

I spread my hands in a gesture of helplessness. "What do I know of these things? I am not an Israelite."

"What are you then?" Hitzig's eyes twinkled with mischief. "You are not Hebrew, nor Philistine, so—"

"I am nothing." I fell silent. I had been thinking that the brothers were vagabonds like me, but they had *people*, a heritage and a history.

I had nothing and no one.

My concentration dissolved in an onslaught of fatigue. I spread the cloak Regnar had loaned me on the sand, then lay on my side, my gaze fixed on the glowing coals in the fire pit. The sight reminded me of the ironworker and my bruised and broken mother. I needed to stay strong for her. I needed to remain fierce with determination, but I could barely hold my eyes open. My eyelids felt as heavy as lead, and the brothers' voices were fading to baritone rumbles in the night.

Hitzig gestured toward the tent. "You should go inside and sleep, girl. It's been a long day."

I barely managed to shake my head. "I just want to rest here."

"You'll do things the hard way then."

Before I could rouse myself enough to imagine what he meant, Hitzig bent, rolled me in the cloak, and carried me to the tent like an oversized loaf of bread. My eyes flew open and I yelled in protest, but Hitzig unrolled me in the tent and walked away.

Even then, I was safe. Unthreatened. And protected by three brothers who cared enough to demonstrate simple kindness.

I curled up on Regnar's cloak and tumbled into a deep sleep.

Chapter Twelve
SAMSON

Rei and I arrived at the innkeeper's house long before my parents. The innkeeper greeted us with wide eyes, apparently startled by my unannounced arrival, but immediately sent servants to summon travelers, neighbors, anyone who would rejoice with me at the wedding feast. Though Rei said I should feel embarrassed that none of my kinsmen had come with me, I approved the innkeeper's plan. If my people didn't want to celebrate my wedding, I would celebrate with any passerby who wanted free food and wine.

Eager to begin married life, I asked the innkeeper if I might see my bride.

He sputtered for a moment, then clasped his hands. "Of course, Samson. Wait here."

A few moments later my golden-haired beauty appeared, her cheeks flushed a lovely pink. I greeted her with a soft kiss, then pulled my satchel from my shoulder. "I have not come empty-handed," I said, feeling suddenly awkward. "I offer this to sweeten the occasion."

She took my satchel, opened it, and astonishment touched her pale face. "Honey!" Her eyes glittered with delight. "This must have been expensive."

"My servant paid a high price for it," I told her, grinning. "But this is a special occasion."

A shout from the courtyard indicated that my parents had arrived, so I stepped outside. The innkeeper greeted them with fresh water and ordered a servant to wash their feet. Once they had been officially welcomed, the innkeeper led us to couches where we could rest while we waited for the other guests to arrive.

"I have killed a calf and baked fresh bread," the innkeeper said, twisting his hands. "Everything will soon be ready. In the meantime, relax, have some wine, and Kesi will entertain you."

My bride returned, dressed in a colorful skirt and an almost-translucent blouse. Her costume, while not unusual by Philistine standards, was not the sort of garment found among the Israelites. My father blushed and lowered his gaze, but I feasted on her loveliness. She had prepared a dance, so while her sister thumped on a small drum, Kesi swayed and moved to the rhythm. I clapped with the drum, more than ready to proclaim the beauty of my bride.

I gave my parents a section of honeycomb I had held back to snack on as I traveled. "I know you are tired," I told them. "This will lift your spirits."

I turned as voices floated in from the courtyard. The innkeeper had done a fine job of assembling a crowd for the feast. Men began to straggle into the room—several travelers, a small company of Philistine soldiers, three local Philistine farmers, and a pair of priests from the Temple of Dagon in Judah. At least thirty men sat at the tables, and all of them seemed delighted at the prospect of free food. None of them, I noticed, appeared to be Israelites.

The innkeeper set a pitcher of wine on the table in front of me. "To Samson," he called, holding a cup aloft. "And to my daughter, Kesi, the bride. Long may they be happy, and many be their children."

"Hear, hear!" While the guests thumped empty cups on the table, the innkeeper's servants hurried to fill them.

The aroma of roasting meat and vegetables warmed the air, and my eyes misted as I beheld the men who cared enough to stop and celebrate my good fortune. My mood was expansive enough to bless every last one of them.

CHAPTER THIRTEEN

DELILAH

I SAT A LITTLE TALLER on the camel when I spied an inn on the road ahead. Animal pens surrounded the expansive building, and someone had erected a large tent some distance from the pens.

"Warati," I called down to the brother who walked beside my camel, "what is that place?"

He grinned up at me. "The inn at Timnah. And before you ask, yes, we are stopping. Most travelers stop there to water their animals, so if the place is busy we might stay a few days—"

"To trade!" Hitzig interrupted, coming alongside his brother. "An inn is a trader's dream. Travelers need goods, and we are loaded with goods they need. And while we are trading, food and drink are readily available."

"Are you not grateful for my cooking?" Regnar called from the lead camel.

"Is that what it is?" Hitzig pointed to his mouth. "Your bread is so hard I lost a tooth." He flashed a big smile, displaying a yawning gap in his front teeth. "You will be glad we stopped here, girl. The innkeeper's daughters are good cooks."

The sounds of merriment and music floated out of the building as we approached. The brothers looked at each other. "Could it be a festival?" Warati asked. "A wedding or a celebration of a birth?"

Hitzig didn't answer, but led our animals to a stand of trees near a stone outbuilding. He helped me off the camel, then secured the donkeys. Before letting me leave the shady area, however, he put Regnar's cloak on my shoulders, pulled the hood up and over my head. "Remain silent and look like a younger brother," he said. "I don't expect trouble, but in strange territory it's always good to remain quiet and do nothing that draws attention."

Before I could speak, Warati nudged me forward, placing me squarely in the middle of their group.

I would have willingly remained outside, but the thought of a decent meal made my mouth water. And this did not look like a safe place for a woman alone. Too many donkeys stood in the courtyard; too many deep voices emanated from the building. Furthermore, I counted three Philistine chariots and six proud Philistine horses browsing a nearby field. Whatever sort of gathering this was, important people were present—and from the sound of it, the important people were loud and inebriated.

I followed Regnar into the crowded gathering. Every eye in the building turned to stare at us, and I hid myself behind his broad shoulders.

"What's this?" Hitzig called, lifting a hand as he entered the room. "We have come for food and drink, and instead we find a party? What is the occasion, friends?"

The innkeeper, a round-faced man with a big belly, hurried forward. "Welcome, welcome, do not worry. You have wandered into my daughter's wedding. She is to marry Samson, and we have plenty of room for you. Welcome, friends, have a seat. Enjoy a cup of wine."

Ah. The tent outside was a bridal tent.

Our group claimed a small table, and Warati sat beside me. "What luck," he said. "Dinner for nothing and wine aplenty."

"Until the bridegroom cannot pay." Hitzig grinned as he looked around the room. "I do believe that man over there is the ceren of Gath. Look, Regnar—is that not him?"

My blood froze as I followed Hitzig's pointing finger. The richly dressed man in question wasn't the ceren of Gath—he was Zaggi, the lord of Gaza. And right next to him, no more than twenty paces away, sat my former stepbrother.

I dropped my head to the table and covered my face.

"What's wrong?" Warati asked. "Aren't you hungry?"

"I think I'm sick." My voice sounded strangled in my own ears. "That man over there is the ceren of Gaza, and the youth next to him is the villain who sold my mother into slavery. Please, I beg you—do not make me remain here. If he sees me, he will claim me as his property. And if he takes me away, I will not survive the night."

Silence fell over our table even as the other guests laughed and taunted the groom. Hitzig leaned over and whispered in my ear, "We cannot leave you outside, for you would be in a different kind of danger out there. Switch places with Regnar and sit in the shadows. Remain quiet, keep your head down, and do not worry. No one will take you from us."

I trembled as Regnar stood so I could slip into the dimly lit spot he had vacated. As the big man sat in my place, his shadow, tall and broad, covered me like a cloak. I don't know what he would have done if Achish had issued a challenge, but after a while I relaxed enough to lift my head and glance around the room. Though I was not brave enough to look in Achish's direction, I could feel him, a malevolent presence amid the happy celebration.

"Do we know the groom?" Hitzig asked, speaking to his brothers. "How did he come to be a friend of Delilah's enemy?"

We all turned to look at the man seated in a place of honor at the front of the room. From what we could see of him, beneath his beard and long plaited hair was an ordinary face—brown eyes, high cheekbones, tanned skin. He appeared to be solidly built, but I'd have wagered that he was neither as tall as Regnar nor as stout as Hitzig. In short, he appeared unremarkable.

The innkeeper stood and lifted a wooden mug. "To Samson, our host! May his fields be bountiful and his bride be fertile! May she give him children and not grief all the days of his life!"

The other men roared with laughter, raised their cups, and drank.

"Samson?" Hitzig's brow rose. "A Hebrew name, right?"

Regnar nodded.

Samson stood and looked around the room. "Before my bride joins us," he said, a smile twitching in and out of his beard, "I wanted to thank you for joining my wedding celebration. As you know, none of my people could come to this feast, so I am grateful to you for sharing my joy. To show my gratitude, I have devised a banquet riddle for your entertainment. If any man can solve the riddle in the next seven days, I will give him thirty linen garments and thirty changes of clothes. But if no one answers correctly, I will take a linen garment and a change of clothes from each of you."

Murmurs of surprise rippled throughout the crowd. On the surface, the wager seemed extremely unfair. If the groom won, each wedding guest would lose only one set of garments, but if the groom lost, he would have to provide thirty sets of clothing—more than any one man could afford.

The groom's father tugged on his son's sleeve, but Samson gently brushed the old man's hand away.

"Propose your riddle!" I flinched at the sound of Achish's voice.

He stood, answering the groom's challenge with a confident smile. "Let's hear your cup question."

The groom studied Achish with an appraising glance. "You seem confident, sir."

Achish crossed his arms. "I am confident in everything I do."

This Samson must have seen something in Achish's nature that pleased him, because he gestured to the empty seat on the dais. "Is it not customary for the groom to have a second? And yet this seat is empty."

Smiling—probably in an effort to impress the ceren—Achish leapt over an empty bench and moved to Samson's side. "Are you going to present the riddle or not? Behold, we stand ready to hear it."

Samson's eyes narrowed as he nodded. "All right, then. Out of the eater came forth food; out of the strong came forth sweet." He stepped back and gracefully spread his hands. "There's your cup question. Solve it, if you can."

Samson dropped into his seat as Achish stood before the group and thoughtfully stroked the small tuft of hair on his chin. "Out of the eater came forth food," he repeated, emphasizing each word. "And out of the strong came forth sweet."

"That's easy," one of the men yelled. "Someone ate his dinner and then belched!"

The crowd roared with laughter, but Achish only smiled. He turned to Samson and inclined his head in a deep nod. "A most interesting riddle. You invented it?"

Samson nodded his dark head. "I did."

"Most interesting," Achish answered. "I will stand here again on the last day of your feast and present you with the answer." With a flick of his robe, Achish stepped off the dais and went back to the ceren's table. Only then did I stop trembling.

After we had eaten, I followed the three brothers into the courtyard. Night had fallen, and I lingered in the shadows as other guests came out, found their mounts, and rode away. I crouched by the camels until Hitzig came over to remove their saddles and turn the animals into a pen.

"Hitzig," I whispered, dogging his footsteps, "are we really safe here? Surely we would be better off if we left at sunrise. Or maybe I should go."

He blinked as if my words had startled him. "No, no, no. You will remain with us so you can be safe. I will set up a tent for you, and you can sleep there. From now on we'll bring food to you so you won't have to go inside. When all is finished here, we will be on our way."

I forced a smile, but I couldn't share the brothers' delight. Seven days meant nothing to them, but they were country people who measured time by seasons, not days. I, on the other hand, had spent most of my life in cities, and I knew the difference a single day could make. A feast of seven days meant innumerable opportunities for Achish to spot me, stumble over me, overhear my voice, or learn that the brothers traveled with a young, dark-skinned girl.

I remained silent as Hitzig led the animals to an empty pen. When he returned, I tugged on his sleeve. "You do remember, don't you, that I am running from a man with important connections?"

Hitzig cocked a dark brow. "I remember."

"So if anyone sees me, word might get back to him. I wouldn't be safe at all."

Hitzig exhaled. "I understand that he is an evil man. I understand that he misused you. But you are with us now. You don't have to keep hiding."

"You don't understand anything." I clenched my fist. "That young man is a wealthy merchant now. He is also a friend of the ceren. He is powerful, and he can arrange things."

"Delilah." Hitzig bent to look me in the eye. "My brothers and I have promised to protect you until we've reached a place where you feel secure. We will take you all the way to Gibeon if need be. But if it makes you feel any better, we will sleep next to your tent. No one will be able to get to you unless they trample over the three of us."

I nodded, somewhat reassured, but I did not feel completely comfortable until after the brothers erected the promised tent and told me to go inside.

After lifting each section of fabric to make certain no one but the brothers slept anywhere near me, I lay down and stared at the fabric walls until sleep finally claimed me.

✦

Time had never passed as slowly as it did the week of the Israelite's wedding. One day slid slowly into the next, and every night that mismatched group of wedding guests descended on the inn to eat, drink, and celebrate with Samson. Every night I lay in my tent, peering through a slit in the fabric until I saw Achish enter the building. Then I could relax for a little while, or until Achish came out again.

I begged Hitzig to quietly make inquiries about why my enemy was here in Timnah, of all places. Hitzig promised he would, and that night he sat by our campfire and gave his report. "The men here," Hitzig said, "are mostly travelers and a few local farmers. You can identify the soldiers because of their uniforms. And they are clean-shaven."

"Why?" I asked.

Hitzig tugged on the hair at his chin. "So the enemy cannot grab them by the beard."

The other brothers laughed, and I couldn't stop a smile.

"I also made discreet inquiries about the young man with the ceren," Hitzig went on. "The merchants were only too happy to talk about him. Apparently he has nearly run through his father's fortune already. They said he gambles, throws lavish parties, and entertains too many foolish friends. If not for Zaggi, who supports him, he would be already ruined. But this Zaggi has appointed that young man commander of the Philistine army. The people on this road will be seeing a lot of him, because he will be patrolling lands occupied by the Israelites, Canaanites"—he looked at his brothers—"and Gibeonites. I have no proof, but I suspect he hopes to rebuild his fortune through bribery and extortion. Zaggi has given him untold opportunities to do so."

I gaped at Hitzig, disbelieving. Why did people like Achish always seem to land on their feet? He deserved to be imprisoned or forced to work at hard labor to pay off his debts. He did not deserve to lead an army or bully innocent people. Allowing him to ride through the land beneath the cerens' banner was like setting a lion loose in a field of sheep. I knew Achish, and I knew he would stop at nothing to obtain whatever he desired.

I clutched at Hitzig's sleeve. "Beware of that snake," I whispered. "Promise me—all of you—that you and your families will stay away from him. He destroys everything he touches."

Hitzig's smile flattened as Regnar and Warati nodded. "Don't worry," Hitzig said, patting my hand. "We Gibeonites are wily people, especially when we have been forewarned. We will not allow ourselves to be abused by that particular Philistine."

Hitzig also shared details about the groom and his bride. Samson and his father were Israelites from the tribe of Dan, Hitzig said, and the groom's parents had not been eager to arrange the marriage. But the son had insisted, so the parents had reluctantly come from Zorah to attend a wedding they did not support and could not approve. The bridegroom's mother had gone home after the first day, unwilling to remain throughout the seven-day feast.

"Is this Samson a rebel?" I asked. "Has he always been quick to dishonor his mother and father?"

"Apparently not," Hitzig said. "He is a judge of Israel and is known as wise and devoted to his God. But apparently"—Hitzig shrugged—"he could not be dissuaded from marrying the innkeeper's daughter."

What sort of woman would motivate an otherwise obedient son to defy his parents? The innkeeper's daughter had to be extraordinarily beautiful or enticing in some way I could not imagine.

The next day, the fourth of the feast, I sat in the stifling heat of my tent and looked out, hoping to catch a glimpse of the beguiling bride. In the middle of the afternoon, I finally spied her with Achish, the groom's first friend. They were standing near the stone building, and Achish had his hand wrapped around the woman's bare arm. "Find out!" he hissed, his lips only inches from her cheek. "Learn the answer or you will pay."

"But he won't tell me." Even from my hiding place, I could see the shimmer of tears on her cheeks. "I've tried everything. I've coaxed and pleaded and begged him—"

"Try something else," Achish warned, "or you will force me to use a more effective means of persuasion." He jerked his thumb toward a tall haystack in the field. "How would you and your father like to burn?"

She cried out and he released her. The girl stumbled backward, then ran for the safety of her bridal tent. I kept my eyes fastened on Achish.

He watched the innkeeper's daughter flee, then he stood alone in the field, his shoulders hunched, his eyes downcast, his hand resting on the hilt of his sword. I leaned forward, wishing I could see from a closer perspective. Something in his posture had changed, and I yearned to know what it was. When I lived with him, he had been extremely social, staying out late to eat and drink with his friends. But now, even though he wore a Philistine military uniform, an air of remoteness surrounded him, an almost visible aura of isolation.

What had changed him? Had he finally begun to grieve for his noble father? Or, like me, had he awakened to the fact that he was alone in the world? Neither of us had any remaining family, but at least I had three Gibeonite friends. Since his wealth had run out, I doubted that Achish had any.

I lowered my head to my folded arms and kept watching until he finally turned and walked back to the inn.

⸎

While the wedding was tedious for me, at least the brothers did a brisk business. When the wedding guests returned for each day's meal, they milled around in the courtyard, conversing in small groups and eying the livestock. Though I remained hidden in my tent, nearly every day I heard boasts about which donkey was the most compliant, which camel could run fastest, and which horse would produce the most valuable offspring.

I had often heard men complain about women's gossip, but I overheard plenty of men gossiping, too. They talked about the innkeeper, wondered about his wealth, and made crude comments about both of his daughters. They cracked jokes about the groom, questioned his paternity, and whispered a rumor involving his mother and a journeying merchant. They criticized the ceren, told rude stories about Philistines in general, and even poked fun at Achish. "He has no enemies," one of the Philistine soldiers said, "but his friends dislike him immensely."

While the guests were outside, relaxed and talking, the brothers conducted business. They had been clever enough to unpack the items they had traded for in Gaza, and these were displayed on blankets in a shady spot near the animal pens. One of the brothers always remained near their wares, so when the wedding guests wandered over to examine the items and inquire about their usefulness, either

Regnar, Hitzig, or Warati was ready to haggle. Many items that were plentiful and cheap in Gaza were rare and expensive in Timnah, so every day certain items left the brothers' stores while others were added to their inventory—pieces of silver, valuable seeds, useful tools. One morning Hitzig accepted a live chicken in exchange for a brass pot, then he brought the chicken to me and told me to keep it happy. I didn't have any idea what to do with a chicken, so I tied the end of a long string around its leg and attached the other end to my ankle. The chicken surprised me by remaining near my tent during the day and roosting in a blanket at night. He wandered away the next day and was never seen again. But that night Hitzig reported finding chicken in his stew at dinner.

I began to believe that the Gibeonite brothers enjoyed trading more than *owning*. One afternoon I watched a merchant with Regnar trade a fine linen tunic for a copper cup. Before the sun set, Warati gave the tunic to another man and received another copper cup in trade.

As the sixth day of the feast drew to a close, the wedding guests gathered inside the inn to lift their mugs and toast the groom. I remained in my tent, clutching the blade Regnar had given me in case a drunken fool crawled in with mischief on his mind. The dagger gave me confidence I sorely lacked, and on at least three occasions I wrapped my fingers around the hilt and hoped Achish would wander by. If he had, I would have welcomed the opportunity to plant my blade into his cold heart.

But Achish came and went by chariot, so he was rarely around in the daylight hours. An unexpected blessing, I think, for both of us.

Chapter Fourteen
SAMSON

"And what did you mean to accomplish by sharing that riddle?" Indignation flared in Rei's eyes as he glared at me. "Were you trying to show off?"

Annoyed, I brushed away his concern. "Do not worry—not a man among them will figure it out."

"I wouldn't be so sure." Rei sat on a fallen rock and rested his head on his hand. "I don't have a good feeling about this wedding, not at all. Your mother disapproves, your father disapproves, all of Israel disapproves."

"I know," I pointed out. "But those people hold no authority over me."

"Would that they did." Rei shook his head. "Would that I could make you listen to your parents. Moses gave us a law, but you seem intent on flouting it."

"I answer only to Adonai. He singled me out before I was born, so He alone is my authority."

"You use Adonai," Rei called as I turned to walk away. "You use His calling as an excuse!"

Leaving Rei and his nagging behind, I strode out to the plowed fields where I could be alone with my thoughts. The bridal tent stood off to the north, the place where tonight I would sleep with my bride. A group of women were inside it now, decorating it with flowers and other feminine foolishness. That motley crew of men had joined me in raising our cups and exchanging ribald jokes for a full seven days, a ritual designed to excite my desire while giving the bride time to say farewell to her parents and siblings.

By this time tomorrow, Kesi and I would be traveling back to Zorah and the house I had built for her.

I smiled in anticipation. I doubted that any of the men at my wedding feast understood that my greatest happiness would come not from the physical fulfillment or my delight in winning a beautiful bride. My greatest joy lay in knowing that Adonai had finally provided someone who would be bone of my bone and blood of my blood. The Philistines might nod and wink, Rei might look at me askance, but they did not understand the ache I had endured for years. From my birth—from my *conception*, my mother was always quick to point out—I had been unlike any other man. Adonai had designed and set me apart for a unique purpose, even though I had nothing but Mother's word about what that purpose might be.

"Samson."

I turned and saw Rei coming through the field. "You followed me?"

"I'm sorry. I don't want to be a nag."

I shrugged away his apology. "I guess you can't help it."

"It's true. Why do I hurt the man I've spent my life serving? I want to help, not hinder."

I sank to the ground and lifted my gaze to the western horizon. Somewhere out there lay the Great Sea and the place from which my bride's people had come. My people had come from the East. How fitting that we should meet in the land between east and west.

Rei cleared his throat. "I only wanted to warn you about the riddle because—"

"Forget about it. No one will guess the answer, so I'm not risking anything. And after I have collected my thirty changes of garments, I will have enough to trade for all the things we need in our new home. Few couples begin their married lives with so much—even those who've had the support of family and friends."

"Do I detect a trace of bitterness in your voice?"

I scowled at him, then shrugged. "I don't want to be bitter. But Adonai placed the image of this woman in my heart, so I am determined to marry her. Is she not beautiful?"

Rei sat but remained an arm's length away. "She is beautiful, yes, certainly. But many beautiful girls live among your own people. Their beauty is not that of artfully painted eyes or reddened cheeks, but of spirit and heart. They worship the God you worship; they understand our laws and our history."

"They cannot surprise me." I confided this with a small smile and then closed my eyes. "I want a woman who is unlike any other . . ."

Because I am unlike any other.

I did not verbalize the thought because Rei would not understand. None of my people did. They knew me as Samson the Nazarite, son of Manoah and Akarah. They knew me as the judge who sought Adonai's advice to settle their disputes and maintain peace among the tribes. They knew me as the shepherd who managed his father's flocks and was occasionally skillful with rhymes and riddles.

But most of them did not know that I had been marked before

birth. Even if they *had* heard my mother's story, they would not understand the significance of my beginning.

I wasn't sure I understood it myself.

❦

With the consummation of our marriage only a few hours away, I went in search of Kesi. I found her inside the bridal tent, where she was directing the women who were decorating the wedding bed with flowers and ribbons.

"Kesi." I slipped my arm around her waist and pulled her close, my heart pounding in anticipation.

"What do you need, Samson? There is so much work to be done."

I pinned her in a long, silent scrutiny, *willing* her to understand the matters uppermost in my mind. My parents were able to read each other's looks and glances—why wasn't she responding to my unspoken message? Perhaps we needed time to learn the language of love. "I want to talk to you," I began. "I want to tell you everything about my past, about how I have longed for you, about how I want to cherish you for the rest of my life—"

She kissed me, her warm lips smothering all the things I wanted to say. When she finally pulled away, she looked up into my eyes and placed her hands on my arms. "I need to talk to you, too. I know I've asked almost every day, but in a few moments we will be husband and wife. And I have to ask, Samson—" she paused and looked down, her lower lip trembling—"because how can you say you love me when you have not fully shared your heart with me?"

The question struck me dumb. Had I not mentioned all the things I wanted to tell her? The secrets I wanted to share? "I want to tell you everything," I repeated, smiling down at her. "But we have a lifetime in which to share our hearts."

"Not a lifetime." Her gaze flitted away from my face, then lingered on my arm. "Your riddle, Samson. You have created a beautiful riddle, but you have not shared the solution with me. I cannot believe you would be so . . . so *stingy* with your heart."

I tipped my head back to better see her face. Her piteous expression seemed sincere and her eyes glowed with innocence, but why was she so fixated on my riddle? Its banality overshadowed the hidden things I yearned to share, but night after night, day after day, all she could think about was that stupid riddle.

"The answer is not in my heart. The answer is here." I tapped the side of my head. "And you, my sweet, will learn the answer when I reveal it."

"Samson." Her lower lip edged forward in a pout. "How can you love me when you aren't willing to share everything with me?"

That's when I saw it. A glint of mischief in her eye, a pout too forced to be natural. My bride was toying with me. I stepped back, as repulsed as if she had poured cold water over my loins.

For six days she had pestered me with her question, and for six days I refused to answer. Now, recognizing my displeasure, she turned on me, not with fury, but with grief. "You hate me!" she cried, her tears a gelding weapon. "You don't love me at all! You proposed a riddle to the sons of my people, yet you haven't explained it to me—and we're supposed to be in love!"

What could I say? I had promised myself to an actress, a woman who would betray me at the first opportunity. I saw the signs clearly. Rei—my parents—I should have listened to them.

But I could not back out without humiliating my bride and her family.

In that hour, as the servants hung flower chains over the opening to the nuptial tent, I gave her the answer. She responded with a flurry of hugs and quick kisses that I bore with quiet equanimity.

A bit later, as the sun came down the sky, the young Philistine captain, Achish, lifted his cup and grinned at me. "What is sweeter than honey?" he said, dipping his finger into a honeypot on the table. "And what is stronger than a lion?"

He had to be the instigator. He might not be the only cheat, but he, the groom's first friend, had been whispering in my bride's ear.

The room went silent as I stood. From the corner of my eye I glimpsed Rei shaking his head *no, no, no*. My beautiful Kesi, seated at my side, went as pale as death. And Achish, the villain who had stolen the answer, shifted his hand to the hilt of his dagger.

"If you hadn't plowed with my heifer"—I threw each word like a stone—"you wouldn't have solved my riddle."

Fueled by frustration, something rose within me, stretched its wings, and yearned to escape from its cage of ribs. I lifted my arms and roared, then stalked out of the room and moved into the hazy, golden air of sunset. As others followed me into the courtyard, I took off, fleeing from the inn, running toward the sea.

CHAPTER FIFTEEN
DELILAH

I HAVE SEEN ANGRY MEN, even violent and cruel men, but I saw no sign of violence or cruelty in the Israelite's face when he stormed out of the inn and started running. I watched him race toward the setting sun and wondered what could have changed his visage from that of happy groom to determined sprinter. Only when Hitzig came out and told me about the riddle did I fully understand.

Within a few moments of the groom's departure, the wedding party dispersed. Since most of the guests remained outside to enjoy the cooler air of dusk, I was able to eavesdrop from the safety of my tent.

"Well, that's that," one of the Philistine soldiers said to the inn-keeper. "We've run off your son-in-law, and all his boasting has gone with him."

The innkeeper turned to the groom's white-haired father. "What have you to say about your faithless son?"

The old man wavered a moment, then shook his head. "My son is not faithless. If he promised to pay a wager, he will pay it."

As the other man guffawed, the old man grabbed a staff and took off, walking over the same road his son had covered only moments before. But instead of taking the western path, the old man turned east. Because of the late hour, I hoped he didn't have far to go.

The Gibeonite brothers strolled casually toward my tent, then sat around their small fire, blocking my view but allowing me to hear their conversation.

"Where do you think Samson is going?" Warati asked.

Hitzig shook his head. "Where can he go? They guessed his riddle. He's probably licking his wounds in the wilderness."

Regnar tugged on his beard. "What about the girl?"

Hitzig snorted. "The innkeeper won't let all that food and wine go to waste. He'll probably give her to someone in the bridal party."

The other two brothers exchanged looks of astonishment.

"Don't worry, he won't give her to either of you," Hitzig said, laughing. "He'll look for someone far more prosperous. Like a Philistine."

The brothers packed their belongings and tended to their animals, then stretched out around the small fire that glowed long into the night. I had been restless all day, eager to leave the ill-fated wedding, but I dreaded the coming morning. The brothers would set out for home, but what was I supposed to do? They had already offered more kindness than I deserved, so I didn't want them to think I planned to move in with them. They had enough mouths to feed; they certainly didn't need to take in an unskilled homeless girl with no place or people of her own.

Seeking fresh air, I lay on my back by the tent flap and thrust my head into the open space. Lying there, accompanied by the brothers' snoring, I didn't feel so cut off from the rest of the world. The air was clearer than it had been earlier, and a thousand sparkles of diamond light brightened the sky's velvet canopy. The moon cast strange shadows through the tree branches. I was trying to imagine familiar faces in the dark shapes when a rhythmic creak reached my ear.

I rolled over, propped myself on my elbows, and looked around, but saw nothing unusual. I closed my eyes, trying to identify the odd noise. It sounded like a wooden wheel, but I'd seen no wagons at the inn, so what could it be? Carefully, I reached out and shook Hitzig awake.

"Wh-what?" He sat up, his eyes wide and alert. "What's wrong?"

"Shh." I held a finger over my lips and pointed toward the road, from where the sound came. "What *is* that?"

He frowned and looked in the direction of the sound, but we did not have to wonder long. A shaft of moonlight revealed a figure coming toward us on the road, a man pulling a two-wheeled cart. The cart was heavily laden, but not until it reached the clearing did I recognize the gleam of fine linen and the glitter of golden threads.

"Rise!" Samson called, his voice resonating in the darkness. "Wake and collect your due. I promised thirty changes of clothing and thirty linen undergarments. Here they are, so rise and claim your prize!"

The innkeeper stumbled out of the inn, followed by several wedding guests. Realizing that the courtyard was about to become very crowded, I crept back into the tent and peeked through the slit in the opening. Samson did not wait around for thanks or ask to speak to his bride. Leaving the pushcart in the center of the road, he jogged back the way he'd come, quickly vanishing in the darkness.

The startled Philistines began to pluck robes from the cart.

"By the crust between Dagon's toes, this tunic is fine!" one man exclaimed. "Where do you think he got such fine garments?"

"I doubt he's wealthy enough to own such clothing—could he have stolen them?"

"Do you think he would kill a man for his cloak?"

"Why not? He's a barbarian."

"At least if he's a killer," Achish said, picking up a vermillion robe with fur at the sleeves, "he was considerate enough to kill without bloodying the fabrics. That was good of him."

At the sight of my former stepbrother, narrow-eyed and scornful in the moonlight, I drew back inside my tent and curled beneath my blanket. But as the wool fibers tickled my nose, one question bedeviled me. How had the Israelite made good on his promise?

⌘

Careful to remain beneath the cover of my veil, the next morning I helped the brothers break camp and pack the donkeys. The men said nothing about their plans for me, and when it came time to depart, Regnar set me on the rear camel as though I belonged there.

I didn't protest, though I was still anxious about the future. Achish had not yet come out of the inn, and I didn't want to be in the courtyard when he did.

Warati urged my camel to stand, and I held tight to the saddle as the animal raised its hind legs, tilting his body and nearly toppling me from my seat. Then the front end came up, and my heart settled back to a relieved rhythm.

We left the inn and moved onto the eastern road, heading toward Gibeon and other places unknown to me. I lifted my face to the warm sun and felt at home among the squeaks of the saddle and the occasional braying of a donkey.

When our caravan stopped at a brook under the blazing midday sun, we watered the donkeys and refilled our waterpots. Regnar reclined beneath the shade of a fig tree, and Hitzig sat beside him. Warati checked the bindings of the camels' saddles, then gestured to me, inviting me to join him and his brothers in the shade.

My nerves tightened. This might be the moment I'd been dreading. They would tell me that we were nearing Gibeon, so I had to go. I was not part of their family or their people. If I left them now and walked north, I might reach Ekron in a few days' time.

"Delilah," Warati began as soon as I filled the gap in their circle, "we have made a decision that concerns you."

"I know." I interrupted in the hope that I might make things easier for them. "I know I can't go home with you. You can leave me here, and I'll . . . I'll find another caravan."

"You would die if we left you here," Hitzig said flatly. "A young woman, alone, in the wilderness? You would not last two days."

"But I'm determined—"

"No," Hitzig snapped. "Many a determined man has died out here."

"We are approaching the Valley of Sorek," Warati said, continuing as if nothing had happened. "The land belongs to the Israelites, but it is occupied by the Philistines, as you will see. But many of the Israelites who live here are devout people. They believe in only one God—Adonai, the invisible God—who is quite powerful. The people have his law, and those who follow it are righteous. You need not fear if you find a home with the people of Israel."

I pointed out the obvious. "But I'm not one of them."

"That doesn't matter." Regnar offered one of his rare smiles. "The righteous children of Abraham are hospitable to all who pass through their land, because they were once slaves themselves. It's part of their law."

"But mark this—not all the Israelites follow their law," Warati insisted. "Many worship the gods of the Canaanites and Philistines, and those people are as lawless as anyone you could name. Recently we heard about an Israelite who offered his concubine to men of Gibeah, who so abused her that—" he swallowed hard and flushed—"she died. We do not want you to meet the same fate."

Perplexed, I looked from one brother to the next. "So you are leaving me . . . where?"

"We know a widow," Warati went on, "an older woman who lives at a well near the entrance to the Valley of Sorek. She is righteous, but she is old. Though her eyes are failing and her fingers are stiff, she weaves well, and we believe she would take you in. You could help her, she could help you, and together you might do each other some good. We are certain you will not do each other harm."

I was grateful, truly, but something in me objected to the idea that Warati and his brothers should decide where I should go. What gave them the right to decide for me? What if I hated this widow? What if she didn't like me? If I couldn't stand living with the old woman, what other choices would I have?

But even as I compiled a list of what-ifs, I realized that I had no other choice. I had nowhere to go and no one to tell me what to do. My mother had been taken from me and my father could not speak from beyond the grave. Even Adinai, whom I'd come to respect, could no longer advise me.

And these three brothers had helped me when no one else would. If they were kind enough to devise a plan that would keep me safe and give me a way to support myself, I ought to be grateful.

So instead of refusing their offer, I lowered my face to the earth and bowed to them, the only way I knew to show my respect.

"Get up," Warati said, nudging my shoulder. "Are we gods that you should bow to us?"

"But you've done so much for—"

"We are friends," Hitzig said, "and friends care for one another."

I sat up and inclined my head in gratitude. "I am grateful to you all. You have saved my life, and I hope I will be able to learn a trade. I plan to gather enough wealth that I can return to Gaza and bargain for my mother's freedom. If I am successful, it will be because of your kindness."

"Don't thank us yet." Warati lifted his hand. "We have not spoken to the widow of Sorek. But we should reach her home before sunset, and then we will learn if she is willing to take you in."

❦

After traveling so long through the coastal plain, my heart lifted to see foothills as we approached the green Valley of Sorek. The land appeared well-watered and more densely populated. As hills began to rise around us, I noticed that many had been planted with rings of trees at the summit. When I asked about them, Warati made a face and spat on the road.

"I wish we could blame the Philistines for those," he said, disdain in his voice, "but those are places where Baal and Asherah are worshiped. The Canaanites worshiped them for years, and some Israelites have followed their example. On certain nights people go up to the hills, burn incense, and make sacrifices before the wooden Asherah poles. They indulge themselves in despicable practices."

"I'm familiar with stone gods and temple prostitutes," I told him. "Egypt had more gods than I could count."

Warati's features hardened in a stare of disapproval. "The people around here have but two, yet those are enough to keep them from worshiping the true God. Some have been known to sacrifice even their babies to Baal."

"Is he a fertility god?" I asked, thinking of Egypt.

"He is the chief god, very old, the god of rain and storms," Warati answered. "Asherah is his mother. According to those who worship her, she is the queen of heaven. The women bake little cakes for her."

"And the true God?" I asked. "Have you discerned which one that is?"

Warati's expression changed as a wry thought tightened the corner of his mouth. "No doubt," he said, "the true God is Adonai, the

God worshiped by righteous Israelites. For fear of him my fore-fathers swore that we Gibeonites would be servants to the children of Israel forever."

I remained silent, not wanting to comment on my host's choice. Mama and I had visited several temples in Egypt, but, as she later said, the rains came and the winds blew no matter which god we worshiped, so what difference did our choice make?

I was about to doze off in the saddle when Warati spoke again. "Not much farther now," he said, pointing to the road ahead. "Soon we'll be at the widow's." He explained that the widow's house was next to a well, so it had become a popular way station for travelers to fill their waterpots. "She has become the guardian of the well, I suppose," he said, glancing up at me as he walked beside my camel. "As such, people revere and respect her. They also trade for her goods, as she is an excellent weaver."

I smiled, eager to learn what I could from a woman who had learned how to support herself.

"People also stop at her place to glean the latest news," Hitzig said, winking. "She knows everything about nearly everyone, so do what you must to remain on her good side."

"I will," I promised.

"She's not wealthy," he added, "but I've never seen her beg, nor have I ever seen her reduced to gleaning from another man's fields. I think she will not suffer hardship if you stay with her."

I managed a timid smile. "I'll try not to eat much."

He laughed. "Eat as much as you like. The widow . . . well, you'll see."

Not much later I spotted a small dwelling to the north of the deeply rutted road. The mud-brick house was small, but a thatched roof had been built onto to it, creating a porch. The shaded area beneath the porch was larger than the house and had to be cooler when the winds blew. A stone fence enclosed both structures, and

behind it a ewe and her lamb stood quietly and watched us approach.
The well, marked by a circular stone wall, stood outside the gate in
the shade of a towering terebinth tree.

Regnar called a halt and made his camel sit. When he had dismounted, he looked at me and his brothers. "Wait here."

Without another word, he went through the gate and stooped
beneath the thatched roof of the open porch. The area beneath was
dense with shadows, not allowing me to see what was transpiring
beneath the dried palm fronds.

While we waited, I turned my face toward the setting sun and
contemplated the odd turn my life had taken. I knew I would be
either dead or locked in Achish's chamber if I had remained in
Gaza—someone would have found me and returned me to Achish's
house or I would have died from starvation in some dark alley. I had
to flee, but if not for these three brothers, I would have perished
alone in the wilderness.

I shuddered. If other men had found me, I might have suffered
like the concubine who was brutally attacked. Warati was correct
when he called the land lawless. The Philistine cerens ruled within
the walls of their city-kingdoms, but outside those walls, men operated as they wished. Nobility and generosity could be found in
some men's hearts, but others sought selfish pleasure above all. To
some, women were of less value than a muscled bull.

I thought of my father and stepfather, both of whom had seen
the beauty of my mother's heart reflected on her lovely face. Because
they had been good and decent, I had expected most men to be so,
but the last few weeks had taught me otherwise. We women might
not be as strong or as swift as men, but did we not have the same
right to live freely and make choices?

My camel stomped his hoof, growing restless, and I wondered
if Regnar had finished presenting my cause. He was not asking a
simple favor—the woman might not want to accept a responsibility

to feed and clothe me. Though she didn't have to extend hospitality to a girl who was not even of her people, I hoped she would. If the brothers were right and the widow was truly righteous, perhaps she would at least agree to shelter me until I found a way to procure my mother's freedom.

"Delilah."

I turned at the sound of Warati's voice. Regnar had stepped out of the thatched porch and was gesturing us forward. Swallowing hard to dislodge the lump in my throat, I wiped my damp palms on my tunic and watched silently as Warati led the caravan toward the widow's home.

Regnar held the gate open long enough for us to bring the camels and donkeys inside the courtyard. The ewe and her lamb scurried away while Hitzig commanded my camel to sit. I clung to the saddle as my mount bent his front legs, positioning me at a perilous angle, then straightened out so I could slide off the saddle.

I studied the house. Only one window in front, closed off by a tightly woven shade. Thick, upright branches served as supports for the porch's thatched roof, and at one point the roof dipped low, forcing any adult of normal height to stoop in order to enter. Did she not have anyone to repair it, or did she lower the roof on purpose? Perhaps she meant to keep prying eyes away from her work.

I stepped beneath the thatched roof, then blinked as my eyes grew accustomed to the deep shade. A quarter of the space was taken up by a large table covered with folded fabrics, spools of thread, piles of fluffy wool, and bits and pieces of cord and string—the worktable of a woman who began many projects before she finished one. Near the table, a wooden loom hung from a ceiling beam. Next to the loom, a woman sat on a stool . . . and she'd been studying me as I looked around her workplace.

When our eyes met, I quickly lowered my head and blushed.

"She'll do," the widow said, nodding at Regnar. "Any girl with the sense to lower her eyes before an old woman is a girl with character. I will keep her. And now, sit, all of you. I have water and honey cakes to serve you."

She gave the brothers a mostly toothless smile, then rose and moved toward a basket near her fire pit, a blackened space at the back edge of the porch. I glanced at Hitzig, who gave me a reassuring nod and pointed to a small grouping of pillows on a straw mat. Mirroring his actions, I sat on a pillow and offered another to Warati.

Regnar helped the widow carry a tray with cups and honey cakes to the mat, where we sipped water and nibbled and smiled our thanks. I had a feeling that the ritual was part of an unspoken agreement between the widow and the brothers.

While I ate, I studied the woman more closely. Her face was red—with exertion or sun exposure, I couldn't tell which—and her uncovered gray hair hung down her back in a long braid. Frizzy tendrils framed her face and floated on the slight breeze. And her eyes, when not darting to and fro in search of something she needed, were faded but kind.

Warati cleared his throat, gestured to the widow and looked at me. "Delilah, the widow has agreed to our request. She will take you in and teach you her craft. In return, you will obey her instructions and help her as much as you can."

"Cheerfully," the widow said, looking straight at me. "I cannot live with a woman who whines."

Warati smiled. "Delilah, you will *cheerfully* obey. And in return, we brothers will stop here each year when we make our trip to the Gaza market. We will supply anything you need, and we will make sure you are both happy with the arrangement. If you are not, we have agreed to take you away."

The widow gave a curt nod, then lifted her cup. "And you brothers will trade for some of my woven goods," she added, her voice ringing with finality.

"Agreed." Hitzig glanced at the stack of fabrics piled on the table. "No one weaves as well as you do."

I waited on my pillow, quietly hoping that the widow's willingness to take me in would not depend on the size of the brothers' purchase. I didn't want her to begrudge every mouthful I ate, but neither did I want the brothers to deprive their families.

"Now." The widow gave the brothers a no-nonsense smile. "How many tunics do you need, Warati?"

Warati glanced at his brothers, then counted on his fingers. "My children, my wives—we need enough for ten."

"Linen or wool?"

"Um . . . wool."

"Fine or rough?"

Warati squinted at the woman. "Rough?"

"I can't hear you, Warati."

He sighed. "Fine."

"Good." She turned to Hitzig. "You are the one who found this girl?"

An uncertain expression passed over his face. Would the widow regard his action on my behalf a credit or a debit?

"I found her and brought her to my brothers."

A smile gathered the woman's cheeks like curtains. "Then you need buy only three tunics, but they shall be of fine linen. You look as though you could use some festival garments."

She turned to Regnar. "My favorite brother—how is your wife?"

Regnar smiled. "She is expecting our fifth child."

"Then you will need swaddling cloths and a new tunic to celebrate. And a fine woolen cloak for your wife."

The widow folded her hands and nodded at her audience. "Are we agreed?"

"We are agreed on what we shall accept," Hitzig said. "Now, what shall we give for such fine linens?"

The widow straightened and looked toward the pack animals standing by the gate. "A jar of honey . . . a sharp blade, if you have one."

Warati's eyes darted toward the dagger in my belt, and he gave me a rueful smile. "We have a blade."

"Good. A duck . . . a rabbit . . . and fat renderings. As much as you can spare."

"We do not have the meat," Hitzig said, "but we have brass bells from Egypt and painted pots from the land across the Great Sea. Come with me to inspect the donkeys and you may see something you didn't realize you needed."

"Lead on, my friend."

Hitzig helped the widow to her feet, and together they walked toward the donkeys.

Warati turned to me. "I suppose you should gather your things."

"I have nothing but the clothes I'm wearing."

The man's eyes softened. "Take anything you need, Delilah. We will not see you until next spring."

Moved to tears by his generosity, I looked to Regnar, whose eyes shone with the same kindness.

I pressed my lips together and determined that I would not cry. I stood and walked out to the rear camel where I had stashed a scarf, a gourd cup, and a pair of papyrus sandals.

When I went back to the porch, the widow looked at me. "Will you collect their goods?" She pointed to a basket filled with folded garments. "You'll find the fine linens there."

"Yes. And thank you."

She smiled at me, and her dark eyes were not unkind. "You'll find the woolen tunics inside the house, in a basket by the window. The swaddling cloths are near the door, and the cloaks hang on wall pegs. Find Regnar's wife a nice color—blue, I think. And Warati's boys are small, so find tunics to fit a child about so high"—she held her hand at the level of her eyes—"and one a little smaller."

And do it cheerfully. Nodding, I went to work inside the house. Though the room looked as though a windstorm had moved through it, I found the items exactly where she said they would be. While I searched, I heard the low rumble of a baritone voice and suspected one of the brothers was filling in the details of my past. After all, the widow had a right to know who would be living in her home.

When I finally stepped out with a stack of woven goods, a much smaller pile of items waited in the center of the porch. "Thank you," the widow told me. "Now you may take the goods out to the brothers and say your farewells."

Yielding to the iron in her voice, I followed Regnar outside and met Warati and Hitzig by the donkeys.

"I will pack those," Warati said, taking the garments from my arms. He set about placing them in saddlebags while I faced Regnar and Hitzig, both of whom had gone silent.

"Well, that's it then." Regnar cleared his throat. "May HaShem bless you."

"Stay out of trouble," Hitzig said. "And mind the widow. She is a wise woman, or so I'm told. I know she's good at trading."

Warati said nothing, but lifted his hand in a silent salute. But when he took the reins of his camel, I could have sworn I saw the glint of tears in his eyes.

"You have been more than generous," I called, lifting my voice so they would all hear me. "I don't think I can ever repay you."

"Be well, Delilah," Hitzig said, taking the reins of the lead donkey. "And look for us next spring. We will be back."

I said good-bye and stood at the widow's gate until the last donkey disappeared behind a hill. I swallowed and became aware of an empty feeling at the center of my chest. I would miss them every day.

Then I drew a deep breath, squared my shoulders, and went into the house to meet my new life.

Chapter Sixteen
DELILAH

WITHIN HOURS OF ARRIVING at the widow's house, I learned that she was not unpleasant, but neither was she as soft and yielding as my mother. I had just returned to the porch after saying good-bye to the brothers when she faced me head-on and said she was grateful to have a helper. In exchange for my help, she added, she would teach me how to weave because "a woman who weaves can do anything."

"Weavers will be in demand for as long as you live," she said, commanding me to sit with a nod of her head. She picked up an oblong piece of fired clay and began to wrap it with thread. "People will always want to cover themselves, and these days most women are too busy grinding grain and raising their children to sit at the loom. So we weave for them, and we create beautiful garments they could never make themselves."

My gaze fell on a pile of rough fabrics that were not at all beautiful. "And what of those?"

A smile lifted the wrinkles at her lips. "If we did not weave commonplace fabrics, fine linen would not be special," she answered. "Just as women like me make women like you even fairer by comparison."

I lifted a brow. I was certain that I hadn't looked beautiful since Adinai's death. When Achish leered at me, I felt humiliated, not complimented. The Gibeonite brothers had barely been able to see me through the grime that covered my face and arms, but the widow, who apparently said what she thought without hesitation, made me long for a looking brass to see what I had missed.

"If we hear the sound of approaching travelers," the widow went on, "we usually stop what we are doing and step out to meet them. If the men are riding with pack animals, bid them welcome and see if they would like to barter for woven goods. If anyone approaches in the company of a Philistine chariot, however, retreat at once—no Philistine warrior ever conducted business with a weaver. If a traveler approaches on foot, we greet them and offer them water and a place to rest in the shade. Do not press them to trading, for if they cannot afford a donkey to carry their provisions, they cannot afford to barter. Give them what you can and bid them Godspeed."

I nodded, committing her instructions to memory. Fortunately, I didn't think that travelers would be so frequent that I wouldn't be able to sit and learn what I needed to know.

"I'm sure you have questions." She tossed me a sidelong glance as she wound her thread. "Ask what you will."

I blinked, uncertain how to proceed, then began with the obvious. The widow wore a simple tunic, but her hair was uncovered. "Are you . . . Philistine?" I asked.

She shook her head in an emphatic *no*. "I am a daughter of Abraham, from the tribe of Dan," she said, keeping her eye on the spool in her hands. "I married a man from Beth-shemesh, but he died after two years. We had no children. We built this house together, and he also built my loom." A note of pleasure entered her voice, and I was sure she counted the loom among her most precious possessions.

"You stayed here after he died? Alone?"

She nodded. "Some of my kinsmen tried to get me to settle in Beth-shemesh, but I had grown used to this place. I didn't want to leave my house, my loom, or the well, so I remained."

I turned toward the empty road that extended beyond her house. Anyone, friend or foe, could come riding up that road to threaten her and no one would know because she lived alone. "Aren't you afraid?" I glanced back at her. "Don't you worry about evil men entering your gate?"

She stopped spooling and dropped her hands into her lap, and her eyes fixed on me with a startling intensity. "I know you've been hurt," she said, maintaining her bluntness even as her tone softened. "And I know evil sometimes rides on that road. But I trust in *El Roi*, the God who sees me when no one else does." She began wrapping the spool again. "What God do you serve?"

I shrugged and carelessly waved my hand. "Dagon, Amun, Isis—"

"All of them?"

I laughed. "When called upon, I worship with my neighbors and do what they do. Because despite all the sacrifices I've left at shrines and altars, I've never seen anything to make me think that anyone watches me."

The widow didn't stop rolling her thread, but smiled. "Perhaps that will change."

~⋆~

Within two days, I came to believe that the widow and I would get along very well. She seemed to enjoy teaching, and I desperately wanted to learn a trade. The faster I could learn how to weave beautiful garments, the sooner I would be able to redeem my mother.

Between lessons, as we stirred the cook pot or folded fabrics, I told her the stories of my life. I told her about growing up in Egypt with my beautiful mother and my seafaring father. I told her about Adinai's kindness and Mother's grief when he died unexpectedly. I did not tell her about Achish because I did not want to speak of that devil in this peaceful place. Bad enough that he had appeared at the wedding in Timnah; I didn't want to evoke his name at the widow's house, too. Besides, I had a strong feeling that Warati had already shared the story with her.

After breaking our fast every morning—every morning but the seventh of each week, that is—the widow taught me about some aspect of weaving. She did not begin with the loom, but insisted that I first learn how to grow the flax we would later spin into thread.

She walked me around to the back of her house, where I found a sizable field of blue flowers. She had dug a system of irrigation ditches that ran through the rows of plants. "Every morning," she said, "we bring buckets from the well and pour them into these ditches to water the field."

I smiled at her use of the word *we*. Each time I heard it, I suspected she meant *me*.

"You know," I said, surveying the land, "in Egypt the farmers used a system called a *shaduf*. It is only feasible on flat fields, but I think it might work here."

The widow crossed her arms as her brows lifted. "What does it do?"

"It's made of a pole with a bucket on one end and a weight on the other. A *shaduf* lifts water from a source, like your well, and empties it in a trench. We'd have to do some digging, but I think we could make it work here."

"That would be good." The widow leaned on a hoe as she smiled at her flowering field. "The rains come in the autumn and winter, but the flowers require water year-round. You would be a tremendous help if you could figure out how to build your . . . what did you call it?"

"*Shaduf*," I reminded her. "And yes, I'll see what I can do."

"So." She smiled at her field again. "What do you think of it?"

"It's beautiful," I whispered.

"This is flax," she said. "I will teach you to plant, harvest, prepare, and spin it."

"And weave it?" I asked, my impatience breaking through.

She shook her head. "You're not ready for weaving. But you can be a big help to me in the garden." She pointed to a corner of the field where most of the flowers had wilted. "Today we begin there. We pull out the plants by the roots, then lay them in the sun to dry."

I sighed. "Sounds simple enough. I think I can do that."

A grin tugged at the older woman's lips. "Go right ahead."

So . . . my first lesson. I walked into the field and tugged on the first wilted plant. It came up easily, but what was I supposed to do next? I looked for the widow, but she had gone back to the porch. So I searched until I spotted a wide basket. I picked it up, set the plant in it, and kept pulling plants until I had cleared the wilted corner. A couple of times I screamed and jumped back when I heard the rustle of a rat, but soon I realized that screaming did no good because the field was alive with the scurrying creatures.

When I had finished, I carried the basket to the porch and smiled gratefully when the widow handed me a cup of water. "You're a good worker," she said. Her eyes crinkled as she grinned. "I take it you found the rats?"

"They found me," I said, repressing a shudder. "I don't know if I'll ever get used to seeing them."

"I don't mind them, so long as they don't eat my flax plants." She peered into my basket and nodded at the plants I'd gathered. "Good. The wool is easy to gather—I have a shearer clip the ewe every spring. The flax takes a bit more work." She hesitated. "Did you work with your mother?"

With difficulty, I swallowed the sudden lump that had risen in my throat. "Before we came to Gaza, we worked together in Egypt. Like you, my mother is creative. She weaves baskets."

"Did she teach you the skill?"

"I can weave simple designs in my lap, but I don't know how to use a loom."

"You'll take to the work naturally, I'm sure."

Her reassuring words comforted me, then the sound of horses' hooves caught my ear. I lowered my cup and pointed to the road. "Someone's coming—I hear horses."

"Really?" The widow turned toward the road. "My ears are not as good as they used to be."

She gestured toward the gate, urging me to greet our guests while she poured water and muttered something about finding the honey cakes.

I smoothed my tunic and stepped out to investigate our visitors.

⁂

Days flew away from me like windblown leaves. Each morning I would water the flax plants and feed the ewe and lamb, and afterward the widow would give me directions and I would head to the field to either plant, harvest, or prepare flax. Once those tasks were done, I would pick up her shovel and work on the trench we needed for the *shaduf*. It would need to run from the well to her flax field, a distance of about fifty paces. I would also have to install some kind of sluice to prevent the well from flooding the fields.

If I wasn't busy with the trench or the plants, I worked on the porch, serving honey cakes to travelers and helping the widow barter for the things we needed. During one quiet afternoon, when the

widow was out delivering a garment, I attempted to organize her
work space, to consolidate some of her piles and organize her spools.
When she returned, she looked around and asked what I was doing.

"I'm . . . I'm trying to organize things out here," I said, indicating
the straw baskets I had emptied and put in order.

"Don't. I know where everything is."

"But it's all in heaps . . ."

"Leave it be—I know what's in the heaps, you see."

I was tempted to point out that we had to search for the last batch
of honey cakes she'd baked, but I kept quiet. Since she was old and
set in her ways, I thought it best if I adjusted to her. I went out to
pick up my shovel and work on the *shaduf*, a project of my own.

At times I was so focused on my various tasks that I forgot about
my enslaved mother. Then I would hear the thunder of a Philistine
chariot and my memories would strike like a slap of cold water.

At night, while the widow snored on her pallet and I struggled
to sleep on my new straw mattress, I would think about Gaza and
try to imagine what Mama was doing. I was never very successful
because my head would fill with the image of how she looked when
I last saw her. My heart would become so heavy with guilt that I
dared not imagine more. What if her brutish master scarred her?
Sold her? Killed her?

As I worked for the widow, I tried to think of a faster way to
redeem my mother, but my imagination proved to be as limited
as my weaving skills. If at some point I was finally able to weave a
garment or two, I would still have to make enough profit to buy
Mama's freedom. I didn't think a couple of garments was enough
to redeem a slave.

Meanwhile, the widow seemed to be in no hurry to teach me
how to weave.

Even though I had mentioned my desire to ransom my mother,
and even though I gazed longingly at the loom, the widow insisted

I wasn't ready. The process of learning to weave was accomplished in natural steps, she kept telling me, like the seasons of earth. First we grew the flax, then we harvested it. Then we dried it, retted it, broke it, and spun it. Only then would we appreciate it enough to weave it.

Two months after the Gibeonite brothers left me with the widow, I was still working with flax. The blue flowers I had considered beautiful now seemed to taunt me, reminding me every morning that I had an entire field of plants to harvest and prepare.

At least I no longer had to haul water for them. The *shaduf* worked beautifully, so all I had to do each morning was open the sluice and let the water run through the trenches.

I learned that flax harvested immediately after the bloom produced a fine fiber that resulted in an elegant, soft fabric. Flax left in the field after the bloom, even for a day or two, resulted in a coarser fabric suitable for working clothes or storage bags. Because the finer fabric was more valuable, I patrolled the flax field every morning, quick to uproot plants with freshly wilted blossoms.

When the harvested plants began to dry and turn yellow, I bound them into tall bundles and stood them upright in the field. Well aware of the rodents in the vicinity, I caught cats and fed them near my flax bundles so they'd remain nearby. I don't know how many rats they caught, but after a while our cats were so fat and lazy that I didn't have to feed them.

Once the bound stalks had dried to crispness, I worked them with a flail, holding the stalks over a thick wool blanket and beating them until the seeds fell free of their pods. I saved most of the seeds for planting; others we added to our bread dough.

Once the seeds had been removed, the stalks were retted—a process that involved arranging them in thin rows on the ground and allowing the sun and dew to rot away the inner core that supported the flax fibers. I had to turn the stalks every few days, but after about three weeks, they were finally ready for retting. "If the flax is dry enough," the widow explained, "the woody core will snap off in your hands. Once that is gone, what you have left is—"

"Ready to be woven?" I asked.

She smiled. "No, ready to be spun."

Retting, I learned, involved breaking each dried stalk in half, then gently peeling the fibers from the inner core on both sides. The process was slow but relaxing, and the long white fibers came out clean. When I had broken more than a dozen stems, I looked at my growing pile of fibers and was reminded of Samson's golden-haired wife. I picked up a group of fibers and ran my fingers through them. What had become of that girl? I had heard no gossip about Samson or his bride from our traveling guests, but neither had I been bold enough to ask.

Finally, the widow sat next to me and told me we were going to learn how to spin. "The Egyptians use spindles," the widow said, rolling her eyes as if the method were needlessly complicated, "but all you need is a piece of leather, your fingers, and some spit. Watch this."

The widow shifted her position so she sat cross-legged on her mat. She picked up a piece of what looked like cowhide, turned it upside down on her bent knee. She placed a bundle of silky fibers at her left and used the fingers of her right hand to pull a small amount of flax onto the leather, then stretched the flax out in a line. "Wool likes to cooperate," she said, rolling the line of fibers with the palms of both hands. "Flax isn't friendly. But you can make it work if you spit on it." I blinked when she lifted her right hand and spat into her palm. "Spittle makes the thread strong," she said and eyed me as her hands resumed rolling. "Always spin it toward the heart, where all good things reside."

Once the thread beneath her palms was tight and thin, she pulled another section of flax onto the leather and began to roll it, too, working it into the first strand. "Do you see?" she asked, studying my reaction. "We spin it twice. First to make the fibers talk to one another, and second to make them strong."

I nodded, and the widow stopped rolling. She picked up the leather and dropped it into my lap. "We've quite a lot of fibers here," she said, grunting as she pulled herself up from the floor. "You'd best get busy."

I wanted to scream with exasperation. I had to spin all this flax before I would begin to learn weaving? I had already learned so much. I had worked hard to learn as much as I could, but I seemed no closer to my goal. My mother could be sick, her master could have beaten her again and again—

In despair, I tossed the leather and flax fibers aside, then went out to the back of the house, sank to the ground and burst into tears. I feared for my mother and for myself. If I pushed the widow, or didn't please her, she would ask me to leave come springtime. I would have to meet the Gibeonite brothers and confess my ineptitude, and then I'd have to go back to Gaza or beg for a place in some other sweltering village.

I lifted my head and sniffed when I heard the widow approaching. Silently, she took my hands and gently pulled me upright. She led me back to the shady porch, then she sat and asked me to tell her why I was so unhappy.

Unaccustomed to personal questions, I was unable to speak at first. How much of my story had Warati told her? Finally I opened my heart and let the entire story flow over my tongue. I told her about Adinai finding us in Egypt. I told her about Achish abusing me and selling my mother into slavery. I told her about finding my mother at the ironworker's shop, and how she'd been beaten, bruised, and ill-used. . . .

When I finished, sorrow marked the widow's face and my loss shadowed her eyes. She gripped my hand. "Something must be done to restore righteousness. Adonai is a God of justice, and He hates those who take advantage of others. I will ask Adonai to guide you, and I am certain He will provide justice in His perfect time."

I did not believe her God would do anything to help a girl who neither knew nor worshiped him, but the widow's compassion touched me deeply.

⁂

The morning after I'd spilled my secrets to the widow, I rose from my pallet and felt the room spin. To steady myself, I thrust out my arm, but instead of reaching the solidity of the wall, I jostled a stack of baskets and brought them tumbling down. Standing in the midst of them, woodenly observing the mess I'd made, I felt a wave of nausea rise within me, ran outside and vomited in the dirt.

Finished, I sat on the soft earth, wiped beads of perspiration from my forehead, and heard the widow's voice. "You didn't tell me everything, Delilah. How long have you known about the baby?"

The word sent a shiver up my backbone. I couldn't be pregnant. Simply could not.

"How long has it been since you bled?" the widow asked, coming closer. She knelt by my side and placed her hand on my back. "Can you remember?"

I closed my eyes, unwilling to remember anything of the last few weeks. "I don't know."

"Think, child. Has it been four weeks? Even longer?"

A memory, a safe one, blew through my mind like a breeze. "I bled just before the ceren's banquet."

"And after that?"

I pressed my lips together and shook my head.

"Ah." The widow patted my back. "That explains things. You

are carrying a child, Delilah. You will have your baby . . . let's see, near harvesttime."

I felt as though some foul flower had blossomed in my chest, stealing all the air I needed to breathe. I leaned forward, struggling to inhale, and wondered if I would vomit again.

"Deep breaths," the widow said, her hand making small circles on my back. "Did you never think that you might be carrying a child?"

Perhaps I had suspected, but I never allowed myself to think about the possibility of pregnancy. Zahra had brought concoctions, and I had readily drunk them down. How could I be pregnant? I was alone in a foreign land, without family, and to bring a baby into a world that terrified me . . .

I gasped as another revelation struck. The child would be Achish's! I closed my eyes, feeling as if I'd been plunged into an all-consuming gulf of despair. How could I mother a child of that devil? Achish was evil, and Mama once said certain traits ran in families. My stepfather had been kind, but I'd never met Achish's mother. Perhaps she was the root of her son's cruelty, and the child in my belly would be as vicious as its father and grandmother.

I placed my hand on my swollen belly and closed my eyes, half expecting to feel movements from the small monster devouring me from within. Soon he would grow and deplete my energy, constricting my lungs in the same way that memories of Achish visited me every night, crouching like a monster on my chest and turning me into a helpless, terrified creature.

I tipped my head back and wailed. The widow's hand stilled, then she stood and went into the house.

That was the end of it, then. I had shamed her, and soon she'd ask me to leave her house. If the Gibeonite brothers had known I was pregnant, they would not have invited me to travel with them. In some communities, or so I'd heard, unmarried pregnant girls were stoned, or their babies were taken out to the wilderness and abandoned, leaving them to the merciless sun and wild animals.

No one would do that sort of thing with my baby because I would gladly die first.

"Take this." Startled, I looked up and saw the widow standing beside me again, a cup in her hand. Still trembling, I took the cup and drank the herbal concoction it held. I didn't know what she'd given me, but I wouldn't have cared if she had brewed a cup of poison.

"Now come inside out of the sun," the widow said, her voice surprisingly gentle. "We need to talk about what is best for you and your baby."

I stared at her through tears. Was she serious?

"Don't look at me as though I've lost my head." A smile twisted the corners of the widow's lined mouth. "Each life is precious, including the one you carry. It's time to think seriously about your future, because now you are making decisions for two."

I stared at her as my mind spun with bewilderment. Why was she talking as though this baby would be something wonderful? It would be cursed, probably even before its birth. I had heard stories about babies born with missing limbs and stunted heads. The son of Achish would undoubtedly be ugly, probably reptilian, and it would die if it didn't kill me first. But until it died, I would have to shoulder the burden of carrying it within my body.

Nausea rippled through my gut and swam up my throat. I bent forward, about to retch in front of the widow, but somehow managed to choke down the urge.

As I pulled myself onto one of the porch pillows, the widow draped a soft shawl around my shoulders and crouched to push my damp hair from my forehead. "If you were an Israelite, we would take your case to the judge," she said. "But you are not of our people and you may not want to travel in your condition. Frankly, I don't know what our judge could do for you, considering that your complaint is against a Philistine. If you had a case against an Israelite, of course, the situation would be different. Samson would be empowered to take action on your behalf."

I lifted my head as the name stirred a memory. "Who?"

"Our judge."

"What did you say his name was?"

"Samson. Have you heard of him?"

I tilted my head as the memory surfaced. "I've seen him. When I was traveling with the brothers, we saw him at Timnah."

"Oh?" The widow bit her lip. "I've heard about what happened there."

"Really? I spent most of the time hiding in my tent, because Achish was one of the guests. But I was awake the night the groom returned with a cartful of garments." I stared at the straw mat beneath my pillow, then gasped as understanding bloomed. "That's the answer! He came here to settle his bet. *You* gave him those garments."

The widow shook her head. "He did not come here—he went to Ashkelon. The Philistines were gathering at the temple to celebrate their god, so Samson killed thirty of their men as they passed through the city gate. I heard the story from one of my kinsmen, but by this time, I'm sure the news has spread throughout all the tribes."

"He killed so many? Truly?" I stared at the older woman. "How can one man kill thirty in the space of a few hours? And travel a distance it would take our caravan a full day to cover? I saw those garments, and they were whole. There was no tearing, no bloodstains, nothing amiss—"

"Samson snapped their necks as easily as I break a dry stalk of flax. Then he carried the clothing back to the greedy men who had cheated him. As to the distance, you might as well ask how Adonai does miracles. I don't know how He does them, but I know He works through Samson."

Could a god really work miracles? Could he take this baby from me? Help me redeem my mother? The questions floated in the air before me, wavering with the breath of the breeze.

"I watched the wedding guests select their tunics," I said, propping my hands on my bent knee. "The material was fine, the ornamentation quite lavish."

The widow barked a laugh. "That alone should have convinced you that he didn't get those tunics from me. What you saw were festival garments from Ashkelon."

"Samson left at sunset," I said, thinking aloud. "And returned well before sunrise. A man cannot walk to Ashkelon in a single day."

"But a man could run it," the widow pointed out. "Especially if that man had been empowered by the Ruach Adonai."

"What?"

"The Holy Spirit of HaShem." A small smile brightened her face. "As one of our judges, Samson is a remarkable man. But when the Ruach Adonai overpowers him, he is a force from God."

My mind vibrated with a thousand thoughts. I needed a supernatural force to undertake my cause. To see me through this unexpected and unwanted pregnancy, to redeem my mother, and help me create a new life in this foreign land.

If Samson could provide a way to do all those things, the widow was right: I did need a judge.

⁓✤⁓

By the time my belly had grown so large that I could no longer stoop to plant or turn flax bundles, the widow decided I was ready to learn the art of weaving. I'd been itching to get my hands on her loom ever since I watched her finish off a woven piece. Amazing, how simple strands of flax or wool could become a beautiful patterned garment or rug. I asked if she ever combined materials in her weaves, and she said no—Adonai had strictly forbidden it.

She began my lesson by fastening the flax thread I'd spent hours spinning to pegs at the top of her loom. The ends of the long vertical threads were wrapped around flat stones and allowed to dangle below. When she had filled the empty space with vertical threads, she turned to me. "These are the *warp* of the fabric," she explained. "The threads you will weave in from left to right are the *weft*. This"—she pointed to a bar that ran horizontally through the warp—"is what allows you to vary the pattern. This beater"—she picked up an oblong piece of wood with a thin edge—"is how you will keep the weave tight. And finally, *this*"—she lifted a wooden needle as wide as my hand, pointed on both ends with a hole in the center—"is the shuttle that allows us to pull a thread through the warp."

She demonstrated by winding a long thread onto the shuttle, then drew it through the warp strands, over a group and under a group, over and under again. When she reached the other side, she picked up the beater and tapped the horizontal strand toward the top of the loom. "The trick of it," she said, smiling, "is keeping the threads even and tight. I've watched you work, and you're quite diligent. I think you're going to be an excellent weaver."

I didn't share her optimism, but I was highly motivated. Not only did I desperately need a trade for survival, I also wanted to be useful to her. Helping the widow carry her workload was the least I could do to repay her many kindnesses toward me.

With my teacher at my side, I practiced for the rest of the day, and by sunset I had woven several rows of uneven threads across the top of the loom. She smiled and pulled my hands from the beater, then pointed to a platter of dried fish near the edge of the fire pit. "Eat," she said. "You'll find bread under the coals. You need to keep up your strength."

I found a pair of tongs to pull my bread from the fire, and the sight of them awakened memories of the ironworker who held my mother captive. How was she faring? Had she learned to please her master? Was she still alive? I had no time to consider the matter because a sudden, sharp pain in my lower back caused me to cry out.

The widow looked up, saw my horrified expression, and eyed me with a calculating squint. "Maybe you should wait a while before eating. I do believe the little one is ready to join us."

~⊹~

Heat. Cold. Pain. Numbness. Agony.

On a chilly night, while rain fell from the sky, a baby boy slid from my womb on a wave of blood and water and landed on the widow's knees. As she caught him in a soft blanket and began to rub him dry, I heard his tiny cry and a feeling of gratitude washed over me. I knew I didn't love the baby—I could not forget who fathered the infant—but I felt grateful for the widow, who had stepped into a maternal role, walking with me during the birth pangs, urging me to breathe, wiping my forehead when I perspired, wrapping me in a blanket when the cold wind blew in through the gaps in the bricks.

I glimpsed the wrinkled body as she lifted him from between my legs, and I felt a cold panic prickle down my spine. I *had* given birth to a monster. But then the widow cut the cord, wiped his face, and assured me that he was perfect.

I received the news with mixed feelings. If he had been reptilian, I could have taken him out and left him in the wilderness. But the widow wouldn't let me abandon a healthy child.

Surrendering to exhaustion, I watched her clean the squalling creature and realized that despite our differences, the widow and I had become close, almost like a mother and daughter. I suffered a twinge of guilt for my mother's sake, then closed my eyes and thanked whatever gods there were for sending me to the widow. If not for her, I don't think I would have survived childbirth.

Once the baby was safely swaddled in soft woolen strips, the widow placed him on my lap. I reflexively lifted my hands, horrified to find my enemy's spawn so close to me. "I don't want him."

The widow arched both brows, then crossed her arms. "He is your son."

"He is Achish's."

"Delilah." Reproach filled her voice. "The father may be a horrible man, but the baby is innocent. Besides, he needs you, not Achish, not me. My breasts have no milk, and we have no goat. If you don't feed this little one, he will die."

Unwillingly, I lowered my gaze and looked at the child. He puckered his little lips, and something inside me responded with a peculiar swoop of yearning. Exasperated, I picked him up and held him to my bare breast, then snorted when he began to suckle. "How long must I do this?"

"Many times a day," the widow said, smiling as if I were the child and she the mother. "Until he can eat meat."

I exhaled noisily, then settled back on a pillow and stared at the ceiling, the walls, the widow's jumbled baskets, *anything* but the swaddled burden in my arms.

"Have you thought of a name?" the widow asked, wistfully watching the baby.

"I know what I *don't* want to name him." I looked down, half expecting to see a miniature Achish attached to my breast. My son was pale, even paler than his father, but perhaps his skin would darken. Tiny flat curls like Achish's adorned his head, and when he opened his eyes they were as dark as midnight. And unless my eyes were playing tricks on me, he also had Achish's long, straight nose.

The widow gave me a conspiratorial smile. "He looks like you."

"No, he doesn't," I answered. "He looks like the devil who fathered him."

While the widow made unintelligible soothing sounds, I voiced my fears. "I know nothing about babies," I confessed. "I know nothing about children. I never had brothers or sisters, so I'm going to need help."

"You needn't worry." The widow bent and cupped her palm around the child's small head, her eyes sparking with kindness. "I will help you all I can. This child will be our shared delight."

I was about to protest, but she cut me off with a look. "I have often thanked Adonai for bringing you to me, Delilah. You have given these limbs new strength and my life new purpose." She closed her eyes and lifted her free hand. "I praise you, Adonai, for looking on me with such mercy. May the earth and everyone on it praise your name for your goodness and love."

Watching her, I said nothing. Though I didn't understand how her God could know anything about me, I was touched by her words. She had spoken from her heart and promised that we would share in the work of caring for this child. Which meant I would not have to love him, and she would not ask me to leave when the Gibeonite brothers stopped at the well in springtime.

I had a home. I had a place to belong. But I had to share it with this needy, dependent creature.

I looked down, marveling at the strength with which the child suckled. "He is a determined little thing," I murmured. *Just like his father.*

"He's like his mama." The widow smoothed the damp curls on the baby's head. "Have you thought about a name for him?"

I looked away. "Why would I name a child I didn't want?"

"Since you have no name in mind, how about Yagil? In the language of my people it means *he will rejoice.*"

I looked into the child's dark eyes and saw my own image reflected there—a timorous, unwilling girl who had no desire to be a mother. "Yagil." I nodded. "He doesn't seem to mind it."

"Good. When he finishes, you can both have a good rest."

I tapped the baby's chin and told him to hurry and finish. The widow stood ready to take care of us.

Chapter Seventeen

Samson

I ROSE IN DARKNESS, dressed in my tunic, sandals, and a cloak, and went outside. Awaiting some sign from Adonai about my decision, I strode forward, only half aware of where I stood. By the time I stopped walking, I was halfway across my father's barley field.

When I heard the snap of a broken stalk, I turned and saw Rei, who was also dressed for travel. Silent and contemplative, he stood behind me, his eyes fixed on the eastern horizon where the sky had begun to glow pink and orange.

"I've been thinking," I told him.

He lifted a brow. "Yes?"

"Everyone is busy with the harvest, so I have no cases to hear today."

Rei shrugged. "So it would seem."

"And my anger against Kesi . . . has abated. So she told them the answer to my riddle. She is, after all, a woman."

"True." Rei folded his hands. "Women are naturally softer and easier to persuade."

"Perhaps it's time I went back to Timnah. After all, I have a wife there, and the house I built for her stands empty."

The corner of Rei's mouth rose in a wry smile. "Ah, autumn," he said simply. "The harvest is nearly done, the air cools, and a young man's thoughts return to love."

I snorted. "Be cynical if you must, but I signed a marriage contract. I can't leave my bride at her father's house."

"No," Rei said, "I suppose you cannot."

"Then let's go."

Realizing that Kesi and her father might still be upset about my abrupt departure from the wedding feast, I selected a young male goat from the herd and set out for Timnah. Rei walked beside me, but remained uncharacteristically silent during the journey.

The sun had risen a quarter of the way across the sky when we approached the inn. A boy in the courtyard saw me and ran inside to announce my arrival, so it was the innkeeper, not Kesi, who came out to greet me.

I held up the kid as a peace offering, then lowered the animal into a pen occupied by a few sheep. "Greetings." I nodded to the innkeeper. "I've come to see my wife. Is she in her room?"

I stepped forward, assuming permission to advance, but the innkeeper stretched out his hand to stop me. "I was certain you hated her," he said, not wasting time with a ceremonial greeting. "So I gave her to your best man."

"You did what?"

"He hasn't taken her away yet, but he slept with her, so . . ."

My abrupt shock yielded almost immediately to fury. When an involuntary growl emerged from my throat, the innkeeper was quick to respond. "Her younger sister is still unmarried," he said, changing tactics. "You saw her; isn't she prettier than my eldest? Please, let her be your wife instead."

Rage heated my chest—not the fast-burning anger that might

have caused me to break the man's neck, but a white-hot rage that had smoldered for months beneath my breastbone. He had given my wife to that arrogant, cheating young man from Gaza. And that man hadn't done the honorable thing and taken Kesi to his home, but had used her and abandoned her. If the innkeeper thought the youth would return to make Kesi a proper wife, he was sorely mistaken.

In that moment my anger flared at the Philistines, the entire race of those cursed sea people. The man from Gaza, the foolish innkeeper, the raucous guests, and my petulant, empty-headed wife.

"This time—" I turned to Rei as my hand curled into a fist— "*this* time I will be blameless when I do something terrible to the Philistines."

The innkeeper protested, his words of apology piling atop one another, but I was done with listening. I turned and walked toward the village of Timnah, then cut through a field and ventured into the wilderness.

This was harvesttime, and many of the Philistine fields were heavy with grain.

❦

I did not see much of Rei over the next several days. My servant remained out of sight for the most part, and I did not go home. I remained in the area near Timnah and slept in caves, caring nothing for my comfort.

I had a job to do, and I would do it or die trying.

As I strode away from the inn at Timnah, I walked past cultivated fields that had belonged to the tribe of Judah until the Philistines came and forced farmers from their land. Now those fields and olive groves were heavy with fruit and weighty with promise. Altars to Baal and Ashtoreth stood in those groves, their very presence an insult to Adonai. Baal had not blessed those fields; Adonai had blessed them for the tribe of Judah and all Israel.

On the first day of my work, I dug a large, deep pit and covered it with the leafy canopy of a fallen tree, Over the next several days I hunted, finding and raiding dozens of jackal dens. Several Philistine farmers saw me at work and applauded my efforts to rid the land of those nocturnal predators of the vineyard and poultry pens. At night, while the moon climbed high and lit the way for my task, I set traps and caught several jackals in each trap. In daylight hours I searched for dens with young pups and added them to the others I had hidden in the pit.

When more than three hundred of the noisy creatures howled and yipped within their hiding place, I gathered dried leaves and sticks to make more than one hundred fifty torches.

Finally, four full days after my visit to Kesi and her father, I stood on the lip of my jackal pit and stared at the anxious creatures below. Tonight these unfortunate animals would be the means of my vengeance on the Philistines of Timnah, many of whom had sat at my wedding feast and participated in the chicanery that cost me a wife.

I waited until after sunset. When the moon spread its silver light over the fields and lamps no longer burned in Philistine houses, I descended into the pit and pulled up jackals by their tails, two in each fist. I slipped a dried torch between my fingers, then used rope to tie the jackals' tails together and secure the torch in place. When finished, I dropped the jackals into the huge baskets the harvesters used to transport grain to the mill.

When all three hundred jackals had been paired and dropped into baskets, I placed the baskets on a wooden sledge and hitched my mule to the front. We left the wilderness and went along the road that ran beside an area filled with Philistine fields, barns, and olive groves. Looking up, I studied the moon-silvered high places where Philistines and some of my own people danced and committed fornication around Asherah poles and statues of Baal.

Every two hundred paces I stopped the mule, pulled a basket from the sledge, lowered my torch into the container, and tipped it over. Then I moved on.

The mule snorted and stomped her hoof when I approached after emptying the last basket. I walked over to stroke her nose, smiling grimly as fires blazed in every direction—in the fields, the groves, and the little huts where Philistine farmers traded by the road. By the time I disconnected the sledge and mounted the mule, all the Philistine crops in the vicinity of Timnah were burning. Unharvested fields of barley, fields dotted by dry shocks of harvested grain, vineyards, and olive groves snapped and crackled in the heat of my vengeance. Asherah poles caught fire and burned while stone statues of Baal cracked and toppled in the heat.

By sunrise, nothing would remain but charred stalks and singed tree stumps.

I clicked my tongue and kicked the mule. She moved forward in a slow trot as I hummed a song from childhood. Mine was a quiet victory, but a satisfying one. The Philistines had cheated me out of what was rightfully mine. They had stolen my duplicitous bride and given her to the worst character of them all.

But they would pay—they would feel the sting of my anger for months.

And the people of Judah would walk along this road, see the ruined fields and high places, and know that Adonai had begun to cleanse the land of the Philistines' evil.

◦❖◦

A full day passed before I heard about the aftermath of my vengeance. A farmer from Zorah returned from the market and shared the story with my parents, who had invited me in to hear the man's report.

"The Philistines from the plain," he began, an aura of melancholy radiating from his features, "the ones with farms outside Timnah—"

My father inclined his head. "I know the area. Go on."

"Early this morning they came up and demanded to know who'd burned them out. Someone said that Samson"—he cut a look to me—"son-in-law of the Timnite, had done it because the innkeeper took his wife and gave her to someone else. So the Philistine mob went up to the inn, bound the innkeeper and his eldest daughter, and burnt them with fire. They burnt the inn, too."

Sorrow struck me like an unexpected blow to the stomach. I lowered my head and swallowed to choke back the bile that rose in my throat. I had been angry with Kesi—yes, I could admit it—but she had done nothing to deserve such a death, nor had her father. How like the cruel Philistines to turn on each other when they should have accepted the consequences of their wrongdoing.

The visiting farmer shook his head. "I'm sorry to bring such bad news, Manoah."

My father patted the man's shoulder, muttered something, and walked him to the door.

When he returned, my father cast baleful eyes on me. "Can you see your fault in this?" he asked, his voice cold and sharp. "Do you understand that this evil is a result of your pursuit of a Philistine woman?"

Stunned by the charge from my own father, I lifted my head and blinked. "How is this my fault?"

"If you had married a daughter of Abraham," Father went on, shaking his gnarled finger in my face, "none of this would have happened."

I stood so abruptly that my stool toppled backward. A dozen objections jostled in my mind, each demanding to be shouted at the old man, but he was my father and I owed him respect. I had wooed Kesi because I loved her, and wasn't love one of God's gifts? I had asked Adonai to make His will clear, and the Lord had not stopped the marriage or removed my love for Kesi. So why was it wrong to love her?

Honor silenced my answers, however, and I said nothing as I pushed my way out of the house. Standing in the heat of the sun, I drew long, deep breaths to calm my pounding heart, then looked toward the southwest where tendrils of black smoke still hung in the sky. Why should I be calm? The beastly Philistines had murdered my wife and father-in-law, and they deserved to die for their sin.

I did not know that I could be angrier than I was on the night I set the fires, but my rage intensified, burning hotter than the sun. I ran over the rocky path to Timnah, scarcely feeling my feet, and when I rounded a corner and looked down on the inn, I saw a group of Philistines gathered around the smoking ruins. A separate scorched spot lay in the courtyard, undoubtedly the place where Kesi and her father had burned.

I held on to a boulder as the world spun and I snatched a wincing breath. I had believed the old farmer's story, but the slaughter seemed more horrific when I beheld the evidence with my own eyes. Gasping with shock and revulsion, I stood still as Philistines cavorted in the clearing below. Some of them had stolen wineskins from the inn, and now they were drinking from brass cups, mockingly saluting each other. One fellow even had the nerve to stand near the charred spot in the courtyard and scream like a woman, fluttering his eyelids and raising his voice as he mocked Kesi, saying, "Please, please don't burn us! I promise I'll get the answer from Samson, I promise!"

They had threatened her . . . with this?

My strength returned as my heart pumped outrage and resentment through my veins. I strode forward, my head high and my step confident. I did not need to get their attention; all of them stared as soon as I began to bellow.

"Since you have acted like this"—I pointed to the darkened spot in the courtyard—"surely I *will* take revenge on you. After that, I will quit."

I had no sooner uttered my promise than the nearest pair of men charged me. Endued with strength by the Ruach Adonai, I took on both men at once, smashed their noses into their brains and then shifted to face the next pair. One by one and two by two they came at me with knives and axes and staves, and one by one and two by two I struck them down with Adonai's strength and my bare hands.

When I alone stood amid the bones and ashes of my wife and my father-in-law, my body dripping with blood and perspiration, I lifted my head and wept. I wept for my bloody fury, and I wept for Kesi's foolishness. She had berated me for not sharing with her, but why hadn't she shared with *me*? She should have told me that the Philistines were threatening her family. I could have—*would* have—called off the wager rather than see it through to this awful conclusion.

As I wept for Kesi, her family, and her foolish people, I tore my tunic and mourned my loss of hope. I thought Adonai had sent me a woman with whom I could share my life, but apparently I'd misunderstood. Maybe I was not meant to share my heart or my bed. Maybe I was meant to live alone.

I looked up. Through tear-blurred eyes I saw Rei standing beyond the bloody circle of bodies. He extended a hand toward the road, inviting me to follow him.

Sometimes Rei was wiser than I realized. The road he gestured toward did not lead to Zorah, but into the heart of Judah, a territory where I could grieve in relative privacy. A place where I could sort through my feelings and find peace.

Nodding at Rei, I stepped over the bodies in my path and followed him.

CHAPTER EIGHTEEN

DELILAH

"NEVER MIND THAT YOU ARE NOT A DAUGHTER OF ISRAEL," the widow said one morning after Yagil's birth, "you are like a daughter to me, and you need help. So I am going to help you find Samson." She would not give a reason for her newly acquired passion for justice, but I suspected it had everything to do with the baby. He was rapidly becoming more her child than mine, and the childless widow felt so grateful she would do almost anything to make me happy.

Yagil had certainly put a new spring in her step. As the months passed, she talked to the baby, taught him to clap, and fed him soft foods she'd chewed herself. She bathed him and put him to bed while singing lullabies in Hebrew, a language I couldn't understand. Little by little, I took over more of the weaving while she cared for the baby. The arrangement pleased me, for the more time I spent at the loom, the more skilled I became.

And I needed practice—the widow had me weaving cloth for storage bags and rugs. My first attempts at weaving flax had resulted in fabrics so lumpy and bumpy they were good for nothing but scrub cloths.

Throughout those months, the widow stopped every Israelite on the road and earnestly inquired about Samson's whereabouts. We heard that the man had fled after burning all the fields around Timnah, but the widow did not grow weary in pursuing justice for me. "People from all over Israel stop at this well," she reminded me, "so I will keep seeking him. Surely someone will know where Samson is staying."

Though I had been impressed when I first saw Samson, his reputation continued to grow as we asked about his whereabouts. We heard all kinds of Samson stories—about his wedding, his attack on the Philistine fields, and his skill in capturing three hundred jackals. Some people bragged about Samson's attacks on the Philistine fields; others were convinced his actions would soon turn the Philistine oppression into ruthless annihilation.

I wanted vengeance on Achish as much as ever, but my priorities shifted with the coming of the baby. I still wanted to rescue my mother, but every day I realized that my most important responsibility was to the little creature who demanded food every time I wanted to do something else. I suckled him out of necessity while the widow talked to him, bathed him, and rocked him. Because she did not want to leave him alone in the house, she asked me to tie him onto my back when I worked in the fields. At first I grumbled, then I discovered that my work actually went more smoothly when the baby snored softly in my ear.

Then a line of camels stopped at the well one afternoon, and the widow's queries finally bore fruit. While a wealthy merchant's wife looked through a stack of folded linens, the widow and I spoke to the husband, who claimed to know where Samson was hiding.

"I would not tell you if you were Philistine," the man said after carefully scrutinizing me, "but Samson is camping among the mountains of Judah. You could find him if you are willing to travel."

"What good is a judge who can't be found?" the widow grumbled. "He should be available to the people."

"And didn't I just tell you where he was?" the merchant answered. "Set out today and you will find him within the week."

A thrill touched the base of my spine. The widow had assured me that if we could find Samson, he would listen to my story and help me free my mother and punish Achish. For a man who had single-handedly ruined the Philistine crops for miles around, the task would seem like nothing. I imagined him running to Gaza, killing Achish, pummeling the ironworker who had enslaved my mother, then scooping her up and running all the way back to the Valley of Sorek, bringing Mama to me.

After the merchant and his wife had gone, I sat on a pillow near the widow's loom. "Do you think," I began, "we might be able to borrow a donkey and go in search of the man?"

The widow harrumphed and picked up her shuttle. "We have a hungry baby who needs tending. We shouldn't be going anywhere."

"Do you think Samson would come here if he knew we needed help? If enough people spread the word that we need him?"

The widow pulled the shuttle through the threads on the loom. "This is a difficult time for everyone. Many people have suffered at the hands of the Philistines. Samson could not possibly go to all of them, but do not lose hope. If he is nearby and thirsty, he will come to the well. Everyone does."

I bit my lip and wondered what I would say if he did come to us. Samson was an Israelite, a judge of Israel, so why should he be concerned about me? Despite the widow's affection for me and Yagil, I wasn't related to her. I had never worshiped the invisible God. All I knew of Israel I had learned from the widow.

She looked over at me, then tipped her head toward the baby sleeping on my pallet. "He is getting another tooth, did you see?"

I felt the corner of my mouth twist. "I did. He bit me."

"He will be walking before we know it."

I gave her a halfhearted nod and twisted to face her. "When we met, you said you had no children. Did you ever want them?"

Her brow wrinkled and something moved in her eyes. "What woman doesn't want children? And what man? I asked Adonai for a baby, but then my husband died. And I realized that sometimes Adonai says *no* for our own good."

Or perhaps Adonai refused her so she could take care of my son. "Did you ever want to leave this place?" I asked. "You must get awfully lonely."

"I used to." Her smile diminished slightly. "But I have buyers for my work because I live by the well of Sorek. I could make the most beautiful linen in the world, but if I lived up in the mountains or on the other side of the Jordan, who would ever see it?" She shook her head. "Besides, if I had gone someplace else, I would never have met you or little Yagil. I am fine here. This is Adonai's place for me."

I smiled, touched by her simple contentment. The widow seemed to consider everything, good and bad, as part of Adonai's will. I didn't understand how anyone could consider a man like Achish as part of a divine plan, but that sort of unquestioning acceptance explained the widow's unflappable demeanor. Though my attempts at working the loom had not yet met her high standards, I had never seen her lose her temper.

For me, however, the loom became a daily torture. The widow had me working with wool, which should have been easy to spin and weave. But even through the thick, heavy fuzz, I could tell that my warp and weft were uneven, my loops either too large or too small. Weaving, I decided, was not as simple as it looked.

Not many days later, a lone traveler appeared on the road. Like most of the men who came through the Valley of Sorek, he walked beside a donkey and carried a staff. Something in his aspect seemed familiar, though, so I stopped spinning to study him closer.

He was approaching the widow's gate when I spotted his long, plaited hair.

"Samson!" I turned to the widow. "That's Samson, isn't it?"

She left the loom and peered toward the gate, then nodded. "Unless my tired eyes deceive me, yes, that could be Manoah's son."

"What should I do? Can I speak to him? Is there something I need to do or say before I ask for his help?"

She narrowed her eyes at me. "First, cover your hair. If he enters the gate, offer water and something to eat. If he seems inclined to talk or relax, then you may tell him about your situation. Otherwise, let him be on his way. For all we know, the Philistines may be pursuing him."

I hesitated. She had been so eager to find Samson, yet now she seemed reluctant for me to have anything to do with him.

"What's wrong?" I asked, searching her face. "Is there some reason I shouldn't speak to Samson?"

She looked away and grimaced. "It's just that . . ."

"What?"

"Aren't we doing fine as we are?" She looked at me, her eyes bright with unshed tears. "If you send Samson after the baby's father, won't that stir up trouble? It might bring the Philistines down on our heads, and if they find out that Yagil is one of them, what's to keep them from taking him from us?"

"But . . . if Samson kills Achish, no one else needs to know anything."

"I can't do it." The widow twisted her hands. "I've never asked anyone to commit murder for me. I don't think I can ask it now, not even for Yagil's sake . . . or yours. 'You shall not commit murder' is one of our laws."

"Samson had no trouble murdering thirty Philistines for their garments."

The widow sighed. "For a judge, it is different. They are warriors sent by Adonai to enact justice on our behalf. The Philistines are our enemies—"

"Achish is a Philistine."

She shook her head. "Somehow it is different. I would not be asking for Israel; I would be asking for me. For you."

I stared at her as another objection filled my tongue. Samson had killed thirty men to pay off a bet, and *that* had nothing to do with Israel . . . unless I had missed the connection.

The widow sat on her stool and hung her head. "Go out and speak to Samson if you wish, and I'll pray that Adonai guides you. I know you want justice, but I'm not sure we're going about it the right way."

Frowning, I reached for a shawl to cover my hair and left the widow on the porch. I strode toward the gate with my heart in my throat, but I wasn't going to let Samson get away without at least trying to speak to him.

The travel-stained man who fumbled with his saddlebags did not look like the young man who had offered toasts for the Philistines at Timnah. This man was the same general shape and size, with the same dark braids down his back, but the light had gone out of his eyes. This man's face, or what I could see of it beneath the beard, was a stretch of sunbaked leather seamed with deep fissures, a face both tired and sad.

What had happened to the happy bridegroom?

I didn't mean to stare, so the touch of his gaze startled me. "I am sorry," I said, a blush burning my cheek. "May I be of service?"

A line of concern appeared in his forehead. "Does the widow still live here?"

"She does. She's in the shade."

He nodded and gestured toward his donkey. "I would like to refill
my water jugs. The widow has always allowed me to use the well."

"Of course. Please." I opened the gate and stepped outside. "Would
you like me to draw the water for you?"

"You should be in the shade, too. I can handle this."

"I'm happy to help. And I know the widow would be honored if
you would come into the shade and sit for a while. We could offer
sweet bread and honey cakes—"

"I need to keep moving." He dropped the bucket into the well,
then pulled it up as easily as if it contained nothing but air. "Perhaps
another time."

I stepped back, feeling oddly rebuffed. Had I done something
to offend him? Perhaps his religion did not allow men to talk to
strange women. Perhaps he was embarrassed because I wasn't an
Israelite. Perhaps I should have said nothing at all.

But I sorely needed a champion.

"I should leave you." I took a backward step, hoping he would
relent and tell me to stay.

He didn't speak, but lowered the bucket again.

I took another step back, and another, then turned and moved
back through the gate. By the time I reached the table where I had
been spinning, my eyes had filled with tears.

The widow clucked in sympathy. "Don't worry," she said, glancing
away from her loom only long enough to see Samson leaving. "If
Adonai means for you to gain victory over the man who wronged
you, He will arrange it . . . when the time is right."

There it was again, simple contentment. With not a trace of
frustration, though I was drowning in it.

Chapter Nineteen
DELILAH

As years passed and my son grew from infancy into boyhood, I became accustomed to life by the well of Sorek. I watched my son take his first steps from the widow's hands to mine, and together we celebrated his first word: *ball*. He played at the widow's feet when I worked in the flax field; during the afternoon he napped with the widow while I struggled to master the loom.

I couldn't help noticing that the widow seemed a little less energetic with every passing week, so I took over the task of greeting visitors at the well. If they were hospitable and kind, I invited them to sit and share honey cakes with us; if they were secretive or potentially threatening, I would point to the well and bucket, then hastily retreat.

Those days would have been completely happy, if not for the misery that regularly landed at our door. Desperate to find Samson, the Philistines began to harass every Israelite on the road, going so far as to create instant "taxes" if the travelers could not offer any useful information about Samson. Nearly every family we met offered a new version of the predictable story: An Israelite family had been traveling in peace until a mounted troop of Philistine soldiers demanded they stop. The soldiers' leader—who was described as looking like Achish in almost every case—dismounted and approached the family with a sword in his hand and a sinister expression on his face. "He snarled at my husband," one weeping woman confessed. "My husband gave him half of all the goods we had with us, but we were still terrified he would take our lives as well."

Two years passed, then three, then four and five, and the number of people on the road gradually decreased. Only those who absolutely *had* to travel dared take a journey, and the brave souls who risked a trip would often avoid the roads and walk across the untamed wilderness. We frequently heard about disasters, too. One family lost a son to lions, another lost three children when their wagon toppled off a cliff. Perhaps the worst story was that of a family who died of thirst when they got lost in the desert.

"These are like the days of Shamgar, son of Anath," the widow said. "The highways are deserted, and travelers walk on the byways. In that day Deborah and Yael rose to defeat the enemy, but who will fight for us today?"

Samson, I wanted to say, but we had heard nothing about him in months. We could almost believe that Israel's judge had vanished from the face of the earth.

Despite all the tragedies reported to us, the widow maintained her faith in Adonai, declaring that her people were bound to suffer for their disloyalty to God. "*Bnei-Yisrael* has done what is evil in Adonai's eyes," she would say, "and He has handed us over to our enemies. When we repent and turn to the Lord our God, He will bless us once again. Then we will rehearse the righteous acts of Adonai and thank Him for His mercy."

While I didn't mind the widow's faith in her invisible God, I preferred to place my trust in people I could see. I watched Yagil like a hawk and eyed strangers with distrust until I was certain they meant no harm. If a man looked at me as Achish had looked at me, even for a second, I would move away and leave him to fill his own waterpots.

Soon Yagil began to grow curious and explore, and the widow became convinced that we should have a dog around as a means of protection for the boy. I shot her a skeptical glance when she returned from a neighbor's home with a scrawny puppy in her arms. She assured me, however, that many a barking dog had served to intimidate intruders. I found it ironic that she'd never thought it necessary to have a dog for her own protection, or for mine, but she would do anything to keep Yagil safe.

As the months passed, my handiwork moved from barely service-able to sturdy and functional. The widow would examine my finished pieces, often bringing the fabric to the end of her nose for a close examination. She began returning my work to me with a simple "*hmm*," and I realized then that she'd found nothing to criticize.

Before long I was as skilled with flax as I was with wool. The widow smiled now with approval at my finished pieces. I wove long strips of fabric for shawls, and wide, rough pieces for curtains and rugs. As the widow's pace slowed due to her stiff fingers, my tempo increased, so in time we exchanged places. She spent more of her day harvesting flax and carding wool while I spent more hours at the loom.

Yagil divided his time between us. He loved running through the furrows as the widow planted and harvested. When he grew tired, he toddled back to the porch and curled up on the rug beside the loom. He was a happy child, mostly obedient and always bright, and though I can't say I *delighted* in him, I saw less and less of Achish in him. Sometimes I could watch Yagil run and play without even thinking of Achish, but on other occasions I would catch Yagil staring into space and he would look so much like his father that my skin pebbled with fear.

I began to despise Achish for new reasons. The old wounds remained, as raw as ever, but I also hated him for destroying my present happiness. My son, who deserved a mother who saw no fault in him, had me, a woman whose joy in her child had been forever marred. My life with the widow should have been happy and fulfilling, yet I could not look at the road without seeing Philistine soldiers and wondering if they knew Achish. I could not look at my son without seeing Achish, and I could not behold the glory of a fiery sunset without remembering the days when sunset meant Achish would soon be approaching the threshold of my prison.

Sometimes when I worked at the loom while thinking of Achish, I found myself slamming the bar against the threads, driving the shuttle through the warp, and chopping the beater against the newly woven rows with such force that the pattern constricted, producing sections of stunted weave—tight little kernels of hate. The widow never asked me to rework those sections, but when she examined those rows I could hear her clicking her tongue against the back of her teeth, quiet taps of rebuke and regret.

One day I told the widow that I would die content if I never saw Achish again, but then I realized my statement was not quite true. I *did* want to see Achish again. I wanted to see him die, because only then would I be able to stop worrying that I would look out at the well and find him standing at our gate.

In quiet hours, as the widow and I settled down and tried to get Yagil to sleep, I often thought of my mother. How was she? Had she learned how to cope with her cruel master? My blood ran thick with guilt every time I thought about the last time I saw her, and I'd pray to whichever gods could hear me. "Let her be safe," I'd whisper. "Let her be well. And do not let her master sell her before I can return to buy back her freedom."

Thoughts of my mother always brought back my most frustrating problem, that while most people bartered goods, expensive purchases were usually paid for with silver. Where was I supposed to get silver when even a huge stack of tunics and rugs wouldn't bring a single silver coin? I considered presenting my problem to the widow, but I didn't want her to feel pressured to help me. She had done so much for Yagil and me; I didn't want her to think she had to supply anything else.

"What should I do if I need silver?" I asked her one afternoon as we worked together in the shade. "I intend to free my mother from slavery, but I don't think her owner will trade her for a stack of tunics."

The widow exhaled a sigh. "This is why Adonai says one Israelite should not enslave another. Slavery is an awful business."

She was right, but the realization did nothing to solve my problem. "I need to free her," I said emphatically. "If the ironworker is reasonable, surely I can convince him to take *something* in exchange for an older woman who has outlived her usefulness."

The widow arched her brow, and her shoulders began to shake—and I saw that she was laughing at me.

"Outlived her usefulness?" she echoed. "Then why bother redeeming her?"

"Because she's my mother." I lifted my chin, amazed at the question. "And I love her."

The widow sighed again, then shifted to look me in the eye. "Delilah, listen to me. Your desire to save your mother is commendable. I'm sure you love her, and I'm sure she loves you. But in this part of the land, all you will get for your hard work are things like pigeons, rabbits, and cheeses. No one who lives around here has ever *seen* silver, so they aren't likely to have any."

"I've seen wealthy Philistines come through here. Surely they have silver."

"And do you see those wealthy Philistines buying our humble fabrics? If they buy anything, they pay for it in trade. In all the years I have worked the loom, I have never earned even a tiny bit of silver for my trouble."

I pressed my lips together. The widow had never lived in a prosperous Philistine city either, but I had. I had traveled on merchant ships and seen royal women clothed in fabrics so fine they shimmered like light on water. Those women paid silver for their garments, *good* silver, and they had lots of it.

My mother's master lived in Gaza, so he knew what silver was . . . and he would want it.

"I will just have to make something exquisite," I said, speaking more to myself than to the widow. But she heard, and her answering cackle did little to bolster my confidence.

"You will have to spend more time at the loom." She tossed me a ball of thread. "And you will have to harvest the flax early and treat it like a baby. You will also have to maintain a more relaxed hand at the loom, so your weave is consistent and calm throughout." Her eyes softened. "I am sure you can accomplish what you are trying to do, but I am also sure you will be working many years. There is much to be said for quality, but sometimes you must barter with quantity. Forget exquisite, Delilah, and focus on making many goods and selling them. The end result is the same."

I closed my eyes and considered her words. I would prefer to create something so amazing that every woman in Gaza would be envious of the wearer, but perhaps that was a prideful wish. Maybe the widow was right—I should take the gift I had developed and create serviceable items. Tunics and rugs and blankets would always be in demand. But how was I supposed to transport a load of linens to the city?

I gasped as an idea lifted its head. I had no way of getting to Gaza, but the Gibeonite brothers did.

Every year, just after the spring rains, a familiar sight appeared on the road from the east. Travelers with one camel at the lead, one at the rear, and a train of donkeys in between. I could usually determine how prosperous the Gibeonite brothers had been by counting the number of donkeys in the caravan, and each year the number grew.

Regnar, Warati, and Hitzig always stopped at the well to water their animals and share a meal with us. They had looked at me with some confusion the year I introduced Yagil as an infant, but after the surprise wore off, they played with him as if he were one of their nephews. The brothers always gently inquired after the widow's health, and they usually brought her a gift—some spun wool, a pot of honey, or a bag of barley seeds.

My heart sang with delight every time I spotted their caravan on the horizon. They had promised to look after me, and they had proven themselves to be men of their word. Each year they asked the widow if I had been a bright pupil; each year she proudly displayed something I had made. The first year she showed them a lumpy rug; last year she showed them a length of flax so tightly woven it flowed like water over her upturned hands.

This year I could give them a basket filled with my woven tunics, and they would sell the goods for me. They and the widow were the only friends I had in the world, so they would help me. I was certain of it.

⁓❧⁓

As the days grew longer and warmer, I spent more time at the loom, cursing the stubborn threads when I tangled them, silently rejoicing when I managed to do something right. I tried not to think about Achish as I wove, struggling to maintain a calm and consistent weave. I devoted my daylight hours to producing serviceable goods like those the widow had recommended. But at the end of the day, after Yagil had fallen asleep and the widow had gone to bed, I lit oil lamps by the loom and struggled to create something extraordinary.

My first attempt at it resulted in a bulky and uneven linen tunic. When the widow saw it, she made a face and suggested that I sell it as a garment to be worn only at home. Yet I promised to fix it by embroidering the neckline and hem with a design so beautiful that no one would notice the uneven weave.

I had nearly finished the embroidery when I heard a familiar cry. I looked up to see a caravan approaching from the east: three men, two camels, and the inevitable train of pack animals. The donkeys were heavily laden with wool, which meant the Gibeonites had had a prosperous year.

The widow stepped outside to invite the brothers in for water and honey cakes. While she prepared a tray, I hurried out to welcome my friends, then led their animals to the watering trough. Our dog yipped in frenzied welcome and danced in delight when Warati bent to scratch his head.

"You still have that dog," Hitzig said, tugging on his beard. "Has it bitten anyone yet?"

"Not unless they bite him first," I teased. "Come out of the sun and rest."

Regnar's eyes lit up when he saw me. "You look well, Delilah."

"This place agrees with you," Warati said. "You have more color in your cheeks this year."

"Because I'm always chasing Yagil," I said, leading them to the porch. "Come and see how big he's gotten."

Yagil squealed when he saw the brothers, then ran forward and hugged their knees. Warati complimented the widow on her beautiful work, and each man made a fuss over my five-year-old while I poured water into gourds. The brothers, I realized as I listened to sounds of happy reunion, were like the uncles and cousins I had never known.

The brothers sat on a woven carpet to enjoy the widow's hospitality while I brought out the tunic I'd just finished. "See?" I held it against me. "It may not be as fine as something you'd see in Gaza . . ."

"It's fine enough," Warati said, nodding. "Good for you, Delilah. Next time we come, you'll be designing tunics for the ceren."

"I'm so glad you've arrived." I put away the tunic and sat in the circle with the brothers. "I was wondering . . . If I made linen and wool garments and gave them to you on your way to Gaza, could you sell them for me? I don't have much prepared this year, but next year I could have a basketful."

Warati looked at Regnar, who looked at Hitzig. Hitzig nodded. "We would be happy to trade for you," he said with a grin. "Your work might bring attention to our wool."

"And there's something else." I drew a deep breath. "I need to ask if you are willing to see my mother again. I know things were difficult last year—"

Regnar clasped his hands and leaned toward me. "We would be happy to visit that place again. But this time we'll approach more carefully."

"Thank you. I need to know that she is well, and I want her to know I haven't forgotten her. I am working hard to earn enough to redeem her because I want to bring her here to live with us."

For the past three years the brothers had gone to the Gaza shipyards to find the ironworker and look for my mother. Not wanting to make trouble, the first year they kept their distance and came back to tell me that Mama was still alive. The second year they saw her when the ironworker was away, and they told her I was alive and safe, that I had a son, and I was working to buy her freedom. She was so delighted to hear their news that she kissed their hands and begged them to come again. Last year, emboldened by Mama's happiness the year before, they walked over to my mother while the ironworker sat at his forge. Hearing their voices, he turned around. Amazed that his slave was receiving messages from outsiders, he threatened the brothers with arrest if they ever appeared at his business again.

An uneasy stillness fell over us as the brothers looked at each other. I was sure they were thinking that I would never earn enough to buy Mother's freedom. But they did not know how determined I could be.

Warati looked up from beneath craggy brows. "We will do what we can, Delilah."

"We will," Regnar echoed. "I don't know what we will find, but we promise to search for her."

Overcome with gratitude, I pressed my hand to my mouth as tears filled my eyes. Aside from the widow, they were the only friends I had, and they had been completely kind in the past. They would find my mother. I trusted them.

The next morning, with anxious hearts the widow and I said farewell to the brothers, who promised to stop again on their way back from Gaza. "I wish I could promise to bring your mother to you," Regnar told me, his eyes flickering with concern. "But we will do our best."

Yagil hugged my leg as their caravan moved away, and I told him the brothers would return. One day, if all went well, they would return with my mother.

⁂

Two weeks passed before we spotted the brothers again. My heart started racing when I saw the caravan approaching from the west. I hurried into the house to awaken the widow and Yagil from their afternoon naps.

All three of us rushed to the courtyard to greet them properly, Yagil bouncing on the balls of his bare feet. As the brothers came through the gate, I could see that their pack animals bulged and clanged with household goods, so their trading had been brisk. As much as I wanted to ask about Mama, I restrained my curiosity until the brothers had dismounted and watered their animals. Finally we stepped into the shade for refreshments.

Yagil plopped himself into Regnar's lap, content to remain there while we talked. I poured cool water into our guests' gourds, then sat while they munched on honey cakes and made appreciative smacking sounds. I studied them carefully, searching for some clue about my mother, but they wore their faces like masks—straight and still.

Their expressionless demeanor filled me with dread.

Finally, Regnar swallowed hard. "We found the ironworker," he said, reluctantly meeting my gaze, "at the docks, same place as last year."

"And?"

His eyes glistened. "It pains me to tell you that your mother is dead. When we could not find her, we spoke to the ironworker. He was not happy to see us, but he answered our questions. He said your mother died a few weeks ago, during the fertility festival."

I brought my hand to my mouth as anguish seared my heart. How could this have happened? I had been working so hard to save her. I had promised that I would free her. For over five years she had waited . . . and I had utterly failed.

A suffocating sensation tightened my throat. "How did she die?" I whispered, looking into Regnar's eyes. "Did that man kill her?"

Regnar looked away, but Warati spoke up. "We talked to other slaves who worked at the docks, and they didn't know much about your mother. But one man said that because your mother was old, she almost certainly died in her sleep. That sounds reasonable to us."

I closed my eyes, realizing that Warati had created a sympathetic lie. Regnar had not been able to look me in the eye and give me the truth. Furthermore, Mama was several years younger than the widow, and I knew of few slaves who died in their sleep—most of them were worked until they dropped. But these men were like brothers to me, and they had inquired about Mother out of kindness. I would forgive the lie and the kind conspiracy that prompted it.

"Thank you," I whispered. "Thank you for asking about her."

I turned away, allowing the widow to guide the conversation. I felt exhausted, drained of will and purpose. What was I to live for now? A tear rolled over my cheek and I swiped it away, not wanting our guests to feel guilty for sharing such a horrible report.

"We have other news," Hitzig said, probably in an effort to distract me from my sorrow. "The road to Gaza is never empty these days. The Philistines maintain a guard outside the gates of the city, and soldiers continually harass those who enter and leave. They stopped us both coming and going and asked if we knew anything about the Israelite called Samson the strongman."

The widow snorted. "Now the roads will be doubly dangerous."

Hitzig released a sour laugh. "I remember the day we met Samson at his wedding in Timnah, do you remember, Delilah? You may find it surprising that the Philistines at Gaza are commanded by that particularly obnoxious young man we met in Timnah, the one who was the groom's first friend."

"Hitzig," Regnar said, a warning in his tone.

"He's a Philistine, of course," Hitzig went on, ignoring his brother. "He rides tall in the saddle and snaps his whip at anyone who dares look him in the eye. The people say he's obsessed. All he cares about is finding Samson."

A spark of alarm touched my spine. I lifted my head and stared at Hitzig. "This captain—is he the same man who leads patrols on the roads?"

Hitzig nodded. "I believe so."

"And he is called Achish?"

He nodded more slowly this time, and his face crumpled in

chagrin. "I forgot," he whispered, cringing before Regnar's hard stare. "I forgot that he was . . ."

"My enemy?" My agitation blazed into a fury that burned my cheeks and tingled my fingertips. "Achish is still in a position of authority? And he is searching for Samson?"

Warati glanced at Hitzig as if for permission to speak, and he nodded.

"Because of the reward," Regnar inserted quickly. "The Philistine lords have offered a handsome reward to whomever brings Samson to them."

I stood and paced in the small space beneath the porch. "I was certain Achish would have come to justice by now, that he would have assaulted some other woman or done something to fall out of Zaggi's favor. I didn't think him bright enough to maintain his position for so many years."

The widow lifted her hand. "I think I missed something. Can someone tell me why Delilah is upset?"

I clenched my fists and stopped pacing. "They're talking about the man who held me captive and killed my mother. He deserves to be in prison or dead, yet he is still doing the Philistines' dirty work."

Regnar closed his eyes. "Your mother's death may be a blessing, Delilah. If you had tried to take her out of Gaza, this captain would have seen her. And if he recognized her . . ." He shook his head. "I'm afraid he would have killed her. He would probably kill you, if he had the chance. You know too much about him."

"I know he's a scoundrel." Hitzig looked around the circle. "When the guards were searching our pack animals, I overhead two of them talking. Apparently their commander is a gambler, and in debt. Now he works to curry favor with the Philistine cerens."

"You should forget him," Warati said. "Now that your mother is gone, you have no reason even to think of Gaza. Put it out of your mind, along with that wretched young man. Look forward, Delilah, not backward. Think about your future."

I sank to the rug as my anger deflated. "Many times," I said, my voice quiet in the unnatural stillness that had overtaken our group, "I have thoughts about the night my stepfather died. In hindsight, I can understand how Achish must have felt. We had only been in Gaza for three months, so Achish barely knew us. I can understand why he hated the idea of our sharing in Adinai's inheritance, the house, the wealth. We were nearly strangers to him."

Lost in memory, I stared at the carpet beneath us. "But Mama was not unreasonable. We were ready to leave; Mother even said we would go and leave him with the house. He could have let us walk away, but instead he decided to *punish* us. He had to humiliate and debase my mother, and he had to break me." I lifted my eyes and met Warati's dark gaze. "That is why I cannot forget what he did to us. That is why I cannot forgive."

I was not a good hostess after that. The brothers sensed my sorrow and said little more that afternoon. An hour before sunset they took their leave so they could camp farther down the road. I said farewell with a heavy heart, then returned to the safety and security of the porch.

The widow sensed my unhappiness and remained inside the house, caring for Yagil and allowing me to struggle privately with my loss. Every once in a while I heard her coughing. I had asked her if she felt sick, but she assured me her persistent cough meant nothing. "It's dust," she said, waving my concern away. "It will pass."

But the brothers' bad news would not pass. My mother was dead and I could do nothing about it.

I went to the loom and picked up the shuttle, moved the bar, and rhythmically tapped the threads into a tight formation. I had learned to weave for my mother's sake; I strived to create gorgeous garments to set her free. Now that I had no mother, I had no reason to keep weaving.

But my hands, accustomed to the rhythms of the loom, kept working even as my heart went numb. Why should I keep living? The widow would say I had a son who needed me, and that was certainly true. But Yagil didn't need *me*—any woman could serve as his mother, and almost any woman would do a better job of mothering him. His skin was fairer than mine, and no one looking at him would ever guess that his grandmother's skin had been the color of a midnight sky. Perhaps another woman should be his mother, because I could not look at Yagil without thinking of . . .

Achish. The mere name brought my blood to a boil. He had destroyed everything I held dear. Even though I took grim pleasure in knowing that he was no longer a wealthy man, he yet breathed and my mother did not. He had power, while Mama and I had none. He had traded his wealth for indebtedness; he traded poverty for a life of service to the lords of the Philistines. But he still carried a whip, and he still snapped it at innocent men and women.

Achish did not deserve power. He did not deserve prosperity. His actions had murdered my mother, so he was indebted to *me* more than anyone. I wanted him to be as powerless as Mama had been, but how could I make that happen? I was no god. I wasn't even sure the gods had that kind of influence.

My enemy deserved to be whipped and confined. He deserved to be in chains. He deserved to be mocked and derided and impoverished, but how could I make those things happen?

I needed a champion. The Gibeonite brothers were helpful and kind, but they were traders, not warriors. They were family men, and I could not endanger them. They had already done too much for me.

I needed a champion who could defeat the Philistines with nothing to lose but his life. . . . I needed Samson the strongman, but after so many years I had no idea where to find him. And I could think of no reason why he would want to help me.

Chapter Twenty

DELILAH

For the next several weeks, sorrow filled my chest like a huge, painful knot. The widow kept claiming that Adonai would deliver justice at the right time, but that time would come too late for my mother. I couldn't help feeling that the burning lump of guilt and sorrow within me would not go away until Achish was dead.

Ever since learning about Mama's death, my thoughts had crystalized into one refrain: Achish was the poison and Samson the antidote. To my knowledge, the strongman had not stopped by our well in years, but occasionally we heard rumors that he'd been spotted in the area. His parents still lived in Zorah, a village not far from us, which probably explained why the Philistines frequently focused their searches in our area.

But why was Achish so obsessed with the Israelite? Regnar had mentioned a reward, but after years of chasing the Israelite judge, one would think that even Achish would grow weary and give up his search.

I learned the answer a couple of months later. A wealthy merchant stopped at the well to water his camels, then he and his wife came to the porch to enjoy the widow's hospitality. While they sipped wine and ate honey cakes, the merchant casually remarked that the Philistine cerens had been so frustrated by their inability to find Samson that they had increased the reward for his capture to eleven hundred pieces of silver. The merchant wiped perspiration from his brow with a cloth. "I cannot remember them ever offering a prize so large."

The number hit me with the force of a blow. Silver was a rare and precious commodity, worth more than its weight in gold. Yet the cerens were willing to pay eleven hundred pieces of silver for Samson?

I gaped at the merchant. "Surely . . . surely you are mistaken. Perhaps you meant eleven pieces?"

His smile deepened into laughter. "You misunderstand, my dear—the reward is eleven hundred pieces of silver *from each ruler*!"

He chuckled while I stared in amazement. "The Philistines have repeatedly been outsmarted by that Israelite fox," he said. "They have sent an army to search for Samson in Judah, but many times they have awakened to find that during the night Samson had drawn his symbol in the dirt at their captain's side!"

"His symbol?" The widow leaned forward, her cheeks turning pink. "What symbol?"

"The image of a rising sun, of course." The merchant leaned over and used his finger to trace a straight line. He then drew a half circle on one side—a rising sun behind the horizon.

"The sun?" I looked at the widow, who seemed pleased by the image. "What has Samson to do with the sun?"

"His name," she said, "comes from our word *shemesh*. Our Samson is like the sun."

"And about as hard to pin down," the merchant added, grinning.

Surprise siphoned the blood from my head as the widow's laughter ended in a coughing fit. I patted her back until she caught her breath, then offered her a cup of water.

"So much silver!" she said when she could finally speak again. "Has any son of Abraham been worth so much? I doubt it."

"But why are they so set on capturing him?" I asked. "He hasn't done anything to them in months."

"The damage he did long ago is still being felt," the merchant answered. "This land produces three main products: grain, new wine, and olive oil. Samson burnt the barley and wheat, and those fields were replanted. But he also burnt the vineyards and olive groves, and newly planted olive trees will not produce fruit until they are between five and twelve years old."

"Grapevines need at least three years before they'll bear fruit," his wife added. "But even then, the fruit is small and sparse."

The merchant shook his head. "The strongman's actions not only affected the people, but now the merchants who deal in olive oil and wine are feeling the pinch. So the cerens have declared Samson an enemy of Philistia. They have declared that if he is not to be captured, the Israelites must pay for his misdeeds."

The merchant's wife placed her hand on her husband's arm. "Yet our people have been paying for years. We have been robbed on the highways and in our homes. Our flocks and crops have been seized as a penalty for Samson's actions. The Philistines are determined to make our people hate Samson so much that we turn him over to the enemy."

The widow flushed. "Isn't it enough they took land Adonai promised to us? Must they take even our heroes?"

"They swear they will stop the harassment if we surrender Samson," the merchant said, his brows pulling into a frown. "And their plan is working. Many Israelites who once counted Samson a hero now consider him a traitor—"

"The Philistine commander," I interrupted. "Is he still . . . ?"

"I know the man." The merchant lowered his voice as if confiding a dreaded secret. "He's well-connected to Zaggi, the ceren of Gaza. A pompous young fool."

"Is he called Achish?" I asked.

"That's him." The merchant snorted in derision. "He's a wily sort, but he's not as clever as Samson."

I turned to the widow. "I wish we knew where Samson was. I could tell him a few things about Achish."

The corner of the merchant's mouth twitched. "You want to know where Samson is?"

I stared at him. "Doesn't everyone?"

"Nearly everyone in Judah knows that Samson is hiding on Etam Mountain." A smile flashed in the merchant's beard. "The Philistines have camped around that mountain, but they're too cowardly to attempt the ascent. They've been trying to convince the elders of Judah to go up and bring Samson down."

My mind stuttered with disbelief. They couldn't do that. I didn't know who or what Judah was, but they had no right to turn on Samson. I looked at the widow. "These people from Judah—are they Israelites?"

She nodded, her expression somber.

"Why would they betray one of their own? How could they be so disloyal?"

The widow opened her mouth as if to answer, then sighed. "I don't know." She swiveled back to the merchant. "Perhaps you do?"

"What can I say?" He shrugged. "The men from Judah are tired of being harassed. They worry about their sons and daughters. They want peace. So they have bargained for it."

"Has it already happened?" I asked. "Is Samson already in the hands of the Philistines?"

"No." To my surprise, the merchant's wife answered first. She cast a quick glance at her husband, then smoothed her tunic and continued. "The men of Judah want a sizable company to approach Samson, so they are waiting for more men to arrive. Like the Philistines, they are afraid of the strongman."

"Where is this happening?" My heart began to beat faster. "Where are they waiting?"

"A well," she answered. "Near the base of Rock Etam. We traveled around the camp a few days ago." The corners of her mouth tipped upward. "Apparently there isn't a Philistine soldier or a son of Abraham willing to confront Samson alone. Both leaders want an army behind them before they will even attempt to climb the rock and speak to him."

"Maybe," the wife said, a teasing light in her eye, "they should send a woman up the mountain."

I listened calmly, but my heart swirled with emotion. How was Samson supposed to survive when both his enemies and his friends wanted him dead? He had proven himself capable at odds of thirty-to-one, but how could he possibly succeed against hundreds of trained warriors? And how would he feel when he realized that half the men arrayed against him were his own people?

For the first time in my life, I felt a surge of gratitude for my lack of connection to a people or a tribe. If a man couldn't trust his kinsmen, who could he trust?

Adonai. I heard the answer as clearly as if the widow had spoken it. Samson would trust his God to save him. If only I could believe that steadfastly.

In the quiet of the afternoon, I was seized by a sudden wish—if only I could go to that well! I would stand before the men from Judah and try to persuade them to support Samson. They had been harassed and robbed, so they knew Achish was evil. Why would they turn against the only effective weapon they had against him?

"Be careful on the road," the widow was saying as the merchant and his wife prepared to leave. "And may Adonai go with you on your journey."

"The Philistines may come through here," the husband warned, "because they're all gathering at Rock Etam."

"After Samson is taken, what will we do?" The widow shook her head. "Without the threat of Samson to restrain the Philistines, they may demand even more of us in the future."

In a daze I watched the couple depart, my thoughts stumbling over an unexpected realization. I had felt detached and purposeless since learning of my mother's death, but why not adopt a new reason for living? Why not make it my goal to destroy the man who had destroyed my family? I would need help to accomplish such a goal, but I could find help. For who had dared to stand against the Philistines? Who was the only man to be victorious in his encounters with them?

Samson.

I turned away from the road as my thoughts raced. I needed Samson to be my champion, but before long he would be in Philistine hands. Would he listen if I warned him? If I told him that I'd been at his wedding feast, would he feel any sort of connection between us?

Years ago, when I met him by the well, Samson had looked like a man with a broken heart. I had also suffered a broken heart, so perhaps he *would* listen to me. If I told him about the injustices my mother and I suffered, surely he would be willing to attack Achish. He would probably kill any Philistines who stood in his way, but I would never blame him for that. Unlike the men of Judah, I would never betray him.

I gazed down the long road that led to Bethlehem, Jerusalem, and Rock Etam. If ever I needed to take action, this was the time.

~⁂~

That evening I poured a handful of lentils into the cook pot, then glanced at the widow. "I don't understand," I told her, stirring the lentils, "why your people are so eager to hand Samson over. Aren't people of the same clan supposed to defend one another?"

The widow drew a breath, then dissolved into a coughing fit. I watched, concerned, until she settled back and blew out a breath.

"Are you all right? I worry about you."

She waved my worries away. "I told you, it's the dust. I've been breathing it for years, and now my body decides to complain." She let out another little cough, then pressed her hand to her chest and looked at me. "There are a great many of us Israelites," she said, patting her chest, "and one of our leaders once said we were a stubborn and stiff-necked race. But not everyone thinks or feels the same way. Some of us have eyes to see and hearts that understand."

"That understand . . . what?"

"Signs, child. Miracles." A smile ruffled her mouth as she shifted to watch Yagil, who was kicking an inflated goat bladder and laughing while the dog chased it. "Our history is filled with miracles, for Adonai does wondrous things. I once talked to a woman who was related to Samson's mother. You are right when you say he is no ordinary man. But he has been different since before his birth."

I pulled the spoon from the pot and crossed my arms. "Go on."

"Samson's father is from the Danite clan. His wife, Akarah, was barren in the early years of their marriage. She suffered with childlessness, but one day the angel of Adonai appeared to her. The angel told Akarah that she would conceive and bear a son, but he would not be an ordinary boy. He would be consecrated to the Lord from the moment of his conception."

I stared in dazed exasperation. "What does that mean?"

"It meant that he would belong to Adonai throughout his life— not to his parents, not to a wife, not to children, but to Adonai first and always."

"But Samson wanted to be married," I argued. "At his wedding feast he seemed happy to be joined with a wife."

The widow tilted her head and smiled as though explaining something to a young child. "But was he actually married? Or did Adonai prevent it?"

I sighed and stirred the lentils again. If the widow's story was true, then the Israelite warrior and I had something in common. He had been set apart from his people on account of his God; I had been set apart by the color of my skin. In that respect we were both separate and alone. In a world of clans and nations, we were aliens.

Maybe that was why some people were so determined to be rid of us.

❧

The next morning I told the widow that I had to go to Etam before Samson was captured. "I'll leave Yagil with you, of course," I said, mentally running though a list of things I would need on my journey. "I should be back in a week or so."

The widow's eyes widened to the point that I thought they would fall out of her head. "You are going *where*?"

"I have to reach Samson before the Philistines do." I lifted a brow, bemused by her astonishment. "He's at Rock Etam, remember?"

"Child, you can't go to Etam—and you can't go anywhere alone. It's not safe even for a man to travel with no escort."

"Then how am I supposed to speak to Samson?" I fisted my hands, frustrated beyond words. "He's a judge, isn't he? He's supposed to enforce justice? I have to see him because someone has to tell him what Achish has done. Samson will soon stand before him, and if he knows how evil Achish is, he will have every reason to kill him. I have to do something—somehow—to take vengeance on the man responsible for my mother's death. Can't you see that?"

I knew I was approaching hysteria, and the widow realized it, too. She walked to the edge of the porch and looked right and left as if she worried about spies on the road. She then glanced behind the house as if Philistines might lurk in the shadows.

When she was satisfied that we were completely alone, she looked up at me, her eyes shining with purpose. "I understand that you have been wounded. But your mother is dead and you are living in occupied territory. The Philistines are our masters. They do with us as they please. We have no king—"

"But you have Samson." A rise of emotion clogged my throat, but I pressed through it. "You're always saying that Adonai will free you from the Philistines in his time, but why not now? You have a champion! He's not far away, but you haven't gone to him, and the men of Judea are planning to hand him over to the executioners! How can that be? Do your people want to be free of the Philistines or not?"

Color flushed the widow's face and she bent over in another coughing spell. When she had finished, she took a deep breath and dropped onto her stool. "It would be—" she snatched a breath—"so much easier if you would simply trust Adonai to handle your hurts. You spend so much energy fretting over your past—wouldn't you like to leave it behind? Let go of the past, Delilah, and look toward the future. You can trust Adonai to take care of your wounds. He is Israel's true king, and He can see into every man's heart and judge righteously—"

Another coughing fit seized her when she gasped for breath, and for several minutes she leaned forward and coughed until my own throat tightened in sympathy. I reached for a gourd and dipped it into the water jug, but the widow shook her head, turning away until she could breathe again.

Finally she sat still, her eyes closed, her breathing shallow. "Sorry," she whispered, shaking her head. "The dust . . ."

I gave her the water. She drank it down and gave me a wavering smile. "Have you seen Samson leading an army?" she asked quietly. "Has he led an attack on a Philistine stronghold? No, because he fights for himself. He doesn't fight for his people. So why, dear girl, should he fight for you?"

She looked at me, pain and regret warring in her eyes, and I knew she hadn't intended to make me feel insignificant. She was simply pointing out the obvious, but still, her words cut deep.

Why would Samson fight for me? I had convinced myself that we shared a connection because I'd been at his wedding and I'd spoken to him at the well. In the darkness at Timnah, I'd watched him return with all those rich garments and I'd marveled at his speed and strength. I had admired him, and I'd feasted on rumors about him. But the fanciful bridge that linked us wasn't real. It was composed of suppositions and illusions.

Samson didn't know me. He didn't know my mother. So why would he listen to my sad story?

My wretchedness must have shown on my face, because the widow stood and rested her hands on my shoulders. "It's folly, love," she said, pushing a strand of hair away from my watery eyes. "But Adonai's ways are marvelous and unexpected. So if you want to find Samson, I'll go with you to help look after Yagil. The next caravan that stops here, we'll ask where they're going. If they're going to Bethlehem or anywhere in that vicinity, we'll ask if we can join them. And when we arrive, we'll figure how to find Samson . . . if we get there in time."

I took a quick breath of astonishment, then squeezed the widow's hand. "Thank you."

She pressed a finger to the tip of my nose and smiled. "Who can say what the will of Adonai is? If we find Samson, we can certainly ask him to avenge your cause. If he says no, we're no worse off than we are now, aye?"

I nodded, grateful that at least one of the gods—who could say which?—had sent me an ally.

Two days later, a caravan bound for Bethlehem stopped at the well. After refreshing the travelers with water and sweetening their mood with honey cakes, the widow asked if we could join them on the journey. The Israelite men who led the group looked at each other, then nodded.

"Only an uncircumcised brute would refuse women with a small child," the widow told me as we hastily gathered our supplies. "My people are commanded to show hospitality to strangers, so we will be in good company."

I held Yagil's hand and carried a basket with fresh clothes, a few small loaves of bread, and some dried beef. The widow had packed a bag as well, so we hurried out to the caravan. One of the men placed Yagil between two water jars on a donkey. The widow and I flanked the animal and carried our baskets. If the widow was worried about leaving everything she owned unguarded at the house, she showed no sign of it. The sparkle in her eyes seemed to indicate that she was delighted to break from routine and indulge in an adventure. "So long as the sheep are still there when we return," she said, grinning, "we'll be fine."

We had barely begun to move when the dog came running from wherever he'd been hunting. One of the camels shied away from the furious blur that was our dog, but Yagil called out to him and the dog veered away from the camel, deciding to trot by our side instead. The man at the head of the caravan narrowed his eyes as if he would say something about our canine companion, but the widow gave him a stern look. If Yagil wanted his dog along, he would have his dog.

I sighed in relief when the man finally turned around.

"How long has it been since you left your house overnight?" I asked the widow.

She chuckled and looked at the sun as if it tracked days rather than hours. "Years. I have not left home in years."

"Not even to visit . . ." I hesitated. "Have you family nearby?"

She shook her head. "My mother died before I was married, and my father soon after I came here. So I've stayed in my little house ever since I married."

I blinked, finding her story hard to believe. Though I was not nearly as old as the widow, I had traveled from Egypt to Gaza, and from Gaza to the Valley of Sorek. I didn't intend to remain in the valley, either. As soon as I found a way to win justice for my mother, I would go back to Gaza and try to claim the estate my mother should have received when Adinai died. Once Yagil and I had means, we might sail to Crete or return to Egypt.

I glanced at my son. Supported by the water jars and the harness that held them, he had stretched out on the donkey's back. The warmth of the day had lulled him to sleep, and the donkey's plodding gait rocked him gently. With any luck, he would sleep until we stopped to rest, where I would allow him to explore a bit. After a day or two, we would be at Rock Etam.

I only hoped we would find Samson before the men of Judah took action.

⁓✺⁓

The journey from the widow's home to Rock Etam would not have taken more than a day if we had traveled over flat terrain. As we moved southeastward, however, the land became uneven and the road more challenging. My basket of supplies, which seemed to weigh practically nothing when we left, now felt as though it were filled with rocks. Yagil, who had been intimidated and shy on the first day, spent the second day fidgeting on the donkey or sulking as he trudged beside me. His whine became an irritating whimper that moved my heart more toward anger than compassion.

More than once, I closed my eyes and wished I'd kept silent about

Samson. I was beginning to believe that the odds of encountering the strongman were no better than my surviving this trek through the territory of Judah.

When at last we entered Bethlehem, the leader of our caravan came back to speak to me and the widow. "Rock Etam lies south of this place," he said. "The road is not heavily traveled, but you will find yourself in a crowd today. The men of Judah are gathering outside the well—you're sure to spot them as you walk southward. The well is a good place to rest. Just be careful to avoid the western fields where the Philistines are encamped."

The widow thanked him for the information, and I looked away, my thoughts racing. I wanted to find Samson before he encountered the men from Judah, but how could I do that? If the well lay between us and Etam, we were more likely to run into the men from Judah or the Philistines than to meet Samson. But if the men from Judah were on the east and the Philistines on the west, maybe we could walk straight toward the rock and reach Samson before the others.

I shared my thoughts with the widow as we left the caravan and started walking south. A flicker of shock widened her eyes, then terror tightened her mouth. "You think we should go forward? Do you have any idea what could happen to us? Philistine spies could see us coming, but we would not see them until we were at their mercy. And how am I supposed to climb a rock at my age? No, Delilah, absolutely not. We are not running ahead of anyone."

"Then why have we come, if not to meet Samson?"

She took a deep breath and forced a smile. "We have come to see if we can talk to him *after* he's come down the mountain."

"*If* he comes down," I said. "And if the men of Judah or the Philistines don't kill him."

A muscle quivered at her jaw. "Trust in Adonai, Delilah. You must learn to trust."

I could not convince her to continue toward Rock Etam. We drank from the well, then sat beneath the spreading canopy of an oak tree. The widow tipped her head back against the tree's wide trunk and fell asleep within minutes. Yagil curled into her lap and slept soundly, despite—or perhaps because of—the widow's steady snoring. The dog lay next to me, panting as he scanned the horizon.

I crossed my arms and sighed. Had we come this far only to nap? Back at the widow's house, my idea had seemed perfectly logical. Find Samson before the others, warn him about Achish, and enlist his aid in avenging my mother's death. I had envisioned a tidy little mountain surrounded by a curving path that spiraled upward from its base. I had imagined myself running up the path, having a quick talk with Samson, and hurrying back down before either the Israelites or the Philistines had finished gathering their forces.

But what did I know? Until today, I had never seen a mountain. And I had certainly never imagined Rock Etam.

I looked across the wide plain before the mountain where Samson was reportedly living. Rock Etam was neither tidy nor little. From where I sat, his refuge appeared to be a large stone that had been hurled to the earth from a great distance. No trees grew on it, no grass or shrubs. I had no idea how anyone could scale that rock, or how they could survive on its stony surface.

I let my head fall back to the oak and closed my eyes. Maybe I wouldn't have to climb the rock. Maybe the widow was right and I'd be able to talk to Samson once the men from Judah brought him down . . . if they brought him down alive.

Maybe I'd been a fool to suggest we come here.

I fell into a shallow doze and didn't wake until the widow nudged my shoulder. When I looked up, she silently gestured toward the western plain. A great cloud of dust had arisen, signaling the approach of men and chariots. Apparently the Philistines had decided to advance.

Keeping an eye on the cloud of dust, the widow pushed herself up from the ground. "I do not think," she said, brushing sand from Yagil's tunic, "that we should stay here and be caught between two armies. Let's go to the well and see if someone can tell us what this is about."

I had no choice but to agree.

CHAPTER TWENTY-ONE
SAMSON

I HEARD THE CRUNCH OF SANDALS on scree and knew that Rei would be returning from his lookout point. "More riders in the distance," he called as he entered the narrow chasm that had become my home. "Apparently the men of Judah are enlisting warriors even as the Philistines ride toward us."

I accepted the insult implicit in those words. The people who had cheered me after burning the Philistine's crops had grown tired of dealing with the aftermath. They were also weary of my presence, even on this uninhabitable rock in their territory.

I understood, of course. Time had eased my grief over Kesi, but the passing years had only increased the Judahites' anxiety.

"What about the Philistines?" I asked.

Rei gestured toward the west. "They're advancing from their camp, but still keeping their distance from Judah's men."

"Of course."

I leaned back and rested my head on a wall of rock. For years I had wandered through the land Adonai promised us, seeking solace for my pain. Grief from Kesi's death clung to me like the soot that covered the bricks of the inn at Timnah. Along with that grief I wrestled with confusion. Why had Adonai ignited feelings of love in my heart if He did not intend Kesi to be my wife? Was I only a tool in His hands, a battle-axe forged for the Philistines? Did Adonai not have any concern for Samson the man, or was I always to be Samson the weapon?

As I wandered through Judah, traveling under star-studded skies to avoid detection, I felt compressed into an ever-shrinking space between the weight of Adonai's purpose for my life and my own needs. I was a man of flesh and bone; I needed love and companionship. I knew my life was consecrated to Adonai. I knew I had been born for the purpose of liberating Israel from the Philistine oppressors. But how could I balance Adonai's plans with my needs and desires?

I had wandered in Judah for over five years, yet the passing time did not bring answers. It did, however, numb my grief and allow me to distance myself from my sorrowful memories.

"Will you do nothing?" Rei squatted next to me, bracing his back on the opposite stone wall only a few paces away. "Are you simply going to sit here and wait for them to prepare for your execution? How do the Philistines do it, impalement? Beheading? Have you decided on the best way to die?"

He was jabbing at me, trying to arouse me to action. But I felt more frustration than anger.

"What would you have me do?" I spread my hands. "They will do what they will do, and I will deal with them when they come for me. Then I will do what Adonai wills, because it will be my only choice."

"Not your only choice. You could move now. You could climb over this rock, head south, go to Gaza or some other city—"

I waved his suggestion away. "Perhaps it would be better for the men of Judah to stop fooling themselves. Let them realize that they responded like sheep, not bulls, when the Philistines challenged them. A tribe—a nation—will not change until it realizes how low it has fallen. When my people realize that they have loved bondage with leisure and sin better than strenuous liberty with righteousness, they will repent and return to the Lord. Until then . . ." I shrugged, feeling the heavy weight of duty on my shoulders. "I suppose Adonai will use me to keep the oppressors in check."

I turned my head as a sound like tumbling boulders caught my ear. Rei heard it too, then leapt up and returned to his lookout. A moment later he was back, his eyes wide.

"A company is climbing the mountain."

"Philistines or Israelites?"

"Men of Judah. And they're carrying weapons."

I stretched out and pillowed my head on my upper arm. "Wake me when they near the halfway point. Then we will go down and spare them the climb to the summit."

I closed my eyes but could not sleep. An inner restlessness consumed me, a sense that Adonai would soon expect something of me. The feeling came over me at certain times, and on each occasion I found myself able to do whatever I could imagine . . . but I had been too late to imagine rescuing Kesi. I tried to avenge her, but a few dead Philistines—killed in self-defense—could not begin to atone for the deaths of two innocents.

I propped my chin on my hand and looked down the length of the cavern. Moses had once hidden in a cleft of a rock, when Adonai had personally shielded him from more glory than he could bear. I had been hiding in the cleft of this rock for months, off and on, and yet all I saw was an empty space two hundred fifty paces long, eighteen paces across, and only eight or so paces high. In some places the walls were only as tall as the average man, so I could stand and peer over the top of the rock, gazing at clouds and green pastures and tan deserts—

"They're halfway up the mountain, Samson."

My attention shifted at the urgent note in Rei's voice. My servant stood next to me, his hand on his walking stick. "Are you sure you want to meet them? We could climb out and cross over. We are familiar with this place and most of these men are not—"

"We're going to meet our brothers, and we're not going to harm them." I sat up, braced my hands on my bent knees, and stared at my faithful servant. Without him, I might have gone mad in this forced isolation. "We are going to speak to them. Adonai wants peace among His people, so we will agree with whatever the men from Judah want us to do."

"But they're not thinking," Rei argued. "They have forgotten about Joshua, who cleared the land, Deborah and Barak, Gideon and Jephthah."

"Men have short memories," I said, standing. "And if I have to die to save my people from destruction, so be it. It may be that I was born for this day."

Born to die. The thought echoed in my head as I climbed out of the chasm and began to follow the footpath. Sacrificial lambs were born to die. Some insects lived so briefly that their lives made little impact on the world, but even flies had a purpose, though I wasn't sure what it was. But surely Adonai, creator of everything good, would create nothing unless it had a reason for being.

I led the way down the path with long, purposeful strides, moving easily over the narrow trail that opened to sharp cliffs. When I paused to look down, I could see a single line of bearded men approaching, most of them concentrating on their footing rather than their weapons. The leaders of the tribe had gathered quite an army—more than three thousand, by my estimation. Had none of them stopped to consider that their real enemy stood on the plain below?

I squinted at the first man in line. Unless my eyes deceived me, the leader was Micah, an elder of the tribe. The men immediately behind him were probably distant kinsmen, and why not? He would want support, and no one supported like a brother.

Yet none of my brothers were fighting beside me.

I shook off the painful thought and kept moving.

Finally, we met on the Etam path. I stopped, my hands empty, and looked at Micah, who carried a shield and a sword, with dozens of armed men standing behind him.

"Samson." Micah halted and nodded in cautious greeting. "Surely you know why we have come."

I dipped my head in recognition. "I understand why *you* have come. What I don't understand is why you are willing to deliver a kinsman to a ruthless enemy."

"You are not from our tribe."

"Yet I am a child of Abraham. I share the same right to dwell in this land."

Exasperation twisted Micah's face. "Don't you realize the Philistines are ruling over us? Every time you act, you think you are injuring the Philistines, but you are injuring *us*. The uncircumcised barbarians intend to make us suffer until you are in their custody."

"As they did to me, so I did to them." I set my jaw. "I have always had good reasons for my actions."

Micah waved my words away. "How odd, then, that the Philistines have camped in our land because *they* want to do to *you* as you did to them."

"They struck first. They cheated me at my own wedding feast."

Micah sighed, his shoulders slumping as if he were weary of carrying an invisible load. "Be that as it may, Samson, we have come to bind you so we can surrender you to the Philistines."

He took a step forward, but I lifted my hand. "Before you come any closer, swear to me that you won't kill me yourself. I see your men are carrying swords, and I would not want one of them to lodge a blade in my back."

Micah looked over the line of men behind him, some of whom had pulled their swords from their scabbards. He motioned for them to put their weapons away, and when the last blade had disappeared, he turned back to me. "Before Adonai, we swear we will not kill you. But we will bind you fast and hand you over to the leader of the Philistines."

I searched his face for signs of duplicity but saw none. As Rei muttered behind me, I tossed my cloak over my shoulder and stepped forward, my palms pressed together. I stood patiently while the men of Judah scrambled to bind my wrists with new ropes. Then I walked quietly as they led me down the rocky trail.

At the bottom of Rock Etam, on the wide plain, the Philistines waited. I couldn't see them, but I could tell when the first of the men of Judah reached the base of the mountain, because at that moment the Philistines released a deafening cheer.

❧

With every step down the path, the fire in my chest burned hotter. The cowardly men from Judah had been altogether too quick to appease the invading Philistines, but so long as they kept their word to me, I would not blame them for this situation. Like blind sheep that did not recognize their shepherd, they were terrified by the wolves howling at their gates.

Let them bleat and let them quake in fear. I had grown weary of the wolves, and I would not allow them to attack any more members of this flock.

"I will bring *shalom* in the land," I said, punctuating each downward step with words from the Book of the Law, "and you will lie down, with no one making you afraid. I will remove dangerous beasts from the land and no sword will pass through your land. You will chase your enemies and they will fall before you by the sword. Five of you will chase one hundred, and one hundred of you will chase ten thousand, and your enemies will fall by the sword before you."

We stopped at a landing just above the final slope. A downward glance revealed a roiling crowd on the plain—rows and rows of cheering Philistines, many in chariots pulled by Arabian stallions. A crowd in simple tunics stood slightly apart from the foreigners, leaders from other tribes perhaps mixed with residents of Bethlehem and other small settlements. Women stood in the crowd, their faces lifted toward Rock Etam in undisguised curiosity. At their feet, children scampered to and fro while brandishing sticks as pretend swords and daggers.

At the front of the Philistines, a man in gleaming brass armor stood in a chariot, his narrow face pointed in my direction. He lifted his sword, aimed it toward my silent companions, and let his arm fall in a dramatic gesture, dispatching the first division of his warriors. On they came, jogging confidently, swords and spears at the ready.

"Forward!" Micah cried, setting my feet in motion again.

My heart surged within me and my hands began to tingle as we continued down the path. At least a thousand Philistines waited for me, assembled and handpicked by Adonai himself. If I allowed them to take me, they would torment me all the way back to the closest Philistine city. Those who could not reach me would bedevil the men from Judah as they journeyed back to their homes. Filled with bravado, the Philistines would imagine themselves lords of the land, when Adonai had decreed that they were not. This Promised Land and its people belonged to Adonai, who ceded it to Abraham in an eternal covenant. The Philistines were and always would be foreigners.

How dare they make merry on this sacred soil!

When the path twisted, a boulder blocked my view of the valley below. Now only a few steps from the base of the rock, the men from Judah slowed their pace as the path narrowed to a point where only two people could cross abreast. We halted, waiting for the men ahead of us to pass through the narrow opening.

I turned to Rei, who had remained behind me on the way down. "Shall we show the Philistines something new?"

His face split into a wide grin. "Shall I alert Micah?"

I laughed. "Let *this* draw his attention."

The rocks themselves seemed to crackle as I lifted my bound arms and pulled my wrists apart. The new rope popped like a bowstring. The unexpected sound startled Micah and the men ahead of me, putting them on the defensive. Before their wide eyes I flexed my arms and heard the resulting snap of the ropes around my biceps.

Realizing that I had dramatically altered their plan, two of the men serving as my guard scrambled up and over the boulder, then leapt to the earth below. Two others, startled by the sight of the Ruach Adonai's work, launched themselves through the narrow passageway, knocking over and trampling their fallen kinsmen.

Micah, the only Judahite remaining, turned to me and lifted his sword, then halted and smiled in exasperation. "I have delivered you to the Philistines," he said, bowing slightly.

"I am ready," I replied. "Tell them their prisoner stands ready."

As Micah hurried down the trail, a silence swept over the area, an eerie stillness that chilled the marrow of my bones. What did Adonai want me to do next?

Because I could not see my enemy, I moved back up the trail until I cleared the obstructing boulder and had a clear view of the plain.

I saw the last of the Judahites coming off the trail. I heard the thunder of their footsteps as they ran for their lives. Those who had panicked and fallen on the rocks had to hobble away.

The Philistines did not run, but they looked up at Rock Etam with uncertainty in their eyes.

"Five of you will chase one hundred," I murmured, "and one hundred of you will chase ten thousand, and your enemies will fall by the sword before you."

I braced my legs, flexed my arms, and stared down the interlopers. The warriors at the bottom of the approach remained motionless, and a moment later I realized why they were waiting. Their leader—the narrow-faced young man who had cheated at my wedding feast—strode forward and hopped up onto a rock. "Samson!" he called, his bold voice echoing between the cliffs. "The Philistines have come for you!"

"Philistine," I called back, "come and get me!"

When the enemy captain lowered his hand, the first line of soldiers charged the path with swords extended and shields raised. Because I had neither sword nor dagger, I cast about for something to use for defense. A rock would be too slippery once wet, but . . . my gaze lit on a donkey skeleton. A layer of desiccated hide covered the head, but I ripped the hide away and picked up the jawbone, still in one piece.

The long bone would make a formidable weapon. And didn't Shamgar, son of Anath, strike down six hundred Philistines with an ox goad?

I was standing a few paces behind the narrow passage when the first Philistines came at me. One blow with the jawbone deflected a sword, a second one crushed a skull. Another warrior followed the first and I dispatched him easily. One by one they came, occasionally two by two, and I met each of them with the jawbone, cracking heads, gnashing throats, severing spines. Rei scrambled onto a high boulder and crouched there, calling encouragement as I crunched and slashed and ripped. The pile of dead Philistines at my feet grew so tall that I was forced to move back up the trail, drawing the Philistines forward. They scrambled over the bodies of their fellows, slipped in streams of blood, and occasionally slid off the steep side of the cliff.

And still I fought. I swung and battled my way through air that seemed to have grown as thick as wool. The muscles of my calves and thighs grew hot with exertion, and I tasted blood from an accidental bite of my own tongue. I whirled in the midst of surging chaos, but my position guaranteed the upper hand. One by one I took them down; one by one they either fell to their deaths or surrendered to the jawbone. I heard nothing save the clash and screams around me. I saw nothing but the wide eyes of the enemies who came at me.

Finally . . . silence. The men around me lay motionless. No other Philistines raced up the path to challenge me, and no men of Judah.

The battle, if it could be called that, was over.

I lowered the jawbone and let it slip away as I stretched my stiff fingers. The bone skittered down the path, sliding over rocks and stones, then it lay still, a bloody half smile gleaming red in the afternoon sun.

"With the jawbone of a donkey, heaps upon heaps." I stretched my arms toward the bodies of Israel's enemies. "With the jawbone of a donkey I have slain a thousand men."

From his perch, Rei clapped, once, twice, thrice. "Good job," he said, grinning because our word for *heaps* was similar to the word for *donkey*. "Not only have you won a great victory, you have immortalized it with clever words."

"I will call this place—" I looked around at the blood-spattered spot—"Ramat-Lehi. And now I thirst." I fell back against the wall, overcome by weakness as the fire of battle departed.

Rei and I searched, but we found nothing in the area but death, blood, and stone. Lifting my face to heaven, I called on the one who had fed the Philistines to me like a mother vulture feeding her young. "Adonai! You have granted this great deliverance by the hand of your servant. So am I now to die of thirst and fall into the hands of the uncircumcised?"

I waited a moment, then Rei pointed to a bowl-shaped rock.

The rock was as dry as that desiccated donkey, yet as I watched, the stone split and water rose from the fissure. Sparkling, delightful, refreshing water.

I drank deeply, then splashed my face and looked over the field of battle. A sudden thought occurred—I had killed every Philistine who came up the path, but the thin-faced commander had not come to face me.

As a measure of strength returned, I climbed onto a boulder for a better view of the plain. The Philistine army had vanished, their camp now nothing but empty tents and abandoned chariots. The men of Judah were taking custody of the stallions, removing them from their harnesses and leading them away. Nothing else moved.

The captain had fled.

The day was over, the battle done, and I was still alive . . . and a free man.

CHAPTER TWENTY-TWO
DELILAH

THE WIDOW, Yagil, the dog, and I rested in a shady spot near the well as the men of Judah brought bodies down the rocky trail. As the empty plain filled with the corpses of dead Philistines, the innkeeper smiled in grim approval.

He tempered his expression, however, when Achish approached, stamping and cursing at the sight of his defeated army.

I pulled my veil over my face and shifted to face my sleeping son. I planned to hide behind the widow if Achish looked my way, but after a while I realized that the widow and I were of no more interest to him than the flies on the dead. We were two poor women with a child and a skinny dog, therefore not worthy of his attention.

The Israelites who handled the corpses wore expressions of pleased surprise—expressions that shifted to broad grins when Achish turned his back on their work. As I eavesdropped on the men's chatter, I began to understand why the children of Israel were thrilled by this one-man victory. Everything Achish had done to me, the Philistines had done to the children of Israel for more than thirty-five years. Samson might have aggravated the oppressors, but he did not cause the oppression.

"Adonai surely sent Samson to us," one man muttered to his companion as they trudged past me.

"Perhaps," his friend answered. "Perhaps they would be gone if Samson loved his people as much as Adonai does."

The widow nudged me. "Unless you want to sleep on the road, perhaps we should begin the walk home?"

I knew she wanted to get back to the house, but I was determined to learn more about the mighty man of the Israelites. So I smiled at the widow, pointed to my sleeping son, and suggested that we let him sleep a little longer.

She settled back with a resigned sigh, and I kept my head low. Achish had vanished, so I was free to eavesdrop.

"I heard Samson's father wanted to betroth him to a woman from Judah," another man said as he and his partner strained to carry Philistine bodies on their backs. "But Samson preferred the Philistines to his own people."

"Can you blame him?" The second man tossed a grin over his shoulder. "Philistine women are pagans, immodest and reckless. What man prefers the tame dove to the wild eagle?" He laughed, then shifted his weight. "Surely Samson has soured on marriage. If he wants a woman, he'll take one."

"Truthfully," the other man called, "I believe Samson must be destined to remain unmarried. How is he supposed to find a daughter of Abraham who will forgive his previous snub?"

As they walked away, I ran my hand through my hair and considered their comments. If Samson felt alone in the world, so did I. If he was acquainted with the feeling of being an outsider, we had much in common.

Perhaps enough to bring us together.

We had been home only two days when the widow took to her bed. Her cough, which had never gone away, grew worse, shifting from an insistent dry bark to a wet, gurgling hack. She would often cough until she gagged, then she'd lay exhausted until the next attack began. She could not sleep, and neither could I. Yagil slept like a stone through those long nights while I kept a vigil by the widow's bedside and wondered what I would do without her.

Daylight brought no relief. The widow did not have the strength to rise from her bed. When she began to cough up blood, I feared that she was sick unto death.

She couldn't die. I needed her, but Yagil needed her even more. Though the boy had come from my body, the widow was more of a mother to him than I was. He loved her more than me, and she loved him because she didn't see Achish every time she looked at him.

I told Yagil to go outside and water the sheep. Then I stood beneath the porch and searched for some sign of movement on the road. If the widow were standing in my place, she would pray for a healer or physician, but I didn't know how to pray. Three or four caravans did stop at the well, and when I asked if they had a healer along, they only shook their heads.

Whenever the widow sank into a fitful doze, I would sit by her bed and stroke the dog's head. He seemed content to keep me company during those long days and nights, and I was grateful for his presence. If the widow died, Yagil and the dog would be my only companions.

And Yagil . . . what would he do without the widow? She had mothered him when I could not. A sense of responsibility had led me to nurse him and occasionally discipline him, but the widow had played with him, taught him, hugged and tickled him. She had told him stories about her people and Adonai. She had given so much of herself that Yagil probably thought he was an Israelite.

I swallowed hard and hugged my arms. I had lost so many people—father, stepfather, and mother. I had always thought of myself as independent, but as the widow teetered on the brink of death, I realized I had always been able to depend on *someone*. When the widow died, I would be completely alone, except for a dog and a little boy who would have no one but me to care for him.

And I was not a good mother.

I helped the widow as much as I could, offering water and broth when she could breathe without coughing, but on the seventh day after our return from Rock Etam, she exhaled a long breath and then breathed no more.

In the hollow of my back, a drop of sweat traced the course of my spine and I shivered despite the heat. I felt an overwhelming urge to turn and go to the loom, to place my hands on it and work the threads, draw the shuttle, beat the rows until the widow woke up and came back out to say that dinner was ready.

But instead I closed the widow's eyes and brought her hands to her chest. I called for Yagil, then brought him to the widow's bedside and told him that she had fallen asleep and would not be waking up. I patted his back as he cried. I told him I would wrap her in a sheet of our finest linen and bury her behind the house.

The urge to run to the loom was so strong that my hands and arms trembled as I ministered to her earthly frame. Though I did not cry when I nursed her, a tear trickled down my cheek as I struggled to dig the grave. I swiped it away, but it was the first of a flood that rained from my eyes, implacable rivers of loss and love. Tears slid between my fingers when I tried to wipe them away, washing the flat rock I was using to dig her grave.

For the first time I realized how much I would miss her. She had taken me in as a stranger, she had trusted me, and my son had been born on her knees. Yagil adored her, and I knew he would miss her terribly. Though we were as different as two women could be, somehow we completed each other.

After carrying her from the house, I sank to the ground and stared at the narrow hole I had labored to dig, then felt a wavering smile creep across my face. If the widow were here, she would show me a better way to dig graves. She had taught me so much.

She taught me how to weave and how to look at the beauty of a sunset and know that Someone lay behind it. She taught me to trust and to do my work calmly and with confidence. She taught me how to cook and how to care for a baby.

If only she could teach me how to love my enemy's son.

I ran my hand over her linen shroud. I couldn't imagine what I brought to the widow's life, but I wouldn't have survived without her.

I rolled her into the earth just before sundown. Yagil, the dog, and I knelt beside her shrouded form, then Yagil dropped blue flax blossoms onto the linen shroud while the dog whined. "We will miss you," I told the widow, clinging to Yagil's small hand. "Godspeed to the world beyond."

After sunset I put my sad son to bed. In the dim glow of an oil lamp, I listened to Yagil weep until his sobbing faded to soft snuffling sounds. When I was certain he slept, I went outside and sat by the loom in the darkness.

What should I do with myself now that the widow was gone? I could return to Gaza to try to establish a trade as a weaver, but I had nowhere to live and no connections. The widow had taken me in because her God commanded her to be kind to strangers, but Dagon had no such commandment. In that bustling city I would be completely on my own with a small child, a dog, and an inherited loom . . . if I could figure out how to move it to Gaza. But where would I grow flax? Where would Yagil play? I had always considered myself a city girl, but six years in the wilderness had changed me.

By the time the sun rose the next morning, I had decided to remain at the widow's house. Travelers had been stopping at this way
station for years, and they would continue to come. They would ask
about the widow, and I would tell them that I planned to continue
her work. I would pick up the spools she had dropped, and I would
tend her flax fields. Until I found a better place, I would remain
in the place I knew.

I could be an honest woman at the well. Detached from any
city or town, unaffiliated with any tribe or clan, I could be myself:
neither Canaanite, Israelite, or Philistine. I belonged in the middle
of nowhere.

So I stayed.

⁓❧⁓

One afternoon a large party of Philistine travelers stopped at the
well. I would not have invited them in, but they greeted me and
offered a basket of pomegranates in exchange for water and a shady
place to rest. I accepted and let them sit on the porch, even though
I could almost feel the widow's disapproving stare on the back of
my neck. I placed the fruit in the house and checked on Yagil and
the dog, then returned to working the loom while I eavesdropped
on my guests' conversation.

"I hear the strongman escaped Gaza again," one Philistine said,
slapping another on the back. "Achish had him trapped like a genie
in a bottle, but his men fell asleep during the night."

"They woke, though," another man interrupted, laughing. "Most
men sleep deeply after visiting a harlot, but Samson didn't linger till
morning. He left the woman's house and would have slipped away,
but the city gates were closed. So what did he do? He grabbed the
iron bars on the two doors and pulled them up, dislodging even
the beams that held the structure erect. Achish and his guards were

struck dumb as the barriers left their place and rose as Samson lifted them over his head. Though a few managed to fire off arrows and spears, by that time the strongman had placed the gates on his back where they acted as a shield. None of Achish's men so much as nicked the strongman."

"Didn't they follow him?" someone asked.

The storyteller laughed. "Why would they? The jawbone battle had already proven that the Philistine army can't touch him. The Israelite kept the gates on his shoulders and carried them to Watchtower Mount, the last in the chain of hills that leads to Hebron."

"Bah." One of the other men spat. "I don't believe it. The story is unbelievable."

"Is it?" The storyteller crossed his arms and smiled. "I myself have seen the gates on that mount. Little children now climb on them and pretend to be Samson, killer of Philistines. If my story is not true, how did the gates come to be on that mountain?"

"Someone could have moved them."

"But why would they?" The storyteller shrugged. "Merchants in the Gaza marketplace swear to the truth of the tale. And anyone can see that Zaggi's beautiful city now boasts of a new temple *and* shiny new gates."

Silence followed the story, a quiet so thick that the only sound was the gentle *tap tap tap* of my beater against the woven threads.

"You have to admit," another Philistine finally said, "Samson was brazen, walking right into Gaza like that. With so many Philistine warriors around, he was practically putting his head into a hungry lion's mouth."

"What you call *brazen* others would call *courageous*," another man said. "Would you have been so bold? Knowing that most people could identify you on sight—"

"Ah, but they couldn't," the storyteller insisted. "Samson doesn't look all that remarkable. He looks like any other man—except for that hair."

"Oh, yes, the hair." Another man laughed. "Why any man would want to grow his hair past his waist . . . it's beyond my comprehension."

The other men joined in the laughter.

Quietly listening at my stool, I smiled at the story. Though I was not particularly pleased to hear that Samson had visited a prostitute in Gaza, I was delighted to know that he had foiled Achish again. The wild-haired Israelite certainly had the courage of a champion.

If that wandering son of Abraham had come into my house at that moment, I think I might have kissed him.

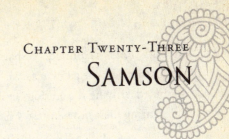

CHAPTER TWENTY-THREE
SAMSON

"You are simpleminded and foolish," Rei said, panting as he jogged beside me. "Time after time, you ignore the laws of our people. You know there are certain prohibitions for a Nazarite—"

"Simpleminded I may be," I admitted, "but I am not foolish. Why should I be bound by laws that don't apply to me?"

"That's no excuse for getting drunk. We should talk about it—" Rei panted—"so stop."

"Not here." I looked around and spotted a knotty pine ahead. I cut diagonally across a field, and Rei sprinted to catch up.

"Here." I dropped into the shade, leaned against the tree, and stretched out my legs. "Sit and rest. You are altogether out of breath."

Rei collapsed beside me, then rolled onto an elbow and shook his head. "I don't understand why we are always in a hurry."

"When there is work to be done someplace, why should I linger in another place and do nothing?"

"Work?" Rei's head lifted. "What work do you mean? Are you planning to repair the gates at Gaza?"

I grinned, reliving the glorious feeling of lifting those bars. Like a spider luring flies into her nest, I had drawn the Philistine guard away from Gaza and scattered them on the road. Unfortunately, they hadn't had the courage to follow me to the mountain where I could have taken them out one by one.

"I don't know what work I'm hurrying toward," I admitted. "But the Ruach Adonai goads me, so I move. I have a feeling something important lies just over the ridge, just around the corner. Something I'm supposed to do."

Exhaling a heavy sigh, Rei rolled onto his back, falling into a bed of pine needles. "One day you will be the death of me."

I laughed. "And you of me, probably. But as to your concerns—I wasn't drunk."

"But you were drinking."

"A cup of wine only, and it wasn't even the good stuff. My conscience is clear."

"But what if someone had seen you?"

"Let them see. I've done nothing to break my vows."

Rei snorted softly, so I leaned toward him. "When Adonai's angel gave my mother instructions, he said nothing about me avoiding dead bodies or wine or vineyards. He placed only one condition on me, and I have observed that one my entire life."

"No other Nazarites touch unclean things or drink wine," Rei challenged. "Are you better than they?"

"Not better," I answered, stretching out on the ground. I closed my eyes. "But different."

CHAPTER TWENTY-FOUR

DELILAH

AFTER FEEDING YAGIL, I let him go out to play with the dog while I prepared my work for the day. As was my habit, before going to the loom I stepped out from the porch and stood near the well, looking east and west for signs of travelers. The people who stopped at the well were now my only connection to the outside world, and from them I learned about current fashions in Gaza, details about the Philistine lords, and the mood among the oppressed Israelites. Occasionally I even heard rumors about Samson, the most sought-after man in the land.

I was just about to go sit at the loom when I spotted a solitary figure on the road. Though the image shimmered in the sun's haze, something in the traveler's posture evoked a memory that began to swim up through the years. Squinting, I saw a man, bearded and clothed in a tunic like those the Israelites favored. He moved with a stalking, purposeful intent in his step, and long braids hung over his shoulders. When he lifted his arm and I glimpsed a bare shoulder, I realized I'd spotted Samson.

Alone and coming toward me.

I stiffened. The one person I'd been hoping to see and I'd done nothing to prepare for him. This was my opportunity, perhaps my only chance. If I wanted to enlist Samson's help, I'd have to hold his attention for more than a few hours. All the stories I'd heard about him had convinced me of one thing—the door to his heart was approached through his eyes. The Israelite strongman enjoyed beautiful women. I was not looking forward to seducing a virtual stranger—Achish had destroyed my desire for intimacy with any man—but if I needed to dress in my finest to win justice for my mother, I would do what had to be done.

"Yagil!" I shrieked my son's name and nearly melted in relief when he appeared on the porch. "Run into the woods and catch us some rabbits for dinner."

"Rabbits?" A wide gap-toothed smile crossed his face. "Can I make a trap?"

"Make whatever you like. Just search until you find one, but be home by dinnertime. Take the dog with you."

He paused only long enough to grab a ball of string, then off he went. I didn't expect him to catch anything, but the quest would keep him occupied for hours.

I darted into the house, yanked off my veil, and shimmied out of my spattered workday tunic. I reached for a new garment I'd been saving for a festival day, a blue garment made of the softest, most fluid linen I'd been able to produce. I'd sewn gemstones around the plunging neckline so they would catch the eye and draw attention to my shape. No mere cord would do for a belt; I reached for a linen strip as soft as a leaf, then tied it around my waist. I kicked off my scuffed sandals and slid my feet into leather shoes with glittering stones on the straps. If Samson happened to look down, he would certainly notice my shapely feet.

I lifted the widow's looking brass and studied my reflection. My skin was clear and smooth, my lips still moist and full. I applied a layer of kohl across my upper eyelids, pinched my cheeks, then blew a kiss for luck to the image in the brass. At the last moment I grabbed a veil so I wouldn't look quite so much like a roadside harlot.

With my heart thudding beneath my breastbone, I stepped onto the porch and went to the edge of the shade. I could see the traveler clearly now—Israel's strongman was walking toward the well.

I moved toward the gate, determined not to let him get away this time. He slowed his pace when he saw me, then glanced right and left as if I might be part of a trap. I was, but this trap had not been set by Philistines.

I passed through the gate, then pulled up the rope at the well. "Greetings, Samson." I dipped a gourd into the bucket and offered it to him. "Thirsty?"

His gaze lingered on me for a moment before settling on the gourd in my hand. "Thank you."

While he drank, I stepped back and studied him. His sandals were dirty and well-worn, so I would offer to wash his feet, and his tunic was of short wool. Linen would be more comfortable in this heat.

"Samson . . ." I deepened my smile and boldly met his gaze. "If you will come into the shade, I will wash the dust from your feet. Then I will give you a tunic of fine linen that will be much cooler as you travel."

He lowered his gourd and looked at me with a glint of humor in his eyes. "What about the cold nights, when a man needs warmth?"

Was that a flirtation?

I considered a saucy answer, then thought of Achish and quickly changed my mind. "If you are cold, I will give you a woolen garment that is thin enough to fold into a satchel." I regarded his current garment with a sad expression. "I'm afraid you are thread-worn and hopelessly out of style. Let me serve you, please. It's the least I can do for the strongman of Israel."

My invitation wavered on the air, and for a moment I was sure he would thank me and move on. But, true to his reputation, Samson returned my smile and gestured to my work area. "You have something to fit me?"

"If not, I will make a tunic for you." In the same way a spider draws a fly, I led the way to my loom. "There's only one problem— you'll need to stay until I have time to complete it. Have you some great need to rush away?"

His eyes were as dark and powerful as the man who owned them, and they focused on my face. "No reason," he said, following me into the shade. "But it would not be good for me to encounter Philistines out here in the open."

"Then I will warn you." I gestured toward the road. "Working at my loom, I can see anyone approaching from the east. If I say, 'Samson! The Philistines are coming,' you should run behind the house and hide in the wilderness." I stepped closer to him and lifted my chin, so close that my lashes stroked his nose. "Do you think that warning would suffice?"

One corner of his mouth rose in a half smile, then he gently took hold of my upper arms. His touch was so soft, so different from what I had known with Achish, that my pulse pounded in my ears.

"Who are you?" he asked, his beautiful eyes searching my face. "Have we met? And what have you done with the widow who lives here?"

"We met once . . . a long time ago." I returned his smile in full measure. "And I am neither your kinswoman nor your enemy. I am from Cush and Crete, but this way station has been my home for years. I am aligned with no particular people, and I belong to no one but my little boy, Yagil."

His brows rose. "Your son has a Hebrew name?"

"Bestowed by the widow who used to live here. Yagil and I will forever be grateful to her for taking us in."

I stood silently, afraid to move too quickly, while his gaze fell to the smooth expanse of my neck and bosom. I think he liked what he saw, but I was caught up in the vitality he radiated like the sun.

"Your name?" he asked.

"Delilah," I answered, my heart hammering in my ears. I moved toward him, compelled by my own interest, then tiptoed my fingers from his chest to his chin. Smiling, I tugged on the fabric at the opening of his tunic. "Off with this, Samson, so I can outfit you in something more comfortable."

He smiled again, and I liked the curve of his mouth, the brilliance of his eyes, and the gentleness of his hands.

Risking everything on the sincerity of that smile, I took his hand and led him into the house.

Chapter Twenty-Five

SAMSON

AFTER BEING MEASURED and told to make myself comfortable amid baskets of fabrics stacked nearly to the ceiling, I sat on the mattress—one of the only available surfaces—then stretched out to relax. I rolled onto my side and propped my head on my hand, intrigued by the woman who had entranced me with a single look. Glancing around the house, I saw proof of Delilah's story everywhere—the rough toys on the floor, the tools of her trade on the porch, half-finished tunics hanging from pegs in the wall. And I had known the widow, a righteous woman who would not have tolerated an evil influence in her home.

I hadn't remembered that a young woman was living with the widow. I was thinking of other things as I approached the well, frustrating thoughts about the Philistines and Adonai's purposes. I looked up, expecting to see the old woman, and saw a vision instead—a young beauty, tall and slender, with skin the color of the river after a heavy rain. She wore a veil, like most modest women, but riotous dark curls escaped it, framing her face and emphasizing her dark eyes.

Of course, I suspected a trap. I looked around, certain I would see shadows on the ground or hear the nicker of hidden horses, but all remained silent.

The beauty had walked forward, looking directly at me, a smile softening her features. "Greetings, Samson," she said in a voice filled with good humor. "Thirsty?"

I looked down and made some sort of reference to the well. In truth, I don't know what I said; I only know that I was besotted from that moment.

"You live alone now?" I asked later, testing her.

She was folding fabrics near the door, and one of her lovely brows flickered as she turned to face me. "Yes—except for Yagil and the dog. The widow died after our return from Etam." A weight of sadness overshadowed her face. "We still miss her."

The mention of Etam triggered something in my brain, but it took a moment for the thought to surface. "Why were you at Etam?"

She smiled, her gaze as soft as a caress. "I had gone in search of you, Samson. Given my situation, I knew I needed a champion. The widow and I could think of no one better than you."

She seemed honest, and not once had she hesitated when I asked about her past. Few women of my acquaintance were as open, and most had a hidden agenda of some sort. But if this woman had a secret, I had yet to discover it.

"Why do you live alone here?" I pressed. "A woman alone is in a precarious position, for danger lurks everywhere, especially in these times."

"I didn't choose to live alone." She took a handsome blue tunic from the wall and ran her hand over it as if evaluating the garment's texture. "But then the widow died, so what choice did I have? I am not an Israelite, so I would probably not be welcomed in one of their villages. I am not Philistine, so even if I could forget the past, I would not feel at home in one of their cities. So I stayed, begging the gods to send someone who might alleviate my loneliness."

"What gods?" I asked.

Her brows flickered. "Any who would listen."

"And whom did you beg the gods to send?"

"Someone"—a dimple appeared in her cheek—"who would want to stay."

The answer, honest and pleasing, made me smile.

"So you belong nowhere . . . and to no tribe," I said, summing up what I'd felt for years.

"Maybe I belong everywhere." Her eyes twinkled with mischief, giving me hope. This woman, a blend of land and sea, north and south, Cushite and Cretan . . . maybe she was the solution to the riddle of my life. I also belonged to a tribe of one, but perhaps my tribe could be expanded. . . .

I exhaled a sigh, rolled onto my back, and laced my fingers across my chest. In the close quarters of the small house I could smell the perfumed oil in her hair, and my fingertips ached to dance over her soft skin. We had already spent hours talking and had shared a simple dinner of bread and goat cheese. When her young son came home, the boy had gaped in surprise to find me wearing one of his mother's colorful robes.

"This tunic you want to make me," I said, speaking to the ceiling, "how long would it take to weave?"

"Do you promise not to burst the threads by flexing your arms?" Her smiling face slid into my field of vision. "I will not make you anything if you intend to destroy it."

"No sleeves," I suggested, reaching out to catch her hand. I pulled her to my side. "So how long would it take?"

She propped her elbow on my chest. "A week," she said, bending low. "Maybe a month. Or, if you want to stay longer, I could stretch the work to fill a year or more."

I caught her head and gently kissed her, amazed to have found such a treasure on the side of the road.

Chapter Twenty-Six
DELILAH

SAMSON POINTED toward the pot of porridge I had pulled from the fire. "More, please."

"More?" I lifted my brows, feigning surprise. "I thought you didn't like my cooking."

"I never said that," Samson answered, his cheeks stuffed with bread. "I said you might want to brush the sand off the loaf the next time you pull it from the fire."

I grimaced. I *had* forgotten to break the sandy crust off the little loaves. But not wanting to admit defeat, I picked up a bit of the offending crust and tossed it at Samson, hitting him squarely between the eyes. The bread bounced off his wide forehead and then hit Yagil, who tipped his head back and howled with delight. Soon we were all whooping with laughter, setting off the dog, who danced in our merriment and barked in happy confusion.

As my laughter died down, I couldn't help wondering why life couldn't consist of a series of such happy moments. If I could forget my past, forget Achish, then Samson, Yagil, and I could be happy forever. But no matter how badly I wanted to, I couldn't forget my tortured past without forgetting the lessons that had formed me. And Samson seemed to love the woman I was.

I told him my story the first day he stayed with us. I told him that I thirsted for justice. But I didn't press him to confront Achish on my account because I wanted him take on my cause out of love, not obligation.

I didn't intend to fall in love with him. I liked him from the start, for he was clever and funny and oddly naïve in his straightforward approach to life. He moved into my heart as easily as he moved into my house, and once he arrived I realized how utterly lonely I had been. He did not demand, nor did he ever threaten me with his extraordinary strength. He was never abusive or cruel, and he did not take pleasure in humiliating me.

But I didn't fall in love with him because of what he *didn't* do.

I fell in love with the things he *did*. While I worked and went about my routine, Samson played with Yagil, brought in fish and meat for our dinner, and crawled through my flax field on his knees, gently pressing seeds into a furrowed row. In a few short weeks he had become my right hand and my delight. Unlike Achish, Samson wanted to give, not take, and protect, not threaten. Achish had made me feel dirty and worthless, but Samson convinced me that I was beautiful and worthy of being cherished.

Yet Samson did not cherish me alone. He seemed to have a special fondness for Yagil, and though I didn't expect him to devote time and attention to the boy, he behaved as though Yagil were the most amazing child in the world. He reserved a special lopsided smile for the lad, and every night when Yagil lay down to sleep, Samson sat by his pallet and told him stories of floods and animals and the creation of the earth. I was fairly certain that Yagil had heard many of the same stories from the widow, but Samson told them with dramatic pauses, artful voices, and grand gestures. Yagil would listen, his eyes glittering with fascination, and when Samson finished, my son would roll over and go to sleep without even a tiny complaint.

By the time Samson had lived with us for a month, I felt as though we'd known him for years. And I knew he would protect Yagil and me from any danger on earth. I thought he might even risk his life to defend the dog.

Without any sort of formal arrangement or discussion, Samson and I made a home together. I did not bring up the subject of marriage, for I understood that Samson had his own store of bad memories. He did not look backward—a discipline I had not mastered—but he taught me to accept each new day with joy and gratitude. We lived in the moment and created a happy family in the widow's little house.

But in our innermost hearts, I think we both knew it couldn't last.

⚜

One day Yagil called us out to the flax field where he'd been puttering for days. He pointed to something hanging from a tree, and after a moment, I saw a net loosely woven from flax fibers. The net hung from a low branch, and inside the net something brown and furry was moving.

"What is it?" I asked, almost afraid to hear the answer.

"A fat rat." Yagil grinned. "I caught him."

I opened my mouth, about to tell him that the rat would soon chew his way out of the net, but Samson threw me a warning glance and interrupted. "A fine net, Yagil. You'll have to show me how to weave such a thing. Maybe we could use it in a creek and catch a fish."

I blew out a breath, watching in silence as Yagil scampered off, leaving his prize in the tree. When he was a good distance away, I turned to Samson. "I was only going to point out the obvious. That rat will be free by sunset, if not sooner."

"So he will. But isn't it better to encourage the boy's skills? He will learn about rats soon enough."

"Better he learn about rats now, before he weaves another useless net."

"He's a child, Delilah. Let him enjoy his innocence."

I pressed my lips together and watched my son run with his dog, both of them completely free from worry or fear. But I knew our enemies waited like rats, and one day they would find us.

We lived out in the open—a good thing, Samson said, because we could see the enemy coming. A bad thing, I countered, because the enemy could see us just as easily.

We were careful, of course. With my loom turned to face the road instead of the house, I could look through the threads and see approaching travelers without having to leave my stool. Never had I been so wary of visitors. We knew that if anyone discovered Samson living in such an accessible spot, the Philistines would be on us before we could grab a walking stick.

Samson and I decided to conceal his whereabouts even to his own people. Rumors were likely to reach his enemies, so we decided it would be safer if not even the Israelites knew where Samson was living. Day by day we maintained our contented conspiracy, keeping everyone but Yagil out of our lovely cocoon. And night after night I found myself content and safe in his arms.

When I lay in his embrace, I couldn't help thinking about the Philistine woman from Timnah. She had dared to love Samson, and she'd been burned alive. If I continued to love this man, would the same sort of fate await me?

I wondered if Samson thought about Achish as he drowsed on the edge of sleep. I certainly did, and never had thoughts of him infuriated me more. I should have been the most secure woman

in Palestine, but Achish was a continual threat to my family and
my happiness.

If the Philistines found us, Achish wouldn't hesitate to kill me,
but his reason would have nothing to do with enforcing the law
of the Philistines. He would kill me simply because he hated me,
just as he hated Samson. Achish hated anyone who threatened his
superiority.

One day when I'd come back from gathering bundles of flax, I
called for Samson and he didn't answer. My pulse quickened as I
ducked into the house, but I only saw Yagil napping on his pallet
with the dog beside him. I ran back outside and called "Hello!" as
loudly as I dared, but no one answered.

I ran out to the road to scout east and west, then I heard a nick-
ering behind me. I whirled in time to see Samson enter the gate,
a young goat in his arms. Sweaty and smiling, his mood did not
match mine.

"Where were you?" I demanded, my face growing hot. "I thought
you'd left us. I thought something had happened to you—"

"Woman, get ahold of yourself." He released the kid, then strode
toward me. "Come sit."

I would have argued, but I was too upset and didn't want to cry
in front of him. So I sat.

Samson sat crossed-legged in front of me, so close our knees
touched. "Delilah"—he caught my hand as his eyes searched mine—
"how could I leave you?"

"Easy," I sputtered, my voice cracking. "You could walk out as
easily as you walked in." I pulled my hands free to push my hair
away from my face, then I turned my head, not wanting to see what
I was certain to lose.

He caught my wrists and held both of them firmly. The touch
of his hands, the pressure of his fingers, only added to my frustration when I could not free myself. A cold shiver spread over me

as I remembered another man holding me in the same way. With a shudder of vivid recollection, I closed my eyes and saw Achish's face, heard his voice, smelled his perfumed oils. Then fear churned my soul, and I panicked. Because I couldn't free my hands, I kicked and screamed as tears rolled over my cheeks—

Samson released me immediately. I scrambled away, curled into a tight ball, and peered at him through tear-clogged lashes. What had I just done?

"Delilah." Regret and sorrow deepened Samson's voice. "I'm sorry."

I closed my eyes again, and after a long moment I finally gained control of my emotions. "I'm the one who should be sorry," I told him, my voice as ragged as my feelings. "You did nothing wrong. It's just . . . Achish used to restrain me like that. I thought I had put the worst of the memories behind me, but it all came rushing back. I'm so sorry."

Samson sat silent and still, his forehead knit in puzzlement, and I knew he was afraid to touch me. What if he set off some other memory?

So I went to him, sat in his lap, slipped my arms around his neck, and buried my face in his throat. His arms surrounded me and held me close to his heart.

When we pulled apart, he used his thumb to wipe tears from my cheeks. "I couldn't leave you if I wanted to." A look of helpless appeal filled his eyes. "How could I? I know when you breathe in and out. Twenty paces away, I can tell when a sneeze is tickling your nose."

"Hush," I said, my heart too raw to be charmed. "Be serious. This is a dangerous life we've chosen. We take a risk each time we step away from the house. If we grow careless for even a moment, anyone could stop here and find you. They would run to the Philistines, who would tell Achish. But I can't allow Achish to find me, Samson, and I can't have him knowing where you are. . . ."

I tried to control myself, but my chin trembled and my eyes filled again. Samson saw the tears and kissed them away. "Sweet Delilah, you worry too much." He let me weep for a moment, then held me as though he could protect me from the world.

When I finally stopped crying, he released his grip and pulled away to look at me. "I will never leave you," he promised, his eyes shining with a light I'd never seen in a man's eyes. "You are the only woman who understands who I am. I will not let anyone separate us, ever."

I pressed my hand against his chest and felt the powerful drumbeat of his heart. "I believe you," I whispered, placing my lips just above his.

CHAPTER TWENTY-SEVEN
SAMSON

DAYS MELTED INTO WEEKS, and weeks into months as my time with Delilah passed. On warm afternoons, while she worked at her loom and the road appeared empty of travelers, Yagil and I went hunting. The boy loved to follow in my footsteps and crouch behind me as we waited for a hare to cross our path. We hunted badgers and rabbits and jackals, and once I even killed an old lion while the boy watched, his eyes wide.

I had my own reasons for hating the Philistine who fathered Delilah's child, but Yagil was a sweet-natured lad, not given to complaining or laziness. He had learned to entertain himself, so he was rarely underfoot, but preferred to play outside—sailing little boats in the irrigation trenches or exploring the area with his dog. I was happy to take him deeper into the wilderness and help him learn what a boy needed to know.

One afternoon we tracked a rabbit that seemed to lead us in

229

circles, then we paused beneath a shelter of oaks to rest. We were only a short distance from home, but I thought Yagil might like to avoid the stuffy house and nap outside, so I spread my cloak on the ground and offered it to him. "You might want to lie down and take a rest."

"I'm not tired," he said, sitting on my cloak, legs bent, back straight. He shot me a curious look. "What are you going to do?"

"Think," I told him. "I want to think up a verse for your mother."

His nose crinkled. "What do you mean?"

"Something like . . ." I closed my eyes. "She rose at dawn . . . and dropped her eyes upon—"

"You can't drop your eyes." Yagil frowned in stern disapproval. "They're stuck in your head."

"Unless you are careless." I held up a warning finger. "I knew a man who lost an eye when he ran into the path of a slingshot. That's why you should always be very careful."

Yagil's eyes went round. "Could he still see?"

"Aye, he had one eye left. But after that he didn't want to hunt anymore." I closed my eyes again. "She rose at dawn and dropped her gaze upon the bed where we last slept."

"Better." Yagil grinned. "But why isn't she looking for breakfast?"

"Because she isn't hungry." I reached over and ruffled his hair. "Now be quiet while I learn this verse—I didn't bring parchment for writing." I looked at a tree and recited the line again: "She rose at dawn and dropped her gaze upon the bed where we last slept."

"Thinking," Yagil said, stretching out on my robe, "is hard work."

I chuckled. "That it is. Now, what else do I want to say about your mother?"

"She makes good stew," Yagil suggested, his eyelids drooping.

"I will have to use that. Might be perfect for the second line." I glanced over at him again and saw that the fringe of his lashes had lowered. He was asleep. Finally.

I sighed and contemplated my verse, but my attention wandered in the rare silence. What was I doing in this place? Though I had fallen in love with the woman and her son, I did not believe I would fulfill my destiny in the Valley of Sorek. Adonai had not sent His angel to my parents to announce that I would fall in love with Delilah.

I lifted my eyes to the wide horizon as memory brought a twisted smile to my face. The angel of Adonai told my mother I would begin to deliver Israel from the Philistines, and what had I accomplished so far? Not much. I'd killed thirty in Ashkelon, a handful in Timnah, and a thousand in Lehi. But the Philistines had not gone away. My strikes against them had only resulted in more suffering for Israel, so how was I supposed to deliver my people?

"There you are." I glanced over my shoulder and saw Rei coming along the path. "You are not easy to find."

"Maybe"—I kept my voice light—"I didn't want to be found."

"Ah, Samson." He chuckled. "I will always be able to find you." He dropped to the earth beside me, then jerked his thumb toward the sleeping boy. "Has he given you any trouble?"

I shook my head. "He's a nice lad. Easy to like."

"If only Israel were as compliant. I saw at least half a dozen statues of Baal on my walk." Rei wrapped his arms around his bent knees. "What are you doing out here?"

"Thinking."

"Of what?"

I shrugged. "I am supposed to begin to deliver my people from the Philistines, but my people don't want me to do anything for them. You remember what happened at Rock Etam."

"Your people are asleep. They will awaken at the proper time."

"Really? And who will wake them?"

Rei gave me an easy, relaxed smile with a good deal of confidence behind it. "Know this, Samson—Adonai never wounds His people without also making preparation for their healing. You were conceived when the Philistines arrived. You are the answer to their oppression."

"I'm glad you think so." I kicked at a pile of dirt near my feet. "I have accomplished nothing of significance."

"Shouldn't that judgment be reserved for HaShem?"

I had no answer for that, so I remained silent.

"Do you think you're the only one Adonai has prepared?" Rei continued. "Surely you've heard the stories about our high priest. A few years after you were born, Adonai answered another barren woman's prayer. She gave birth to a boy and consecrated him to Adonai, just as your mother did you."

I snorted. "I suppose he has also forsworn razors."

"Along with wine, yes. He lives in Shiloh and serves Adonai with extraordinary strength, though his strength is not like yours. Adonai will use both of you to free Israel. You may not see the end of the occupation, but you can trust that freedom for Israel is part of the Lord's plan."

"And Israel is the apple of HaShem's eye." I tilted my head and studied Rei, who rarely spoke so openly. "How do I know you're telling me the truth? You could be saying these things to lift my dour mood."

"And when have I ever done that?" Rei's grin flashed, dazzling against his olive skin. "Adonai does not whisper obscurities, Samson. He would not have told the people of Israel to seek Him if he could not be found. What He said, He will do, both for you and for the prophet in Shiloh."

The reminder that other men also shared the burden of leadership alleviated some of my distress. For years I had imagined myself alone in my task, but if Adonai was also using another man with long plaited hair, maybe the responsibility wasn't as heavy as I feared.

I glanced at Rei. "This other Nazarite, has he won any victories?"

Rei gave me a small, tentative smile. "He doesn't count victories like you do. But do you remember when the army of Israel tried to throw off the Philistine yoke in the latter days of Eli the high priest?"

"I'd hardly count that a victory. Our people were slaughtered and the Ark of the Covenant stolen."

"Yet that is when the Nazarite Samuel became our high priest. When he was small, he learned how to listen for the voice of Adonai. He was our spiritual leader when the Philistines placed the Ark in Ashdod's Temple of Dagon."

I couldn't stop a smile. "I remember hearing about that. Dagon fell on his face before the Ark, and his hands and feet were cut off."

"Exactly. Samuel was praying during that time. Because the hand of Adonai moved against the people of Ashdod, they sent the Ark to Gath, but the hand of Adonai afflicted the people of that city, too. So they sent the Ark to Ekron—"

"And those people panicked." I grinned at the thought of the Philistines' fear. "My father knew one of the men who was in the field when the Philistines sent the Ark back to us."

"Didn't he feel a deep and abiding joy when the Ark returned to Israel? Didn't you?"

I looked at Delilah's sleeping son, then sighed. "I'm afraid I gave little thought to Philistines in those days. I was more concerned with crops and flocks."

"And women." Rei chuckled. "You have always been a man with—"

"An eye for beautiful things," I finished. "Surely there's nothing wrong with appreciating God's glorious creations."

"Not as long as those glorious creations are yours to appreciate," Rei countered. "You should be more careful. Some women are like suckerfish. If you catch one, there are sure to be ugly things attached. Consider your present woman—"

"Keep Delilah out of this." I lifted a warning brow. "She is beautiful in every way."

"Really?" He gave me a bland look, with only a twitch of his eye to reveal that he knew he was treading dangerous ground. "Can you see into her heart? Do you know the sort of person she is beneath that lovely exterior?"

"I know her," I insisted. "I have lived with her for months, and I know her."

"Really? Tell me about her."

I frowned at him, skeptical of the motivation behind his request, but his expression remained open and guileless.

"Delilah," I began, "is as courageous as any man I've ever met in a fight. Once she decides to do or make something, she sets to work with fierce determination, not quitting until she's reached her goal."

"Fierce determination," Rei said. "How feminine."

I ignored his jibe. "In quiet moments," I went on, "if she's talking to me or the boy, she can be sweetness itself. The veneer of determination falls away, and I see a young woman who is struggling to rise up from the ashes of loss. But she loves me. With all my flaws, she loves me completely."

"Ah, Samson." Rei's squint tightened. "If woman is man's greatest help, she is also his greatest danger."

"What do you mean?"

"I think you can figure that one out." He tilted his head. "Here's another riddle for you. What do you get when you squeeze a lemon?"

I blinked, surprised by the riddle's simplicity. "Lemon juice."

"I'm afraid not." Rei stood. "When you squeeze a lemon, you get whatever is inside. So make sure she loves you as much as you love her."

"What do you mean?"

He gave me a knowing smile. "And I thought you were the puzzle master."

Chapter Twenty-Eight

DELILAH

I shifted my basket to my other hand and paused before I climbed the sandy hill. I could hear Samson's voice echoing among the rocks beyond, so apparently he and Yagil had decided to stop for a rest. I took a step, then halted again when I heard my name.

"Keep Delilah out of this. She is beautiful in every way."

Who was Samson talking to? Yagil was supposed to be with him, but Samson wouldn't speak of me as "Delilah" in a conversation with my son. I tilted my head and leaned closer to listen.

"I have spent a lifetime waiting for her. She holds my heart."

I traveled another five steps up the hill, more curious than ever. Had Samson run across someone from Zorah?

I lowered my basket and took a moment to smooth my hair and adjust my veil. I wouldn't want to appear unkempt in front of Samson's neighbors.

I took another step, then frowned when I heard Samson speak again.

"Of course, I love the lad, too. He's a good boy."

I lifted my chin and marched ahead, eager to satisfy my curiosity. I climbed to the top of the hill and spotted Samson below, at the base of the slope. Yagil lay beside him, stretched out on Samson's cloak.

"Samson!" I pasted on a smile and ducked beneath the low-hanging branches of an terebinth tree. "I can't believe I found you. I thought you and Yagil might be hungry after your long hunt." I glanced around, searching for whomever Samson had been addressing, but saw no one.

"I'm always hungry." Samson grinned and reached for my basket. "You've thought of everything. Bread, olives, dried beef—"

"Who were you talking to?" I'd meant to be more discreet, but the question popped out of my mouth before I could stop it.

"Hmm?" Samson halted, a loaf of bread in his hand.

"As I came over the hill, I heard you talking. Who was here?"

"Oh." Samson chuckled and broke the small loaf in half. "My servant, Rei. He doesn't come around much because he doesn't exactly approve of—" Samson pointed to me, then to himself—"you know. But he brings me news every now and then."

"He doesn't approve of us?" I sank to the ground between Samson and my sleeping son. "Why does he object to me?"

"Rei is very devout." Samson tore at the crusty bread with his teeth, then chewed. "But sometimes he makes no sense at all."

Perplexed, I turned to look behind me. Nothing stirred beyond the trees. I glanced past Samson and Yagil; again, I saw nothing. I studied the thin layer of sand where we sat, but I saw no evidence that anyone else had been near the place. I saw only two sets of footprints, one small, one large.

I turned back to Samson, who had begun to eat the olives. "How long have you known this—this servant?"

"All my life." His lips curled in a one-sided smile. "Ever since I can remember, Rei has been around."

"You've never mentioned him."

"Like I said"—he popped another olive into his mouth—"he doesn't exactly approve."

I made a small sound of dismay and looked around again. Nothing and no one. "Well," I said, kneeling next to Yagil, "the next time Rei comes around, invite him to stay for dinner. I would love to meet him."

Samson grinned as I gently shook Yagil awake.

⚜

A few months later, a man and his wife came from the road and tied their donkey to a hitching post by the well. The husband slipped an arm around his red-eyed wife and brought her through the gate, asking if she could rest in the shade while he watered the donkey.

Samson remained in the house, out of sight, while I led the woman to a pillow, then bent to ask if she needed anything else. The woman, who was hugging her shoulders in a posture of grief, suddenly lowered her arms and began to sob. "He . . . took . . . my . . . baby," she sputtered, barely able to speak. Struggling to push the words out, she told me a story that made my blood run cold.

She and her husband had been traveling from Jerusalem to Ekron with their infant son. A Philistine captain on horseback stopped them and drunkenly demanded to know where Samson was hiding. When they replied that they didn't know anything about Samson, the soldier snatched the baby from its mother's arms, then gripped the feet and swung it, bashing the child's head against a rock.

As the woman wept inconsolably, my gaze went to her tunic, which was wet with milk and blood. I reached out to comfort her when Samson emerged from the house. I flashed him a warning look, but he ignored it and strode out to speak to the husband. I didn't realize what he was doing until he returned with a tiny body in his arms. He held a finger over his lips when he caught my eye, and with his free hand he pulled a rectangle of my finest linen from a basket. With his back to us, he cleaned the body, wrapped it in the linen, then secured the shroud with narrow strips. When he had finished, he knelt before the woman and offered the mother an opportunity to weep over her child, its dreadful wounds now artfully concealed.

The mother held the tiny body to her breast and keened, rocking back and forth, swaying beneath the weight of her sorrow. I stared at Samson and marveled. Had any man ever shown such compassion for a mother's grief? Perhaps, but I'd never seen anyone even come close.

The husband came in and fell to his knees beside his wife. Samson pressed his hand to the man's back. "Would you like to bury him here?"

The father's first inclination was to say no—I saw it in his eyes. But then he must have thought of the road ahead, of the hours he and his wife would pass with the dead child. The father dipped his chin in a slow nod.

Just minutes later, Samson and I stood with the couple beside a small grave. The father recited a prayer, and I embraced the wife. And while I stood there, watching Samson pray over the tiny boy who had barely even begun to live, a realization crashed into my consciousness like the surf hurling itself upon shore. Samson didn't know these people, but he was a well of compassion and kindness. He was demonstrating love, and they were receiving it, taking comfort from his words and generosity of spirit.

He had demonstrated that same love for Yagil, a boy unrelated to him who was, in fact, the son of a man Samson hated. But he didn't care who Yagil's father was; instead he showered my son with attention and affection, just as the widow had.

Couldn't I do the same? Since the widow's death, I had been

wondering how I could compensate for Yagil's loss of the woman who loved him unconditionally, then Samson had appeared and lavished all kinds of love on the boy.

Why couldn't I do the same thing?

I could not forget who Yagil's father was, but I could stop blaming the child for being Achish's son. If I was going to be a proper mother, I would have to love my son like the widow did, like Samson did.

I shifted my attention to Yagil, who stood in front of Samson, his feet set apart at the same angle as Samson's, his little hands clinging to Samson's hands, which rested on Yagil's shoulders. I found myself studying Yagil's face, and as I looked at the combination of eyes and nose and mouth, that face no longer looked like Achish's. His eyes were slightly rounded, like mine, and his lips were full, like Mama's. His mouth rose at the corner, an imitation of Samson's lopsided smile.

Yagil's dark gaze connected with mine for an instant, then moved away, drifting off to safer territory.

Poor boy. Had I ever looked at him with love?

Samson finished his prayer, and the husband comforted his wife. They thanked Samson for what he had done, and I picked up the stone I'd selected as a grave marker. I placed it over the grave and took comfort from the thought of the baby lying next to the widow.

When the couple departed, I walked over to Yagil, wrapped my arms around my long-legged son, and hugged him so tightly he complained. Then I let him go, and through a veil of tears I watched him drop into Samson's lap.

That was okay. He wasn't accustomed to affection from me, so I'd have to be vigilant and not fall into my old habits. But if Samson could love my boy, surely I could.

"That particular Philistine captain has gone too far," Samson muttered, speaking as if Yagil would recognize Achish's name. "Adonai will surely punish him."

I barked a laugh. I loved and respected Samson, but I had not yet been impressed by his God. "What do you think your Adonai will do?" I asked. "Strike him on the road? Burn him with living fire?"

"I don't know." Samson's voice brimmed with confidence. "But HaShem will not allow his evil to continue forever."

One afternoon I was at my loom when I saw riders approaching— two riders on horseback accompanied by an iron chariot, which meant the passenger was a Philistine of high rank. I pursed my lips and blew a long, low whistle, the signal Samson and I had agreed on to warn of a threat on the road. Without turning, I heard the quiet creak of the door to the house and knew that Samson had hidden himself away.

The widow had always remained near the house whenever Philistine chariots appeared, so I forced myself to remain at the loom as the riders came on. Perhaps the Philistines would simply ride by. They may have come from Timnah or one of the closer villages, so they might not need to stop for water.

Ghost spiders crawled down my spine as the lead rider reined in his horse and turned toward the well. They were stopping.

I pulled my veil over my hair and hunched over the loom. The dog remained at my side, but his ears pricked to attention. Neither of the Philistine horsemen even glanced my way, but I gasped when I recognized the profile of the passenger in the chariot.

Achish.

My stomach dropped, and fear blew down the back of my neck. I could not remain; I ought to go inside. I slipped from my stool and turned on the ball of my foot, then halted when I heard a commanding voice. "Woman!"

With my heart in my throat, I pulled my veil over the lower half of my face. Maybe he wouldn't recognize me. After all, we had both aged six years, and I was no longer a thin girl. Holding my veil firmly in place, I turned toward the chariot and answered in the deepest voice I could manage. "Do you need something, sir?"

"Draw water for us."

Like a tree rooted to the earth, I stood motionless, pride struggling with common sense. The widow would have told me to obey so that the Philistines would soon be on their way, but pride wanted me to tell Achish to draw his own water. If he protested, I would laugh because I had created a life over which he had no control.

Then I remembered the woman with the dead baby and knew that the Philistines controlled everything.

As the riders dismounted and led their horses to the trough, I kept my veil over my face and suggested that *all* the riders lead their horses to water. "A walk will do you good," I said, speaking in my roughest voice. "And now, I have work to do."

Achish sputtered in indignation, but I turned and walked into the deepest shade of the porch and ducked behind a stack of baskets. I saw Achish say something to his driver. The man answered with a weary shrug, perhaps suggesting that it *would* feel good to walk around.

I remained out of sight until the Philistines mounted and rode away. I sighed as the chariot rumbled over the road, then relaxed and returned to the loom, grateful that I had avoided speaking directly to Achish.

When the door creaked, I turned to see Samson and Yagil. "Are they gone?" Samson asked, his eyes snapping.

"Yes." I blew out a breath and smiled. "All gone."

"Did they give you any trouble?"

"Not a bit." I crossed my arms, not wanting to worry Samson. "You can come out now."

"Good. We're going hunting." Samson patted the satchel in which he carried his slingshot. "Maybe we'll bring back a rabbit for dinner."

"Make it two rabbits," I said, giving the growing boy a smile that might have been slightly frayed. "My growing son needs meat."

I moved my beater to the rhythm of their retreating footsteps, then stopped to thread the shuttle with a different color. Once I had established the new thread, I ran the shuttle through and watched the road, alert for any signs of movement. A warm wind blew over the sand, creating a whirlwind that swayed over the road before disappearing. I had not seen many travelers that morning, and now I understood why. Who would want to travel with Philistines nearby?

I worked the loom, stopping occasionally to evaluate the new color, and hummed quietly, determined to maintain the illusion of peace. A warm kernel of contentment settled into the center of my chest because I'd met my enemy and fooled him, escaping unscathed. I had handled the situation without even having to call on Samson. Now, if only my jittery nerves would settle . . .

The dog, who had remained with me, let out a sudden low woof, then trotted away. I glanced around to see what had caught his attention, but saw nothing. He had probably spotted a mouse.

I reached for the shuttle and felt an iron hand clasp my wrist. I turned, heart pounding, and found Achish standing behind me. I snatched a breath, about to scream, but his free hand clapped over my mouth. Far braver than I used to be, I bit his finger, but Achish released my wrist and struck me, momentarily making my knees give way and the world go dark.

I did not faint, but when the world brightened and the earth resumed its proper place, I was on the ground. Achish was crouched behind me, one hand over my mouth, the other holding a bloody blade near my throat.

"It is good to see you again, Delilah," he whispered, his breath burning my ear. "Did you think I wouldn't recognize you? Those eyes of yours will give you away every time. I thought about taking you right away, but one of my companions thought subtlety would be more successful. So here I am, and now you are mine again." His voice was low but filled with a restrained menace all the more terrifying for its control.

I closed my eyes as fear and anger knotted inside my chest. Where was Samson when I needed him?

"I am actually delighted to find you here," Achish said, leaning forward so I could see him. "I have long needed cooperative eyes and ears in this region, and who would make a better spy than you? People stop here often, don't they? You could ask questions, and no one would think you anything but curious. So if you don't already know where Samson is, I'm sure you *will* know. It's only a matter of time."

A hank of dark hair fell into his eyes as he grinned at me. "So, *sister*, this is what we will do. I will visit you here every month, say, around the time of the full moon. If you cannot tell me where Samson is the next time I come, I will use you like I did in Gaza for, say—" he shrugged—"two or three days. If you cannot locate Samson by the *next* full moon, I will remain with you for a week. And if by my third visit you cannot tell me where to find Samson, I will punish you most severely, and then . . . I will kill you just as surely as I killed your dog."

He shifted, turning me until I saw the dog lying in a pool of blood at the back of the house. A horse stood there as well, which explained how Achish managed to return so quietly. He must have traded places with one of the horsemen farther up the road and then doubled back.

A scream rose in my throat, but I choked it off. Achish thrived on the fear of others, and I would not feed his thirst for power. I lowered my eyelids lest he glimpse the terror his touch aroused in me.

He removed his hand from my mouth, then swung around to

hold his blade just over my heart. "Have I made myself clear, Delilah? Look at me."

I opened my eyes. Despite my trembling limbs, somehow I found the defiance I had developed over the passing years. "I will do *nothing* for you!"

"Yes, you will." He squeezed my neck with his free hand, threatening to cut off my breath. "You will do everything I ask. If you run, I will find you and sell you at the slave market. The agent paid a good price for your mother."

Fury threatened to choke me. "Why do you seek the Israelite? You had him at Rock Etam, but you ran."

"You know nothing about Etam."

"I saw everything. Even if I were to present Samson trussed up like a chicken, how would that help you? He would break free of his bonds and strike you dead. Finding Samson will do you no good, not even if you bring a thousand men. Bring two thousand and two thousand will die."

I thought my retort would silence him, but Achish's smile broadened. "You don't understand." He lowered his voice and brought his forehead to mine, so close that I could smell his sour sweat. "I know I can't capture Samson in the usual way. What I want is his secret. Find the secret of his great strength so I can subdue him. If you accomplish your task, I will give you your life. Willingly."

"Wh-what secret?" I stammered. "He was born a strongman."

"He was *not*." Achish squeezed my throat. "Have you seen him? He is no giant, no warrior, and definitely no god. He is a man like any other, yet he can do things that should not be possible. Why is that?"

He tilted his head to study me, but all I could do was tremble. "Why do you want him? He hasn't done anything to you."

Achish smirked and answered, "Why do I want Samson? I'll tell you why. After my father died, I tried to live the life he'd lived—

merchant, businessman, friend to the ceren—and I discovered that my father's life didn't fit. The business went away, along with the wealth, the house, and the servants. So I decided to create another life, the one I'm enjoying now, and I discovered that it's better to be feared than respected, or even loved. People fear me even more than they fear their gods. Samson doesn't fear me . . . but he will."

"I don't think so." I pulled away. "They say his strength comes from his God."

"The invisible God of the Israelites?" Achish's voice turned to pure rage. "If that God is so strong, why are his people so weak? No! Samson's strength definitely has a source, be it potion or talisman or spell. I want you to find Samson, go to him, and use your womanly wiles to discover the source of his strength. Destroy it, if you can. Then the strongman will be as weak as anyone else."

Finally he released me and stood straight, his eyes lazily raking my form. "By the crust between Dagon's toes, you are still a beautiful creature. I have no doubt that you are up to the task." He slipped his blade into his belt. "By the way, your maid—what was her name?"

His expression made my blood run cold. "Has something happened to Zahra?"

"That's it. Zahra." He snapped his fingers, then gave me a polished smile. "Zahra took your place in my bedroom, but she lasted only a month or so. She didn't have your stamina."

He turned and walked away while I remained in a silent huddle on the ground, too frightened to open my eyes lest I see him again.

Some time passed before I heard the sound of footsteps. The shivering at my core resumed, especially when the footsteps quickened. I was about to scream, but when I finally looked up, Samson was staring down at me.

"Delilah?" He crouched before me, alarm lighting his eyes. "What happened here?"

I rose on unsteady legs and clung to him. Then I heard Yagil scream . . . he had found the dog.

Samson's eyes remained focused on me. "Are you all right?"

"Go to Yagil. I'm fine."

Samson looked at me with those dark, watchful eyes that missed nothing. "What's wrong?"

I pushed at his arm. "Please, tend to the boy."

He nodded and raised his voice to tell Yagil he was coming.

As he hurried away, I pressed my hands over my face and struggled to come up with a believable lie. How was I supposed to explain my terror and a dead dog? If I told Samson about Achish's threats, Samson would run off to kill more Philistines, but that wouldn't help. Nothing short of killing Achish would solve my problem, but I didn't know where to find him. And I would not risk Samson's life by sending him off on a vain search. . . .

"What happened here, Delilah?" Samson was back again, his voice firm and his eyes burning.

"The dog," I whispered, "I think . . . I heard a sound like a wild animal, so I crouched down by the loom to hide. Will you clean up the mess?"

Samson straightened, his eyes gleaming dark and dangerous in the fading light. He had to know I was lying, but I couldn't tell him the truth. If Achish heard even the slightest rumor linking me with Samson, he would return with an army. By the time Samson found Achish, he might have ten thousand men, and not even Samson the strongman could take on so many, especially in an open area like this.

"I'll take care of the dog and the boy," Samson said, "while you decide if you want to tell me the truth."

As he walked away, I reach for a pillow and hugged it as tears streamed from my eyes. What was I going to do?

Achish knew where I lived. He would not give up; he would haunt me until he found Samson. And he would soon return to my house.

I stood, brushed sand from my tunic, and looked toward the back of the house. Yagil stood at our little cemetery, where Samson was digging a grave next to the stone over the travelers' baby. Samson was comforting Yagil, assuring him of something that seemed to ease my son's pain.

Oh, Samson. Anguish flooded my heart as I watched him. Our time together was coming to an end, and apparently I alone realized it.

⁂

For several days I imagined myself walking a road that ended with forking paths. Until Samson arrived, I had believed that I could remain in the widow's little house for the rest of my life, but I was beginning to see that a future with Samson was a foolish dream. Though he had become part of my family, we could never be happy as long as we lived in Philistia. Even if Samson hid himself every time people stopped at the well, eventually he would be spotted. He would leave his gigantic sandals out in the open, or his big voice would boom through the countryside as he crested the hill after a hunt. His enormous personality could not be hidden forever, and we lived under a regime that wanted his head on a platter.

I raked my hand through my hair, frustrated beyond belief. I wanted a life with Samson and I wanted Achish dead. How could I have both? I could ask Samson to find Achish and kill him, but what if Achish saw him coming? What if he set a trap from which Samson could not escape?

I stood at the edge of the porch and stared into the wilderness. What was I to do?

Achish had told me to find the secret of Samson's strength, and I had never seen any sign of an outward source. Samson kept insisting that his strength was a gift from God, and perhaps it was. But I had been at the wedding and at Rock Etam, and I had seen no lightning bolts or supernatural apparitions. I don't know how Samson killed those thirty men when he took their garments, but maybe he attacked drunken fools. And according to the men of Judah, at Etam Samson had positioned himself behind a narrow passageway so he could kill his enemies one by one. Adonai had not destroyed the Philistines' crops; Samson had spent days collecting jackals. And the story of the gates of Gaza was a mythical tale that grew more exaggerated with every telling.

Samson was strong and a devout believer in his God, but no man was invincible. If I sent Samson after Achish, I could be sending him to his death . . . and I loved him too much to do that.

Furthermore, while killing Achish might end the threat against me and satisfy my thirst for justice, it wouldn't keep the Philistines from hunting Samson. Some other Philistine warrior would appear on these roads, and Samson would have to hide every time we heard the sound of horses' hooves. The cerens of Philistia would not be happy until the Israelite strongman was dead. So long as Samson was part of my family, Yagil and I would never know peace.

If I did nothing, Achish would return and eventually he would find Samson. This time Achish would be smarter—he wouldn't send his men up a mountain or have them engage in hand-to-hand fighting. He'd reconnoiter the area and realize that Samson lived here. Then he'd send for archers and spear throwers and have them attack Samson as soon as he stepped out of the house. Sheer strength could do little to protect against the barb of an arrow or a well-aimed spear.

Maybe we should leave. We might move to one of the Jewish settlements, though moving would force us to meet people, any one of whom could be greedy for silver. I had watched the men from Judah parlay with the Philistines, so I knew Samson's kinsmen could not be trusted. Neither could we move to a settlement near one of the Philistine cities, for the Philistines spread gossip as easily as children spread sniffles. Within days Achish would know where we were.

We could move to Egypt . . . but Samson loved his people, and he wouldn't want to go so far from his parents. He was keenly aware of his position as a leader in Israel, and to remove him from his tribe would be like cutting the heart out of a thoroughbred racehorse. Samson wouldn't be himself if I led him away from this land, and he wouldn't be happy.

So what choices remained?

I sat at my loom and picked up the shuttle, then fingered the vertical threads. "Know your enemy," my mother once told me. "Know them so you can be prepared to survive them."

I knew Achish all too well. I knew what he loved—pleasure—and I knew what he hated—me. Samson. The Israelites. Anyone who had more power or resources or skill than he had.

A memory broke through the surface of my thoughts. The Philistine lords had promised 5,500 pieces of silver to anyone who captured Samson. Achish was doing everything he could to claim that reward, and he hoped to use me to win it. But what if someone else brought Samson in? What if, for instance, *I* did?

I looked into the distance, where the wind swept the dust along the side of the road. *Betrayal* . . . the word left a horrible taste in my mouth, and I wasn't blind to an obvious irony. I had despised the men of Judah for betraying Samson, but they hadn't acted to save themselves from the kind of abuse Achish intended for me. Most of them would never know that kind of humiliation.

So . . . what if I handed Samson over to the cerens instead of Achish? Achish was evil incarnate, but the cerens were practical rulers. In exchange for my cooperation, I would demand that they spare Samson's life, and they would listen to me. I had never forgotten the way men lost their reason when I dressed to appeal to a man's senses. . . .

I stared at my weave, imagining a scene on the threads. If I went to the Philistine lords and told them I could deliver Samson, I would defeat Achish on several levels. I would win the reward he coveted, forcing him to look elsewhere for silver to pay his debts. He would be humiliated if a mere woman succeeded where a commander of the Philistine army had failed, and the Philistine cerens would realize that he'd accomplished nothing in all the years he commanded the militia. I could testify to his cruelty and heavy-handed methods. The cerens would be so horrified by his evil that they'd remove him from his post.

I could ask that he be executed. Perhaps, finally, he would drink from a bitter cup of his own brewing, and I would win justice for my mother. I could accomplish all those things . . . if I betrayed my lover.

I searched the recesses of my mind for other ideas that might save Samson from the Philistines but came up with nothing.

If I *didn't* surrender Samson to the cerens, we would all likely die. And in the future, if by some miracle we managed to escape Achish's plot, any Philistine with a knife to my throat or Yagil's could force Samson's surrender. Love would disarm his strength every time. His marriage to the girl at Timnah had already proven the point. So long as Samson loved, he and his loved ones would be in danger.

Samson had intertwined his life with mine and Yagil's, and I could see no way to separate the threads without causing pain.

Sitting at my loom, I weighed the odds and made a decision. While I would love to live with Samson forever, I couldn't rest until I achieved safety for my son and justice for my mother. If I couldn't have those things *and* Samson, I would take safety and justice alone. Because I could not be happy knowing my enemy thrived while our lives were in constant peril.

Later that night, as I sat with Samson's head in my lap, I ran my finger over a line in his forehead. "Samson, if you were forced to leave me—"

"Impossible," he murmured, snaking his arm behind me to hug my hips. "I would not leave you, Delilah, no matter what. I have promised."

"But what if—" a lump rose in my throat and I struggled to push past it—"what if it became necessary for us to part? What if the Philistines were after you?"

"Let them come." He tilted his head back and looked at me with his big, compelling eyes. "I would defeat the entire world rather than let you go."

"What if I had to leave? What if Yagil and I—"

"Don't even speak of such things." He hugged me more tightly. "In all my wandering, Delilah, I never belonged anywhere until I found you. You understand me."

I tugged on one of the plaits of his hair. "Sometimes, old man, you speak nonsense."

He smiled. "I'm not the one talking about foolish things." He closed his eyes and let himself relax. "I love it when you play with my hair."

"Your braids need to be tightened. You look like a wild man."

"Tomorrow," he said, his voice husky with drowsiness. "Let nothing disturb us now."

I worked my fingers into the silky strands at the top of his head, knowing I would not always be able to comfort him.

Because Achish would soon return.

～❦～

Once I had decided to surrender Samson, I had to work out a way of delivering him to the cerens. I had never faced such a tough challenge—how could I bind Samson so he could be taken away?

My thoughts kept returning to Achish's conviction that Samson could be stripped of his strength. I had been living with Samson for months, and I'd never seen him do anything to receive or maintain his strength. Other than simple prayers, I'd not seen him perform any religious rituals. He didn't wear a talisman; he didn't chant spells. He didn't smoke plants or inhale ground powders. He *did* go outside to pray, but his prayers consisted of words, not rituals or dances or self-mutilation. If Samson's strength came from an outside source, I had no idea what it could be.

I shifted my gaze to the courtyard, where Yagil was opening the sluice and Samson was repairing the stone wall. Studying Samson's frame, I saw why Achish believed Samson's strength was supernatural. Nothing in Samson's appearance indicated that he might be stronger than any other man. He was not particularly broad across the shoulders or thick through the thighs. The only unusual thing about him was his hair, which he seemed to take inordinate pleasure in growing. It fell from his scalp in dark waves, which he wove into seven braids and tied together with a leather band. He'd worn his hair that way since childhood, he told me, because he could pull it back and keep it out of his way while hunting.

To all appearances, he was an ordinary man. He was a good hunter but not a good fisherman. His singing was tolerable, his step often a tad clumsy. He had a tendency to talk to himself, and he snored so loudly that I couldn't sleep without wool in my ears. His temperament was as bright as his name implied, and he had a knack for puns and riddles. He had beautiful eyes, rimmed with long lashes, and though he was no giant, he *was* unusually strong.

Was his supernatural strength a gift from his God? I was reluctant to credit Samson's victories to a divine source, because Adonai made no sense to me. If Adonai supplied Samson with strength, why hadn't he killed *all* of Samson's enemies? Why didn't Adonai cleanse the land so the Israelites didn't have to cower in fear of the Philistines? I simply could not reconcile Samson's beliefs with the reality of life as I knew it.

But if Samson's strength did not flow from Adonai, from where then did it come? Some men drew power from their convictions, and Samson certainly did. So I told myself he was strong because he believed in his causes. He killed thousands because he believed his God gave him the strength to kill thousands.

What would it take to kill his belief?

I shifted my gaze as Samson stepped into the shade, a stone in his hand. He looked around as if searching for something.

"Can I help?" I asked.

He stopped and scratched his head. "Mortar," he said. "I mixed some this morning."

I left my table and stood before him, then slid my arms around his waist. "Samson." I smiled up at him. "Have I thanked you for coming into our lives?"

He grinned down at me. "I'll keep forgetting the mortar if you keep welcoming me like that."

I kissed him, then pulled away and tapped the end of his nose. "I've been meaning to ask you . . . though you are the most handsome man I've ever met, you don't appear to be especially strong. Where does that fabled strength of yours come from?"

He lifted a brow. "So you love me for my strength?"

"I love you for you," I answered truthfully. "And I want to know all about the man I love."

His grin broadened as he leaned back and tightened his arms around me, lifting me off my feet.

"Put me down," I said, "and tell me your secret."

"That's easy." He set me on the ground, then lifted his hand and delicately pushed a stray hair from my eyes. "My strength comes from Adonai. When strength is needed, He empowers me."

"Your God empowers you." I gave him the same disbelieving look I gave Yagil when he claimed that a lion broke my waterpot.

"You don't believe me?"

"I believe you believe . . . but I find it hard to accept an invisible God."

"Do you love me?"

"Haven't I said so?"

"My love is invisible." He lowered his forehead to mine. "And you have no trouble believing in that."

"I see evidence of your love every day," I answered. "But your Adonai is more elusive—"

Samson bent to nibble my earlobe, but I playfully swatted him away. "You have a wall to repair," I reminded him. "So apply your strength to the wall, my mighty man."

He nodded and went out to work while I returned to my fabrics. But my throat ached with regret as I drew a deep breath and prepared for the most difficult task of my life. Before I could implement my plan, I would have to go to Gaza and present my offer to the cerens. If I didn't have their support before I acted, Achish could always claim that *he* had found Samson and I had nothing to do with the Israelite's surrender.

In the courtyard, Samson kicked an inflated cow's bladder and invited Yagil to join in the game. I clamped my eyes shut over a sudden rise of tears. If my plan was successful, we would not enjoy many more days like this.

As I set a pot of stewed rabbit before my family that night, Samson leaned on his elbow and gave me a curious look. "Is something on your mind?" he asked, studying my face. "You have been distant these last few days."

"Nonsense." I gave him a smile and passed the bread. "I was thinking about my weaving, that's all."

"And what do you think about?" He grinned at Yagil, whose round cheeks were stuffed with food. "Do you think as much as your mother?"

"I dfthik shek aldfkys tinks." The boy giggled at the silly sounds that came out of his overloaded mouth.

I had been thinking, of course, about my decision and its consequences. And at one point I realized that while the details of my
plan were crucial, I could never be at peace with myself unless the
motivation for it was appropriate.

"Samson," I said, propping my chin on my hand, "why did you
kill the thirty men in Gaza?"

His bushy brows lifted. "To get their garments, of course."

"Very practical of you. And why did you kill the Philistines at
Timnah?"

"You know why. They killed Kesi and her father."

"So it was revenge. The pursuit of justice."

"I suppose, yes."

"Why did you kill a thousand Philistines at Rock Etam?"

His frown deepened. "They were going to kill me."

"Self-defense, then."

"In a way."

"You killed them to prevent them from killing you."

"And others. That's a thousand Philistines who won't be murdering Israelite babies."

I nodded. I was about to implement my plan for the exact same
reasons.

I hoped Samson would understand.

Chapter Twenty-Nine
DELILAH

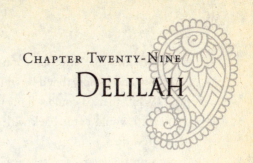

OVER THE COURSE OF THE NEXT SEVERAL DAYS, I gathered all the garments I had made and proceeded to finish them off in a style worthy of a well-dressed Philistine woman. I left fringes at the hem of the garments and sewed brilliant bits of rock around the hemlines. I embroidered elaborate patterns around necklines and sleeves and created stunning belts of the softest leather. I folded each garment carefully and inserted fragrant herbs into the folds. Then I packed them into baskets and stacked them on a table.

When I had finished, I set my proposition before Samson. "I have woven all these garments for the market at Gaza," I said, avoiding his direct gaze by pretending to examine the stitching at a tunic's neckline. "I would like to take them to market myself."

Samson brought his hand to his chin, and I knew he was figuring out a way to get me to the city. He'd insist on his plan if I didn't quickly offer an alternative.

"My friends, the three Gibeonite brothers, will be coming this way soon, and I know they'd be willing to escort me to the market-place. While there, I could sell my garments and trade for supplies we need. I would come back with the brothers, so I will only be gone a few days."

Samson frowned. "You talk as if you plan to go alone."

"I *am* going alone." I drew a deep breath and looked directly into his eyes. "I know you want to go, but Gaza would be dangerous for you. Furthermore, I need someone to watch Yagil. I can't take care of him and sell my wares at the same time. Please—will you stay with him? I need both of you to be safe, and I promise to be careful."

Samson's eyes narrowed as I held my breath, terrified that he had intuited my plan. He had come to know me well in the months we'd been together, and it wouldn't be the first time he'd appeared to read my mind.

But after a long moment he nodded, then held up a warning finger. "I must meet these brothers," he said, his eyes snapping. "I must meet and approve them before you go."

I exhaled on a tide of relief. "You will adore them." I moved closer and playfully tugged one of the plaits of his hair. "They saved my life, you know."

"Then I am sure I will like them." His arms went around me and drew me closer. "Since I owe them such a great debt."

Chapter Thirty
SAMSON

THE THREE GIBEONITE BROTHERS ARRIVED three days before the full moon. I stood in the shadows, remaining out of sight as they hailed the house, calling Delilah by name. Their boldness set me on edge, for who would be so familiar with another man's woman?

But I had not known Delilah last spring, so perhaps I should remain silent.

The leader, a tall man with a dark beard, brought the caravan inside the courtyard, then sat his camel and slid off the saddle. Delilah hurried forward to meet him, lightly embracing him and his two brothers, none of whom held her any longer than was proper. I pulled myself off the wall and was about to step out and meet them, but Delilah brought them into the shade of the porch. They stood in a straight line, blinking as their eyes adjusted to the light. Their mouths fell open when they saw me standing against the house.

The tallest one gave me a nod, then turned to Delilah. "You did not tell us that you had married."

Delilah smiled and linked her arm through mine. "Brothers, I'd like you to meet Samson, judge of Israel. He has been living with me for the past several months."

The trio blinked at this information as Delilah continued, "You have actually met him before—"

"I remember," the tallest brother said. He dipped his head again. "We were present at your wedding feast in Timnah. We did not, however, participate in the cheating."

"We didn't take any of the garments," the second brother assured me, lifting empty hands. "Not a one."

I uncrossed my arms and returned his acknowledgment. "The cheaters were Philistines, and Delilah assures me that you are not cheaters." I forced a smile. "It is good to see you again."

"It's terribly important that you don't breathe a word of Samson's whereabouts to anyone, no matter how insignificant they may seem," Delilah went on. "He has been safe here, and I do not want him harmed."

The middle brother stammered in apparent confusion. "I don't understand why the strongman stays here, out in the open—"

"The Philistines have spent years searching for him," Delilah interrupted. "And that brings me to the question I must ask you. Will you take me with you to Gaza? I have goods to trade, and I will not put Samson's life at risk for one of my errands. He is going to stay here and take care of Yagil while I'm gone. I'll be ready to leave as soon as you have sold your wool. Please, brothers, allow me to go with you and promise me that you will not share my secret."

The three men looked at each other, then gave their assent.

"Thank you." Smiling, Delilah moved to the straw mat, where she had already set out pillows and cups. "Please join us for a meal. I knew you would be coming, so for the last several days I've been preparing your favorite dishes. We have been eating so well that I'm afraid Samson is getting fat."

I shot a glance at her—was she teasing? She was probably trying to make her guests feel comfortable, but I wished she hadn't mentioned me.

The brothers turned toward the feast, but the shortest man kept glancing over his shoulder as if I made him nervous. I smiled, hoping to put him at ease, but my effort seemed to have the opposite effect. He jumped ahead of his brothers and took the far pillow, then sat facing me as if he wanted to keep me under surveillance.

Why was the fellow so nervous? Delilah had insisted that the brothers were harmless, righteous men, but now she seemed anxious, too. She brought a clay pot of meat and vegetables to the carpet and set it before us, but when she stood I saw that her hands trembled. I searched her face, and she purposely looked away.

Was she nervous about the journey? I reminded myself that she did not travel regularly, and I didn't think she had ever been parted from Yagil. Was that the reason for her apprehension?

I picked up a dried fig and chewed it thoughtfully as Delilah chatted with the brothers. She seemed especially bright and shiny, as if she had polished her veneer to hide a deep-seated flaw. She did not need to hide anything from me, so perhaps she was keeping a secret from the brothers . . . but what?

My thoughts drifted to Rei's confusing advice. He told me to be sure Delilah loved me as much as I loved her, but there were moments when I wondered if she loved at all. Sometimes, when she was working the loom or spinning flax, a distant expression occupied her face and hardness glittered in her eyes. In those moments I knew her thoughts were far away, wandering among people I had probably never met. For a woman who claimed to have shared her complete history with me, I counted far too many moments when she was not with me at all.

Was she dreaming of a former lover? Of her childhood home? Probably not, for pleasant memories would have brought a soft glow to her eyes, not the callous glint I saw so often.

"Samson?"

I took the small loaf of bread she offered, dipped it into the pot. Though I hoped all was well, something secret and significant seemed to be stirring beneath her beautiful features.

⌇⋇⌇

"Samson." Wearing her veil and cloak, Delilah turned to face me one last time. She pressed her hands to my chest and looked up into my eyes. "You know I hate to say good-bye."

Then why had she been so eager to leave?

I kissed her forehead. "Go, so you can come back. We will miss you."

My hand rested on Yagil's head, and she bent to kiss her son again. "Mama will be back in a few days. Be a good boy."

Yagil nodded and wrapped his arm around my leg.

Delilah took a step back, then turned to me again. "Samson"— her brow wrinkled with worry—"the full moon is coming. The Philistines increase their patrols around that time, and I wouldn't be surprised if one of them stopped here to inquire about you. Be extra careful, will you? Perhaps you should cover my work and make the place look deserted."

I glanced at her loom, which sat empty, as was the table that usually held her fabrics. "The place already looks abandoned," I pointed out. "Except for your cook fire."

"Smother it." She rose on tiptoe to give me another kiss. "And stay safe until I return. Perhaps you should camp in the wilderness."

I stared at her, still perplexed by her anxiety. "Are you worried? If you're worried, you don't have to go—"

"I'm not worried, but I've never left my son before. Leaving him feels . . . odd. Like I'm leaving part of my heart behind."

She knelt to give Yagil another kiss, then turned and strode toward the animals. The tallest brother helped her into the saddle, and the camel stood. The youngest brother grabbed the reins of the lead donkey, and away they went, heading west.

I waited until they disappeared from sight and then I scooped up the boy and held him so that we were eye to eye. "How would you like to visit Zorah?" I asked. "My mother and father live there, and I think it's time we enjoyed another woman's cooking."

Yagil laughed as I tossed him in the air and kicked sand onto Delilah's smoldering fire. My heart warmed. Perhaps her departure was a good thing. If I was going to be the man in Yagil's life, we needed to get to know each other better.

Taking time only to grab a cloak for myself and shoes for the boy, we set out and walked south.

CHAPTER THIRTY-ONE
DELILAH

THE JOURNEY TO GAZA PASSED UNEVENTFULLY, and within three days our caravan entered the city gates. We spent that first night in the marketplace, bedded down in straw near our animals, and the next morning we rose early. The brothers unloaded the wool and prepared for a busy day of barter while I pulled a special tunic from one of my baskets. I had woven this garment soon after the widow died, and it was by far the finest, most luxurious linen I had ever produced. I dyed it green to match my eyes, and though I'd only worn it once, Samson's reaction convinced me it was an especially effective choice.

I stepped behind a half wall, slipped out of the tunic I'd slept in, and pulled the tunic on. I ran a comb through my unruly hair and pulled it into a knot at the back of my head. As a finishing touch, I tugged some tendrils free to float around my face. I would not dress for modesty today; no veil would cover my hair.

The Philistines loved beauty, and Philistine men loved a long, exposed neck.

I pulled the widow's looking brass from the bottom of my basket and held it up. My reflection looked back at me, eyes narrow. *Why do you have to do this? You should stay at the market and focus on trading. When you've finished, you can go home to Samson and Yagil. You do not have to fear Achish because Samson will be with you, and he trusts in his God.*

I dropped the brass back into my basket and tossed a blanket over it. The girl in the reflection was less realistic than I. She had forgotten how it felt when Achish's hand clapped over her mouth. She had forgotten the nights of pain and humiliation and how she'd been forced to beg Adinai's servants for scraps of food. She'd forgotten what Achish did to her mother.

That girl was only a figment, not flesh and blood. She had no memory, but I did. My memory was long and elastic and it did not forget.

I slipped into my finest sandals, stepped out and thanked the brothers for displaying my garments alongside their wool. I promised to return as soon as I'd attended to an important errand.

I slipped away from the marketplace, stopping by a familiar fountain to get my bearings. I had washed here when I was frantically fleeing Achish, after I'd spent the night hiding in a boat. So much had happened since then and I had no idea what had happened in Gaza. For all I knew, all the ceren's daughters had married and were living with their husbands, but Sapha had implied that she was her father's favorite and he would be reluctant to let her go. I could only hope that she still resided in her father's household and that she would remember me.

Much had changed in the years I'd been away from the city. The massive Temple of Dagon had been completed, and it dominated the skyline near the docks. The structure was the tallest I'd ever

seen in my life, with half of the bottom floor left open to the sun.
The second floor featured a balcony that ran along three walls,
and a rooftop mezzanine topped off the section closest to the
street. A colossal statue of Dagon, half fish and half man, stood
before a solid wall at the head of the building, and I imagined
that Temple-goers on the roof could look directly into the statue's
wide eyes. From the street I could see men and women leaning
over the railing of the balcony. I suspected that they'd climbed
all those stairs not to show devotion to Dagon, but to enjoy the
best views of the city.

After wandering the streets and searching for familiar sights, I
finally found the ceren's house. The privacy wall had been beautifully covered with tiles painted in the colors of the sea, probably in
homage to Dagon. The unmistakable ornamental gate brought back
a shiver of recollection as I moved closer. This house was the last
place I visited with Adinai before he died and my nightmare began.

I held my breath and rang the bell. When the answering servant
asked what I wanted, I said I was a friend of Sapha's and wished
to speak to her.

"Come in," the servant said. I sighed in relief, grateful my hunch
had proved correct. The ceren's eldest daughter had not yet married.

I waited in the exquisite garden until Sapha came out to greet me.

"Yes?" She looked me up and down and then frowned, a question in her eyes.

"You don't remember me." I smiled at her, then took her hand
and held it. "We met at a banquet several years ago. I attended with
my stepfather and Achish, my stepbrother. You and your sisters were
quite taken with him."

A warning cloud settled over her features, and I had a feeling
Achish was no longer welcome in this household. But I hadn't come
here to discuss him.

"I think I do remember you." She gave me a careful smile and gestured toward a stone bench. "Would you like to sit a moment? Then I am expected somewhere else—"

I dismissed the bench with a wave that fluttered the fine fringe at my wrists. "I won't keep you. I'm visiting Gaza only for a few days, but I'd like to see your father."

"That is a beautiful tunic." Her eyes had not left the swaying fringe. "Where did you find it?"

"I made it." I pushed a bit of hair away from my face, setting the fringe in motion again. "I will be selling tunics in the marketplace for the next few days. But if your father will be home tomorrow, I'd love to bring you one—in blue, I think, to contrast with your brown eyes."

The color in her cheeks darkened as she smiled brighter. "Father will be home tomorrow. Come early and I will hold him here until you arrive. We will look forward to seeing you."

"Thank you."

My heart pounded as I left the house. One step taken, with many more to come.

                      ~⁂~

The next morning, before the sun had crested the neighboring homes, I rang the bell at the ceren's gate. A sleepy servant allowed me to enter, and one of Zaggi's younger daughters gaped at me as I followed the servant over the tiled pathway. Sapha was waiting and welcomed me with open arms, her eyes fastened greedily on the package in my basket. Smiling, I handed over the gift, then smiled as she opened it and shook out a lovely linen tunic with knotted fringe at the neckline, sleeves, and hem.

"Isn't it beautiful, Father?" She held it to her body and sashayed around the table where they were enjoying breakfast. "Have you seen such an elegant tunic in Gaza?"

He barked out a noncommittal response, then looked up and squinted at me. "Do I know you?" he asked, his nasal voice sharpening my memories of his banquet.

"You do, my lord ceren." I knelt and bowed my head, then straightened. "We met in this house several years ago. I had come with my stepfather, Adinai, and my stepbrother, Achish."

He coughed, leading me to wonder if his conscience troubled him. Then he looked at me again, his eyes watering as if his breakfast bread had stuck in his throat. "If you want to address an old grievance—"

"I've come, my lord, because I understand that the Philistines would like to take custody of an Israelite called Samson. Would you—" I forced the difficult words over the lump in my throat— "would you be pleased if I handed the man over to you?"

Despite his obvious discomfort with my presence, interest gleamed in the depths of his deep-set eyes. "And how would you know anything about the strongman?"

"I know a great deal, my lord." I bowed my head again. "And I could hand Samson over if you agree to my terms. But you are lord over only one city. I must have agreement from all the Philistine lords, for I cannot proceed unless all the cerens agree to pull back their forces and let me work. I will not tolerate interference from roaming Philistine soldiers while I carry out my plan."

Zaggi harrumphed, but he did not dismiss me. "And what are your terms?"

I smiled, thrilled to achieve this small but satisfying victory. "First, you must restore my rightful place as Adinai's legal daughter and grant me anything that remains of his estate. Second, you must promise that you will arrest and execute Achish for selling my mother into slavery and causing her death. And third, you must swear that you will not kill Samson. Once he has been captured, he will no longer be loyal to his God. He will be but an ordinary man then, one who cannot hurt you."

The ceren stroked the bit of beard on his chin. "And how are we to arrange this surrender?"

"Give me your word and call the other cerens. In two days I will return. If the other cerens are present and agree to my terms, then I will give you details."

Zaggi tilted his head as a strange half smile twisted his mouth. "You are nothing like the young girl who came to my house with Adinai."

"True. I am a wiser woman now." I matched his smile with one of my own. "I want our agreement written on parchment. Only then, before all the other cerens, will I share details of how you will capture the strongman of Israel."

⁂

Two days later, as the brothers packed up the goods they'd bartered for at the marketplace, I stood in Zaggi's house before five self-important men. The lords of Gaza, Gath, Ashdod, Ashkelon, and Ekron sat in a semicircle of thrones, all of them waiting to hear my proposal.

"My lords." I bowed before them, then stood and swept my gaze over the group. "I bring you a proposal concerning Samson, the judge of the Israelites. Once I have stripped him of his great strength, I will turn him over to you and you alone. You will pay me the promised reward of fifty-five hundred pieces of silver. You will also restore any possessions that should have gone to my mother as the widow of Adinai of Gaza, and you will guarantee that Achish, who is well known to you, will be arrested and executed for selling my mother as a slave and causing her death. You will also promise not to kill Samson." I smiled at the somber men. "Do we have an agreement?"

A frown knitted Zaggi's brows, but I knew his displeasure was only an act. He and the others had already discussed my proposal.

After a moment, Zaggi sent a servant for parchment and ink. When the man returned, a scribe filled the page with words, dripped wax onto the page, and offered it to Zaggi, who pressed his ring in the soft wax. The document went around the semicircle until all the cerens had signed it.

"Is this acceptable?" Zaggi handed me the parchment written in Akkadian, the language I'd learned to read in Egypt. I skimmed the text, then nodded. "I am living at a small house by the well at the entrance to the Valley of Sorek. The spot is a way station well known to travelers. In seven days, your men should set up a camp in the wilderness and wait for my signal."

"What if Samson sees our camp?" Zaggi asked. "He will flee the area."

I shook my head. "Better that he see you and avoid you than catch your men hiding in the brush. Establish your camp near the well of Sorek, but not so close that Samson feels trapped."

"And after we establish this camp?"

"Keep most of your men and their horses hidden in tents, so Samson will not be able to estimate your strength. When I have subdued him, I will give the signal. You and your men should ride out and approach the house, where I will give you the final details. But do not let yourselves be seen at the well until I signal you."

"And what is the signal?"

"White smoke. I have a fire pit. When I release a plume of white smoke, you should come to the house at once."

Zaggi closed his eyes as if memorizing the details. He lifted his head and nodded at me, a gleam of appreciation in his eyes. "What a manipulative woman you've become," he said, with no trace of malice in his voice. "I don't know that I've ever met a woman as beautiful or as clever."

"You shouldn't be surprised," I said, slipping the parchment into my basket. "I have learned from your people, the best of teachers."

⁂

Drained by the heat and lulled into lethargy by the rocking motion of the camel, I was nearly asleep when Warati spoke my name. Startled, I looked down to see him walking beside me.

He squinted up at me. "Did I wake you?"

"No." I shook my head in an attempt to cast off my drowsiness.

"Good." He looked ahead and smiled, and for a moment I thought he had seen something funny on the road. "I doubt we will have time to talk when we reach the Valley of Sorek," he said. "So I thought we could talk now."

I glanced down at him, confused by the odd request. "I am happy to talk," I told him. "Do you want to talk about something particular?"

He shrugged. "I am happy to see you're not living alone. But what happened to the widow?"

"She died." I struggled to speak over the thickening that clogged my throat whenever I thought of her. "She was old and full of years, and she wasn't well."

"Do you miss her?"

"Of course. She taught me everything I know about weaving. She taught me how to live as a woman alone. If she hadn't . . ." I waved the thought away. "I would not have survived without her."

Warati walked for a while without speaking, then he cast me a sideways look. "How did you come to meet the strongman?"

I laughed. "You are responsible for that. The first time I ever saw him was at Timnah, when we stopped at the inn, remember?"

"I remember. But you did not speak to any of the men at the feast."

"I saw a great many things while hiding in my tent. That was the first time I saw proof of Samson's strength."

"And after that?"

"After that, like everyone else I heard stories. So when he stopped by the well a few months ago, I went out to help him draw water. We talked"—I couldn't stop a smile—"and he has been with me ever since."

Warati dropped my camel's reins. "I was afraid Samson was using you in the same way your—"

"No," I interrupted. "Samson has never been like Achish. They are as different as light and dark. Samson respects me. Achish does not respect any woman."

A niggling doubt rose in my mind as my own words mocked me. Samson had been nothing but good to me, yet I was planning to turn him over to his enemies. Was I repaying his goodness with evil?

I rode the rest of the way home in silence.

Chapter Thirty-Two
Samson

Struggling to contain an armful of dried flax, I stepped into the shade of Delilah's porch and saw my manservant sitting at her worktable while absently chewing a fingernail. "You could offer to help."

Rei shrugged. "You seemed to be managing well without me."

I dropped the dried stalks in a corner and brushed the dust from my hands. "So what do you think of the place?"

Rei stopped chewing long enough to look around and shrug. "It's no palace, but it has to be better than sleeping on the ground. I can see why you're comfortable here."

"You could be comfortable, too. We could use an extra pair of hands."

Rei spat in the dirt, then gave his nails an appraising glance. "If I stay. When you're with her, I might as well be invisible." He jerked his chin toward the long bench that had replaced the widow's pillows on the straw rug. "That looks new."

"I finished it yesterday. Found saplings, bent and cut them, then wove them together. It's rough, but it's a bench. She's going to love it."

"If you say so."

I dropped onto the bench and looked out at Delilah's blossoming flax field. "You've never been in love. If you could feel what I'm feeling—"

"I would have more sense, I think." Rei lowered his hand and stared at me. "Have you stopped to think about how disastrous this is? She is not of your people."

"I'm not of my people, either." Rei gaped at me, but I'd spoken the truth as I knew it. "None of my people have had to deal with the constraints on my life. Every other Nazarite *chose* to take the vow of dedication, but I was never allowed choice. Most of them take the vow for a period of years. I was not allowed choice in that, either. I am the only man on earth who has been a Nazarite from before birth until death, and for all I know I may be the last."

"I haven't noticed that vow slowing you down," Rei countered, his voice dry. "Most Nazarites don't drink wine or even step inside a vineyard. They cannot touch an unclean thing, but you have handled dead lions, cattle, and donkeys, not to mention dead men."

"They take the vow for seven years," I went on. "I was put under the vow for a lifetime. And as a lifetime slave to Adonai, perhaps His grace requires me to keep only one vow. *That* one I will not break."

"Your life is not over, Samson." Rei's eyes narrowed as he studied my face. "You love her, yet you have been in love before. You remember how the woman from Timnah manipulated and wept and chided. Your Delilah will eventually do the same. And the ending of this love story might be more tragic than the last."

I closed my eyes, unable to look at him. Rei knew me better than I knew myself, and he was usually right about such things. I could handle any number of screaming, brawling men, but I had never been able to remain strong before a weeping woman. I didn't have time to consider the implication of his words, because his next comment brought me to my feet.

"I see a caravan approaching," Rei said. "Two camels and several pack animals. Could it be your woman's escort?"

"I hope so." I stood and moved to the shade. When the caravan reached the fork in the road, the lead camel turned toward the well, coming close enough for me to recognize Warati's thick beard. "Praise be to Adonai. She's home."

I turned to share a smile with Rei, but he had already made himself scarce.

꿍

Delilah greeted Yagil and me with a kiss and invited the brothers to share a meal with us. They dismounted and watered the animals while Delilah set out dried fish and aged goat cheese, delicacies from the market in Gaza. "Have you butchered the kid yet?" she asked, glancing over her shoulder.

"No."

"Good. There's no need, since I traded for dried beef and fish in Gaza." She sent me a teasing smile. "I know you were ready for something different."

I smiled too, trying to figure out what was different about her. She seemed brighter somehow, as if she'd developed a hard sheen. She wore more cosmetics than usual, and the lush fringe at her sleeves kept getting in the way as she worked.

"You're going to catch fire." I gestured to the fringe that wavered only inches from the red-hot coals in the fire pit. "Shouldn't you put on something less elaborate?"

She blew out an exasperated breath and disappeared into the house—to change, hopefully.

Several hours later, after the brothers had departed for Gibeon,

Delilah and I sat on the bench I had built for her. She wore the comfortable tunic she usually wore at home, and she seemed more like herself in the familiar garment. Crickets filled the early evening with their insistent chirring and beckoned me toward sleep. I rested my head in Delilah's lap and closed my eyes as she played with my braids.

Yagil had been asleep for some time, so Delilah and I were quite alone.

"I'm glad I'm back," Delilah said, her fingers tunneling through my hair. "And I love my new bench. It's beautiful."

"We will sit here every night, and you can do just what you're doing now."

"Really? And when will it be *my* turn to lie down and relax?"

I rolled onto my back to see her better. "Anytime you like. Just say the word."

She trailed her fingertips over the side of my face. "I was teasing. You do so much for me—I will happily massage your scalp."

I closed my eyes again and gloried in the moment, then said the words I'd been trying to say ever since she returned. "Things weren't the same without you."

She smiled down at me. "I heard your name more than once in Gaza. People are amazed by the stories about you. They keep wondering about the source of your great strength." Gently she traced my brows with her fingertip. "In all the time we've been together, you've never told me."

"Told you what?"

"The secret of your strength. You look like an ordinary man, and yet . . ."

I opened my eyes. "I *did* tell you—the Spirit of Adonai comes upon me."

"But *why* does the Spirit come over you? And why *you*, and not someone else? Surely there's someway you could be bound and subdued."

"I could be bound in your arms."

"That's not what I mean and you know it. There must be some reason for your power. Something you do, some spell you recite to build up your confidence and courage."

I shrugged. "I keep my vow, and Adonai keeps His."

"But what vow have you made? What is the key to this agreement with your God?"

I lifted my heavy eyelids and snuggled closer to her. "If you were to bind me with seven fresh bowstrings that have never been used, I would be weak and like any other man."

"Now, was sharing that so hard?" She bent and kissed my ear. "Sleep, my love. Your Delilah is home again."

CHAPTER THIRTY-THREE

DELILAH

EIGHT MORNINGS AFTER I had made my promise to the cerens of Gaza, I waited until Samson and Yagil left the house, then dropped a handful of green leaves into my fire pit. The resulting cloud of smoke was dense enough to send me running for fresh air, but a few moments later a contingent of Philistine warriors arrived on foot. "Quickly," I said, "I need seven fresh bowstrings that have never been used."

The warriors rummaged among their supplies, but found themselves five strings short. "You must bring me five more," I hissed. "Nothing can be done until you do."

The man in charge sent his servant to the nearest village while the others hurried back to their camp. I paced and tried to remain calm. What if Samson and Yagil saw the soldiers' tracks in the sand? What if they approached the camp? What if they saw the man who'd gone for bowstrings approaching the well?

Treacherous Beauty

I set up my loom and arranged the threads for a linen scarf, but my fingers trembled and I kept dropping the shuttle. My thoughts darted toward possibilities, the myriad things that could go wrong. . . .

Finally, the Philistine warriors returned, panting and perspiring. One of them dropped five additional bowstrings onto my palm. I told the others to hide inside the house. "And you must keep silent," I told them. "Samson won't be back until evening."

If he ever returned to that room.

When Samson and Yagil arrived with a rabbit, I skinned and cleaned the creature, then put it in a clay pot in the fire pit. Samson stretched out on our new bench while Yagil went to catch mice in the flax field. I sat next to Samson and picked up my sewing.

Samson lifted a brow. "No weaving today?"

"There's a time for weaving," I said, keeping my eye on my needle, "and a time for embroidery." Impulsively, I leaned down and kissed him, long and hard, a small penance for what I was about to do.

Afterward he settled back and was asleep within moments.

When I was certain that he breathed deeply and evenly, I took the bowstrings from my sewing basket and held them in my open palms. They were nothing, powerless in themselves, but apparently Samson believed that his supernatural strength was tied up in them. And because a man's faith could spur him to greatness, I would use these bowstrings to undo his belief.

Kneeling by the bench, I threaded them around his ankles, knees, thighs, wrists, and elbows. My sleeping strongman twitched every time the cords tickled his flesh, but he had always been a sound sleeper.

When I had made the knots as tight as I could, I sat on my stool and took a long look at the man I loved. When he woke, would he understand my reasons for this? Would he listen to my explanations? Or would his hate for me burn hotter than his love?

282

I closed my eyes and felt yet another tear roll down my cheek. I drew a breath and reluctantly said his name. "Samson."

He didn't wake. I would have to be firmer and more determined if I wanted to pull off this charade. I said more loudly, "The Philistines are upon you, Samson!"

No sooner had the words left my lips than Samson sat upright and flexed, snapping the bowstrings as if they had been dried flax. I gaped at him, honestly surprised, as he looked around and then settled his gaze on me. "Did you say Philistines?"

I blinked, then frowned. "Liar."

I went back to my sewing, but a few moments later, I knelt by Samson's side. "You deceived me," I said, my voice breaking. "You lied to me. So tell me, please—what is the secret of your strength?"

He caught my fingers and kissed them. "Delilah, I have told you almost everything about me."

"Do you truly love me?" I asked. "If you love me as I love you, there would be no secrets between us."

He heaved a sigh, followed by a smile. "If they bind me with new ropes that have never been used for work, then I will be weak like any other man."

I leaned forward and kissed him on the forehead. "Thank you. Now rest, darling."

After he slept, I went into the house and whispered to the Philistines. One of them produced a length of new rope, and another cut it into two pieces. I immediately went to work—one rope to bind his feet, the other to lash his wrists. When I had finished, I stood back and shouted again, "The Philistines are upon you, Samson!"

Hearing the panic in my voice, he sat up and snapped the ropes as if they were threads from my loom.

"You've done it again!" I cried, both amazed and frustrated. "You have mocked me and told me lies! So tell me how you can be bound!"

He rested his elbows on his bent knees. "Must we do this?" He reached for my hands and held them in his strong grasp. "I can think of more enjoyable ways to spend the afternoon."

The feel of his hands on my wrists, so like the way Achish had gripped me, sent waves of alarm up my spine. I wrenched away from him, pulled back, and regarded him like the enemy.

My reaction startled him, but only for an instant. "I'm sorry, I forgot." He bit his lip and slumped forward. "If you weave the seven locks of my hair within the web of a loom . . ." He shrugged, then stood and stretched. "I'm going for water," he said, picking up a jug. "And to look for the boy. He should be making his way home now."

My energy drained away as he walked to the well. What made me think I could do this? Samson was going to find the Philistines in the house. He was going to see through my charade. He had already been more patient than I had any right to expect, and only his sunny, amiable nature had kept him from growing angry with my little game.

When Samson walked toward the hills, I hurried into the house. "Go!" I told the waiting Philistines, pointing them toward the door. "Come back tomorrow if you like. But I am too spent to commit treachery today."

Chapter Thirty-Four

SAMSON

THAT NIGHT, as Delilah lay by my side and Yagil snored on his pallet, the woman turned to me.

"Woven into my loom, you say?" She reached over and tugged on one of my braids, her eyes twinkling like pools in the semidarkness.

I snorted in response. I did not want to keep lying to her, but I didn't know how to answer. I had given her the larger truth and she had refused to accept it. I had shared nearly every detail of my life story, excluding only one detail. My status as a Nazarite—the requirement that had been thrust upon me and made me unique—was so singular that only Rei and my parents knew about it. I wasn't sure I could explain it, and I wasn't sure Delilah could understand. How could she when she refused to believe in my God?

Delilah snuggled closer and rested her head on my upper arm. "Tell me about your mother," she said, her voice like a warm song in the night.

"My mother?"

"When you were a little boy, what sort of child were you?"

I tipped my head back to better see her. She had been full of questions all day, yet this query seemed innocent enough.

"My mother," I began, "fears Adonai more than anyone I have ever met. When I was young, she began every day with prayer and ended it with a blessing on my head. My father is a devout man and watched over me carefully. He loves my mother a great deal."

"They are both still living?"

"They have a farm in Zorah. Yagil and I went to visit them while you were in Gaza." I gave her a chagrined smile. "Maybe I should have asked you before taking the boy."

She shook her head. "No, I'm glad you didn't stay in this very public place." She pressed her fingertips to my lips. "I would love to meet your parents, but something tells me they would not approve."

"Of you? My parents grudgingly approved my choice of a Philistine bride, so *you* would be a relief. If you decided to follow Adonai"—I lightened my tone—"you would be a cause for rejoicing."

She evaded my blatant suggestion and snuggled closer. "Were you born early in their marriage, or late?"

I sighed, realizing she had picked up the scent of my secret. She would question me until she had heard the entire story.

"I was born later," I told her. "For a long time my mother was barren. But then the angel of Adonai appeared to her and said she would conceive and bear a son. She should therefore not drink wine or any strong drink, or eat any unclean thing. I would be a Nazarite of God from the womb."

Delilah lifted her head. "What's that?"

I attempted an explanation. "The word means *to separate*, and it applies to a person who separates himself unto the Lord. We give up certain things in order to be dedicated to God."

Her smile gleamed in the dim light. "You didn't give up women."

"No," I admitted, "though my parents probably wish I had."

"The angel of Adonai." She propped herself on an elbow. "Was this a woman?"

"A man."

"Did he look like a Hebrew or a Philistine?"

"He simply looked like a man. When my father asked his name, the angel of Adonai answered, 'Why do you ask for my name? It is wonderful.'"

Delilah walked her fingers from my belly to my throat. "What was so wonderful about him?"

"You'll have to ask my mother." Then, in an effort to stop her queries, I took her in my arms and thoroughly kissed her.

CHAPTER THIRTY-FIVE

DELILAH

BECAUSE WE HAD NOT SLEPT MUCH the night before, I put pillows on Samson's beautiful bench and prepared a large pot of rabbit stew to break his fast. I brewed a fresh tea that he enjoyed at morning, and to the resulting brew I added several leaves from a leafy plant known to make men sleep. I sent Yagil out with his slingshot to look for rabbits, then went in and woke Samson with a kiss. "Come and eat," I told him, pulling him out of bed. "You need your strength."

I set up my loom while he breakfasted and smiled when he lay down on the bench and looked at me. As I suspected, a night of love, the warmth of the day, and the bounty of the breakfast combined to lull him to sleep. While he slept, I moved my loom closer to the bench and worked the loose ends of his seven braids into the pattern of my linen, stark strands standing out against the light flax, like sin next to holiness.

A lump rose in my throat. How many more times would we enact this charade? Didn't he realize that he was breaking my heart each time he sidestepped the truth? I had found it difficult to go to the cerens, but to endure this act of betrayal again and again and again—

"Samson!" I called. "The Philistines have come for you!"

He sat up so abruptly that he pulled the loom's pin and fabric from their places. The loom toppled over, striking the new bench. Samson looked at me, confusion and bewilderment warring in his eyes.

I burst into honest tears, my heart as wounded as my loom. "How can you say you love me when you aren't truthful with me?" I cried. "Three times you've made fun of me, and not once have you told me the real source of your strength."

"Come here," he said, his voice gentle. "Release me from this thing."

Like a scolded child I knelt at his feet, picked up my ruined fabric, and began to pluck at the threads, freeing his plaits from the weave. Samson braced his elbows on his knees and leaned toward me, his hands folded, his chin on his chest. Finally he lifted his head and looked at me. "Is it really so important that you know everything about me?"

I hiccupped a sob. "There should be nothing between us."

"Have you told me everything about yourself?"

"I have told you—" I hiccupped again and thought about the heavy secret I had not shared—"more than I have told any man."

He sighed, took my hand, and pressed it against his chest. "I have learned one thing about women—they do not surrender easily. So I will tell you what you want to know, even though you should have already recognized the truth. It is this: when the angel of Adonai appeared to my mother, he told her that no razor should ever touch my head. My hair is the symbol of my obedience to Adonai. If I allow someone to shave me, my strength will leave . . . and I will be like any other man."

I saw resignation on his face, and something in his eyes that looked like forgiveness for my prying too deeply.

"Samson." I rose to my knees and cradled his head against my breast. "You're right—I should have seen it. Now be at peace." I kissed his forehead and his lips, then urged him to lie down again on his bench. "Sleep, my love," I told him, "while I work the rest of your braids out of the linen."

My lover slept while I worked to set the loom right again. When I had finished, I went to my fire pit and dropped a fistful of green weeds on the coals. Within a moment the flames belched billows of white smoke.

The Philistines appeared within minutes. I held my finger to my lips and gestured to the sleeping Samson, then whispered that I needed someone with a sharp blade to shave Samson's head. A burly soldier stepped forward, a razor in his hand, but I took it and gave the razor to a man who appeared less likely to cut Samson's throat as he worked. To assist in the deception, I knelt by Samson's side and massaged his temples while the soldier focused on removing Samson's braids. "What will he look like without hair?" I whispered to the barber, attempting to cover my anguish with banter. "I'm not sure I will know him."

I studied my sleeping strongman. Samson appeared surprisingly vulnerable without his beard and mantle of hair. In his shaven face, for the first time I saw traces of the child in the man—the round cheeks, unusually long lashes, and sweetly curved lips of an innocent.

I was not foolish enough to believe that Samson's strength came from the braids now lying on the floor. His strength came from his faith in the God who had asked him to grow his hair, and a man stripped of his faith was a man who could be defeated. . . .

I looked away as my ears filled with the soft murmurs of the waiting Philistines and an occasional snort from one of their horses. I could easily stand and tell the Philistines that I'd been mistaken; I was wrong about the secret of Samson's strength. They would return to Gaza and I would sit by Samson's side until he woke, and I'd do my best to console him. He might feel as weak as any other man, but I would tell him that he had not changed, and if he believed in me, in *us*, he could still rise up and defend our home. His parents had told him a story, no more, and his strength had come from their belief in him. But I believed in him too, and so did Yagil.

But Achish was coming here again, and if Samson did not believe in himself, he would not defeat Achish and his men. We would all be killed or taken prisoner, so I could not back out now.

I had no choice. I had to hand over my lover and my future in exchange for knowing that Achish would be stopped and punished for what he'd done to me, my mother, and countless others. He would finally receive the justice he had managed to evade.

I would find myself alone again . . . but I had been alone before. I would survive.

When he finished, the man with the blade looked at me and nodded. I waited until he left the porch. Then, with tears streaming over my cheeks, I braced myself and shouted, "Samson! The Philistines have come for you!"

Samson opened his eyes and then leapt up, his arms tense when he saw the circle of armed men around the porch. Without hesitation, he picked up a stick of firewood and advanced toward the closest warriors, but they grabbed his arms while a third man drew his spear and placed the tip at Samson's throat. Samson flexed, undoubtedly expecting to throw his captors off, but he could not move.

He dropped the stick of firewood and stared at the carpet, littered with his dark braids.

Samson turned and looked at me. Such horror and pain filled his eyes that I recoiled, stepping backward. Samson might have lost the strength of his arms, but the look in his eyes was as powerful as ever.

"Samson," I cried, forcing myself to move toward him as my

heart rioted within me. "This is not as bad as it seems. The cerens have promised to preserve your life, and they'll execute Achish for all the evil he's done. You must understand why I had to do this . . ."

Samson did not reply, for at that moment a chariot rolled up to the well and Lord Zaggi descended. He greeted me with a curt nod, then gestured to a servant, who strode through the courtyard and dropped five black bags at my feet. I heard the chink of metal on metal and wanted the earth to swallow me alive.

"Payment for a job well done." The ceren's mouth curved in a smile. "I should have sent a beautiful woman after Samson long before this. You have proven your courage today, Delilah. Congratulations."

I stepped over the bags, more concerned about Samson than the silver. "You will remember your promises," I told the ceren. "You will spare Samson's life."

Zaggi nodded. "Of course. But when one has taken so many Philistine lives, something must be taken from him."

"Isn't it enough that you have taken his freedom?"

Zaggi lifted a shaggy brow. "Is it enough that Achish will be humiliated by a woman? No, you asked for more. Even so, Samson must pay what is due."

When I turned, two of the ceren's men had bound Samson's arms behind his back. Zaggi nodded to the burly soldier who had first volunteered to shave Samson. Grinning, the man walked over to the prisoner. The soldiers forced Samson to his knees, and one of them stepped between Samson's bent legs and held my lover's head tight against his chest. The burly soldier fisted his hands, lifted his thumbs, and held them before Samson's eyes. Samson's jaw clamped and his eyes narrowed. While I blinked in confusion, the soldier thrust his thumbs into Samson's eye sockets and swept out the eyeballs with one smooth motion. I gaped in horror as color ran out of the world and my legs turned to water.

I landed on my knees, gulping deep breaths, inhaling sand and smoke and pain. A dull roar filled my ears, muffling the sound of Samson's screams.

Ignoring me, Zaggi returned to his chariot. His warriors dragged Samson through the courtyard and used a simple rope to tie the prisoner's hands to a horse's saddle. The image was disturbing, but worse by far was Samson's frenzied calling for someone named Rei. I looked around, but all I could see were Philistines. Who was Rei?

"Rei!" Samson called again, his voice in tatters. "Rei, are you coming with me?"

"Shut up," one of the Philistines called, checking the rope that connected Samson to the saddle. "There's no one here but us and Delilah."

"Please . . ." Samson's head lolled over his shoulders as if he were trying to see someone. "My servant is never far from me."

The soldier turned to me. "Has he a servant?"

Sitting in the dirt, I closed my eyes and returned to the memory of a recent afternoon as if to a deep dream. Samson had been talking to his servant, and for a moment I believed that the man really existed.

But he didn't. Rei was about as real as Samson's invisible God. I looked at the soldier and shook my head.

"Will you *tell* him there's no servant? I can't stand that yelling all the way back to Gaza."

Had Samson lost his mind? I shook my head, pressed my hands over my ears, and stumbled toward the porch. I had not expected this, nor had I wanted it. I couldn't look at Samson's bloodied face.

One of the soldiers cracked a whip, and the chariot and horsemen began moving forward.

"Rei! Where are you?"

"Shut up, fool!"

"There is no servant!" I whirled and screamed the truth, the wind catching my voice and flinging it back at me. "And there is no Adonai to save you."

I hurried to the security of the porch, looked down and saw the gelatinous orbs on the carpet near my loom. Samson's eyes stared, silently accusing me of betrayal and torture and murder. I may not have killed the man, but I had murdered the family we created.

I should have known the Philistines would never be content to merely take him into custody. They were, after all, the pragmatic culture that had produced Achish, so I should have expected them to maim Samson so he would never again be a threat. They had stolen his sight—the sense that had brought him the most pleasure.

Never again would he look on me with delight. Never again would he behold the world his Adonai had created. And never again would I lose myself in the pool of those beautiful, lash-fringed eyes.

I staggered into the house and found Yagil whimpering on his pallet. I didn't know when he'd come home, but clearly he'd seen enough to break his heart.

"Yagil—"

"Get away from me!" he shouted. Then he turned his back on me, buried his face in his pillow, and quietly went to pieces.

Chapter Thirty-Six

DELILAH

For seven days, Yagil and I did not speak—not to each other, not to ourselves, not to the wind. We woke, we worked, we picked at our food, we went to bed when the sun left us in darkness.

I think we both sensed that it felt wrong to utter trivial words while Samson suffered. So we went about our lives in silence, and when I lay down on my mattress, I turned my back to the spot where he once slept.

As for Yagil, he scarcely lived during those days. He did not go out to play; he did not hunt. Instead he sat beneath the terebinth tree by the well, his gaze fixed on the western road as if he could bring Samson back through the sheer force of will.

After the Philistines left, I cleaned up the bloody mess on the porch, burying Samson's eyes next to the widow. I worked slowly, arms and legs and back moving woodenly while my heart pounded thick and heavy in my chest.

Over the following days I tried to practice our ordinary routines, but despair had moved into our home. The house was thick with it, and even the porch seemed shrouded with a gray fog of loss and anguish. I set out food, worked at the loom, and tended the animals. I didn't fuss at Yagil for neglecting his chores in the flax field, but tended the plants myself. How could I chide him for mourning the man he loved?

I mourned too, but I was determined not to look back. So I carried on as usual, though sometimes I buried my face in Samson's pillow and breathed in his scent, my throat aching. One night, desperate to know I had done the right thing, I lifted my voice and called on Adonai . . . but then a moment later rolled over and closed my eyes. Why should Samson's God answer me? If Adonai really existed, if he was as powerful as Samson said, then I dared not address him. I had betrayed one of his judges, and loneliness was a small price to pay for so great a sin.

After a full week without Samson, Yagil stopped watching the road. His tongue loosened and he spoke, though he spoke of nothing important, and once again he left the house to go hunting with his slingshot.

He was sitting on the porch with me when a Philistine chariot pulled up to the well and a soldier in gleaming brass armor stepped down. He waved for my attention, then asked if he might come through the gate. I gave my permission, a bit warily, and the man walked toward me with a burlap bag over his shoulder.

"Greetings, Delilah of Sorek," he said, his face a mask of cold dignity. "I bring a message from Lord Zaggi, ceren of Gaza."

He handed me a sealed papyrus parchment. While Yagil stood pale and wide-eyed by my side, I broke the seal and hastily skimmed the words:

To Delilah at the Valley of Sorek, Greetings!
    With the greatest pleasure I am writing to inform you that we have met all three of your conditions. You have been reinstated as

*the legal heir to the title and properties of Adinai the merchant.
Though I am sorry to inform you that nothing remains of those
properties, as his stepdaughter you will be considered a citizen of
Gaza should you choose to live in the city.*

We have spared Samson's life, as you will see if you visit us.

*And yesterday, at sunrise, we led the traitor Achish to the Temple
of Dagon where he was publicly executed.*

*I trust you will be satisfied that we have honored the terms of
our agreement. Long life and good fortune to you, lady!*

When I had finished reading, the messenger pulled the burlap
bag off his shoulder, opened it, and offered me a look. Curious, I
peered inside and saw Achish's head.

I blinked in astonished silence, then turned away, fell to my
knees, and vomited.

"Mama?" Yagil placed his hand on my shoulder. "Are you all
right?"

I wiped my mouth with the back of my hand and nodded.

The soldier closed the bag. "Any response for Lord Zaggi?"

"No." My voice broke in a rattling gurgle. "Just take that thing
away."

The man slung the bag over his shoulder, nodded and walked
off. Within a few moments the chariot had turned and was on its
way back to Gaza.

Feeling as though I'd aged ten years, on shaky legs I walked to
Samson's bench and sat. A sough of wind blew past me and vibrated
the strings of my loom, creating a strangely musical moan.

I closed my eyes and waited for the dark surge of joy I had long
anticipated. Achish was gone. The man who abused me and murdered my mother had finally been eliminated. I had waited years for
this moment and sacrificed the love of my life for this victory. . . .

I sat motionless, head cocked, heart receptive, but felt nothing.

Nothing changed in my surroundings; nothing shifted in my heart. Despair still hovered around us, and my son's face was still tight with concern. I might have experienced a dark little pleasure if I'd been able to watch the execution—no, I would not. I had never been able to find joy in the sufferings of others.

Sighing, I stood, cupped my hand around Yagil's cheek, and went back to my work.

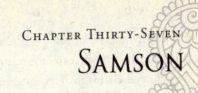

CHAPTER THIRTY-SEVEN
SAMSON

THOUGH I HAD VISITED GAZA MANY TIMES, I had never noticed the myriad sounds of the city. When I woke in my prison cell, my ears informed me about the time of day. If darkness still covered the city, I heard the squeak of rats and the clatter of roaches as they rattled across the damp stone floor. Sometimes I heard the chink of chains, accompanied by the sobs of prisoners or a bronze bracelet knocking at an iron post in the floor.

If the sun had risen, I heard the rumble of carts outside my window or the tinkling of bells from a young lady's dainty ankle. Early morning brought the *clip-clop* of donkey's feet and the yawns of merchants who had reluctantly risen to open their shops. I heard the slap and slide of planks as our breakfast slid beneath our cell doors, and the jingle of keys at the jailer's belt.

I learned to be grateful for the sound of those keys. Many prisoners did nothing but sit in their cells all day, a tedium that drove some to madness. Because I was as much spectacle as prisoner, my jailers hauled me up each morning and told me to stand still as they slipped chains through the bronze bracelets at my wrists and ankles. When I had been hobbled, unseen escorts led me from my cell, prodded me down a flight of stone steps, and escorted me to the public mill. There they placed my hands on a wooden bar and told me to push. Straining with every muscle in my scarred back, I pushed the bar that turned the grindstone, an effort that became easier once the massive circular rock had begun to move. On and on I pushed, my bare feet braced against the wet stone floor. I breathed in dampness and mold; I heard the grind of the stone and the onlookers' laughter; I tasted dry bread and sometimes the tang of blood. I felt the smoothness of wood beneath my palm, the texture of damp stone beneath my feet, and the throbbing of my wounded heart.

Nothing passed before my eyes but darkness and memories.

I had not noticed the mill in my previous visits to Gaza, but over time my senses informed me about its details. We were situated near the waterfront, but not *too* near, for though I could smell the stench of rotting garbage, we were not so close that I could hear the waves. Occasionally a gull would alight somewhere near my window, probably in hope of gleaning a kernel of wheat or barley, but usually the air was quiet save for the steady grind of the millstones. On festival days, the mill opened its doors to the public and my senses were overburdened with taunts, blows from rotten fruit, the assault of spittle, and splatters from streams of warm urine.

I was a prized exhibit in the mightiest of the Philistine cities, but the crowds thinned after a few months because I had become old news and unfashionable. The women who used to exclaim or call out suggestive comments disappeared, probably because I had become unkempt and unpleasant. The prison did not bathe its residents, nor did they shave us. Even I could smell the rank odor of my unwashed body. And at the end of the day, when I was free of the grindstone, my questing fingers felt soft hair returning to my face and head.

During the night, when I wandered in that shadowed place halfway between sleep and waking, I found Delilah. I breathed in the lavender scent of her hair and felt the softness of her skin beneath my lips. Yagil also wandered in that place and looked at me with a child's bright, hope-filled gaze. On other nights my parents appeared in my dreams, saying nothing, looking at me with sorrowful expressions. *What a waste*, their eyes seemed to say, *what a deliverer you could have been.*

Whether waking or sleeping, my thoughts always returned to Delilah. As in Rei's riddle about the lemon, life pressured Delilah, and her desire for vengeance poured out. I know she loved me, but she loved vengeance more.

Many a night I argued with her. I railed against her, cursed her, tried to reason with her, and wept with her. Over time I ran out of things to say and knew that nothing I said would have changed anything. In the end, her hatred for Achish, her desire to conquer him, overruled everything, even her love for Yagil and me. And that determination—that perverse refusal to yield—was one of the things I loved about her.

I might have been content to remain in Delilah's house forever, hiding from the Philistines and from my responsibility. I had been distracted from my task, and for that sin I begged forgiveness from Adonai. I had let a woman interfere with my sacred covenant with Adonai.

Yet even in my despair I found hope for the future. Joseph had been imprisoned, too. He was also betrayed by a woman, yet he rose to sit on a throne nearly equal to Pharaoh's.

I had been temporarily sidelined, but Samuel, my Nazarite brother, was preparing the people of Israel for spiritual battle.

From defeat came victory. When we went down into the earth, we rose to fight with renewed strength.

I was Adonai's instrument, His Nazarite, His son, and in Him I placed my trust. I would tell Delilah as much . . . if Adonai allowed me to see her again.

CHAPTER THIRTY-EIGHT

DELILAH

SIX MONTHS PASSED—six months in which my five bags of silver lay under the earth, covered by the widow's tattered carpet. What was I supposed to do with so much silver? The marketplaces were jammed with merchants who bartered in materials, not precious metals, and I could buy more with linen than with silver.

When I could buy, that is. After our first visit to Zorah, the closest Israelite town, I realized that I had become a pariah among Samson's people. News traveled fast and gossip even faster, so everyone knew what I had done. They did not know my reasons, but after the Philistines carried Samson away, the people of Israel forgot that they had betrayed Samson only a few months before. They wanted to be rid of him so they could be meeker slaves, but once the Philistines eased their harassment, all the Israelites wanted to do was shame the harlot who betrayed the man of God.

At least, I told myself, I still had friends in Gibeon.

Yagil and I kept to ourselves and tried to follow our routines. I kept an eye out for the Gibeonite brothers, who would soon be riding up to my door. They weren't Israelites, so surely they would rally to my cause once they learned the reasons behind my actions.

As the land warmed in the promise of spring, I rose every morning and scanned the road, searching for a caravan of camels and donkeys. Finally I spotted the brothers in the distance. I hurried to set out pillows and honey cakes, new tunics and blankets. When they were close enough to hail, I ran to the well and pulled up the bucket, eager to serve my friends.

But Warati, who sat on the lead camel, rode by without even looking in my direction. When Regnar and Hitzig did the same, grief pooled in my heart. Had the story reached as far as Gibeon? And had even my best friends turned against me?

I walked slowly back to the porch and dropped onto Samson's bench, my shoulders slumping with the weight of crushing disappointment. Yagil watched the caravan go by, then he looked at me. "Aren't the uncles stopping?"

"No, my son." I forced a smile. "They must be in a great hurry."

Being rejected by the brothers broke my heart, but I managed to set my anguish aside and go about my work. The next morning an older man and woman traveling with only a donkey stopped by the well. I went out to help them water their beast, but when the old woman saw me, she stepped back as if I were a poisonous snake. "The dark *tob* woman!" she said, her expression hard and resentful. "Get away!"

Astonished, I turned to her husband, who was even less cordial. "Adonai sent us a champion," he said, his words as sharp as thorns, "and you sold him to our enemies."

As my chin wobbled uncontrollably, I pulled up the bucket, set it on the well, and walked back to the porch.

That night I told Yagil we were moving to Gaza.

Yagil and I sat together high atop a camel, a seat for which I'd
paid a small fortune. The caravan had come through just after I'd
finished packing our few belongings. Within a few minutes of settling on a price, Yagil and I were en route to the Philistine city.

Since the Israelites clearly did not want me in their territory, I
thought the Philistines might be more welcoming. After all, I was
now officially related to Adinai, who had been well respected in the
business community. And I had money, so I could buy a nice house,
perhaps near Sapha and her family, or maybe I could find a place
near the sea. Anything would be better and safer than remaining
alone in hostile territory.

As the camel plodded over the road, I tried to ignore a fact that
kept buzzing in my brain. Not so many months ago, Samson had
walked over this same road at the end of a rope, bleeding and in
horrible pain. I could not imagine the agonies he endured that night.
I knew what I suffered, and if his pain had equaled or surpassed
mine, then I had made a poor bargain. I had exchanged a relationship that filled my life with light for victory over a hateful man.

What else had I gained? Silver I would never spend. Ties to a
businessman few people would remember. And the knowledge that
my enemy would never trouble me again. I did appreciate that
knowledge, but my life was far from trouble-free. Instead of avoiding one man, I found myself avoiding dozens of men and women
who hated me for my part in Samson's capture.

I leaned back in the tall saddle and told myself that things would
be different in Gaza. No Israelites lived in Gaza, and my Philistine
neighbors might actually value my contribution to the security
of their people. I would find a home that held no memories of
Samson, and Yagil would find friends his own age. Later, when we
were settled and happy, I would inquire as to where Samson was

being housed. Perhaps, if I could find the courage, we would visit. Perhaps we would even speak.

After arriving in Gaza, I found a woman who knew a man with a house for sale. Yagil and I met the man on the street, and he took us to a large residence across from the Temple of Dagon. "When you open the shutters, you can hear music from the temple festivals," he said. "And from your balcony, you can view the spring sacrifices without fighting the crowds."

The house pleased me, not because it overlooked the temple, but because of its proximity to the water. We were far enough away that I wouldn't have to breathe in the odors of dead fish and rotting vegetables, yet we were close enough that I could open the upstairs shutters and glimpse the endless Great Sea. My father had loved the sea, and the view would make me feel close to him. As he grew, Yagil might even forget the years we spent in the Valley of Sorek . . . and Samson along with them.

I furnished the house, bought clothes like those of our neighbors, and traded a few garments at the marketplace. I did not advertise my name or my association with Samson, and for a few weeks Yagil and I were happy.

Until Zaggi learned I was in Gaza and invited me to the Temple of Dagon.

CHAPTER THIRTY-NINE

SAMSON

ON A HOT, dry morning that made me dream of lizards sunning themselves on warm rocks, I woke and listened to a variety of sounds I'd not heard before. Dozens of people were moving about on the street outside. Had I slept later than usual? If so, why hadn't the jailers come to take me to the mill?

I sat up and placed my hands over my empty eye sockets, a gesture that seemed to help me concentrate on hearing. Somewhere a distant trumpet played a flourish, then was joined by others. The footsteps in the alley quickened, and the murmur of the crowd increased to a confused babble. Drums pounded in a walking rhythm as somewhere a crowd cheered.

I lowered my hands, tipped my head back, and parsed the atmosphere. My nose might be playing tricks on me, but I thought I smelled roasting meats.

A crowd, music, food . . . a festival. Gaza was celebrating.

Quick steps came down the hallway outside my cell, sandals slapping against the stone floor. "Always the last minute," my jailer said, his words accompanied by the jangle of keys and the creak of the lock.

"Samson!" His voice held a cheery note. "You've been invited to the festival. If you're lucky, they'll bring a bull or goat for the sacrifice. If you're not lucky, I pray you enjoy the afterlife." The door creaked and a length of chain struck the floor. "Come, your escorts will be here soon."

I sat stock-still, unwilling to hurry toward any event where I might be a sacrifice. "What if I don't want to go?"

"Ha ha ha, hee hee!" The old man cackled, then broke into a cough that ended in spastic wheezing. "That's a good one, strongman," he said when he finally caught his breath. "Give me your hand, let me link these two bands together . . ."

Other footsteps came from the hallway—six or more men, I guessed, and they were walking as a unit. An official escort.

"Is the prisoner ready?"

"Just about. Wait . . . okay, that's it." My jailer stepped away. "Here's your man, Captain. Just be gentle going around corners. He can't see to avoid them—careful! Samson, try to cooperate, will you?"

I was pushed, pulled, and jerked by the chains on my wrists and ankles. They treated me as if I were an unreasoning farm animal, accustomed to bit and bridle. My temper flared, then cooled nearly as quickly. Didn't they have every right to see me as a beast? I did a donkey's work by day, and at night I slept on the floor like a dog. Why not be their ox, goaded toward whatever pen they intended for me?

I stumbled through the prison passageways and felt the uneven stones of a muddy road beneath my bare feet. We walked for a while, then we stopped in a large space—an enclosure tall and wide, because every sound vibrated in the cavernous place. I dropped down the well of memory and visualized Dagon's temple in Gaza, the only structure large enough to hold a festival crowd. While music played and distant voices ran together in a stream of sound, we waited . . . and Rei whispered in my ear.

"Adonai is with you, Samson."

I nodded, a single tear running over my cheek. "I know."

CHAPTER FORTY

DELILAH

THE WEATHER USHERED IN a marvelous day for the festival. High clouds sudsed the sky and filtered most of the sun, while occasional shafts of sunlight burst through the cloud cover like spears. I held tight to Yagil's hand and joined the crowd on the street, all of us eager to enter the temple and find a good seat.

"Will we see lions?" Yagil asked, rising on tiptoe in an attempt to see over the mob. "Tigers?"

"I don't know," I answered, a thread of irritation in my voice. "I've never been to a festival."

Apparently the gates had not been opened, because the mob was not moving. I smoothed my varicolored skirt, which would soon be limp, and inhaled the odors of sweat and waste from the open gutters.

How long would we have to wait?

After what felt like an eternity, my stomach swayed and I feared

I would have to sit down or faint. I looked around for an empty space, then heard a murmur and felt the crowd surge forward. Up ahead, the double doors had opened. We streamed in, a pressing tide of people eager to view whatever entertainment the priests of Dagon could provide.

A corps of acrobats and jugglers had filled the open floor by the time we entered. They flipped, jumped, and cartwheeled as the crowd poured in and clamored for seats. Slaves in white tunics stood at the openings to various aisles, so I asked one of them where I could find Lord Zaggi's seats. The slave pointed toward a box at the center of second floor, and with one glance I saw that the ceren and at least two of his daughters had already arrived.

Keeping a firm grip on Yagil's hand, I threaded my way through the multitude until I arrived at the ceren's box. I bowed to the ceren, then smiled at Sapha and one of her sisters. "Here," Sapha said, gesturing to two empty seats on the first row. "Please take the front seats."

We did, though Yagil was so excited by the idea of a spectacle that he could barely hold still. I held on to the back of his tunic, worried that he might lean over the railing and tumble into the sandy arena below.

"My son is not accustomed to the city," I confided to Sapha, who looked cool and lovely in her linen tunic. "He has never seen so many dancers and acrobats."

"Gaza is home to many performing artists." Zaggi leaned over his daughter to address me. "But we have prepared something special for you, Delilah." He smiled, and his hazel eyes held more than a hint of flirtation. "I was overjoyed to hear that you had moved to Gaza. This should be your home. It's what Adinai would have wanted."

I smiled and politely inclined my head at the mention of my late stepfather but resolved to keep my distance from the ceren. I had not moved to Gaza to entertain powerful men. If the cerens considered me a harlot—and I understood why they might—I would have to correct their impressions.

I turned away from the ceren and ran my hand through Yagil's tousled curls, drawing him close to my side. I would be a mother in Gaza, nothing more.

"Here it comes." Zaggi pointed to a pair of doors at the front of the building, directly beneath the colossal statue of Dagon. "The main attraction."

I twisted in my seat and shoved my troubling thoughts away.

CHAPTER FORTY-ONE

SAMSON

DOORS OPENED—a hot breeze ruffled the hair on my head—and a nasal voice made some kind of announcement. The resulting roar tumbled out at us, nearly knocking me over. Then the mob began to sing:

> "Our god has handed over to us our enemy Samson.
> Our god has handed over the one they call *judge*.
> He destroyed our land and killed so many of us that we say:
> Who's the strong man now, Samson?
> Who is the stronger god?"

The guards goaded me into a cavern of living sound that seemed to vibrate around, over, and beneath me. The floor trembled with it; mocking voices rode the wind that whipped around my ears. Confused, I turned my head, seeking the warmth of the sun, the source of the breeze, anything that might identify my location. Then it hit me—I was standing at the *back* of the temple, the area with box seats above it and a rooftop patio over the box seats. The building had been under construction the last time I visited Gaza, and I had been astounded to see its unique structure. At the time I'd been impressed with the wizardry of the Philistines, yet now their breathtaking building made me smile.

The escorts pulled me forward, and in the confusion I lost my balance and fell. My assailants dragged me over hot sand until I felt the living sun on my face. My smile broadened because I knew I was in the center of the temple, under the sun and sky.

The chains holding me relaxed, then ran like a metallic river through the hasps on my wrist and ankle bands. I was free.

I sat up, then stood as the crowd cheered and applauded. For a moment I was able to stand in relative peace as music began to play and the games began. Lassos whirled through the air, stinging ropes that tried to snag my arms, my head, my feet. I tried to keep my feet on the ground, but in my effort to feel the ropes, one caught my left hand and tightened on my wrist. The man who wielded the rope ran behind me, forcing me to turn or risk breaking my arm. Another rope kept smacking my head, and I only had my right hand to throw it off. As I stumbled and struggled to remain upright, another lasso caught my foot and pulled me down.

At some silent signal, the ropes went limp. I sat up and pulled them off one by one, standing to my feet. Jeers, catcalls, singing surrounded me, and someone, guards or performers, began jabbing my legs with sharpened sticks, forcing me to sidestep and turn and shift to avoid the pricks. I evaded the painful jabs until I realized that's what the crowd wanted—they wanted a dancing monkey, and the monkey was me.

I stopped moving and gritted my teeth, resolving to bear the pain rather than provide pleasure for my enemies. The Philistines

were amusing themselves at my—no, at *my God's* expense. I was
His vessel, to use as He saw fit, and at the moment, He saw fit to
have me stand in the center of Dagon's temple.

"Even before birth," Rei whispered, "you belonged to Him. You
were given life for His purposes, you were dedicated to Him and
only one thing was required of you—faithfulness. And you were
faithful until the moment you placed your love for a woman over
your love for God."

I fell to one knee and bowed my head, inadvertently silencing
the crowd.

Adonai, forgive me.

"He has," Rei assured me.

For a moment, an unnatural silence prevailed, and then laughter
penetrated the silence, beginning with a titter and swelling into a
deafening chorus.

Someone struck a gong, and silence reigned again.

I lifted my head, sensing a change in the atmosphere. "And now,"
someone called, and I felt an instinctive stab of fear. I had heard
that voice before, at Delilah's house. The nasal tones belonged to
Lord Zaggi, ceren of Gaza. "As the highlight of the day," the ceren
continued, "I give you the woman who charmed the killer of thousands, the destroyer of gates, the ox of Israel. Let me present . . .
the beautiful Delilah!"

I froze, paralyzed by the mention of her name.

Chapter Forty-Two
DELILAH

My heart had stuttered when the doors opened to reveal Samson, and it nearly stopped when Zaggi announced my name. I had moved to Gaza to escape continual reminders of my actions, but Zaggi had just reminded everyone that I was responsible for the blind man standing helpless in the center of the temple—the man I had loved and wronged.

I couldn't move.

"Delilah?" Zaggi turned to me, a subtle rebuke in his tone. "The staircase is to your right."

"Go on, give them a show." Sapha prodded my shoulder. "The entire city is waiting to see what you'll do with him."

Had I not done enough injury to the man? How could they expect me to go down and face him? For a quarter of an hour I had been watching priests of Dagon's temple torture the man I loved. In watching them stab, trip, and torment Samson, I'd suffered a jab of memory from childhood. Like the beautiful stallion who broke his neck rather than submit to his handlers, I knew Samson would rather die than submit to the priests who wanted him to entertain this mob.

"I can't go down there." I lowered my head, aware that nearly every eye in the stadium was fixed on me. "I can't face Samson now—"

"Don't fret, Delilah," Zaggi said. "He won't even know you are there. We took his eyes, remember?"

My gorge rose. I brought my hand to my mouth, about to refuse the ceren altogether, but Yagil wasn't hampered by guilt. While I struggled with my conscience, my son slipped out of the row and was halfway down the staircase by the time I noticed that he'd gone.

"Yagil!" I screamed.

The crowd saw me stand. They cheered, calling my name, as I left the box and followed my son down the staircase and—after an instant of indecision—onto the sandy floor of the arena.

I stopped at the periphery, however, remaining against the wall while Yagil sprinted toward Samson. I shouted my son's name, but the chanting crowd swallowed up my voice. When I saw Yagil wrap his arms around Samson's leg, I knew I had no choice—I would have to go out there and pry him away from the man he loved.

On trembling legs—was this some kind of divine punishment?—I went after my boy, moving toward the man I had betrayed.

CHAPTER FORTY-THREE
SAMSON

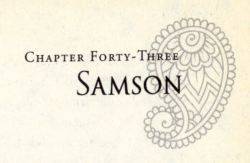

As the multitude shouted Delilah's name, I braced myself for whatever torture might ensue next. I did not believe Delilah was present—the Philistines were probably sending in a costumed harlot or a soldier with a whip and a painted face. So I spread my feet, extended my arms, and turned my head from one side to the other, listening for some clue that might grant me an extra hour of life.

I was completely unprepared for the soft body that collided with my leg and clung to me like moss to a stone. "Samson! We miss you so much!"

My mouth went dry. "Yagil?" I tunneled my fingers through his hair, then knelt to meet him on his level. "Is that really you?" How could it be? Yagil would not be here without his mother. So Delilah had to be here as well . . .

"Is your mother—?"

He threw his arms around my neck, and I could not speak as I held him. I had hoped to raise this boy, but Adonai had not called me to be a father.

"We love you, Samson." His voice quavered in my ear. "Can't you come home with us?"

My heart squeezed so tightly I could barely draw breath to speak. "I'm sorry, Yagil. I have to do what Adonai has called me to do."

He sobbed. "But I don't want you to stay away."

"I know. I don't want to be away, but sometimes we have no choice. We have to be brave. Can you . . . do you think we can do that?"

Yagil sniffed, then loosened his grip on my leg. "Okay."

"That doesn't mean I don't love you." I clung to the sleeve of his tunic, unwilling to let him go. "I love you, understand? I always will."

He was still weeping, and I needed him to be strong . . . for what must come next. "Yagil"—I pulled him closer so he could hear me above the crowd—"am I in the center of the open area?"

"Yes."

"Do you see two pillars close together—maybe beneath the ceren's seats?"

I felt his nod.

"Good boy. Can you lead me over there so that I can rest against the pillars?"

The crowd fell silent as Yagil took my hand and led me toward the back of the temple. I trailed behind him and might have looked as if I were following some sort of script as I walked toward the important guests with one arm outstretched and the other wrapped around Yagil's small hand.

When Yagil stopped, I groped through empty air. The sun was still on my face, so why had we stopped in the open?

"Samson?" Delilah's voice, soft and tortured, was instantly overwhelmed by the murmurs of the crowd.

I swallowed to bring my heart down from my throat. "I didn't think I would ever hear your voice again."

"Samson"—her words, spoken in my ear, came out in a rush—"I am so sorry. I would never have allowed them to take—"

"Don't worry," I answered, pitching my voice for her ears alone. "This is what Adonai wanted."

"How can you say that? This is all my fault."

May heaven help me, I nearly laughed. How like Delilah to claim HaShem's work as her own. "Delilah . . ." I smiled from the sheer joy of saying her name. "I forgave you weeks ago. And trust me when I tell you that this is part of Adonai's plan. Today marks the beginning of my people's deliverance from the Philistines."

My smile broadened as I imagined her standing there, her cheekbones wet with tears, a frown line between her elegant brows, her full lips pulled tight with argument, even though the time for squabbling had long passed.

I reached out and caught her arm, eliciting a gasp from the crowd. "They expect me to hurt you," I said, keeping my voice low as I drew her close, "but I would never, not even now. You need to leave this place, Delilah, the moment I release you. Take the boy and flee the city. Don't stop to gather your things, don't worry about your loom. Just take Yagil and run."

"Why?"

"Because today I will ask Adonai to destroy my enemies. I will bring this place down upon the Philistines' heads." I gave her a confident smile. "I was born for this day."

CHAPTER FORTY-FOUR

DELILAH

I STARED AT SAMSON as outlandish and unexpected thoughts careened in my head. Adonai was going to allow him to destroy the Philistines? He was going to bring the temple down? And even more outrageous, he wanted to spare me?

In a breathless moment, I realized a startling truth. In this brief moment when life was reduced to its base elements, what remained for Samson were his calling, his God, and his love for Yagil and me. And somehow that love allowed him to *forgive*. I didn't deserve it, hadn't expected it, and wouldn't have offered it if the situation were reversed.

And yet Samson followed a God who delivered the unexpected. And though I could see no way Samson could destroy this temple through confidence or human power, I knew he would accomplish what he promised.

Like blood out of a wound, silence surrounded us and spread

through the temple as hundreds of Philistines leaned forward to eavesdrop on our conversation. But Samson hadn't spoken to them.

His sightless eyes turned in my direction. "Do you understand?"

A sob broke from my lips, and I whispered, "Yes. Yes, I understand. And I believe you will do what you say."

My heart, so burdened with shame and guilt, lightened when a smile shone through the thicket of Samson's dark beard.

CHAPTER FORTY-FIVE
SAMSON

"Now"—I turned my head toward the boy—"Yagil, can you lead me to those pillars?"

I released Delilah and caught Yagil's hand. We walked, and when I felt the coolness of shade on my skin, I knew we had reached the right spot. Yagil stopped, and I bent to kiss the top of his head. "Go, my son. Find your mother. You will make a fine man one day."

I waited, listening, and when I heard the crowd cheer, I extended my arms until I felt the cool touch of marble beneath each palm.

To divert the crowd's attention from Delilah's exit, I threw my head back and roared. A moment later, the men with sharp sticks surrounded me again, but I stood perfectly still, enduring the pricks and cuts because I dared not lose my bearings.

As musicians played and onlookers jeered, I envisioned Yagil and Delilah leaving the temple. I saw them hurrying along the inner passageway, exiting through a side entrance, running down an alley.

I imagined them stopping to catch their breath, approaching the city gates, and taking time to fix a loose sandal. And when I was sure I'd given them more than enough time to get out of the walled city, I lifted my head and addressed HaShem, whose glorious handiwork I could no longer see. "Adonai Elohim, just this once, please, think of me, and please give me strength so that I can take revenge on the Philistines for at least one of my two eyes."

In my imagination I saw myself as Adonai saw me—dirty and disheveled but with new hair on my head and a renewed commitment in my heart.

"Let me die with the Philistines!" I shouted. Then I shoved with all my might.

Chapter Forty-Six
Delilah

Standing on an elevated mound outside the city walls, Yagil and I watched the Temple of Dagon tremble, shatter, and implode. We heard the screams and saw a cloud of dust rise from the spot where all of Gaza had gathered to mock Samson and his God.

I did not deserve to escape the death they suffered, but I did . . . because Samson loved me.

When the rumbling finally stopped, I sat on the mound and wrapped my son in a fierce hug. "Tell me again what Samson said," I whispered. "Remind me, please."

Yagil looked at me with eyes that seemed far too old to be in a child's face. "He said we should run out of the temple—"

"Before that."

Yagil held his finger to his lips, thinking. "He said today marks the start of his people's deliverance from the Philistines."

I felt the truth all at once, like a tingle in my stomach. Because

Gaza was the largest and oldest Philistine city, and because everyone of importance had been at the festival, Samson had just killed the majority of the Philistine military leaders. Zaggi, who probably lay beneath tons of stone, had been the most influential of the cerens. This had been the newest and most glorious of Dagon's temples, and Dagon the merman now lay in the dust. In a single hour, Samson had delivered a deathblow to Gaza and a mortal wound to Philistia and its chief god.

Hysterical laughter bubbled up from my throat. I hugged Yagil again, overcome by Samson's unexpected forgiveness and Adonai's mercy.

As my laughter dissolved into tears, I released my son and rested my head on my crossed arms, weeping until I could weep no more. I had never met a man like Samson. Without him, I would have never learned to love my son, and I would never have understood the essence of faith.

I had thought that I could strip Samson of his faith by eliminating the outward symbol of it, but I was wrong. Samson's faith went deeper than his scalp, deeper even than his emotions. He did not merely *believe* in Adonai; he *knew* his God and trusted completely in His purposes. The Egyptians and Philistines worshiped fickle gods who changed with every season, but Samson's Adonai was unshakable.

As were the deliverers He called to save His people from their oppressors.

When at last I lifted my head, Yagil sat next to me, his elbow on his bent knee, his chin on his hand. I tilted my head, suddenly aware that in his face I could see the beginnings of a man.

Samson had been responsible for that, too.

"What are you thinking, son?"

"I miss home," he said. "I think we should go back to our house by the well."

I nodded, realizing that my little boy was wiser than his years.

DELILAH

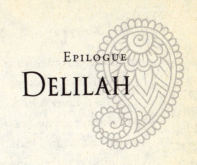

SAMSON JUDGED ISRAEL FOR TWENTY YEARS. After his death, his family heard about what happened at the Temple of Dagon. His brothers and all his father's family went down to Gaza, found his body, brought him up and buried him between Zorah and Eshtaol in the tomb of his father, Manoah.

And the people realized that Samson had killed more of Israel's enemies in his death than in his life.

As the angel of Adonai had foretold, he did begin to deliver Israel from the hand of the Philistines. Following his death, the whole house of Israel yearned after Adonai.

The High Priest Samuel spoke to the house of Israel, saying, "If you are returning to Adonai with all your heart, then remove the foreign gods and the ashtaroth from among you, direct your hearts to Adonai and serve Him alone. Then He will deliver you from the hand of the Philistines." So Bnei-Yisrael removed the idols of Baal and Ashtaroth, along with the Asherah poles, and served Adonai only.

Then Samuel said, "Gather all Israel to Mizpah, and I will pray to Adonai for you." So they gathered together at Mizpah, drew water, and poured it out before Adonai. They fasted on that day and confessed their sins.

When the Philistines heard that Israel had assembled at Mizpah, the lords of the Philistines sent their armies against Israel. Hearing the news, the Israelites became afraid, and they said to Samuel, "Don't stop crying out to Adonai our God for us, so that He may save us from the hand of the Philistines!"

Samuel took a nursing lamb and offered it whole as a burnt offering to Adonai. He cried out to Adonai for Israel, and Adonai answered him. As Samuel was offering the lamb, the Philistines drew near to fight against Israel. But Adonai thundered against the Philistines and confused them so they were defeated. Afterward the men of Israel left Mizpah and pursued the Philistines, striking them down all the way to below Beth-car.

Then Samuel took a large stone and set it between Mizpah and Shen. He named it Ebenezer, saying, "Thus far Adonai has helped us."

So the Philistines were subdued and did not invade the borders of Israel anymore. The hand of Adonai was against the Philistines all the days of Samuel. The towns that the Philistines had taken from Israel, from Ekron to Gath, were restored, and Israel recovered its territory from the Philistines.

After the destruction of Dagon's temple, I stood outside the gates of Gaza and considered my choice. On one hand, a life with the Philistines, the money I'd hidden in our house, and status as Adinai's daughter and the ceren's friend. On the other hand, a life amid the children of Israel, a well where I could serve and show hospitality, and an old loom on which I could make a living . . . and a life.

Yagil and I returned to the little house in the Valley of Sorek. We had seen everything Adonai did for the Israelites, and we believed in the power and authority of the Israelites' invisible God. One day, when I breathe my last, I will not be afraid to step from this life into the next, because Samson opened my eyes to things that could not be seen with human eyes. Adonai may be invisible, but as Samson said, so is love, and nothing is more powerful.

When he was of age, Yagil built a room onto the house and took a wife from the tribe of Dan, Samson's tribe.

And I taught his wife how to weave.

DISCUSSION QUESTIONS

1. Angela Hunt has said that she tries to invent as little as possible when writing about historical characters. But since Scripture tells us so little about Delilah, she had to invent a plausible backstory in keeping with Samson's historical and political era. In your opinion, did the story feel appropriate to the time and place?

2. The biblical book of Judges gives us a bare-bones outline of Samson's life and tells us very little about Delilah. Before reading this novel, what was your opinion of Delilah? Of Samson? How did reading this novel alter your perception of these characters?

3. As in the other Dangerous Beauty books, Hunt chose to tell this story from only two characters' viewpoints: Delilah and Samson. Do you think the story should have been told from another point of view? Which other character would you like to hear from?

4. Is this story similar to other biblical historical fiction you have read? How was it similar or different? Do you prefer historical fiction or contemporary fiction?

5. Prior to reading this novel, how much did you know about the time of Israel's judges, before God allowed the nation to

have a king? While we think of judges as arbitrators, and they certainly filled that role, Scripture makes much of their roles as *saviors* who acted to deliver Israel from her oppressors. In what ways did Samson deliver his people?

6. What did you think about the character of Rei, whose name means *mirror* in Hebrew? Why do you think the author wrote Rei into the story?

7. After suffering great harm from her Philistine stepbrother, Delilah encounters other people who extend grace to her—the Gibeonite brothers and the widow, for example. How do they positively influence Delilah's life? Is their influence enough to steer Delilah away from her desire for vengeance? Why or why not?

8. Why do you think the men from Judah agreed to hand Samson over to the Philistines? In speaking of them, Samson says, "A tribe—a nation—will not change until it realizes how low it has fallen. When my people realize that they have loved bondage with leisure and sin better than strenuous liberty with righteousness, they will repent and return to the Lord." What other nations have gone through periods of loving "bondage with leisure and sin" more than "strenuous liberty with righteousness"?

9. What lessons or ideas will you take away from this novel? If you read the biblical account of Samson again (Judges 13–16), how will the story be different for you?

10. Who was your favorite character? Who was your least favorite?

11. Would you recommend this book to a friend? Why or why not?

Author's Note

In researching novels set in ancient times, I frequently run across contradictory accounts of ancient peoples, places, and customs. But rarely have I encountered so many differing opinions as in my research on Samson and Delilah.

Many, if not most, of the articles and books I read about Samson portrayed him as a lust-crazed man who fell far short of God's purpose for his life. Though Scripture tells us that Samson judged Israel for twenty years, the writers who depict Samson in negative terms focus on three accounts of his dalliances with women. Other writers say that Samson's story is included in the Bible to warn us against immoral choices.

But consider Hebrews 11, where Samson is given a place of honor in the "roll call of faith":

What more shall I say? For time would fail me if I tell of Gideon, Barak, Samson, Jephthah, also of David and Samuel and the prophets. By faith they conquered kingdoms, administered justice, obtained promises, shut the mouths of lions, quenched the power of fire, escaped the edge of the sword, were made strong out of weakness, became mighty in war, and made foreign armies flee (Hebrews 11:32–34).

Many of those noteworthy accomplishments belonged to Samson. He administered justice, shut the mouth of at least one lion, escaped the edge of the sword numerous times, was made strong out of weakness, became mighty in war, made foreign armies flee—and those are only the things we know about.

Samson was not a perfect man, but neither were other Bible characters. Only Jesus has been a perfect role model.

And Scripture clearly demonstrates how God used Samson's foibles to work His divine will. When Samson desired a Philistine wife, for instance, his parents protested: ". . . but his father and mother did not know that it [Samson's desire] was of Adonai, for He was seeking a pretext against the Philistines" (Judges 14:4). Furthermore, Samson's strength did not emanate from overdeveloped muscles. His strength appeared when "the *Ruach Adonai* [the Holy Spirit] came mightily upon him. . . ." (Judges 14:8, 19; 15:14).

Scripture says very little about Delilah. In fact, we are not told if she was Philistine, Jewish, or from some other nation. Some scholars are certain she was Philistine, for who else would betray a Jewish hero? Other scholars are just as certain she was an Israelite, for how else could Samson trust her with the secret of his strength?

No matter what her heritage, some scholars are convinced she was a fiend from hell:

> This Philistine courtesan was a woman of unholy persistence and devilish deceit, who had personal charm, mental ability, self-command, and nerve, but who used all her qualities for one purpose—*money*. She and womanly honor and love had never met, for behind her beautiful face was a heart as dark as hell, and full of viperous treachery. Her supreme wickedness lay not in betraying Samson to his enemies but in causing him to break faith with his ideals.[1]

Having no description of Delilah's nature in Scripture, and having never met the woman, I am reluctant to describe her in the

---

1. "All the Women of the Bible," Bible Gateway, https://www.biblegateway.com /resources/all-women-bible/Delilah, accessed 3/23/2015.

terms used above. Through years of living, observing, and studying, however, I have learned that unless someone is a sociopath with no empathy whatsoever, human nature demands that we rationalize our actions.

The teenager who steals a car will claim that the driver deserved to lose his vehicle if he was stupid enough to leave his keys in the ignition.

The man who cheats on his wife will convince himself that he deserves to seek love and affection because his wife has been cold in the bedroom.

The woman who steals from a department store will believe that the store overcharges to make up for shoplifting losses, so she might as well take her fair share.

Even serial killers depersonalize their victims to obviate the moral sting of murder.

Yes, Delilah betrayed Samson. And Samson murdered thirty men and stole their clothing just to satisfy a bet. In both cases, the perpetrators managed to convince themselves that they had legitimate reasons for their actions.

Because that's what humans do.

The pages of this book contain a carefully researched, biblically faithful story of Delilah and Samson. Think of the Bible account as a pencil sketch and the novel a completed oil painting. Naturally, I have used my imagination to fill in missing details, but I have worked hard to ensure the characters remain true to Scripture and also to human nature.

Samson and Delilah were not heroes or villains. They were *people* . . . because people, with all their flaws, are what God uses to work His divine will.

—Angela Hunt

REFERENCES

Achtemeier, Paul J., and Harper & Row and Society of Biblical Literature. *Harper's Bible Dictionary*, 1st ed. San Francisco: Harper & Row, 1985.

Acolatse, Joachim. *Samson: God's Mighty Man of Faith*. Mustang, OK: Tate Publishing, 2010.

Adler, Conrad. *The Book of Judges in the Jewish Tradition*. New York: Funk and Wagnalls, 1906.

"All the Women of the Bible," Bible Gateway, https://www.biblegateway.com/resources/all-women-bible/Delilah, accessed 3/23/2015.

Block, Daniel Isaac. *Judges, Ruth, The New American Commentary*. Nashville, TN: Broadman & Holman Publishers, 1999.

Cheung, Vincent. *Samson and His Faith*. 2003.

Criswell, W. A., Paige Patterson, E. Ray Clendenen, eds. *Believer's Study Bible*. Nashville, TN: Thomas Nelson, 1991.

Day, Colin A. *Collins Thesaurus of the Bible*. Bellingham, WA: Logos Bible Software, 2009.

Deere, Jack S. "Song of Songs" in *The Bible Knowledge Commentary: An Exposition of the Scriptures*. Wheaton, IL: Victor Books, 1985.

Easley, Kendell H. *Holman QuickSource Guide to Understanding the Bible*. Nashville, TN: Holman Bible Publishers, 2002.

Easton, M. G. *Easton's Bible Dictionary*. New York: Harper & Brothers, 1893.

Elwell, Walter A., and Philip Wesley Comfort. *Tyndale Bible Dictionary*. Wheaton, IL: Tyndale House Publishers, 2001.

Exum, J. Cheryl. "Delilah," in *The Anchor Yale Bible Dictionary*. New York: Doubleday, 1992.

Ferris, Paul Wayne. "Sorek, Valley of (Place)," in vol. 6, *The Anchor*

Yale Bible Dictionary, ed. David Noel Freedman. New York: Doubleday, 1992.

Freeman, James M., and Harold J. Chadwick. *Manners & Customs of the Bible*. North Brunswick, NJ: Bridge-Logos Publishers, 1998.

Fruchtenbaum, Arnold G. *Ariel's Bible Commentary: The Books of Judges and Ruth*. San Antonio, TX: Ariel Ministries, 2006.

Goslinga, C. J. *Joshua, Judges, Ruth*. Grand Rapids, MI: Zondervan, 1986.

Grossman, David. *Lion's Honey: The Myth of Samson*. New York: Cannongate, 2005.

Harris, D. R. *Samson: The Beast of Dan*. Mustang, OK: Tate Publishing, 2013.

Jeffrey, David L. *A Dictionary of Biblical Tradition in English Literature*. Grand Rapids, MI: Eerdmans, 1992.

Jenkins, Simon. *Nelson's 3-D Bible Mapbook*. Nashville, TN: Thomas Nelson, 1995.

Kirk, Thomas. *Samson: His Life and Work*. Edinburgh: Andrew Elliot, 1891.

Lindsey, F. Duane. *The Bible Knowledge Commentary: An Exposition of the Scriptures*. Wheaton, IL: Victor Books, 1985.

Macalister, R. A. S. *The Philistines: Their History and Civilization*. 1913.

McGee, Vernon. *Thru the Bible Commentary*. Nashville, TN: Thomas Nelson, 1997.

Milton, John. "Samson Agonistes." *Complete Poems*. The Harvard Classics. Lines 270–71.

Richards, Sue Poorman, and Larry Richards. *Every Woman in the Bible*. Nashville, TN: Thomas Nelson, 1999.

Robinson, Simon J. *Opening Up Judges, Opening Up Commentary*. Leominster: Day One Publications, 2006.

Scott, W. A. *The Giant Judge* or, *The Story of Samson*. Philadelphia, PA: Presbyterian Board of Publication, 1858.

Smith, James E. *The Books of History, Old Testament Survey Series*. Joplin, MO: College Press, 1995.

Smith, William. *Smith's Bible Dictionary*. Nashville, TN: Thomas Nelson, 1986.

Thomas, Robert L., and The Lockman Foundation, *New American Standard Exhaustive Concordance of the Bible: Updated Edition.* Anaheim, CA: Foundation Publications, 1998.

Youngblood, Ronald F., F. F. Bruce, R. K. Harrison. *Nelson's New Illustrated Bible Dictionary.* Nashville, TN: Thomas Nelson, 1995.

Zodhiates, Spiros. *The Complete Word Study Dictionary: New Testament.* Chattanooga, TN: AMG Publishers, 2000.

Angela Hunt has published more than one hundred books, with sales nearing five million copies worldwide. She's the *New York Times* bestselling author of *The Tale of Three Trees*, *The Note*, and *The Nativity Story*. Angela's novels have won or been nominated for several prestigious industry awards, such as the RITA Award, the Christy Award, the ECPA Christian Book Award, and the HOLT Medallion Award. Romantic Times Book Club presented her with a Lifetime Achievement Award in 2006. She holds both a doctorate in Biblical Studies and a Th.D. degree. Angela and her husband live in Florida, along with their mastiffs. For a complete list of the author's books, visit angelahuntbooks.com.

More Biblical Fiction From Angela Hunt

Visit angelahuntbooks.com for a full list of titles.

After she is forcibly taken to the palace of the king, a beautiful young Jewish woman, known to the Persians as Esther, wins a queen's crown and then must risk everything in order to save her people . . . and bind her husband's heart.

Esther: Royal Beauty
A DANGEROUS BEAUTY NOVEL

When King David forces himself on Bathsheba, a loyal soldier's wife, she loses the husband—and the life— she's always known. Now, pregnant with the king's child, she struggles to protect her son and navigate the dangers of the king's household.

Bathsheba: Reluctant Beauty
A DANGEROUS BEAUTY NOVEL

Roman Tribune Clavius is assigned by Pilate to keep the radical followers of the recently executed Yeshua from stealing the body and inciting revolution. When the body goes missing despite his precautions, Clavius sets out on a quest for the truth that will shake not only his life but echo throughout all of history.

Risen: The Novelization of the Major Motion Picture

BETHANYHOUSE

Stay up-to-date on your favorite books and authors with our free e-newsletters. Sign up today at bethanyhouse.com.

Find us on Facebook. facebook.com/bethanyhousepublishers

Free exclusive resources for your book group! bethanyhouse.com/anopenbook

You May Also Enjoy . . .

The young Egyptian slave Kiya leads a miserable life. When terrifying plagues strike Egypt, she's in the middle of it all. Choosing to flee with the Hebrews, Kiya finds herself reliant on a strange God and developing feelings for a man who despises her people. Facing the trials of the desert, will she turn back toward Egypt—or find a new place to belong?

Counted With the Stars by Connilyn Cossette
OUT FROM EGYPT #1
connilyncossette.com

For the sake of his new God and his friend Joshua, Caleb will battle the enemies of God's people until his dying breath. From his early days as a mercenary for Pharaoh in Egypt to his flight with the Hebrews through the Red Sea, Caleb recounts, with graphic detail, the supernatural events leading up to the Exodus.

Shadow of the Mountain: Exodus by Cliff Graham
SHADOW OF THE MOUNTAIN #1
cliffgraham.com

After years of exile in Babylon, faithful Jews Iddo and Zechariah are among the first to return to Jerusalem. After the arduous journey, they—and the women they love—struggle to rebuild their lives in obedience to the God who beckons them home.

Return to Me by Lynn Austin
THE RESTORATION CHRONICLES #1
lynnaustin.org

◈ BETHANYHOUSE